NO DEED UNPUNISHED

NO DEED UNPUNISHED

Richard Anders

authorHOUSE®

AuthorHouse™
1663 Liberty Drive
Bloomington, IN 47403
www.authorhouse.com
Phone: 1-800-839-8640

First published by AuthorHouse   10/28/2011

ISBN: 978-1-4670-4350-2 (sc)
ISBN: 978-1-4670-4349-6 (ebk)

Library of Congress Control Number: 2011917687

Printed in the United States of America

Any people depicted in stock imagery provided by Thinkstock are models, and such images are being used for illustrative purposes only.
Certain stock imagery © Thinkstock.

"Whatever our creed, we feel that no good deed can by any possibility go unrewarded, no evil deed unpunished."

Orison Swett Marden

Chapter 1

(The Present)

"See you tomorrow, Jen. Drive carefully," said Max as he stared trance-like at the young woman leaving the bar. "God, what I wouldn't give," he thought.

"I will, Max. Thanks," said Jennifer Sands as she slipped into her plastic raincoat, tucking an umbrella under her arm. With her back against the heavy wooden door, she pushed it open, and stepped outside and into a cold, driving rain.

Max looked longingly at her as she exited the bar. He admired her young body, her long, blonde hair. She was a sweet kid and one of his best, most reliable waitresses. Max thought to himself, "If only I was twenty years younger and thirty pounds lighter." Then, with a shrug and a shake of his head, he turned back to the small sink behind the bar. He continued cleaning the beer mugs and whiskey glasses left behind by the night's crowd.

Jennifer Sands, Jen, as she was called at the club, was a single mother who worked nights at the topless bar to make ends meet. Her son, Troy was almost three years old. Her son was her whole life. She'd do anything for him, including working in a dump like that to make ends meet. When she worked she'd have a neighbor's daughter watch him until she got home. Unfortunately, the girl wasn't very reliable. One night the babysitter failed to show up and Jen was forced to bring her son to work with her. He didn't cause any trouble sleeping most of the time.

No one said anything to her about it; however someone must have seen him and called Child Protective Services. A few days later two women from the New York City Department of Social Services showed up at her apartment. She tried to explain that it was an isolated incident and would never happen again. They took her son from her that day. After a court hearing her son was placed with a foster family.

Initially, she thought one of the "topless dancers" had made the call. There was often friction between the waitresses and dancers, because each was vying for the patrons' attention and their money. After questioning the other girls she began to think her earlier assumption had been wrong. She now had a strong suspicion it was her "ex," Bruce Krane, who filed the complaint with DSS. One of his buddies must have been in the bar, seen the boy and told Bruce. He was probably trying to get back at her because she'd brought him into court for nonpayment of child support, that had been six months ago. Jen's plan was to work hard, save enough money to, get a decent apartment in a good neighborhood and land a "respectable" job. Then the agency would have to return her son to her. The rain, which started around ten, brought with it a drastic drop in temperature.

The lousy weather kept the flow of customers down. Only a small number of regulars sat at the bar. They'd come not for the dancers but for the warmth and companionship of a familiar place.

Tired from standing on his feet for several hours, Max decided to close for the night.

"Last call! Last dance!" he announced.

The customers grumbled but eventually slid off their stools and headed home.

The dancers didn't bother hanging around. As soon as they finished their last dance, they dressed and headed home, having separated most of the customers from their money with lap dances.

Jen stood outside huddled under a canvas overhang which gave her some protection from the driving rain. She fumbled with a jammed button on the umbrella. When she finally got it to open, as a gust of wind swept past, almost pulling it from her grip. She hung on and managed to raise it over her head, closing her hand tighter on its slender metal handle. Suddenly another strong gust of wind caught the umbrella pulling her out from under her cover into a driving, icy rain.

She'd worked the late shift and the parking lot was nearly full when she came in. Now, there were only a couple of cars left in the lot. She took a moment, trying to remember where she'd parked the car. In the distance and across the empty asphalt, she could barely see her beat-up VW as it sat forlornly in the driving rain, and darkness.

"Well, here goes," she said to herself, as she pulled her head into her raincoat and began running across the lot. When she reached the car, slightly out of breath, she started rummaging around in her cluttered pocketbook looking for her car keys. Holding the umbrella with one hand and trying to find her keys with the other was impossible. As she tried to tuck the umbrella under her arm it slipped from her fingers, flipped upside down falling to the ground next to her feet. The cold rain whipped around her face and down the neck of her coat. Her hair became wet and plastered against her head.

Reaching deep into her bag she found the car keys.

"Ah, at last," she thought.

She managed to get the keys out and located the one that would unlock the door. She tucked her pocketbook under her arm and after two tries she managed to get the key into the lock and turned it. Through the misted-over window, she could see the lock button inside pop up, releasing the lock. Jen reached for the door handle to open the door. Suddenly, she felt a sharp blow to her lower back.

At first it felt like a punch. But, then she was seized by an excruciating, sharp pain. Her pocket book fell to the ground. More startled than in pain, she turned around to see who or what had caused it. As she did a hand was clasped roughly across her mouth. It was too dark to see who it was, but she could tell it was a man by the roughness of the hand and by his strength. The man, whoever he was, pressed his body against hers, pinning her to the side of the car. Eyes wide with fear, she tried to comprehend what was happening and why. She sensed the man's face was only inches from her own because she could feel his breath on her face. It smelled of beer and garlic.

"Could it be one of the guys who'd been in the bar earlier?" she thought. "Is he going to rape me?"

She wanted to recoil from his breath, but couldn't. As she stood there shivering and frightened, the man shoved his face against hers. She could feel the stiff bristles of his beard scratching her cheek.

"Did you really think you'd get away with it?" the voiced asked. His voice was familiar, but from where?

"Get away with what?" she thought. "What did I do?" she wanted to ask, but his hand prevented it.

Her assailant continued to press his palm hard against her mouth cutting her lip on her teeth. She could taste her own blood.

Before she had a chance to think of what to do, she felt another sharp pain. This time it came from her stomach. Then her attacker eased off her, ever so slightly.

"Is he going to leave me alone?" she wondered. Before she completed this thought, she felt as if her attacker punched her in the abdomen.

"This is for your son," grunted the man, as he shoved into her.

Jen felt something sharp being thrust deep inside her stomach. She felt and heard a ripping noise, like her shirt was being cut. Now the pain had become more severe, a burning. It was unlike anything she'd ever felt before. She remembered the pain of child birth. This was ten times worse, much worse.

Finally, the man eased off her. Removing his hand from her mouth, he turned and started to leave. She couldn't see his face in the dark but noticed he was dressed in black, some kind of hood pulled over his head.

"He was in the bar earlier," she thought.

As he ran away she heard his feet slap against the wet pavement, the sound receding into the distance. The sound of the rain beating on her car's roof seemed to be fading away as well. Now she became aware of a different beating, not the rain. This sound was coming from deep inside her. She heard and felt a pulsing, throbbing sound in her ears. It was her own heart beat.

Sliding to her right she reached for the door handle. It was unlocked, her keys still dangled from the lock. With shaking hand she pulled the keys free from the lock. As she turned about to get into the car she saw her pocketbook on the ground. "I need that," she thought and started to bend over to pick it up, but was hit with excruciating pain. Unable to bend she knelt down, grabbed the pocketbook, then using the door for support, pulled herself upright again.

"Once I get inside, I can lock the door. I'll be able to start the car, and get away from here. I'll be safe," Jen said out loud.

She grabbed the handle and pulled. The door swung open and the inside dome light came on. She suddenly felt very weak and staggered back, almost falling to the ground. She felt woozy, like she was going to faint. Everything seemed to be spinning. It was getting darker, like the distant street lamp was slowly being turned off. She also felt tired, very tired, and cold. Regaining her balance, she spotted her umbrella on the ground.

"Now why didn't I think to use that as a weapon?. Stupid!" she said out loud to herself. Hearing her own voice, it sounded like she'd slurred the words, like she was drunk. But Jen rarely drank alcohol, especially when working.

She grabbed the handle and succeeded in closing the umbrella. She shoved it behind the front car seat. Throwing her pocketbook onto the passenger's seat, she turned sideways and, plopped onto the driver's seat. A sharp pain shot up through her abdomen as she pivoted in the seat and lifted her feet inside. With each movement the pain grew worse.

As she closed the door she noticed something dark and glistening sitting on her lap. Reaching down with her hand, she tentatively touched it. It felt warm.

"It feels wet and coiled, like a snake," she thought. She began to shiver uncontrollably.

"Well, whatever it is, I don't want it in my car," she said, her teeth chattering. Again, her own voice sounded strange to her, like someone else was using her mouth to talk.

Jen reached down, sliding her fingers underneath the coiled mass, and started to lift it, intending to toss whatever it was outside the car. But, as she tried to lift it, she found it was caught on something.

"What is this? What's holding it?"

Then, in the dim light from a nearby lamp post, Jen realized what it was.

If one were standing across the parking lot one would have heard an unearthly, high-pitched scream piercing the night air. It was a scream of sheer terror, the likes of which one might imagine coming only from the depths of hell.

The scream came from a small, isolated car, parked in the far corner of a parking lot, outside a topless bar. The car's side door stood open, a faint light coming from inside. The scream continued for about a half minute. Almost muffled by the sound of the falling rain, a woman's voice could barely be heard.

"Oh God! Dear God, someone help me!!!"

But there was no one there to hear her prayers. No one to help her. She was alone. She began to pray, plead that someone, God, would hear her cries and help her. Finally, even the prayer stopped. All was silent, except for the continued patter of the rain.

Inside the bar, Max finished washing the last of the glasses and put them under the bar. He went into the small kitchen in the rear, checked the back door to be sure it was locked, and shut the light off. Walking through the front of the bar towards the door, he cursed as he realized he didn't have his rain coat or an umbrella. As he held the door open he leaned back inside and shut the main lights off. The faint glow of a fluorescent light behind the bar cast a ghostly glow over the empty bar and, the raised dance platform.

Max yanked the door closed tight, locked the double dead bolts, and lowered his head against the rain.

"At least she's close by," he thought, as he turned to his right and ran the short distance to his eight-year-old Caddy. He grabbed the handle, pulled open the door, and slowly eased his large bulk in behind the wheel. Leaning outside, he grabbed the door's handle and yanked it closed.

Max never bothered to lock his cars. He thought car locks were for honest people. The crooks would just smash the glass to get in.

He turned the key in the ignition and he was happy to hear the engine kick over immediately. He leaned forward and tried to wipe some of the fog off the large front windshield. He only succeeded in smudging the glass, making it worse. He turned on his head lights and wipers, put the car into drive, and slowly eased the ancient behemoth around to the right and out of the parking lot.

"No one else on the roads this time of night, but you never know," he said. "I'll just take my time and drive slowly. That way I'll get home in one piece."

Max hadn't bothered to look over to his left before leaving the bar's parking lot. If he had, he may have noticed a small, faded-blue VW, someone sitting behind the wheel. But he didn't. He drove down the narrow, poorly lit road. The radio was on, a sad country song playing on the radio. The clock on the dash board read 1:45 A.M.

"Maybe I'll get six or seven hours sleep before I have to be back to open for the lunch crowd," he thought to himself.

As he drove down the dark streets his thoughts returned to Jen.

"She'll be on again tomorrow night," he murmured, a smile forming on his lips.

Chapter 2

(The 1960's)

Newspaper headlines cited stories of boycotts, demonstrations, and race riots. It was a time for acts of civil disobedience, voter registration drives and the battle for civil rights. Vietnam was still a far away place, unknown to most Americans. "Pot" was no longer a place to cook food. The "Beetles" were still playing small clubs in Liverpool, England. The "Good Times" were drawing to an end. A new age was dawning.

Airlines were still for the "rich." The common man's means of transportation were trains and buses. In the sixties the sunshine state of Florida was just beginning to emerge as the Mecca for retirement. Interstate 95 was yet to be completed. Great silver buses ran up and down US 1, taking people from one place to another. One of the most widely used and profitable bus companies had a picture of a racing dog on its side, a sprinting greyhound. The company offered safe, comfortable, and reliable transportation at a reasonable price.

Clarence Brown had been a driver for Greyhound for over twenty years. He was proud of his safety record. He took pride in what he did. He made sure his grey uniform was spotless and the brim of his hat shined. His salt-and-pepper hair was cut short in keeping with company regulations. He couldn't understand the popular "Afro"—style hair cut sported by his teenaged son, Clarence Jr.

He worried about him, concerned about his participation in marches with the other young people. He was afraid he'd get himself in trouble some day and lose his scholarship at N.Y.U., Clarence Jr. was a freshman there and preferred that people called him "JR, rather than Junior. JR was his only child he and his wife's pride and joy. Knowing JR was getting a good education and would have opportunities he'd never dreamed of made the lonely job of driving a bus tolerable.

Although Clarence Brown hadn't graduated from high school, he was a proud man. He thought of himself as a professional. He wore his uniform proudly and would never be caught with dirty shoes or a dirty bus. In his years of driving for Greyhound, he'd seen all sorts of people. This particular trip would be nothing out of the ordinary for him. But, for one passenger, it was a trip that would have lasting repercussions for her and for many others in years to come.

The trip from the New York Port Authority Building had taken just under twenty hours. There had been driver changes around the South Carolina-, Georgia border. Clarence Brown had the last leg of this trip. He followed US 1 into Florida and then drove across to the state's west coast. There were cattle farms in the middle of the state now, but in a few years a mouse would come here and cause a building boom that would change the countryside.

Mr. Brown drove through the downtown area of St. Petersburg, Florida. Swinging wide to avoid parked cars, he skillfully maneuvered the long Greyhound bus around the corner and down the block to the terminal. As he pulled up to the platform he tapped the brakes and brought the huge bus to a gentle stop. The long, loud hiss of released compressed air announced to the passengers that they'd reached their destination. Despite his directions to wait until the bus had fully stopped, some passengers had already begun moving out of their seats and were removing items from the overhead compartments. They began shuffling down the narrow aisle towards the front of the bus. Clarence glanced up into his rear view mirror. Seeing the people pushing to be "the first off," he just shook his head. "What's their hurry?" he wondered.

He turned in his seat and nodded to the passengers as they filed by. Some nodded back, bid him good bye with a smile, and thanked him for a safe trip, while others just ignored him. The passengers, many of them elderly, slowly climbed down the stairs and stepped onto the cement platform. Moving towards the middle on the side of the bus, they waited as handlers unloaded their luggage from compartments underneath the body of the bus. Once they'd retrieved their belongings, they scattered, eager to move on to the next phase of their lives.

Once the last passenger had disembarked, Clarence Brown rose and began his routine of moving down the aisle, checking to see if someone had left anything behind. As he passed the rows of seats, he bent down, picking up empty coffee cups, candy wrappers, and soda cans.

As he approached the last row of seats, he found a small, teenage girl, huddled against the right outside wall. Her jacket was draped over her chest and she clutched it tightly under her chin. She was sound asleep. Not wanting to frighten her, he gently touched her arm and shook it.

"Hey. We're here. It's time to wake up," he said softly.

The girl moved slightly. Her head turned towards him and her eyes fluttered open. They were blue. She had blonde, almost white, hair. Bangs hung over her brow and two pigtails dangled from either side of her head. Opening her eyes fully, the girl bolted upright.

"Hey, it's okay. I didn't mean to scare you. You were asleep and . . . . Well, we're at the end of the road. This is where you get off," he said with a smile.

The girl looked up at the driver. She saw a man, of about sixty with sad-looking brown eyes, but with a gentle smile. She smiled back and yawned. Taking the back of her hand, she covered her mouth.

"Excuse me. I must have dozed off," she said and stretched her arms over her head.

The driver guessed that she was twelve, maybe thirteen years old. She wore sneakers, baggy, blue sweat pants, and a matching sweatshirt. Her face, arms, and legs appeared thin, but when she stretched her arms over her head, her jacket slid off her chest onto the floor. Her stretching had lifted the bottom of her sweatshirt up, exposing her bare, white belly. It appeared swollen, "too large for such a skinny kid," he thought. She noticed his gaze and immediately lowered her arms, pulling her sweatshirt down over her stomach.

"I'll be going then," she said. "Thanks, mister."

She rose from her seat, reached underneath, and pulled out a worn, faded-blue knapsack. She took one of the straps, slid her arm through it, and hefted it over one shoulder. As the driver stepped back away from her row, she wiggled out into the aisle and headed down and off the bus.

"Hmm. Poor kid. Probably pregnant and running away from her family," he thought. He'd seen a lot of kids, both boys and girls, riding his southbound bus. From time to time he'd remember a particular face and wonder whatever happened to the kid, how he or she was making out. But, in the spring of 1964 there seemed to be more of them, each looking younger than the one before.

He followed her towards the front of the bus and threw the garbage he'd picked up into a plastic bag. Then he picked up a clipboard with several forms on it, his uniform hat, and the bag of garbage and exited the bus.

Stepping down onto the platform, he put on his hat, walked to a nearby trash can, and dropped the plastic bag inside. He was about to head into the company's office when the sound of voices made him turn around. He saw the young girl from the bus talking to two people at the other end of the platform. The girl seemed nervous. The couple she met reminded Clarence of that painting, "American Gothic, the one that shows an elderly couple, thin and stern looking, the man was holding a pitch fork in his hand and, the woman staring straight ahead, a blank expression on her worn face.

The people in the picture didn't seem to give off any warmth. Neither did the couple talking to the girl. The man stood very erect, arms folded across his chest. He wore a faded, plaid flannel shirt, bib overalls, and work boots. The woman was in a faded house dress, her hair grey and pulled into a bun at the back of her head, a few loose strands fluttering in the warm breeze. On her feet she wore comfortable looking black shoes with thick, short heels.

The woman bent down and began to talk to the girl, who simply smiled and nodded in reply.

The two people who'd met Lori at the bus terminal were her aunt and uncle on her step father's side. Lori's step father, Charles Edgar, had two brothers, both younger. This one's name was Herbert.

Clarence could overhear part of the conversation.

"I'm Edith Edgar. This here is my husband Herbert. Herbert is your dad's brother," said the woman.

"He's not my father," snapped the girl.

"Well you're kin all the same. We've been looking forward to meeting you. You'll be staying with us for a while," the woman snapped back.

Upon hearing this Clarence became aware that he was intruding on a private conversation.

"None of my business," he thought. She's lucky to have someone meet her. Most kids taking the overnight from up north were usually runaways. His wife often said her husband was a big "softee."

"He'd pick up every stray off the street and bring it home if I'd let him," she tell people.

It was true. Clarence felt a responsibility for his passengers that often went beyond the bus. He would see a youngster slouched down in his or her seat.

Sometimes they'd talk to another passenger, but usually they remained silent, ignoring everyone around them.

As they left his bus he would wonder what was going to happened to them. Would they be safe? He had the same thought now about this young girl. What was her story? He'd never know. Instead he turned and headed into the terminal. Clarence Brown had a few hours off before turning the big bus around for its return trip.

The girl and the couple walked to the parking lot and climbed into a Ford pickup truck. She was squished between them. The truck had a floor shift. The lever was a long, metal rod that extended up through the floor. On the top of the lever was a wooden knob. Each time Herbert moved the lever, his hand would brush against her leg. His touch was driving her crazy, but she bit her tongue and kept quiet.

After several minutes riding in silence, the woman spoke up.

"So Laurel, how was the trip?"

"Lori."

"Excuse me?" said the woman.

"My name's Lori, not Laurel," said the girl.

"Sorry. Okay, Lori. How was your trip? How long of a ride was it?" she asked.

"It was okay. I slept most of the time," she lied. "I think it took about twenty-four hours. Yeah, we left at 10 A.M. from the city and it's what, 11 A.M. now? Twenty-four hours."

"Did you eat anything?" asked the woman.

"We stopped a few times along the way."

Lori, didn't tell them she hadn't eaten since she got on the bus. She'd felt nauseous almost as soon as the bus started moving. She guessed it was either the smell of diesel fumes from the bus or motion sickness. She'd thrown up a couple of times in the small, smelly bathroom on the bus. Even if she had gotten some food at one of the stops, she didn't think she'd have been able to keep it down.

"Well, I'm sure you're tired after your long trip. A nice hot bath and nap will set you right," promised the woman. Lori wasn't so sure, but forced a smile anyway.

Herbert Edgar was in his mid-forties and worked in construction. Right now, there was a building boom going on in Florida. The men who fought in World War II were approaching retirement age. Up and down both the east and west coasts one housing development after another was going up. In a few areas, builders would be experimenting with what was to be the next big building boom, condominiums. As a result, Herbert Edgar worked full-time and many weekends as well.

Although they didn't have children, Herbert insisted that his wife, Edith "stay home and tend to the house."

For her part, Edith rarely complained. The only draw back she saw was that Herbert made all the money and took care of all the bills. It was like pulling teeth to get him to part with a dollar. Oh, he didn't spend money foolishly on himself, either. He had no vices and made sure to put a percentage of every pay check into their savings account. Yes, you might say the Edgar's lived frugally. Behind their backs, neighbors said he was just cheap.

Herbert had his pick up truck, which came in handy considering the type of work he was in. Besides, there were only the two of them, so they didn't need anything bigger.

"It got them where they were going," was Herbert's favorite expression when it came to his truck.

Unlike the state's east coast, which was flat with palm trees, the west coast was different. It had low, rolling hills. Instead of palm trees, there were pine. The winters were cooler, but they rarely suffered the damage from hurricanes like the east coast. Some considered it "red neck" country. However, it wouldn't be long before the folks from the central United States and Canada discovered the west coast and turned it into retirement communities. But back then things never seemed to change and life was predictable for the Edgars. That is until his brother's kid came to town.

The Edgars lived in a two bedroom, one bath bungalow on a dirt road just outside Tarpon Springs, Florida. The back of their property ran down to a canal that led out to the Gulf of Mexico. Most homes had a small dock and a small open boat for fishing. To those who had visited both coasts of Florida the west seemed to be stuck in the past century. It was more rural and laid back not like the east coast. Change wouldn't come to that coast for another decade or more.

Once they reached what they called home Herbert parked the truck on the dirt driveway. He grabbed some bags from the back of the pickup and followed the girls into the house. Once inside Edith led Lori to the spare bedroom in the back of the house.

"This is your room, Lori," said Edith. "Tomorrow, maybe we'll go shopping for clothes. I'm guessing, what with your condition and all, the clothes you're wearing now will be too tight for you in no time at all"

Lori could feel her face blush. She wasn't comfortable with people knowing she was pregnant.

When Herbert heard this, he grumbled, "What the hell for? She'll only out grow them."

"Shush," said Edith. "Don't you be saying those things," she warned.

"Well it's true," he said.

"Shush, I said!" warned Edith, raising her voice.

Edith rarely raised her voice, let alone disagreed with her husband. She'd learned after twenty-two years of marriage that it didn't pay to argue with Herbert. It just made him dig his heels in and be more stubborn. Instead, Edith would throw something out in conversation. Like tossing a balloon into the air.

"Wouldn't it be nice if we had a washing machine? Then you wouldn't have to drive me down to the Laundromat on the weekend. You work so hard all week you deserve a rest weekends. Why it'd give you time for fishing." Having said that, Edith left it hanging. Eventually, Herbert would take it in, mull it over in his heard. Later, perhaps over dinner he'd "come up with the idea" as if he'd thought of it first. Whatever! It worked for Edith.

In mid March, Herbert had received a call from his brother, Charles. It was a rare occasion when the brothers talked to one another and neither one ever talked to the third brother, Luther.

Luther lived in Kentucky. He'd married a "mountain girl," as Charles called her.

"He's a woodchuck now," Charles would say despairingly of his brother. Charles rarely had any contact with him either. Maybe an occasional card at Christmas time.

So when he heard his voice, Herbert knew that Charles wasn't calling to pass the time. It usually meant there was trouble. Of the three brothers, Charles was the worst of the men. "He has a mean streak in him," Herbert would tell people warning them to stay out of his way. Charles worked construction like Herbert and was married to a barmaid named Ann Marie. She was a few years younger then him and worked. She had a good figure, but her hair was dry and coarse from constant bleaching. Ann Marie had acne as a teen. As a teen she'd spend hours in the sun trying to get a tan which she hoped would help conceal the scars. Now she resorted to heavy make up. Between the late hours, the heavy cigarette smoke at work and the acne Ann Marie was aging fast. Her skin was dry and she was starting to wrinkle. She looked about ten years older than she was.

The night they'd met, he'd had more than a few beers and was looking for companionship. Ann Marie had flirted with him, as she did with all her customers. But Charles seemed different from the usual customers. He had a nice smile and rugged good looks. They had hit it off. He was funny and charming compared to some of the other losers who passed through the place. Besides, she had a kid to support and so they got married.

Her daughter, from a previous marriage, was named Lori Ann. Lori was a toddler when Ann Marie met Charles. Some said, "Poor Charlie didn't know what he was getting himself into when he married Ann Marie." But that was a two-way street.

Oh, Charles had a good job, but he liked to drink and play the horses. As a result, Mary Ann had to continue to work nights at the bar to help pay the bills. She made arrangements with Charles for him to stay home to watch Lori while she worked. When Lori got old enough for school, Ann Marie got a break and could sleep during the days until she came home. Ann Marie thought Charles was a good father to Lori. Even though she wasn't his own, he didn't seem to mind taking care of her. When Ann Marie came home from work, she'd find Lori all washed and asleep in her bed.

Despite their ups and downs, mostly caused by their mutual abuse of alcohol, Charles and Ann Marie seemed to have a good marriage. But as is the case in so many homes, there were secrets, deep, dark secrets hidden behind closed doors.

When Lori was a small child, her step father often bathed her. He'd often spend an inordinate amount of time cleaning her "private parts" as her mother called this area between her legs. Not knowing any better, the small girl didn't say anything to her mother, her teachers, or her classmates. What was she going to say? My father bathes me funny?. No, she didn't say anything. But in time the small child knew or began to sense it was wrong. As she grew older, her body began to change and she was no longer dependent upon her step father for her baths. She could wash herself. But now her step fathered began to take a different interest in her. She'd find him staring at her in an odd way.

On more than one occasion she awakened in the middle of the night to find him, fully clothed and sitting next to her in bed.

"I thought I heard you crying so I came in to make sure you were okay," he'd say.

At first she found it comforting to know that her "Dad" was always there for her. That is until she awakened one night to find him stroking her cheek, smelling her hair, rubbing her leg. This became more frequent, especially when her mother wasn't around. Again she said nothing to anyone.

Finally one night her step father did something that confused and frightened her. On that particular night her mother was working late.

Charles came into her room as he'd done before but this time he was wearing a robe. As he stood at the foot of her bed, he dropped the robe from his shoulders. Lori pretended to be asleep. He reached down, grabbing a fist full of the thin blanket that covered her small body. He yanked it off her body and threw it across the room. He stood there in the semi-dark, swaying back and forth, as if he were trying to make up his mind what to do next. Lori wrapped her arms around her body, shivering. Suddenly, with a loud grunt, Lori's step father fell on top of her. Lori, squeezed her eyes shut. She clenched her teeth and tried to curl up into a ball, but the full weight of his body prevented her from doing that. Instead, her step father cursed at her, then he grabbed her legs and pulled them apart. What he did next was something so vile that would cause her to have nightmares about it for the rest of her life. Lori's step father, Charles Edgar, raped his twelve-year-old step daughter. Lori stifled her sobs, tears rolling down her cheeks.

She could smell the alcohol on his breath, his body thrusting against her. With each thrust, Lori thought to herself, "Please God, make him stop."

But Lori's prayer went unanswered. Afterwards, he rose from the bed and wiped the sweat and spittle from his face and mouth. He was breathing heavy from his exertion. "Keep your mouth shut about this or you'll be sorry," he warned as he left her room.

She waited in the dark, shivering, hoping he wasn't coming back. When he didn't, she quietly got out of her bed and tip toed down the hall to the bath room. She closed the door before putting on the light. Standing in front of the vanity, she looked at herself in the mirror. Her eyes were red and swollen from crying, her pale, white cheeks raw from the irritation caused by his whiskers. Lori looked down at her little bare feet sticking out from beneath her nightgown. Reaching to her knees, she took the loose fabric and raised her gown up to her chin. Then she cautiously looked down between her legs. There was blood smeared on the insides of her thighs. She took a wash cloth, turned on the faucet, and let the water run until it felt warm. She wet a wash rag and lathered it up with soap. She proceeded to gingerly cleanse herself between her legs. For several minutes she scrubbed and rinsed the area, over and over again, as if trying to get a stain out.

Although she was only twelve, Lori knew that what had happened was wrong. It was a horrible thing, but something she feared sharing with another person. In her innocent, immature mind, she thought it was her fault.

She didn't tell anyone what her step father did. Over the next year and a half, Charles Edgar frequently entered her bedroom in the night. On one occasion while he was on top of her, Lori happened to look towards the door. There, in the hallway, was her mother. She stood there, not saying a word, just watching. Lori couldn't see in the dim light, but a tear was slowly running down her mother's cheek. But who was she crying for?

From that day on, Lori prayed that something would happen to her step father, something that would make him stop coming to her room. After each encounter, her hatred and disgust grew stronger.

"Some day I'll get even. I'll make him stop and no man will ever do to me, what he did. I swear I'd kill him first." This she vowed to herself.

The sexual abuse continued until, a few months after her thirteenth birthday, Lori began to feel strange changes taking place within her body. She'd get out of bed in the morning and have to run to the bathroom to vomit. She felt very tired and "out of sorts," as her mother would say when speaking of her period.

But this was different. Plus, Lori had missed her period. Thinking she had nothing more than a stomach virus, she told her mother. Her mother took her to see a doctor. But this wasn't her regular doctor. She took her to an old man who saw her in the back room of a motel. He examined her, made her pee in a container, and sent them on their way. A week later, her mother received a call from the man at the motel. He told her that her daughter was pregnant. Lori's mother began to cry. When Lori's step father came home that afternoon, her mother sent her to her bedroom.

Lori could hear them arguing in the kitchen. Her mother's voice grew louder. She was calling Charles terrible names and crying as she screamed. Then Lori heard a chair overturn, a loud slap, and her mother fell silent. Charles walked down the hall towards Lori's bedroom. Her step father stopped in her doorway, looked at her for what seemed forever but said nothing. He just glared at her. It was as if he blamed her for what just happened in the kitchen. Lori just sat in her bed, knees pulled up tight against her chest, fearing his wrath would be turned on her. After glaring at her for a moment he continued towards their bedroom.

The next morning, her mother kept her home from school. She didn't understand why. She wasn't sick. She felt fine.

"Lori come here. I need to talk to you," her mother called from the kitchen.

As she entered the kitchen Lori's mother motioned for her to sit down at the kitchen table. She obviously had something on her mind, but hesitated speaking. Apparently she was finding it difficult to put her thoughts into words so that the girl could understand.

Finally, her mother took a deep breath and spoke. She explained to her things about her body and the difference between her body and boys' bodies. Lori already knew about some of these things. She'd overheard girls talking in the locker room after gym class one day. She knew what a period was. In fact, she'd started menstruating over six months before. She knew that girls had babies, boys didn't. Then, while tears streamed down her face, Lori's mother told her that she was going to have a baby.

"How could that be?" she asked.

"It doesn't matter how. What matters is what we are going to do about it," said her mother. Lori didn't know at the time, but her mother had explored the possibility of an abortion. The doctor said he'd perform one, but admitted it was very dangerous. It was also illegal. After much thought, her mother had come up with a different plan.

Ann Marie made her husband call his brother, Herbert in Florida. He told Herbert that his step daughter was pregnant by a boy in her school. He wanted to send her to live with him and his wife, to stay there until she had the baby. Naturally, Charles said he'd pay for her lodging and medical expenses. He told his brother he didn't care what they did with the baby after it was born.

Herbert spoke to his wife Edith, who agreed. Edith said they could probably arrange for a couple from their church to adopt the child. Herbert Edgar knew his brother Charles very well. It wasn't like him to step in to rescue anyone, least of all some one else's kid. He didn't buy that story of the girl getting "knocked up" by a boy in school. If that had been the case, he knew his brother Charles would be all over the kid's family. One way or another he'd get them to pay and he'd manage to make some thing for himself as well. This didn't sound right. It was Herbert's guess that the kid she was carrying was probably his own brother's. He found the very idea revolting, but possible. He kept these thoughts to himself. He never told his wife, Edith what he thought.

So, everything was arranged. At the start of the Easter break, Lori was sent to live with her aunt and uncle in Florida. She would have the baby and return in time for school in September. No one would ever need to know the truth. No one that is except her mother, her step father, and now Herbert and Edith Edgar.

Lori was a very shy and withdrawn child. She had no close friends at school, much less a boyfriend. Once Lori settled in at her aunt and uncle's house, she made herself useful around the house. She did chores and was very respectful towards them. Her aunt found a doctor to look after Lori until she had the baby. It seemed to Lori that the doctors in Florida were younger and nicer than those she'd met at home. No one judged her, even though her pregnancy was becoming apparent to all.

About the only thing that bothered her was the fact that Herbert and Edith made Lori attend church with them every Sunday. They belonged to some kind of "Evangelical" church. Worse yet, they insisted on getting there early and sitting up front in the first pew. As Lori's belly swelled, she became more self-conscious and thought all eyes were on her. The "pastor" seemed to look straight at her when he preached his sermons. He'd raise his voice, warning them about hell. He described a place of fire and torment, the place where all sinners would go, to suffer for all eternity. Listening to him preach, Lori couldn't help feeling like one of these sinners. She did get comfort from the choir, which sang songs "that moved one's soul," as her aunt would say. Lori would clap along, tapping her foot, and join in singing with the rest of the parishioners. Then they'd attend a "social" in the church hall. Here Lori noticed that the people were kind and friendly towards her, never judging or casting an accusing eye.

The months passed and Lori grew in size. By the time she was ready to have the child, it was difficult just getting out of a chair. She'd waddle when she walked, which caused her Uncle Herbert no end of amusement. Uncle Herbert was nothing like her stepfather.

To people he'd meet he came across as stern. However, she saw a gentle side to him. He'd tease her by making the quacking sound of a duck when she'd walk through the room. Lori knew he didn't mean anything by it and actually liked the attention. She saw a gentle side to Herbert and would laugh along with him.

"You look like a turtle trying to walk on its hind legs," he'd sometimes say laughing. "I bet if I rolled you over on your back you wouldn't be able to get up." And then his laughing would become so hard that he'd have trouble catching his breath and tears would roll down his cheeks.

But not all was fun with the pregnancy. She found the summer heat and humidity unbearable. At night, the air was still and insects and frogs could be heard in the nearby canal. Her uncle didn't believe in air-conditioning. So Lori would lie in bed at night, the covers thrown back, the window wide open, hoping to catch a breeze. Her sheets and night gown would be drenched with sweat when she'd roll out of bed in the morning. She found it more and more difficult to get comfortable, whether sitting or lying down.

Her due date came and passed. As the second week of August came, Lori desperately wanted it to be over. The pregnancy, the heat, and the inability to go out and have fun like a normal teenager became unbearable. Lori had begun to think that this baby might never come, that she'd look like this for the rest of her life. But nature took its course and soon the baby was ready to join the human race.

It was one of those typical hot and humid nights. They'd all gone to bed. About two hours later, Lori was awakened by a strange sensation between her legs. When she reached down between her legs and drew her hand away, it was wet.

In fact, the whole sheet was wet. Lori started to cry, not knowing what was wrong with her. She hadn't wet the bed since she was a little girl. She got out of bed and started removing the wet sheets. Her Aunt Edith must have heard her crying and moving around. She came down the hall, walked into Lori's room, and flipped on the overhead light.

"What happened, Lori? Why are you taking the covers off your bed?" asked Edith.

"Oh, Aunt Edith," said Lori, sobbing. "I'm so embarrassed. I must have had an accident. The whole bed is wet."

Edith walked closer and looked down at the soiled bed sheets. She looked at Lori and smiled. She opened her arms and held the little girl tight.

"It's all right, honey. You didn't have an accident. Your water broke, that's all." Edith saw she didn't understand and seemed even more frightened. "It's normal. The water breaks just before you have the baby," she said softly.

"You mean I'm going to have a baby now, here?" she asked.

"Well, I hope not right now, here. We have to get you to the hospital. "Here, put on a clean nightgown and put your robe over your shoulders. I'll wake Uncle Herbert."

Edith woke her husband and then called the doctor to let him know they were headed for the hospital. He told them he'd meet them at the emergency entrance. They drove to the hospital in the old pick up truck. Edith held her close, allowing Lori to rest her head on her shoulder.

"You'll be okay. You'll be just fine, Lori," said Edith, stroking her hair with her free hand.

Once Herbert brought the pick up to a halt, an orderly and a nurse emerged from the hospital. The orderly steadied a wheel chair, while the nurse opened the door and helped Lori get out.

"I can walk," she complained.

"It's hospital rules," the nurse replied with a smile. Lori gave in and eased down into the chair. "You folks can wait in the lobby while we take her up to the labor room. Will anyone be joining her?" asked the nurse. Edith and Herbert just looked at each other and shook their heads, no. They had never heard of anyone going in with a mother in labor before and they weren't about to be the first. It wasn't common practice yet for couples to remain together during labor and delivery.

As she was wheeled down the hall towards an elevator, Lori looked over her shoulder, eyes wide with fear. Edith could only look and throw her a kiss. "Good luck," she mouthed towards Lori. They wheeled her down the hall and onto an elevator. As the door closed, the nurse put her hand on her shoulder.

"Your first?" she asked.

"That's a stupid question. How young do girls get pregnant around here?" thought Lori. Lori just nodded her head.

"You'll do fine honey," assured the nurse.

The elevator stopped and the door opened. In the distance she could hear screaming. It sounded like someone was being tortured.

"Don't mind them," said the orderly. "Some of those women think they have to carry on like that. They're not really in that much pain," he added.

The nurse gave him a look that could have cut through steel. "A lot you know about giving birth. Until you've been through it, keep your mouth shut," she commanded.

The orderly just bowed his head and averted the nurse's eye. Lori was brought over to the nurse's' station and given a bunch of forms to sign. One of the forms was colored yellow, the others all white. Not knowing any better, Lori signed them all. The nurse handed them to the woman behind the desk, who looked them over. When she got to the yellow form, she stopped. She read it, looked at Lori, and then to the nurse. The nurse glanced over as the woman waved the yellow paper in front of her and nodded. The nurse nodded back.

"Is everything all right?" asked Lori.

"Everything's fine," said the nurse and turned her chair away from the desk and moved down the hall.

Lori was wheeled into a small room with two beds in it. One was already occupied. As Lori got out of the chair, the nurse handed her a gown and a large brown paper bag.

"Now I want you to take off all your cloths, underwear too. Also any jewelry and put them into the bag. Then put the gown on so it's open in the back. Then hop up in bed," said the nurse. Before Lori could respond, the nurse drew the curtain closed around her. From the other side of the curtain the nurse said, "The doctor will be in to see you shortly."

Lori proceeded to get undressed and shove her things inside the bag as instructed. Then she took the gown, which was neatly folded on the bed, shook it open, and looked at it.

"Oh well," she thought, never having seen or worn a hospital gown before. After she put it on, she opened the curtains and climbed up into the hospital bed.

She lay back on the hard, flat bed. When she put her head on the pillow, it made a crinkling noise as if it were covered in heavy plastic. She closed her eyes and waited. Thoughts streamed through her mind. From the next bed, she could hear the other woman's regular breathing.

"Ah, this isn't so bad," she thought. With that, the other woman let out with a blood-curdling scream. At the end of the scream, the woman took a deep breath and began to shout a string of curse words, some Lori had never heard before. Then she yelled out a doctor's name and demanded something for the pain. This went on for several minutes before a nurse entered the room. It was not the same one who accompanied Lori to the room.

"What's the matter, honey?" asked the nurse.

"Give me something for the pain now," the woman growled. To Lori she sounded possessed.

"Now calm down, honey. The doctor is on his way."

The nurse left and within a matter of seconds reentered the room with a young man she assumed was a doctor.

"Hi, I'm Dr. Colson. Are you in pain?" he asked.

"Son of a bitch! Yes, I'm in pain," screamed the woman, grabbing the young doctor by his jacket. "Now you get me something to put me out. Do you understand?! If you don't, I'm going to rip this IV tube out of my arm. Then I'm going to come down that hall and find you. When I do, I'm going to rip off your head and use it for a soccer ball. Now do I get something or not?" asked the woman, releasing her grip on the now shaking doctor.

"Of course. Certainly. Something for pain. Nurse, get the anesthesiologist and give her a saddle block, STAT."

"Yes, doctor, immediately," said the nurse, turning on her heels and leaving the room.

The doctor turned to Lori. "As soon as the nurse returns, we'll see about you," he said nervously. Seeing how young his new patient was and the fact she wasn't screaming and threatening to give him a new airway, he sat down next to Lori and took her hand. He proceeded to take her pulse and with the stethoscope listened to her chest, both front and back.

"Can I get one of those saddle things?" asked Lori.

"Maybe, we'll see. But later," he added, glancing over at the other woman who was still staring daggers at him.

The nurse returned, accompanied by a woman who had a long lab coat on. Lori assumed she was a doctor. She carried a small tray of instruments, long needles and clear, glass bottles, which she placed on the table between the two beds.

"Now I understand you're ready for some pain medication?" announced the woman. Before the patient could respond, the nurse pulled the curtain closed. Lori heard the woman tell the patient to roll over on her side and tuck her knees up to her chest real tight.

"There, that should do it," said the woman in the white lab coat, pulling the curtains open. "Now try to lie perfectly still. That will take effect in a moment. Don't try to get out of bed. If you need anything, just push the call button," added the doctor.

"Nurse, could you assist me with this patient, please?"

"Of course, doctor," replied the nurse. She pulled the curtain closed and directed Lori to "Scooch on down" in the bed with her knees up. Lori complied. She could feel the doctor's cold hands on her thighs and inside her vagina.

"A few more centimeters and we should be all set. You're doing fine, Mrs . . . . ?" Here he stopped to confer the chart. "Oh, Miss Edgar," he corrected himself, emphasizing the word "Miss."

As he stood up, she noticed the doctor thumbing through her charts. When he came to the yellow form, he paused and looked at the nurse, who nodded back at him.

"What's so interesting about that yellow form?" Lori wondered.

Lori remained in bed for several hours more. The other woman was taken out shortly after getting her saddle block, never to be seen again.

"She never did scream after that saddle thing," thought Lori. In time, she began feeling severe cramps in her stomach like she had to go to the bathroom.

The pain increased and became more frequent. She tried to keep from screaming. She didn't want to sound like that other woman who'd been next to her. However, the pain grew to a point where she could no longer hold it in.

Finally, she let out a loud moan. A nurse must have heard her and came running in with the same young doctor. He examined her and listened to her swollen belly with his stethoscope.

"She's ready nurse. Take her up to delivery," ordered the doctor.

"What about that saddle thing the other woman got?" asked Lori.

"I don't think you're going to need it. Besides, it's better for the baby if you take as few drugs as possible." Not knowing any better, she listened to the doctor and prepared for the next step in child birth.

What happened over the next few hours was a blur to Lori. She was moved onto a narrow bed-on-wheels, they called a gurney. They rolled her down the hall and into a small white room. There was what looked like a padded table with two metal arms jutting out of one end. She remembered being helped off the gurney and onto the other bed. She recalled lifting her legs up and placing them in the cold, metal contraptions. Lori overheard one nurse call them stirrups. She remembered thinking at the time that stirrups belonged on horses not a hospital.

"OK start the drip," she heard someone say. She looked around the room, trying to get oriented, to see if there were any familiar faces. She thought maybe her aunt would come up to see her at some point in the long day.

Hanging over her head was a large, bright lamp suspended from the ceiling. Lori gazed at it. As she did, it seemed to grow in intensity, get bigger, and then receded in size and distance until the room was in total darkness. "I wonder how they'll see what they're doing," thought Lori. That was the last thing she remembered about that afternoon.

Almost twelve hours after entering the hospital, Lori Edgar gave birth to a child, a child that she never saw. She didn't know it was a boy. She didn't know he was just under seven pounds, about twenty-one inches long, all pink and beautiful.

After giving birth, the baby was carefully examined by a doctor and passed off to a nurse, who cleaned and wrapped him in blankets. He was removed from the delivery room and put into the nursery.

Through the large glass window peered Edith and Herbert. The infant was wrapped in a blue blanket and a matching stocking cap had been placed on his head. The name over the bassinet simply said, "Baby Edgar." Edith began to cry.

"Come on, Edith," said Herbert. "There'll be none of that," he said as he turned her away from the viewing window and walked her down the hall.

Months earlier, and shortly after arriving in Florida, Lori had agreed to give the baby up for adoption. Her aunt told her that it would be best if she didn't see her child after it was born; that it would make it easier that way.

Lori remained in the hospital for three days. The nurses were attentive to her needs, but Lori was sad, depressed. When Lori saw the other new mothers holding and feeding their newborns, she would simply turn away. She'd cover her face in the pillow so they wouldn't hear her crying.

Lori was discharged and returned to her uncle's place to rest.

When she asked about the baby, they would say "it" was fine. "It" was with a good, "church family." She was told to forget she ever had "it." They made sure never to talk about it, never saying whether it was a boy or a girl. She had to settle for the knowledge that it was well and being cared for.

Lori stayed with Herbert and Edith, resting another week before returning home. Herbert and Edith Edgar saw Lori off at the bus terminal. They made her promise to call them once she reached home. "Don't be a stranger. You're family," they said. But Lori knew she'd probably never see them again.

Lori took the Greyhound bus home. By coincidence, she had the same driver as when she came down to Florida. As she boarded the bus, she recognized him and smiled. The driver glanced at her, a puzzled look on his face. He wasn't sure, but she looked familiar to him so he nodded back to her with a smile. But he didn't recognize the blonde girl who smiled at him. The last time he'd seen her she was several months pregnant, very pale, and extremely shy. The girl who boarded his bus today was slim, tanned, and seemed older than her looks. He never connected the two. He guessed she was just being polite.

Lori found a seat in the rear where she could stretch out. For the next twenty four hours she dozed on and off. When she did sleep she'd have crazy, mixed up dreams. She dreamed of babies and pretty clothes, of her step father and horrible things. She wanted to return home, to see her mother, have her own room and clothes again, start school. But then there would be her step father to ruin it. How she hated him.

She knew, of course, how she'd gotten pregnant and who the father was. It made her stomach turn and she felt like she would throw up when she thought of him putting his hands on her again.

She remembered times when she'd go to church with her aunt and uncle. She found herself thinking of her step father. She hated him for what he'd done to her, but felt shame and guilt, because at times she liked it. She was confused about these conflicting emotions. She couldn't understand how she could so hate some one and yet enjoy what that person did to her. Lori recalled listening to the pastor speak of the devil. He described how Satan was the "master of deceit." How the devil could tempt us.

"He even tempted Jesus in the desert," the preacher had said.

Listening to these sermons, she would see her step father as Satan himself. She realized what had happened wasn't her fault, but that didn't take away the shame. Some how she had to cleanse her life of this shame, guilt, and hatred.

One passage from scripture kept returning to her thoughts. "Vengeance is mine, sayeth the Lord."

Not in this case, she promised herself. She knew her step father needed to be punished. He needed to be hurt bad for what he'd done to her. She'd wait until she was older. Then, she'd find a way to punish him. She couldn't wait for that day to come.

However, fate would deprive her of that satisfaction. Lori returned to what she called home. Her hatred was pushed down into the deepest recesses of her soul.

Lori wasn't home more than ten minutes when her step father came to her in the kitchen and put his arms awkwardly around her.

"It's so good to have you home, Lori," he said into her ear. He pressed his body against her, pinning Lori to the counter top.

All the old fears and revulsion flooded back into her mind. Desperate to escape, she reached behind her back, groping for anything to use as a weapon. Suddenly, she felt the form of the wooden handle of a knife. She wrapped her fingers around it and brought it around to his face. His eyes opened wide as he glared at the shining steel blade.

"You ever come near me again and I'll kill you," said Lori through gritted teeth.

Charles Edgar saw the fire in her eyes and knew she meant it. He released her and his body seemed to physically deflate before her eyes. He turned and walked from the room. Lori's step father never tried to touch her again. Lori often thought about what he'd done to her. She fantasized about ways to punish him. To make him pay for what he'd done.

Then one day, fate or God answered one of Lori's prayers.

Her step father had continued to work in construction. The "accident" happened while Edgar was working on a partially completed brick wall.

Without warning, the scaffolding Edgar was standing on weakened and fell. The steel supports and wood planks struck the side of the new wall. Edgar was dropped hard on the ground below. Where the scaffolding hit the wall, the mortar hadn't hardened. The entire side collapsed. Tons of brick, mortar, steel, and timber scaffolding fell on top of Charles Edgar. Co workers rushed to get the material off him. They could hear his screams, hear his labored efforts to breathe. He was obviously in a lot of pain.

The fifteen foot drop hadn't killed him. Instead, he had been slowly crushed to death under the enormous weight of the debris. It took almost an hour to reach him.

When they did, he was already dead.

Even at his funeral, Lori couldn't cry. She actually had to cover her face with a tissue to conceal a smile that occasionally appeared on her face. Her step father was dead and could no longer touch her.

But, Lori felt she'd been cheated. Cheated from getting her revenge. Standing at his grave, looking down into the earthly pit where he'd soon rest, she made a solemn vow. Some day she'd have her revenge for what that "man" had done to her.

In time life returned to some semblance of normalcy. In September, she went back to school. She found the boys looking at her differently. She was still slim, but now her blonde hair was lighter, bleached from the Florida sun. Her skin had a healthy tan and her blue eyes took on a dazzling appearance. Maybe it was the pregnancy, or just nature, but Lori's body had blossomed over the summer. Now she had curves where a young woman most wants them. She seemed to be more developed than the other girls. Some were jealous and made crakes behind her back. Lori didn't care. She didn't need their kind for friendship anyway.

With the attention came self-confidence. She felt good about herself, proud of her body. It was evident in her erect posture and big, toothy smile. Lori Edgar was the most popular girl in the class. The memory of her having given birth to a child slowly faded into the recesses of her memory. She rarely, if ever, thought about it in the ensuing years.

She never called her Aunt to see if she knew how the baby was doing. She had justified her act as being in the best interest of the child. The thought that she'd "abandoned" her son never entered her mind. It was as if those nine months never happened.

Through the years that followed, Lori had many relationships. However, the mark her step father placed on her heart was always there. She could never truly "open up" to a man; never leave herself "vulnerable" again. She had erected a wall and no man would ever be able to get close enough to Lori to inflict that type of pain again.

After graduating from high school, Lori moved out of her mother's home, found an apartment in New York City, and started a new life for herself. She never returned to the home where she'd grown up and rarely telephoned her mother. She would meet and marry a much older man, a very wealthy man. She would be offered a life free of want. Unfortunately Lori would also want excitement in her life, excitement that only a younger man could offer.

Over the years those months spent in Florida with the Edgars became a distant, faded memory. That period in her life never happened. She'd never go back there.

There is an expression, "Never say Never." This would be proven true for Lori.

While she pledged never to have anything to do with the Edgars there would come a time when she would desperately need their help. Again she'd seek refuge in Florida. Like before her presence in their life would create waves, waves that would grow into a tsunami, a tidal wave with devastating results.

Chapter 3

Life for the Edgars of Florida took a dramatic turn after Lori's departure. Edith and Herbert had never had children. They never sought out medical counsel or assistance. Herbert felt it was something good Christian people didn't talk about. Besides, he was of the opinion that it was Edith's fault and not his. At first Edith was extremely disheartened to think she'd never have her own child, never be a mother. Then she suggested to Herbert that they adopt. Herbert, who was always quick with the sarcasm, said, "Adopted kids are like used cars, you're only getting someone else's cast off. They're nothing but trouble."

So Edith resigned herself to a life with Herbert and made the best of it. Edith was a good church woman and, as such, read her Bible daily. There were several women mentioned in the Bible who had been "barren." Then, in their later years, had been blessed with a child. Edith prayed she would be one such woman.

However, when she was about forty-three years. old, she began to miss her period. After about a year of uncertainty, she decided to seek medical advice. She'd gotten the name of a good "women's" doctor from one of the other ladies in her church, a Dr. Feellgord.

Yes, that was his name. Patients used to kid with his receptionist. They'd ask if Dr. "Feel Good" was available to see them. Because of his polite manner and age (he was in his sixties), Edith felt more comfortable going to him with her problem. She didn't tell Herbert. Edith was sure she had cancer. She shared this fear with the doctor as he examined her. He started to laugh. From her position at the time, Edith couldn't see what was so funny.

"Mrs. Edgar, you don't have cancer," he said, peeking his head around her leg.

"I don't?" said Edith.

"Of course not. You're going through your change of life. That's all."

"Oh, doctor, I was so sure I had cancer. Now tell me, what is this change?" she asked blushing.

The doctor realized Edith was naive about certain aspects of life. After completing the exam, he had her get dressed and join him in his office. There he slowly explained what was happening to her body. He was reassuring and patient with her questions. As she was leaving, he gave her a pamphlet to read. He also gave her a prescription to help her with what he called "hot flashes."

Edith left the office relieved, but sad. One of the things Dr. Feellgord had told her was that she could no longer have children.

"I guess my prayer isn't going to be answered," she thought.

Edith wasn't one to be bitter, though. She continued going to church and praising the Lord. She believed

God had a purpose for all things and all people. There was a reason things happened the way they did. Edith totally believed that.

Rather than question God's plan, as many did, she accepted it.

"Leave it up to God," was her belief. It made for a much more contented life.

And so the years passed and the Edgar's, Edith and Herbert, were happy in their own way. Though Herbert wasn't one to show his emotions, she knew he loved her. Besides, he was a good man, a good provider, and didn't fool around with other women. So he drank a little too much sometimes. That seemed to be a trait in the Edgar family tree. Both his brothers drank too much and got mean when they did.

She remembered Herbert's father, Randolf, who died many years ago. When alive, he use to come home on Friday nights, sit down, and drink a quart of whiskey. Then, if he didn't fall asleep in his chair, he'd take to beating either his wife, or one of the boys. He didn't need an excuse. It was just something that happened.

But Herbert was never abusive when he drank. He'd just sit like his father did, but he'd usually stop before he got too bad. Now, as he aged and he had steady work, his drinking became less frequent. It was actually became a rarity to see Herbert drink, let alone get drunk. Yes, Edith and Herbert had a good marriage as far as she was concerned. Then Herbert got that call from his brother, Charles and everything changed. Lori had come down to stay with them while she waited to have the baby. Edith watched her niece's belly swell, growing bigger and bigger with each passing week.

Sometimes when it was just the two of them, Lori would let her aunt put her hand on her belly and feel the baby kick. Edith thought that was just divine. She tried not to think of the day when the baby was born, for it would be a sad day for them all. Edith knew Lori would have to give up the baby.

So, one evening, after dinner, Herbert and Edith Edgar sat Lori down and discussed what would happen to the baby, once it was born. It didn't require much effort on the part of the Edgars before Lori admitted she didn't want the responsibility or shame associated with being an unwed mother, especially at her age. After a brief phone call to Lori's mother back in New Jersey, who never wanted to have anything to do with a "bastard" grandchild it was decided to put the baby up for adoption.

Edith told her that she'd speak to their pastor. She was sure he could help them find a good, Christian family to adopt it. As it turned out, they never did.

Edith thought Lori was being very mature about the whole situation. What she didn't know was that Lori secretly hated the little person growing inside her. She hated where it had come from and couldn't wait to get rid of it.

Edith had worked on her husband, trying to convince him that they should keep the baby. After all, it was family. And if it was a boy, Herbert would have some one to help with the chores. He could teach him building skills. Make a construction man out of him. A boy to be proud of. Someone who'd look after them when they were in their old age. Edith worked her magic on Herbert. Finally, one night, as they lay in bed, he turned to her and made an announcement.

45

"You know, Edith, I've been thinking," he said.

Edith remained on her side. Her back to him, wondering what he was about to say. She knew from past experience that this was the way Herbert made life-changing announcements.

"What is it, dear? What have you decided?" she asked with the emphasis on the "you."

"That Lori is a good kid. She's polite, bright, has a nice smile, and she ain't homely looking." Here he stopped for a moment, searching for the right words. Edith knew this was his way and didn't interrupt.

"Now we don't know who the father is, do we?" said Herbert without conviction in his voice. Edith had her suspicions but kept her mouth shut anyway.

"Charles said it was a boy in her school. If it's some kid in high school, he can't be all that dumb. He sure wouldn't be no retard in high school. Hell, you got to be smart to graduate from high school these days," he reasoned. Herbert never did graduate from high school. When he was a teen, it was the Depression and kids were sent out to look for work by fourteen. He prided himself on being a self-taught man with a degree from the college of life.

"And seeing as how Lori's a pretty little thing, the boy must be good-looking too.

"I guess what I'm saying is, if you really want a kid that bad, we could keep it, just for a while, though. You know, try it out, see if it's okay and all. It's going to be work. It will be your responsibility. You'll have to feed it, change, it, wash it. Do all that stuff."

Edith almost laughed out loud. It sounded like he was giving a speech to a small child on the responsibility of owning a puppy.

"Well, what do you think?" he asked.

Edith waited a moment to catch her breath and allow her heart to slow down.

"Herbert, if you think it would be all right, then it's fine by me. It's the Christian thing to do," she added.

With that, she leaned across the bed and kissed her husband gently on the cheek. Herbert grinned from ear to ear.

"Yep, it's the Christian thing to do," he thought to himself before rolling onto his side and going to sleep.

Edith couldn't wait now for the baby to be born. She had to bite her tongue to keep from saying anything to anyone, especially Lori. She didn't want Lori to change her mind about giving up the baby.

Finally, the day came and they rushed Lori to the hospital. Lori was in labor for several hours before a nurse came out to announce the birth. The nurse led them down the hall where the newborns were kept. Edith was in awe. Glancing at her husband, she saw he was smiling broadly, a tear at the edge of his eye. She couldn't believe how beautiful the infant was. She couldn't wait to hold it in her arms.

As they peered through the window, looking at the baby, a woman around Edith's age stood next to her.

"Your grandchild?" the woman asked.

Edith looked up, surprised, but caught herself before saying anything. She just smiled back at the woman and nodded.

On the morning Lori was being released from the hospital, Edith and Herbert drove up to the hospital. It had been decided that they would not tell Lori they were the ones adopting the baby.

They feared that if Lori ever knew they were the family taking care of her child, she might want the baby returned. On the other hand, if she thought strangers adopted the baby, she would be less likely to seek them out.

Edith and Herbert had met with the hospital social worker several weeks earlier. They'd explained that the mother was a distant relation who had made a mistake and wanted to give the baby up for adoption. However, she wanted the baby to be with a good family and had pleaded with them to take her child and raise it as their own. They said that they'd, "reluctantly" agreed.

The social worker had a stack of papers and forms that needed to be filled out. A yellow page sat prominently on top.

"Now if you'll sign here, at the bottom of the yellow form," she said, handing Mr. Edgar a pen and pointing to a line with a red "x" next to it.

Herbert signed his name.

"Now you, Mrs. Edgar," said the woman, passing the papers to Edith.

With shaking hands, Edith scrawled her signature as directed.

"Now these forms make you the foster parents of the baby born to Lori Edgar, your niece. The yellow paper you signed also has a place for your niece's signature and it will be witnessed by an attending nurse. With Miss Edgar's signature, she gives up all legal rights to the child. However, by law and because of her age, she has six months to change her mind."

She saw the worried look on Edith's face.

"Now don't be concerned. In most of these cases the girl is happy to know the child will be well cared for and rarely changes her mind. Then, at the end of that period, you may adopt the child. Any questions?"

Edith ignored the question. Instead, she thanked the woman profusely for all her help, complimented her on the wonderful staff, and shook her hand several times with both her hands. The administrator was beginning to get uncomfortable with this out pouring of gratitude and just wanted the matter to be closed. The woman rose, signaling the meeting was over. She placed copies of the forms into a large brown manila envelope and handed it to Mr. Edgar. Then she showed them to her door.

"Now the nurse will bring the baby down for you. I understand from what you've told me that, you drive a pick up."

"That's right," said Herbert. "We can't fit everyone in at the same time. We're going to take the baby home first. Edith will stay with him while I come back for Lori."

"That will be fine," concluded the woman. There was another round of hand shaking before the administrator could return to her office.

Edith and Herbert waited anxiously at the nurses' station in the rear of the hospital, where Herbert's pick up was parked. Finally, a nurse from Lori's floor came down carrying the baby, bundled up in blue. She handed the baby carefully to Edith, who held it like she was holding the baby Jesus Himself. From off her arm the nurse slipped the strap of a blue canvas bag with the hospital's name and emblem on the front.

"This is a complimentary bag of baby items we give the new parents when they leave the hospital. I might as well give it to you now, rather than when the mother leaves," said the nurse.

"Thank you kindly," said Herbert as he took the bag from her.

"We better get going. I don't want this bundle of heaven to catch a cold in the breeze way here," said Edith. They waved good bye to the nurse as they pulled out of the hospital driveway.

Instead of turning right towards their home, Herbert turned left. They drove across town and into the "back country," which was mostly cattle farms and orange grooves. After about twenty minutes on the main highway, they pulled off onto a dirt road and followed it up to a small farm house.

As Herbert walked around to open the passenger-side door for Edith, the front door to the house opened.

A woman, who could pass for Edith's sister, if she had a sister, stepped out onto the porch. A small dirty-faced child clung to her dress.

"You're early," said the woman.

"Yes. We wanted to be sure our niece didn't come in contact with the baby," said Edith, which wasn't entirely false.

"Come in the house. I have a crib all set up in our room," said the woman.

"Are you sure it's okay?" asked Edith.

"No trouble. What are fellow church members for if not to help their own." she added.

"Strange, though. I ain't never heard of a mother coming down with the measles just before giving birth. But I guess I can understand why the doctor would want to keep them apart, at least until the mother's safe again. Ya know what I mean?" she added.

"We certainly do," said Edith. "Now, don't you worry about the baby having the measles," said Edith. "The doctor tested him and said he was fine."

"Doesn't matter even if he wasn't. All mine have had it already," she said and wiped her nose on her sleeve. Seeing this, Edith cringed, but kept it to herself.

"I'm sure the baby will be fine. It's only for a few days," she thought.

Edith and Herbert thanked the woman and turned the truck around. They went down the driveway and, turned right, heading back towards the main road and town.

Once they got to the hospital, Edith stayed in the truck, while Herbert went inside to get Lori. A few minutes passed and Edith saw Lori being wheeled to the door by an elderly woman. "Probably a volunteer," thought Edith.

Hanging on to Herbert's elbow, Lori hesitantly rose from the wheelchair. Edith got out of the truck and helped her niece, as she stepped on the running board and slid onto the seat. Edith squeezed in next to her and banged the door shut.

"You okay?" asked Edith.

Lori nodded.

With Lori safely seated between them, Herbert headed away from the hospital and towards their house. Standing by her office window, the hospital administrator who'd helped Mr. and Mrs. Edgar with the paperwork saw Edith, Lori, and Herbert pulling away in the pick up truck.

"Odd," she thought. "I guess they got someone to watch the baby while they came back for the mother. Oh, well," she said and returned to her desk.

Driving home, Edith noticed Lori wiping tears from her eyes.

"What is it, Lori?" asked Edith, putting an arm around her.

Sobbing, she said, "I never even got to see him."

Edith just patted her on the shoulder. She glanced up at her husband with a look that said, "Are we doing the right thing?"

Herbert knew what the look meant and nodded his consent. Lori never mentioned the baby again after that day.

Neither did Edith or Herbert, not in front of Lori, that is.

Lori rested at the Edgars' place for a few more days until it was time to return to New Jersey. She didn't speak of it to her aunt or uncle, but it was something Lori dreaded. She feared the abuse at the hands of her step father would resume. But, she told herself it was almost September and a new school year would begin.

Lori would be entering high school and with that a new beginning. The whole experience of having the baby had matured her, both physically as well as emotionally. She began to look forward to the return home.

For Lori, the days after the delivery flew by. But not fast enough for Aunt Edith,. For her the time seemed like an eternity. The day finally came for Lori to leave. Herbert and Edith drove her to the bus terminal. After hugs all around, she boarded the north bound bus. The Edgars waited patiently for the bus to leave and waved goodbye to their niece.

That same afternoon, Edith and Herbert drove out to the farm and picked up the little boy. As they drove home, Herbert looked over at his wife as she held the baby in her arms. "You look so pretty sitting there, Edith," he said.

"Why thank you, Herbert. Thank you very much." she smiled head down as she gazed at "her" baby.

Chapter 4

It was near the end of February, 1965 when Herbert and Edith filed the final adoption papers with the court. The baby was legally theirs. During the months since Lori left, they'd lived in fear every time the phone rang. Edith dreaded it would be Lori calling to say she'd changed her mind and wanted her baby back. But the call never came. In fact, it would be many years before they would even hear of Lori Edgar again.

Edith and Herbert had settled down to their new role as parents. The members of the church and their neighbors never questioned them about the new baby. They'd seen the young girl living with them and knew she was pregnant. Most assumed the girl was a relative and that Mr. and Mrs. Edgar had adopted the child.

Edith chose the name Jacob. In the Bible, Jacob had been chosen by God to be the patriarch of the twelve tribes, later he would be renamed "Israel." Edith thought "Israel" was too "Jewish" for a Christian baby, so he was baptized in their church, "Jacob Herbert." Edith would often rock him in her arms, telling him how she chose his name and how he too would be "famous" some day. Maybe "infamous" would have been a more appropriate term but Edith had no idea what the future would hold for her "son."

For the Edgar family, life went on. Herbert continued to work at construction. Edith remained home to take care of the house and "her" son. She never seemed to tire of catering to his every whim.

As was her habit, Edith would wake up before sunrise. She could hear Herbert snoring softly on the other side of their "full size" bed. She slid her feet into a pair of worn house slippers and throwing a flimsy cotton robe over her shoulders softly walked from the bedroom; down the hall to the kitchen to prepare breakfast.

A small night-light plugged into a wall outlet in the kitchen cast just enough light to see. Edith opened the refrigerator and removed a can of baby formula. She poured its contents into a small sauce pan and turned on the gas burner. A blue ring of fire flared up around its sides. Turning the knob on the front of the stove, she gradually lowered the flame. She stood there for a moment, staring, wondering what it was she was supposed to get. Suddenly it dawned on her and she reached up and removed a bottle from the shelf. She returned to the stove and stuck a finger into the milky liquid. "Hmm," she said out loud. She shut off the flame and carefully poured the warm liquid into the bottle and put a top on it. As if on cue she could hear Jacob start to cry.

"I swear he can smell this stuff," she said with a smile.

Grabbing a clean dish towel off a rake and headed down the hall testing the temperature of the formula with a few drops on her wrist as she walked. "Ah, just

55

right." The small guest bedroom where Lori had stayed a short time ago had been turned into the nursery. In the faint light cast into the room by the rising sun, she made her way across the room to the crib.

"There, there, now, Jacob, my big boy. Mommy's here. Don't you fuss."

She bent down and gently lifted the small infant from its crib. Cradling him in the crook of her arm, she carried the child out of the room and down the hall to the living room. There she switched on the TV, adjusting the volume so she could barely hear it. Backing up, she sank into her arm chair, the baby cushioned in her arms.

"Is this what you want?" asked Edith. "Just a minute, my precious," she said as she turned the baby bottle upside down and shook a few drops from the rubber nipple onto the inside of her arm.

"Just right," she said to the baby and placed the tip of the nipple next to his lips. The baby eagerly grabbed hold of it with its mouth and began to suck.

"Not so fast," warned Edith. "You'll get a tummy ache."

She sat for a while just looking at the infant suck on the nipple, a feeling of contentment falling over her.

Finally, she noticed the TV and began watching what was on the screen. It was one of those religious revival meetings they held in tents. A preacher was moving through a crowd of mostly older folks. For the most part they had sad weary expressions on their faces. He had a microphone attached to a long cord and was speaking to his congregation. He must have been at it for a while because Edith could see the sweat dripping off his face, the collar of his shirt wet from perspiration.

He stopped what he was saying long enough to wipe his entire face with a large blue-and-white handkerchief. It too was soaking wet.

"And the Lord cast down fire and brimstone on those two cities. Why? Because they were wicked. They'd committed every vile act known to man. They were an abomination. God spared a chosen few because they repented and were forgiven. He allowed those few to leave before he destroyed that wicked place and all who inhabited there," screamed the preacher into the microphone.

Edith noticed that he had a worn leather-covered Bible in his other hand. From time to time he'd open it, allowing the pages to fall by themselves, opening to just the spot he wanted to read from. The preacher slapped the Bible and continued.

"We are not on this earth to have joy and happiness. We are not here to gather up wealth or possessions. We are not here to follow in the foot steps of the evil one, the one caste down into the fires of hell. No, my brothers and sisters, God put us here on this earth to suffer and toil, to pray for repentance, to beg God for forgiveness, and in the end enter into His kingdom where He awaits the righteous. Now I ask you, are you ready to give it up for God? I said, are you ready to walk in the footsteps of the Lord?" he screamed louder.

The people began to respond, some saying "yes," others saying "amen."

On a signal, the choir began to sing. The people stood, swayed, and clapped. Soon they joined in the singing. As they followed the sounds of the music, a basket was being passed among them. Men and women who looked too poor to even own a wallet or pocketbook dropped wads of bills into the baskets.

Edith was distracted when the baby began crying in her arms. "See. I told you so. You drank too fast, and now you have gas. Now don't you fret none., Mommy will take care of that," she said, lifting him up over her shoulder. She began rubbing the child's small back and patting gently, humming to the music coming from the TV.

A deep rumble came from deep within the baby. "Burp!!"

"Where did that come from?," laughed Edith. "That's a mighty burp for such a little boy. Now, I have to change you. It's time and it's back to bed."

Edith carried the baby back into the bedroom, where she changed his diaper and laid him down to sleep. She stood there as he lay on his stomach, his little face turned towards her. "My little angel," said Edith as she rubbed his back. After a while, Edith returned to her bedroom. She removed her robe and hung it on the door knob. Then she slipped out of her house slippers and carefully got back into bed. As she pulled the covers up to her chin Herbert rolled over onto his other side, his snoring ceasing for a moment. Waiting for sleep to take over her body, Edith thought about her baby boy. A smile formed on her lips and she thanked God for answering her prayers.

Chapter 5

In the years since the adoption, the Edgar family went about their lives. From the very beginning, little Jacob was schooled in the mysteries of the church his parents attended. At night, while other parents read nursery rhymes to their children before bed time, Edith would sit with Jacob and read to him from the Bible. As soon as he could understand, Jacob was lead to believe that God was a "vengeful God." Their church preached that the "End," or "Rapture," was near, that when the "Rapture" came, God would gather all the "true" believers and sweep them off to be with him in paradise. Those remaining would endure years of unspeakable torment. God would purify those left behind with fire, floods, plague, and other calamities before the Final Day.

Jacob would listen wide-eyed to every detail of these stories. He was taught that it was the responsibility of the righteous to do God's will. He was told the world was divided between the "chosen" and the lost. It was the mission of the "chosen" to win over the souls of the lost.

To Edith, her son was perfect. She'd often say to neighbors, "He's such a good child. Why, he doesn't even get cavities, as if the boy had some control over this, other than brushing regularly. But it was true. Jacob was one of those lucky people who had perfect teeth. In fact, he only visited the dentist once or twice in his entire life and never required a filling or an X-ray.

Jacob was raised a "good Christian." He listened to his pastor and believed. He listened to his "mother" and believed. He was an good student, getting mostly "A's" and "B's." He was rarely a discipline problem in school. However, on a few occasions, Edith was called to the school because Jacob had been fighting with one of his classmates. As one teacher put it, Jacob acted like he was "possessed." What troubled the teachers most was the vicious and savage way Jacob would respond to these taunts of his classmates. He would have to be physically restrained by an adult. He was described in one teacher's report as "wild eyed, almost foaming at the mouth, and acting like he was trying to kill the other student."

By the time Edith reached school on these occasions, her son would have calmed down. As a result, she couldn't believe their assertions. Instead she believed her son had been taunted by the other students and that the description of the fight had been, exaggerated by the school personnel. No way could her little boy be capable of such a display of anger or rage. She refused their suggestions that they seek counseling for the boy.

As he got older, Jacob became more of a "loner." He was not involved in after-school activities. He didn't participate in sports. He didn't join scouting groups or any clubs, for that matter. He was content to go home and spend as much time as possible with his mother. Jacob loved his mother more than anyone or anything in the world.

Jacob loved his father, Herbert, but it was different. Herbert wasn't affectionate and, rarely praised him, as his mother did. In fact, Jacob looked at Herbert as a rival in some ways. He felt he had to compete with his father for Edith's attention.

Jacob found it difficult to conceal his feelings for his mother. As a result, the other boys teased him and called him a "momma's boy." When Edith and Herbert first attended open-school nights, they were mistaken for his grandparents and this only added to the teasing. The place Jacob felt most comfortable was in church. He thought he might want to be a preacher. After all, he knew all the passages of the Bible. He admired his pastor and saw the way people hung on every word he spoke. He was a respected member of the community. So Jacob decided to speak to his pastor after church one Sunday.

After Sunday services, Jacob's parents joined the other parishioners in the hall for coffee and cake. The pastor took Jacob next door to his house. Once they were alone, the pastor invited Jacob to sit on the sofa. When he did, the pastor sat down next to him.

"Now tell me, Jacob, why do you think you want to be a preacher?" he asked. Jacob sat quietly, trying to think of an appropriate answer to so serious a question. As he did, he noticed the pastor rest his arm behind him across the back of the sofa, behind him. Then the man took his other hand and placed it gently on Jacob's leg. Jacob didn't know what to think or say.

He turned and looked at the pastor. The man was staring down at him, smiling. He stroked Jacob's blonde hair and ran his hand over the boy's shoulder. Then the pastor leaned over and kissed him on top of his head. Jacob was shocked to feel the man's hand on his crotch.

He just sat there dumbstruck. He didn't know what to do, what to say. This was his pastor, a man of God. Suddenly, this man of God pulled Jacob's pant's zipper down and reached inside. He started to rub the boy, causing him to feel a tingling sensation in his loins. Jacob was all of ten years old and was very confused by what was happening. "No!" he yelled and jumped to his feet. He didn't know what the man was doing. He just knew it was wrong. He ran from the house and across the yard to his father's pick up. He opened the door and climbed inside, locking both doors. He sat there shaking all over.

In time, the people began coming out of the hall and he saw his parents approaching the truck. He unlocked the doors and they got in and closed their doors. Edith looked down at Jacob. "Are you all right, Jacob?" she asked.

"Yeah, why?" he stammered.

"Your face is so red. Do you have a fever? Come here," she ordered and pressed her lips against his forehead. "No. You feel fine. What happened with Pastor Ruben?"

"Nothing," Jacob blurted out.

"Are you sure? When he came over to the hall after your talk, he looked upset about something. I swear he made a point to avoid us as we left the gathering," she said.

"Nothing happened, Mom, really. We had a nice talk and then I left. That's all," he said.

"Well that's good. Your dad and I were talking and we think it would be good for you to spend more time with Pastor Ruben. It will keep you occupied and out of trouble. That way you could talk to him about your thoughts of becoming a minister and see what it's like to live that kind of life."

Jacob sat quietly, fear churning in his stomach.

Several weekends passed before Edith insisted that Jacob visit the pastor again. She had Herbert drive him over to the parish house and drop him off in front. Jacob stood there alone, as his father pulled away. He didn't know what to do. He was about to run away when the door opened. It was Pastor Ruben.

"Well, Jacob, how good to see you. Please come in. I was just going to have a cup of tea. Would you care to join me?" he asked.

"I don't like tea, sir," said Jacob.

"That's all right. I have milk. How about a glass of milk and some cookies, then?"

"OK," said Jacob.

"Good. Well, come in, boy. Don't stand out there all day," he said, holding the door wide for him to enter.

Over the next several months, Edith made sure her son spent Saturdays with the pastor. In time, Jacob began to feel less fearful of his sessions with his pastor. He found the man was a kind and gentle. He wasn't hurting him. He began to see the pastor's occasional fondling as just his way of showing he cared. So Jacob and the pastor continued to spend time together. At the conclusion of their sessions together the pastor would offer to give Jacob a massage. Pastor Ruben said it was a way to relax after all their "learning." They seemed innocent enough and Jacob found it relaxing. Sometimes the pastor would have Jacob remove his shirt before he'd rub his back. At the end of each visit, Pastor Ruben would hug Jacob, holding him tight to himself. But that was all.

Then one day Pastor Ruben did something that frightened the little boy beyond words. It was a warm summer day. Pastor Ruben was wearing shorts, but no shirts. He had Jacob lying on his stomach on the sofa and was giving him a massage.

Since Jacob's eyes were closed, he didn't notice the pastor slip out of his shorts. When he turned his head to the other side he was shocked to see the man standing there totally naked. But worse yet was what the pastor tried to get Jacob to do. He wanted the boy to touch him.

"No!" Jacob yelled, and pushed himself up and off the sofa. Now Pastor Ruben's face turned beet red. His eyes were wide and his nostrils flared.

"Come here, boy," he commanded.

"No!" screamed Jacob again and ran from the room. He went into the kitchen and hid behind the pantry door. Pastor Ruben came into the room screaming for Jacob to come out. Noticing the door to the basement ajar, the pastor walked over and opened it all the way.

"Come up here, Jacob. I'm not going to hurt you," called the pastor down the stairs.

With the pastor's back to him, Jacob tried to run out of the kitchen. Pastor Ruben heard him and spun around to grab him. He caught the sleeve of the boy's shirt and held on. In sheer terror, Jacob whirled around and shoved the man away from him with all his might.

The pastor released his grip on Jacob's shirt. Off balance, his hands swinging like a windmill in the air, he struggled to grab something in order to regain his balance.

Jacob watched him teetering on the top step of the basement stairs. He didn't try to help him.

"Go to hell, you bastard!" he thought. As if in slow motion, Pastor Ruben lost his balance and fell backwards down the stairs. Jacob could hear him bouncing on the wooden steps, something metal crashing down the stairs also. Then there was silence. Jacob stood back, expecting to see the man climbing back up the stairs. He was ready to run just in case. Nothing. He waited to see if he could hear the pastor moaning or calling for help. Nothing. Slowly, the boy walked over to the open door, which lead down into the basement. He peered down.

It was dark and Jacob couldn't see the bottom. Feeling along the wall, he found the light switch and pushed it up. A small light bulb at the foot of the stairs illuminated the bottom. Jacob could see Pastor Ruben lying there, his head twisted at a strange angle, blood forming a pool around his head.

"Pastor Ruben, are you okay?," yelled Jacob.

The man didn't move. Not knowing what to do, Jacob panicked. He turned around and returned to the other room to retrieve his shirt, then put it on and went running from the house. He ran as fast as he could down the road to a neighbor's house.

"Help! Help!" he shouted, pounding his little fists on the door.

A woman Jacob recognized from the church came to the door, drying her wet hands on a dish towel.

"What is it? What's the matter?" she asked.

"There's been an accident at Pastor Ruben's. He fell down the cellar stairs. I think he's hurt bad," the boy blurted out.

"David, come here quick," she yelled to her husband, who was in the back yard. In a moment, a man came to stand beside the woman.

"Go over to the pastor's place and see what's going on. This little boy says there's been an accident." Jacob followed the man back to the pastor's place. But once there, he refused to go inside.

"Maybe the pastor was all right. Maybe he was just stunned," thought Jacob.

When the man emerged from the pastor's house, his face was ashen.

"Wait here. Don't go inside. I'm going to call for help," said the man, running off to his own home to call the police.

With sirens wailing, the police arrived just before the town ambulance. The tall uniformed policeman went in, followed by two medics. Several minutes later, the medics returned to the ambulance and departed.

Some time later, another police car came. Jacob's parents were in the back. Edith immediately ran to hold her son and, make sure he was okay. After about two hours, Jacob and his parents were taken back to their home by the policeman.

They surmised that the church's pastor had started downstairs, tripped over some gardening tools, and fallen down the stairs. He'd banged his head hard on the concrete floor, causing a deep gash. But it wasn't a blow to the head that killed the pastor. Rather, a broken neck had caused his death. The police determined that there had been a tragic accident. They never considered any other possibility as the cause of death.

A strange thing happened to Jacob as a result of that incident. He reasoned that despite what he'd been told, Pastor Ruben was evil and had done bad things. God had seen it and wanted him punished. Jacob was merely the hand of a "vengeful God." He'd been taught for years that, "all things have a purpose and come from God." Jacob rationalized in his young mind that he did God's "doing." Jacob acted on behalf of God. It wasn't his fault.

Chapter 6

The years passed and Jacob enjoyed a relatively uneventful life following the sudden death of Pastor Ruben. It took almost a year before a search committee found a new preacher. The new pastor seemed to have the same beliefs as the members of the congregation. He fit in very well.

The Edgar family continued to attend services on Sunday. However, there was never any more talk about Jacob becoming a preacher. Nor was the topic of the "tragedy," as Edith Edgar liked to refer to it, ever discussed.

Jacob grew in size, but not in personality. To his teachers and classmates, he remained withdrawn and isolated from the rest of the students. He was no longer picked on by the other boys. They'd seen his violent side and were afraid of it. He was called the "sleeping giant" back by the other students because he was nearly six feet tall by the age of seventeen. Edith said he must have taken after his father's side of the family. Jacob never questioned her about that, or thought anything strange about what she said. He just assumed she was referring to his "father' Herbert, who was of average height.

As Jacob grew older he continued to spend more time with his father, always seeking his approval. He quickly picked up the skills needed for construction and began working part time and summers with his father on projects. The work was hard, but Jacob enjoyed it. By the time September rolled around and it was time for him to return to school his body was muscled and tanned from working out doors. In Edith's eyes, "her" son looked like a bronzed god, with his blonde hair.

In addition to working together, Herbert took the boy on hunting and fishing trips with him. They'd travel to the interior of the state where there was still open land and forests. They'd hunt deer in season and fish in the canals and off shore in the Gulf, when the weather permitted. Herbert taught Jacob how to use a knife, how to skin and gut deer and how to clean fish. For his seventeenth birthday, Herbert gave his son a hunting knife. It had a six-inch blade and folded closed. It had a bone handle and when opened measured almost a foot long. It had a two-sided blade. One side of the blade was slightly curved upward and tapered at the end. It was extremely sharp. The other side was serrated for sawing or scaling. The handle was made from an elk antler. The knife came in a leather case with a loop attached so it could be slipped onto Jacob's belt. The boy was very proud of his gift. To Jacob it was like a right of passage. He was now a man and his father had given him his blessing, something most boys cherished.

Edith would frequently find him sitting with a stone, sharpening the blade. He worked on the blade until it was as sharp as a razor and could easily slice through a piece of paper. She didn't approve of the knife or the hunting, but she felt it was a good time for the men to "bond." Besides it kept him out of trouble.

When Jacob graduated from high school he decided to follow in his father's foot steps and go into construction work, full time. Edith wasn't pleased by this. She wanted him to go to college.

"Be the first in the family," she'd say.

But Jacob showed no interest in furthering his education. He wanted to get out, make money. Buy his own car.

Then when Jacob was nineteen years old, something happened that would destroy everything Edith and Herbert had worked for and would change Jacob's life forever.

They'd been sitting at the kitchen table finishing up dinner, when the telephone rang. Edith answered, as she always did. Herbert would always say, "It's not for me," half as a joke, but usually he was right.

Most of the time it was one of the women from the church group calling to gossip. But not this night. After she took the call, she turned to Herbert and said, "It's for you," a questioning look on her face. Jacob looked on, wondering who it was. Herbert took the phone, wondering who'd be calling him.

"Hello," he said. After listening for a moment he said, "Just a minute," and turned to Jacob. "Son, do me a favor. I was thinking of going fishing tomorrow. Would you get our rods down from the garage and check them out. Make sure everything's okay."

"Sure, Dad," said Jacob and excused himself from the table. Edith continued to look at her husband, wondering what was going on.

Herbert stayed on the phone for about five minutes, occasionally jotting down information on a piece of paper he'd pulled from one of the kitchen drawers. He said little, mostly listening. When he finally hung up, he sat down and stared off across the kitchen.

"What is it, Herbert? Who was that?" she asked. Herbert remained quiet for another minute before speaking.

"That was a guy named Murray Siegel. He said he was Lori's husband. Lori, my brother, Charles' kid," said Herbert. "He said he and Lori were on their way here by plane. He wants us to meet them. He said something about Lori staying with us for a while."

"Lori Edgar, coming here? Why?" asked Edith, her face drained of blood.

"He didn't say, just that they'd be arriving at Tampa Airport on Delta flight #300."

"When?"

"Tomorrow at 2:20 P.M.," replied Herbert.

"What about Jacob? Did he say anything? Did he ask about the boy? What do we do with him? What do we tell him? Tell her?" asked Edith, her hands shaking, her voice trembling.

"I don't know.? I'll think of something,?" said Herbert without much conviction in his voice.

After several minutes of silence Herbert looked up, a sad and dejected look on his face.

"We tell her the truth," he said.

"The truth! We can't. We'll lose Jacob. I can't allow that," she said and began to cry.

"Now, Edith, we knew some day this might come back to haunt us."

"But not now! Like this?" she moaned.

"I'm afraid we have no choice. We'll meet them at the airport and see where we go from there," said Herbert.

They didn't say anything to Jacob that night. The next day Herbert explained that a "distant" relative had called and was coming to visit them for a while. They avoided answering his questions. They said it was unexpected and they didn't have all the answers yet.

But Jacob saw the worried looks on their faces. He saw his mother's red eyes and knew she'd been crying. He knew something was up.

The next day Edith and Herbert drove down to Tampa to meet Lori. They left Jacob home because there was little room in the truck for all of them. They drove the half hour's drive in silence. When they arrived, Herbert parked the truck and they headed towards the Delta arrivals terminal. The bulletin board said flight #300 was on time and arriving at Gate 3. They walked to the gate and waited, not knowing what to expect as they watched as the passengers disembarked. They didn't see anyone who looked like Lori as they remembered her. But then that was eighteen years ago.

They were about to leave when a voice over the public address system announced, "Will Mr. or Mrs. Herbert Edgar please come to the information desk at the baggage claim center."

"Now what?" said Herbert as they headed in that direction. When they found the information desk Herbert went up and identified himself to the girl behind the counter.

"Yes, Mr. Edgar. That gentleman over there is looking for you," she said with a smile.

Herbert turned to look where she was pointing. Standing alone near the baggage carousel was an elderly man, dressed in casual, but expensive looking, clothes. He wore large, dark sun glasses, which seemed odd because they were indoors. Herbert walked over to the man and extended his right hand.

"I'm Herbert Edgar. I understand you paged me."

The man turned nervously. Seeing Herbert's out stretched hand, he took it in his and shook it.

"Thank you for coming, Mr. Edgar. I'm Murray Siegel. We spoke on the phone yesterday."

"Yes, Mr. Siegel. Where's Lori?" he asked, looking over the man's shoulder towards the exit ramp.

"Are you alone?" asked Mr. Siegel.

"No. My wife Edith is here," he replied, turning towards Edith, who was standing off to the side. Herbert waved for her to join them. When she did, he introduced her to Mr. Siegel.

"Come this way, please," said Murray Siegel. He lead them a short distance to a group of chairs where several people sat. Murray walked over to a woman who was seated with her back towards them. Edith could see she was wearing dark glasses, like Mr. Siegel. She had a kerchief on her head. Mr. Siegel bent down, touching the woman's shoulder and saying something to her.

"Lori, this is your uncle and aunt, Herbert and Edith Edgar," said Murray, as he gently took her hand. The woman rose from her seat, turned, and lifted her sunglasses from her eyes. She had a confused look on her face.

Herbert didn't think she recognized them. Edith couldn't believe it was the same girl who'd stayed with them almost twenty years ago. Although she knew Lori was in her early to mid-thirties now, this woman looked much older. Her face was thin and drawn, her eyes glassy, lacking any life in them. Deep, dark circles formed under each eye. Lori extended her hand as Murray lead her towards Herbert and Edith.

"Hello, Lori. How are you, honey? I'm your Aunt Edith. Don't you remember me?" asked Edith, extending her hand to take Lori's. The woman's hand was weak and cold to the touch. After shaking her hand Lori backed away, arms wrapped tightly around her chest. Edith felt Lori had no idea who they were. Herbert stood back a step and looked in shock at Lori. He couldn't believe this was the same little girl who'd stayed with them, who'd given birth to the boy they called their son. Herbert looked towards Murray Siegel for some kind of explanation.

"Please, why don't we go somewhere that's more private and we can talk," suggested Murray.

"There's a coffee shop just down the walkway. We could go there," said Herbert.

"That would be fine," answered Murray. He went down and spoke softly to Lori.

Neither Edith, nor Herbert could hear what he said. Lori picked up a small pocketbook from where she'd been sitting and followed them towards the coffee shop. No one said anything further until they were seated and the waitress had taken their order.

Herbert and Edith sat across from Murray and Lori.

"By the looks on your faces, I can see your confusion," started Murray.

"Lori is my wife. We've been married for almost eight years now. She's been through some trauma recently that's left her rather shaken. She's not dangerous or anything. Her doctor has her on antidepressants for her nerves. She took some Valium before boarding the plane. That's why she's so quiet. I assure you, once the medication wears off, she'll be her old self again."

"I wonder what her old self is like," thought Herbert.

"What was this trauma you mentioned?" asked Edith.

"I'm afraid it's of a personal nature and better not discussed. Her doctor feels she just needed a change of scenery," responded Murray. He could see they were a little taken aback by his response.

"Please, don't misunderstand. I would love to share with you the whole story, but I'm afraid for many reasons I can't. I know this may not be acceptable to you, but I ask your indulgence. If it were at all possible I wouldn't be putting you in this position."

"You look like you could afford to take Lori anywhere, a cruise, one of those fancy islands. Why bring her here?" asked Herbert, a slight edge to his voice. He felt Edith bump his leg with her knee under the table.

"The truth is, I'm afraid the press would find out if I took Lori to one of those places. You know how relentless the press can be. You see, publicity, any kind of publicity, could have a negative impact on my business right now. A lot of people depend upon me for their livelihoods. I needed to get Lori away from all the pressures she's been under lately. She'd spoken so fondly of you in the past. I thought a short stay with you would be good for her. I'm desperate. Won't you please help her? Of course, I'll see that all her expenses are more than taken care of."

Murray let that thought hang in the air. He could see that Herbert was thinking this over. In the mean time, Edith was looking at Lori, her head tilted to one side, a look of compassion in her eyes. Finally, Edith spoke up.

"Herbert, Lori is family. We can't turn our backs on family. Besides, it's the Christian thing to do," she added.

Herbert looked at her for a moment. "What could the press possibly want with them?" he wondered. Then he turned towards his wife and smiled. "OK. Lori is family and we Edgars take care of our own."

"Thank you. Thank you both. You won't regret this. Lori will be no bother, I promise," declared Murray.

"So, she got any bags?" asked Herbert.

Murray ignored the question, a nervous, almost frightened look on his face.

"You understand, no one is to know she's down here with you," warned Murray.

"No problem," said Herbert. He didn't understand, but wanted to be out of the airport. All the crowds and noise were making him feel ill at ease.

Murray reached into his pocket, extracted a wad of bills, and threw a twenty on the table. "Here, let me take care of the coffee. Her bag is probably unloaded by now."

"Twenty bucks. Pretty free with his money," thought Herbert, looking at the crisp bill on the table.

Edith took Lori by the hand and lead her back to the baggage area. When they reached the baggage carousel, there was only one medium-size bag left, slowly being carried around and around. Murray reached down and grabbed it by the handle.

"Is that it?" asked Herbert, expecting more.

"Yes. We left in somewhat of a hurry," answered Murray.

Herbert took the bag from him. Murray reached into his inside jacket pocket and took out his wallet. He removed several bills, folded them, and thrust them into Herbert's hand.

"Take this. It will help cover your expenses for now. Perhaps Mrs. Edgar wouldn't mind taking her shopping for some clothes while she's down here," whispered Murray.

Herbert didn't look at the money, but just shoved it into his pocket.

"I'm afraid we're going to be a little crowded. All I have is a pick up truck outside," said Herbert apologetically.

"Oh, I'm not coming. I have to catch the next flight back north," replied Murray.

Edith was a little surprised that the man was dropping his wife off with people he knew nothing about. But she figured her questions would be answered in time. Herbert left them inside the terminal while he went to fetch the truck. Stepping out into the glaring Florida sun, Herbert squinted his eyes as he walked towards the parking lot. He found the pick up in the lot, opened the driver's side door, and started to get into the cab. Then he remembered the money Murray had given him. He was curious to see how much he'd given him for "expenses." He reached into his pocket and withdrew the money. Opening the folded bills, he noticed the top one was a hundred dollar bill. Then, as he peeled each one back, he counted out nine more hundred dollar bills.

"A thousand bucks," Herbert gasped out loud, then nervously glanced around to see if anyone noticed the money. Assured that he wasn't being watched, he counted the money again. He came up with the same total. With a big grin on his face, Herbert got into the truck and headed over to where he'd left the others.

He found Murray and the two women standing by the curb of the "arrivals" building. As he pulled up and came to a stop, Murray hefted the suitcase into the back of the truck and walked around to the driver's side.

"Thank you again, Mr. Edgar. You have no idea what this means to me," he said, shaking Herbert's hand.

"By the way, is there a phone number where we can reach you in case we have to call," said Herbert.

"I'd give you my number, but I'm out of town a lot. I'll call you on a regular basis. I'll be sending you a money order every couple of weeks in the same amount I just gave you, if that's okay with you?" asked Murray.

"That'll be fine," was Hebert's reply. "Every couple of weeks?," wondered Herbert. "How long is he planning on leaving her here?" he thought, scratching his head.

Murray walked back around the truck where he also thanked Edith. Then he turned to Lori. He bent his head and took her chin gently in his hand. Raising her head so he could look her in the eyes, he smiled.

"Lori, I'm going to leave you with Herbert and Edith now. You'll be fine with them. Don't worry about anything. I love you, sweetheart," he said and kissed her on the cheek. Lori didn't respond. She still didn't seem to act like she knew what was going on around her. Edith helped Lori into the truck and climbed in beside her.

"Well, I better run or I'll miss my flight. I'll talk to you in a couple of weeks," Murray said as he closed the truck's door for Edith. With that, he turned and walked quickly back inside the terminal.

Herbert put the truck in gear and headed towards the exit of the airport.

"What did he say? Did he tell you how long Lori will be staying?" asked Edith.

"Nope. Just that he'd call."

They drove the rest of the way in silence. Edith glanced at Lori a few times and tried to make eye contact. But Lori just stared straight ahead, a slight smile on her face.

When they got home Edith put Lori's suitcase in a small, back room that she'd used for her sewing. It was sparsely furnished with a bed, dresser, and an old sewing machine. In a corner sat a basket of dirty wash, which Edith quickly removed.

"Why don't you lie down for a while, Lori. Take a nap. When you wake up we can get acquainted over a nice cup of tea. How's that?" asked Edith, not expecting a response.

"That will be fine, Edith," said Lori.

Edith was taken aback by her words.

"You can speak!" Edith let slip out. "Oh, I'm sorry, honey. I didn't mean anything by that. It's just . . . I thought," stammered Edith.

"I know," said Lori. "This must be very confusing for you. We'll have our little talk later, okay?" asked Lori, not expecting an answer.

Edith turned and walked out of the room. She found Herbert in the kitchen, sitting at the table.

"So?" he asked.

"She talked to me," said Edith.

"Did she now? I guess she ain't as crazy as we first thought," commented Herbert.

"Now you stop that, Herbert. Don't you be calling nobody crazy. Hear?" warned Edith. "How much did he give you?" she asked.

"A thousand bucks," was his reply.

"A thousand?" was all Edith could say.

"And he said he'd be sending more every couple of weeks."

"How long do you think she'll be staying?," asked Edith.

"I don't know," said Herbert. "But for this kind of money she can stay as long as she likes."

Edith was silent for a moment, head bowed, starring down at the top of the table.

"Do you think she remembers?" asked Edith.

"How could she forget?" responded Herbert.

"But she didn't say a word. She acted like she didn't know who we were at first," said Edith.

"Well, we'll have to wait and see," said Herbert.

Edith turned and looked down the hall to where Lori was lying down. "I wonder what kind of trouble that girl's gotten herself into now?" she thought.

Chapter 7

Never one to just sit around the house, Jacob was next door helping their neighbor, Mr. Shaw. He had offered to unload some chicken feed from his neighbor's truck. It was a typically hot and humid Florida afternoon but Jacob knew to pace himself. As he was about to lift another fifty-pound bag onto his shoulder, when he heard the familiar sound of his father's pickup. He looked up to see it pull into their front yard. He watched as his father exited the cab, hefted a bag from the rear of the pick up, and carried it inside their house. The passenger side door opened and his mother slowly lowered herself from the seat onto the tarred driveway. Edith held the door while another women squeezed out. Jacob guessed it was their "house guest." Wiping the sweat from his brow with a red bandanna, he returned to his task.

About an hour later, he walked into the house and was surprised to find his parents sitting alone in the kitchen.

"What happened?" he asked as he joined them at the table.

Edith had her back to him and didn't see or hear him come in. When she heard his voice she visibly jumped. She turned, eyes wide, mouth open.

"What's the matter, Mom? Did I scare you?" asked Jacob.

"I didn't hear you come in, I guess," she answered.

"Where's the folks you were supposed to pick up?"

"No folks, just one person. Here name is Lori Siegel. She's in the back room taking a nap," answered Herbert.

"Who is she? How long is she going to be here?" asked Jacob.

"My you are full of questions, aren't you?" said Herbert, teasing. "You'll have your questions answered in due time. For now, her name is Mrs. Lori Siegel. She's an Edgar. She had some kind of 'break down' and is here to rest up. Sort of get back on her feet," said Herbert.

"Okay. When's dinner?" asked Jacob.

"About seven. Why?" asked Edith.

"No reason. I'm going to take a shower. Call me when dinner's ready," said Jacob as he turned and walked out of the room.

"What do we tell him?" asked Edith.

"Nothing for now. Let's see if Lori says anything first," was all Herbert said and left the room as well.

Edith remained seated at the table. She looked around at the kitchen ashamed of the appearance of her place. Many of their neighbors had it much worse than them. At least her husband always had a job. Still to Edith's eyes everything looked shabby. She noticed the worn and faded linoleum floor, the cabinets which needed painting and the old wall paper. The fifteen year old refrigerator worked fine. The newest appliance she had was the washing machine and that was a five-year-old Kenmore from Sears.

But then she thought, "Everything is clean and functional. So the living room furniture is a little thread bare. It's comfortable and there aren't any springs sticking out of it. No, I guess I should be satisfied with what I have." But still, she felt inferior. She was impressed with the clothes and jewelry she saw on Lori. Then a thought came to her.

"As poor as we are, they turn to us when they need help. I guess in some ways God has blessed us. We're better off than they are in some ways." For some reason, she felt things were going to work out just fine.

At a quarter to seven, Edith called everyone to the kitchen table for dinner. She'd cooked a large roasted chicken with mashed potatoes, gravy and fresh mixed vegetables. She cheated a little, getting the gravy from a can. A moment later the men came into the kitchen.

"Ain't she eating with us?" asked Jacob.

"Go knock on the door. See if she's awake and wants to join us," said Edith.

With some reluctance, he shuffled off to the back room. Jacob wasn't one for socializing. He was shy and ill at ease when meeting new people. He softly tapped on the door. It wasn't closed tight. Jacob waited for a reply. When none was heard, he pushed the door open a little more and stuck his head in. In the dim light from the hallway he could see the outline of a woman lying on the bed. He was about to close the door and leave when the woman rolled over and looked at him. She couldn't see who the person was in the doorway because the light was coming from behind him. Reaching over, she turned on the small lamp on the night table.

Jacob was taken aback by the woman on the bed. She was blonde, very pretty, and from where he stood had a "dynamite" figure.

Still groggy from sleep, Lori asked, "Who are you?"

"I'm Jacob, Edith and Herbert's son. Mom wanted me to see if you wanted to join us for dinner."

"Yes, that would be nice, thank you. Where is the bathroom?"

Slightly embarrassed, but not knowing why, he said it was just down the hall way. He turned and went back to the kitchen.

"Is she coming?" asked Herbert.

"She's using the bathroom. She said she'd be right here."

A few moment later Lori walked into the kitchen. Edith looked at her and smiled.

"Why don't you sit on this side, Lori," she said, offering a chair.

"Thanks," said Lori shyly. She sat down and looked around the table.

"This here is Jacob," said Herbert.

Lori smiled and looked Jacob straight in the eyes.

"Nice to meet you, Jacob," said Lori, extending her hand across the table to Jacob.

"Hi, Mrs. Siegel," said Jacob, bashfully.

"Just call me Lori, that's what my friends call me," she said with a toothy smile.

Edith felt her pressure rise and her face redden. "Did she recognize him?" she wondered.

"You have a very handsome son, Mrs. Edgar," said Lori.

Now it was Jacob's face that turned bright red.

Edith finally exhaled and smiled. "Thank you, Lori. Now, why don't you call us by our first names. Call me Edith and this here is Herbert," she said, nodding towards her husband.

"Nice to meet you all," said Lori.

During the entire exchange Jacob just stared at Lori. He couldn't get over how pretty she was. He'd expected an older person for some reason. This was a pleasant surprise. Edith noticed Jacob's stare.

"Why don't you pass the vegetables, Jacob?" said Edith, breaking his concentration.

The rest of the meal went smoothly. There was pleasant, polite conversation. No serious or penetrating questions were raised by anyone at the table. Afterwards, Lori offered to help Edith clear the table while the men went into the living room and watched TV. Edith feared this would be when Lori asked the "big" question."

But she didn't. She acted like her prior visit so many years ago had never taken place. Later that night, after everyone had retired to their rooms, Herbert asked his wife if she had learned anything.

"She was very pleasant, much more outgoing than when we met her at the airport. She never asked anything about Jacob. Never asked about her own child she'd left behind so long ago."

"Well, if she doesn't bring it up, don't you," warned Herbert.

"You needn't worry about that," said Edith. She reflected on Lori's behavior at the airport and how different she was after her nap. Maybe she was tired from the flight down. She didn't seem to be suffering from any kind of "break down."

"I guess it was the Valium that made her seem so out of it. But why is she really here?" Edith wondered.

The days slowly passed and became weeks. The weeks turned into months. True to his word, Murray sent a money order payable to Herbert Edgar in the amount of one thousand dollars every couple of weeks. Occasionally, Murray called, but only stayed on a moment. He rarely asked to speak to Lori or inquired about her condition. Lori never asked about him. In fact, Lori didn't ask many questions at all. She seemed to accept each day as it came. Sometimes, when returning from a late-night trip to the bathroom, Edith would hear noises coming from Lori's room, like she was talking to someone in her sleep. Edith couldn't tell what she was saying. Although once in a while she'd pick up a word or two. She felt she distinctly heard Lori say the name "Raymond." Edith kept these things to herself.

About three months had passed since Lori's arrival. It was a Saturday morning, about eleven o'clock. Edith was busy running her old Hoover around the living room. She didn't hear the door bell over the noise. Suddenly, she was startled by a man's voice.

"Hello! Anyone home?!" Someone was yelling through the front door. Edith shut off the vacuum cleaner and went to the door. When she opened it, she saw a young man, neatly dressed in a blue blazer and grey slacks, a white dress shirt, and dark-red tie.

"Hello, are you Mrs. Edith Edgar?" he asked, a big smile on his face.

"Yes, I am. What can I do for you?" she asked.

"I have a delivery for you. Would you please sign here," he said, handing her a clipboard with a form attached to it. "Here, at the bottom," he said, pointing to the spot and handing her a pen.

Edith took the board and signed her name and returned the clip board and pen to the man. He removed the form, peeled off the top copy, and handed her the carbon copy underneath. Edith looked at him quizzically, waiting for him to hand her a package.

"Here you go," he said and held out his hand. A set of car keys dangled from a ring.

"What's this?" she asked surprised.

"They're for you," he said.

Seeing the confusion on her face, the man stepped aside and motioned with a sweep of his hand towards the driveway behind him.

"They go with that," he said.

"That," he said.

There in the bright sun sat a brand new car.

"There must be some mistake," she said.

"No mistake, ma'am. It's all your's."

"But who? Who is it from?" she asked.

"You're Mrs. Edgar, right?" He didn't wait for an answer. "All I know is I'm to deliver it to you. I don't know anything else. All the paperwork is in a large manila envelope on the front seat," he said.

With that he turned, walked down the driveway, and got into a car, which had been waiting for him, and sped off.

Edith stood on the porch, the keys still sitting in her upturned hand, her mouth hanging open.

And that's how Herbert found her minutes later when he appeared from around the side of the house, a greasy rag in his hand. He'd been in the garage working on their old pick up when he heard the sound of the car tires on the "blue-stoned" driveway.

"Who's here?" he asked.

Startled by his voice, Edith came out of her shocked trance. "No one," she replied.

"No one? Then who owns that car in the driveway?"

"We do," said Edith, still stunned.

"What? What are you talking about, woman?," asked Herbert.

"I don't know. A man came to the door and, had me sign this form," she said, waving the paper in her hand, "and gave me this set of keys. He said the car's for us. The paper work is in the car."

"Let me see that," said Herbert, grabbing the paper from her hand. Holding the form at arm's length, he tried to read the print, but couldn't without his glasses.

"It's some kind of a mistake. No one just gives a car away," he said. "I'm going to get my reading glasses. Then we'll get to the bottom of this."

Herbert went inside and returned a few moments later, a pair of half reading glasses perched on the end of his nose. Slowly, carefully, he read the form, his mouth moving as he read.

"I'll be damned," he said when he finished.

"What is it?" asked Edith.

"It's from Murray Siegel. He said he thought we could use a second car while Lori was here. He says not only can we use it, but it's in our name. In fact, the insurance on it is paid up for a year. Well I'll be," said Herbert. Now he stood on the porch beside his wife with his mouth hanging open. But he was the first to recover his wits.

"Come on. Let's go have a look—see," he said, taking the keys from Edith's hand.

They walked around the car several times. It was a brand new Cadillac, deep grey, four door, fully equipped. It had 120 miles on it.

"We can't accept this," said Edith.

"Why not? He can afford it. Besides, Lori can use it. It will get her out of the house once in a while. It will be good for her," advised Herbert.

"Okay, but when she leaves, she takes the car with her," added Edith.

"I don't know," said Herbert. "We don't want to insult the man." He opened the car, slid onto the leather bucket seat, and rested his calloused hands on the leather-wrapped steering wheel. Gazing out the front windshield, he inhaled deeply. "Ah, ya gotta love that smell of a new car," he said to himself. Glancing to his right he found the brown envelope with the paperwork inside.

In time, Edith accepted this enormous gift. For the next several months they all took turns driving the new car. All, that is, except Edith. She'd never learned how to drive.

The first time Lori invited Jacob to join her, indicating she didn't know her way around and might get lost.

Initially, Edith hesitated. She was afraid Lori would say something to Jacob. She dreaded the thought of her son finding out who her real mother was. But then, Edith decided Lori could have talked to him any time over the past few months. She didn't have to wait to get him away in the car. So far, Lori hadn't asked about the baby or discussed her previous visit so many years ago.

Jacob was totally in awe of Lori. He got a big kick out of going driving with her. She often let him drive and insisted he drive fast, the windows down, and the radio blasting. Although she was much older than he was ("old enough to be his mother," he figured), to him she was the prettiest woman he'd ever met. He'd find himself looking at her as she sat in the seat next to him the window opened and her short, light-brown hair blowing in the breeze. She was perhaps five foot two, a cute face, small turned up nose, big blue eyes and full lips. To him she was the "all-American" girl. She had a good figure with strong, well-shaped legs, a nice rounded rear, and good-sized breasts. He fantasized about what it would be like to hold her in his arms, to feel her breasts pressed against him. Sometimes, Lori would turn and catch him looking at her. She'd smile and giggle like a school girl, causing him to blush. When he did, she said she thought it was cute, which made him turn even redder.

"If I didn't know better, I'd swear she was flirting with me. But that couldn't be. Dad says we're related," he thought.

Herbert Edgar loved his new car. Over his wife's objections, he insisted on taking it to church on Sunday. Herbert would beam as the other parishioners admired his car when they pulled into the church parking lot.

When folks asked about it he'd say a rich relative passed away and left it to him.

At first, Lori joined the Edgars on Sundays. She was attentive, listened to the sermons, and joined in some of the hymns. Then one Sunday she announced she was going to stay home and "keep the Lord's day in her own way."

The next Sunday, Jacob said he wasn't feeling well and wanted to skip church. He complained he had a stomach ache. Besides, the next day was work and he didn't want to lose a day's pay being sick. Reluctantly, Edith gave in. She and her husband headed off to church by themselves.

Once the car was out of the driveway, Jacob threw on a pair of jeans and a "T" shirt. He headed out to the front porch, where he found Lori sitting in a metal rocking chair. She was rocking back and forth humming a song Jacob didn't recognize.

"How are you feeling, Jacob?" asked Lori.

"Better. Do you mind if I sit out here with you?"

"No, of course not," she said with a smile.

Jacob sat there for a while, quiet, thinking to himself. Finally, Lori broke the ice.

"Do you have a girl friend, Jacob?"

"Nope"

"A good-looking young man like you! I'd think you'd have plenty of girlfriends. You do like girls don't you?" she asked.

"Oh yeah. Of course I like girls. I date a few girls, but nothing steady."

"How old are you now, Jacob, twenty-three, twenty-four?" she asked.

"Naw, I'm seventeen," he said, adding quickly "But I'll be eighteen come August."

"Really. You look much older. Do you lift weights?"

"No. But my job gives me a good work out."

"I can tell. You have big muscles," commented Lori, reaching over and squeezing his left bicep with her fingers.

Jacob felt his face flush and began to feel sweat trickle down his back. He knew it was warm, but not that warm. Feeling uncomfortable, he said he was going to take a quick shower and excused himself and walked back inside.

Jacob had just finished showering and was about to step out of the shower when there was a knock at the door. Before he could answer, the door opened and Lori stepped in. Jacob gasped. He didn't know what to do and just stood there. Lori looked at him with a smile on her face.

"I thought you were finished," she said, slowly moving her eyes over his wet, muscled body.

Instead of leaving, Lori just stood there. Then she asked, "Do I make you nervous?"

"No. It's just that . . . I wasn't expecting . . ." he stammered.

Lori moved closer to him. She took her hand and let the tips of her fingernails glide over his tanned chest.,

"You are a very good looking man," she said, emphasizing the word "man." She moved both hands to either side of his chest and moved her nails down his sides and across his ribs. Then she leaned her head back, eyes half closed, and looked up at Jacob.

Jacob felt his head start to spin as he stared into Lori's eyes. He quickly found himself fully aroused by her touch. Finally, he couldn't contain himself any longer. Breathing heavily, he grabbed Lori and pulled her against his naked body. He pressed his lips hard against her mouth kissing her lips, her neck, and moving down to her shoulders.

"Hey! Easy big boy," said Lori as she pulled away. "Come with me," she said, as she began leading him back to her room. She made Jacob sit on the side of her bed as she slowly removed her clothes.

Jacob's dreams and fantasies were about to come true. He stared, afraid to blink. Afraid if he did she'd disappear or he'd wake up and find this was just a dream. But this was real and Lori's body was as beautiful as he'd imagined. Naked now, she moved closer to Jacob, standing in front of him. She took his head in her hands and pressed his face against her flat stomach. Jacob kissed her smooth skin. Then Lori lifted his head up and looked into his eyes. She leaned down and kissed him full on the lips. Then she pushed Jacob down on his back and knelt down straddling his legs. The next half hour would be the most passionate, exhilarating experiences of Jacob's young life and his first time with a woman.

Afterwards, Jacob sat up in bed, staring across the room into a mirror over a dresser. Lori lay next to him, the sheet pulled up to her waist, leaving her breasts exposed. Jacob couldn't take his eyes off her.

Lori caught his gaze and smiled. "It was your first time, wasn't it?" she asked gently.

"Yes," he admitted.

Richard Anders

"You were very good for your first time," she commented.

Jacob couldn't help but smile. Although he wondered how he could have been good since she did all the "doing."

"What are you thinking?" she finally asked.

At first Jacob didn't reply. Then, hesitantly, he turned to look at her. "What if you get pregnant?" he blurted out.

Lori laughed. Jacob found her laughter intoxicating, yet disconcerting. "Was she laughing at him?" he wondered.

"I can't get pregnant. I'm on the pill. But why did you ask?"

"Well, I always thought if you had sex with a relative and she got pregnant, the kids would be born with two heads or something," he said.

Lori really burst out laughing after hearing that. "Who told you that?" she asked.

"It's in the Bible. You can't have sex within your third kindred," said Jacob, proud of his knowledge of the Bible.

"Well, first of all, it's within the third degree of kindred. That means you can't have sex with your sister. Someone like that. Do you see me as a sister?" she teased.

Red faced he said "No way. But I . . . ." he stammered.

"Don't worry. I don't think it would apply in our case," she added.

Somewhat relieved, Jacob smiled and slid down in the bed. Suddenly, under the covers, he felt Lori's hand moving across his right thigh. He immediately felt himself grow erect.

"You ready for seconds?" Lori asked, rolling on top of him without waiting for a reply.

Since his encounter with Pastor Ruben, Jacob had wondered about his sexuality. Was something wrong with him? Was he "queer," as some boys used to tease? He'd never had the courage, or chance, for that matter, to make love with a girl. Now, all his doubts were dispelled. Jacob was no longer a virgin. Lori changed all that. Jacob knew he was a "normal" man.

There were numerous other secret encounters between Jacob and Lori over the next few months. Once, they'd snuck away in the new car to a secluded beach and swam naked in the warm waters of the Gulf of Mexico. Afterwards, they laid a blanket down on the sandy beach and had sex in the dark. Doing it out in the open made it all the more exciting for him.

On another occasion, Lori had slipped into his bedroom after everyone had gone to sleep. He thought for sure his mother was going to walk in and catch them. It seemed Lori thrived on taking chances. To be honest, so did Jacob. But what he couldn't understand was why Lori insisted on being on top. For Lori it meant being in control. It was perhaps one of the lasting effects from her having been molested by her step father. She had to be the dominant one during sex.

Then one day it all came to a sudden end. Jacob was working at a construction site with his father all day. That evening, when they returned home, Edith was sitting on the battered living room sofa, trembling all over. Jacob hadn't noticed her and walked through the house directly to his room. He was in a hurry to wash, change, and see Lori. But Herbert saw his wife and realized something had happened. He walked into the room and sat across from her in his recliner.

"What's the matter, Edith? What's wrong?"

"She's gone," was all she said.

"Who, Lori?" he asked.

"The police were here. They said she was arrested."

"Arrested! For what? Did they say?" asked Herbert.

"They said she's a fugitive from justice. They think we were hiding her. They want us to come down to the police station to answer some questions," said Edith.

Herbert sat quietly, reflecting on what he'd just heard.

"I knew there was something wrong. No way does anyone come down here, stay with us to recuperate. Especially when they have the kind of money they have. Well, we have nothing to worry about. As far as we're concerned, we were just helping a family member in need. When do they want us to come down?" asked Herbert.

"As soon as you got home from work," she replied.

"Okay, then let's go. We might as well get this over with." Herbert walked down the hall to Jacob's bedroom. He pushed the door open without knocking and told Jacob they were going out for a while. They took the pick up truck because the police had picked up Lori while she had the new car.

When they arrived at the station, they were taken to a back room where a detective interviewed them. He explained Lori Edgar Siegel escaped from a mental facility in New York. She was a suspect in a murder case and was out on bail. When she walked out of the hospital she'd violated the conditions of her bail and a warrant had been issued for her arrest. She'd been missing for several months.

Herbert assured them that they didn't know any of this. He said they met Lori at the airport and took her in as a guest. After about an hour, the police realized that if the Edgars had known any of this they wouldn't have been driving all over the county with her, taking her to church socials, and such. Finally, the police let them go. They'd been told that Lori was being held at the county jail until she could be sent back north. They returned the keys to the new car to Herbert, because it was registered in his name.

Shaken by this new revelation, they drove back home. Herbert would have to get Jacob to come with him to retrieve the other car. When they got home, they found Jacob sitting in the kitchen eating a sandwich.

"What was that all about?" he asked between bites.

"It seems our sweet cousin Lori is wanted by the police," said Herbert matter-of-factly.

"What! What for?" asked Jacob.

"It was something she did back in New York. The police back there wanted to question her," was Edith's guarded reply.

"They didn't say what she did?" asked Jacob.

"Just that they had a warrant out for her and they were taking her back. You'll have to come with me after dinner to get the car back. It's at the police station," said Herbert.

"Can we see her?" asked Jacob.

"No. She's being sent right back," said Herbert hastily. He'd decided the less they had to do with her

97

at this point the better. Later that evening, the two men picked up the other car and drove home.

Jacob was devastated by the news. He felt like his heart had been broken. In his own, young way, he'd fallen in love with Lori Siegel. Jacob continued to ask questions about Lori after they got home. Edith and Herbert offered little in the way of explanation. About a week later, Herbert got a call from Murray Siegel. Murray apologized for their inconvenience without explaining what the real story was. Another week passed and the last money orders came to the Edgar house by messenger. This time it was in the amount of ten thousand dollars. There was no note of explanation.

Over a year passed without any news regarding Lori Siegel. Life returned to some semblance of normalcy for the Edgar family. Then one day, while Edith was waiting in the check out lane at the supermarket, she happened to pick up a week-old copy of a New York newspaper.

She idly scanned the different stories, absently flipping through the paper to kill time. Then she read something that made her heart stop in her chest. It was a story on page three. It even included a picture of Lori that looked nothing like she did while she was with them. In this picture she had long, bleached, blonde hair. She wore heavy make up and jewelry. She looked "hard."

Edith doubted that any of her friends, who'd met Lori, would recognize her from the picture. She began reading the story. After a few lines, Edith's hands began to shake. She looked around to see if anyone had noticed. Then she closed the paper and added it to her items. She couldn't believe what she'd read. When she got home, she unpacked the groceries and put them away. The house was deathly quiet and she was the only one home. She took the newspaper, went into her sewing room, and read the entire article.

Later that night, after dinner, Edith waited until Jacob went out. It was one of the rare occasions that he was joining some of the local boys at the neighborhood pool hall. She got the New York paper and showed the newspaper article to Herbert. She sat across the room as he read the story.

Herbert's lips moved as he read the article to himself. From time to time he'd shake his head as if in disbelief. When he finished, he dropped the paper on his lap.

"Wow! Can you imagine? And she was living here under this very roof. It just shows, you never know," he commented.

"We have to make sure Jacob doesn't see this. If he reads it he may start asking questions," said Edith.

Herbert agreed. He gave the paper back to his wife, assuming she'd throw it out. Later, Herbert went outside to the driveway where the Caddy was parked. He backed it into their garage and closed the door. When he returned to the house he went into the kitchen and threw the keys into a small drawer under the kitchen counter. Seeing this, Edith inquired, "Why'd you put the car away? You never put it in the garage before."

"I don't want to use it anymore. There's blood on that car," was all he said. Edith didn't question him, but thought to herself, "Wasn't there blood on the money also?"

Several days later, Jacob realized they hadn't been using the "new" car.

"What's up with the Caddy, Dad?" he asked.

"Nothing. I just don't want to use it anymore."

"Is there something wrong with it?" asked Jacob.

"It's fine. I just have no use for it."

"Then can I use it?" asked Jacob.

Herbert didn't reply.

"Well?" asked Jacob.

"Sure. If you want it. It's yours more than mine," said Herbert, but didn't explain. "Tomorrow I'll transfer the plates over to you. But you've got to pay the insurance," he warned.

"Great! Thanks! Where are the keys?"

"They're in the kitchen drawer with the junk."

Jacob ran into the kitchen, found the keys, and headed out the door to the garage.

"My own car!" he yelled at the top of his lungs.

As it turned out the car was a good distraction for Jacob. He stopped asking questions about Lori and spent his time caring for his new car.

Chapter 8

The next few years passed quickly for Jacob. He rarely thought of the mysterious visitor, Lori. The few times he did, was to recall the passionate moments he'd shared with her. Herbert and Jacob continued to work together on construction jobs. But Herbert was getting on in years. A few weeks after turning sixty-six he announced he was going to retire. Edith thought he should continue to work for as long as he was physically able. She was afraid that he'd end up like all the other retired men in the community. She'd been talking to some of her lady friends at church. They all said the same thing. Most of the men sat around the house all day and night. They'd drink too much, do too little, and complain about everything. It was like they were just waiting to die. But Herbert didn't share her concerns. He said he was different. He put in his papers and started collecting his small pension, and Social Security. She tried to get Herbert to go fishing or hunting with Jacob, but he showed no interest. She was sure he was heading for an early grave.

As it turned out, Edith's concerns about her husband's health were misdirected because it was around this same time that Edith's health began to decline. She lost weight, which seemed impossible for a woman considered "frail" all her life. Her skin took on a pale, transparent look to it. Deep circles developed under her eyes that wouldn't go away, no matter how much sleep she got. Yet, she refused to see a doctor.

Then one day, while getting an annual flu shot, her doctor noticed her appearance. He insisted on drawing some blood, just to make sure. A week later, Edith got a call from the doctor's office. He wanted to see her in his office right away.

While Edith sat nervously in the doctor's office, he explained what her blood tests had revealed. It was what Edith feared and had been trying to deny. She had cancer.

It was a kind that attacked the blood. It affected all parts of the body and there was no cure. He suggested they try chemotherapy. When Edith asked if it would cure her, he admitted it probably would not. He said with all honesty that it would only prolong the disease and could make her feel sicker. Edith declined treatment.

Her doctor gave her some medication to help with the pain and sent her home to die. When Edith told Herbert, he cried like a baby. She'd never seen him cry like that before and it frightened her. She actually felt worse about leaving him alone than about the thought of dying. She wanted to keep it from Jacob, but Herbert convinced her he was old enough to know and should be prepared for what was to come. Finally, after more thought, she agreed.

Like her husband, Jacob wept openly and uncontrollably when told about her illness. Both men admitted they didn't know how they'd survive without her around. For solace, Edith turned to the only source of comfort she'd ever known. Her faith. She felt she had led a good, long life and now it was time to turn to the Lord. "It was in His hands now," she'd say. She believed this down to the bottom of her soul.

As it turned out Edith lasted six months after being diagnosed with the cancer. The pain medication helped and she remained alert and aware.

For Edith, the end came fittingly enough on a Sunday morning. On that morning Herbert lay beside his wife waiting for her to stir. It was her habit to get up at seven. She'd get finished in the bathroom, then get Herbert and Jacob up and ready for church. But this morning she didn't move.

Herbert waited a while, thinking she was just tired and needed a few more minutes rest. After almost a half hour, Herbert rolled over to face Edith. Her head was turned towards him, resting on her pillow, her eyes closed, a slight smile on her face. She looked better to him some how, peaceful even.

"Hey, sleepy head! You staying in bed all day? What about church?," he asked.

Edith didn't open her eyes. Herbert sat up, leaning on one elbow. He touched the side of her cheek and stroked it with the back of his hand. That usually woke her up without a start. Edith didn't wake up. He rested his palm against her forehead. It felt cold. Edith Edgar was dead.

Herbert couldn't bring himself to get up, call for help, or do anything. He took his wife of over forty years into his arms and rocked her back and forth, his head resting against her. Tears slowly rolled down his cheek.

"Oh, Edith. I'm so sorry. I rarely told you I loved you. Now it's too late."

Edith's funeral was a simple service with an internment in the cemetery next to their church. The church ladies arranged for a gathering in the hall, where sandwiches and coffee were served. Afterwards Herbert and Jacob rode back to the house in silence. They went into separate rooms, alone with their grief. Jacob seemed to be taking it better than his father. The next day, Jacob got up, as usual, and went to work. That evening Jacob found his father lying on Edith's side of their bed, asleep. He left him be and fixed a bowl of soup for himself. The next evening, Jacob found his father, passed out in his recliner, a half-empty bottle of scotch opened in the kitchen. Jacob let his father be for the remainder of the week, hoping he just needed time to grieve and would eventually come out of it. A few weeks passed before decided it was time for them to move on with their lives.

He asked his father to help him clear out his mother's clothes. He would pack them in cartons, take them down to the church on Sunday and donate them for the next clothing drive. Herbert insisted only the clothing be removed, none of her personal things. Jacob agreed.

Jacob soon discovered that he was doing most of the work himself. Each time he removed an item and handed it to his father, Herbert would just sit on the edge of the bed holding it to his chest In frustration, Jacob sent his father to the garage for twine and more boxes. As Jacob folded each article of clothing, he was reminded of his mother. Her smell was in all her clothes. Edith wasn't one for perfume, but she did use dusting powder after her bath. The smell was clean, not over powering like some perfumes. From the time he was a small child, Jacob had identified that smell with his mother.

Finally, after nearly two hours, he'd folded everything and placed the clothes carefully in cartons that were scattered about the floor. He lifted the cartons and took them out to the kitchen, where his father was tying them closed with twine. Once he'd finished, he noticed that the closet had dust and litter on the shelves and floor. Taking a small broom and pan, he swept up the floor and deposited the litter in a garbage bag. Then he got a rag and some ammonia from under the kitchen sink and went back to wipe off the shelves. The smell of the ammonia irritated his eyes. But the tears that ran down his cheeks were not from the ammonia fumes.

Jacob finally removed everything from the closet and shelf. Now he began to wipe the surfaces down with a damp cloth to remove the accumulated dust. Standing on his tiptoes he reached towards up and wiped, but as he moved his hand across the surface it struck an item he'd apparently missed. Stretching as far as he could, he still couldn't grasp the object. He got a chair from the kitchen and returned to the bedroom. Placing the chair in the doorway of the closet he climbed up to see what he'd missed.

There, pushed far to the rear of the shelf, he found an old, battered shoe box. He removed the box, climbed down from the chair, and placed the box on the bed., then returned to cleaning the closet. When he'd finished he picked up the items from the bed, intending to put everything inside one of the larger cartons. As he lifted the shoe box, he wondered what secrets it held.

It didn't feel heavy enough for shoes. He took the shoe box into his bedroom and sat on the bed. Jacob stared at the object on his lap for several moments.

"What could be in it?" he thought.

With a slight tremble in his hands, Jacob pulled the old, yellowed strip of Scotch tape that secured the top. He removed the tape and lifted the top. Peering inside he saw assorted papers and forms, some rolled up, others clipped together. He removed the papers and set them aside. Underneath, he discovered a brown manila envelope, the label sealed shut. He placed this on the bed next to the papers.

There, in the bottom was a small white envelope with the name "Jacob" written on the front. Jacob recognized his mother's handwriting. He slowly opened the envelope.

Inside he found strands of blonde hair and a note, "Jacob's first haircut, 4/17/65." He also found a baby's tooth that he assumed was his. He returned the hair to its envelope and turned to the other items. He unrolled the first paper. It was a marriage certificate dated over forty years ago and belonging to his parents. There was also a small life insurance policy in his mother's name and a larger one ion his father's name. The remaining papers were ownership documents for their pick up and the deed for their house. Then he turned his attention to the large manila envelope.

He hesitated at first, turning it over several times in his hand. Holding it up to the over head light, he tried to see what was inside. Eventually, he made up his mind and carefully pulled the sealed flap open. He turned it upside down on the bed and shook the contents onto the bed spread. He looked down at what appeared to be official looking forms and some old photos. He picked them up one at a time and examined them.

The first photo was a close up of his mother and a young girl. It was in black and white, but Jacob could tell the girl had blonde hair. She was hugging Edith and smiling broadly into the camera. Edith also smiled. Jacob could see that the girl was shorter than his mother. The girl was thin and looked to be no more than twelve or thirteen years old. There were no names or dates on the back. Then he looked at the second picture. This was of the same girl by herself. She was sitting on their porch in a metal rocking chair. Her head was tilted back and her eyes were closed. She seemed to be sleeping. She looked peaceful and pretty. Then he noticed her stomach. It was swollen. She was pregnant. Jacob turned the picture over to the other side but it was blank. But something about the girl was familiar. He'd seen her before, but where?

Jacob felt that he was looking at something not meant for his eyes. He didn't recall his mother ever mentioning a girl, especially a pregnant one. After all, his mother had always been truthful with him. She'd never had any secrets that he knew. She would share everything with him, or so he thought. But why wouldn't she have put these pictures in the old, tattered family album with the rest of their pictures? Maybe she was a neighbor's kid. He decided to look at the rest of the papers in the box.

One of them was from the community hospital. The paper had turned yellow with age. It was a carbon copy and some of the ink had faded making it difficult to read. He turned it one way, then another, trying to catch the best light so he could read it all. It was some kind of legal document. He couldn't read the signatures at the bottom. Whoever signed it had terrible penmanship.

He returned his gaze to the top and tried to read it from the beginning. He was able to determine that the paper had something to do with "guardianship" and he saw the names Herbert and Edith Edgar. The rest of the page was too faded to read.

But guardianship of who?" wondered Jacob.

He set this form aside and unfolded the next. This one was printed on thicker paper and had a raised seal on it. Again the name of the hospital was at the top. It was a birth certificate.

He carefully read each word hoping it would clear up the mystery of the girl. But then he froze, his eyes transfixed on the middle of the paper.

There was a date. "August 15, 1964." His birthday.

Where his name should have been was typed just one word, "MALE." Then he looked for his mother and father's names. They weren't there. Where the father's name should have been it read, "unknown." Where he would expect to see his mother's name was another

The name entered next to mother was, "Lori Ann Edgar."

A chill ran down his spine. He picked up the black-and-white picture of the teenaged girl taken with his mother.

"Lori Edgar? Is she the mother of this baby born on the same day as my birthday?" he wondered. Jacob could feel his blood rising, his face getting hot, his stomach churning.

"What's going on here?" he asked himself.

He quickly rummaged through the rest of the papers. There were more legal papers stapled together.

They were long and filled with "wherefores" and "henceforth."

The names Edith and Herbert Edgar were repeated several times. Then, towards the end, was his name, Jacob Edgar, his date of birth, and the date the papers were signed, October 2, 1964.

He began to understand why he'd never seen any of these papers. The people he'd been raised by, the man and woman who he'd grown up thinking were his mother and father, were not. He'd been adopted. He looked at the birth certificate again. "This Lori Edgar was my real mother," he concluded.

Stunned by this revelation, he sat motionless for several moments. Shaking his head, he began to feel his eyes stinging. He knew they'd lied to him, but why?

Then he found a newspaper article. It was from a New York newspaper. Blinking back tears, he slowly read the story. As he read the story his tears flowed even more, his face turning redder. At last he understood what these papers, the pictures, and the news story meant, and this knowledge horrified him. He felt bile rising up from his stomach and thought he was going to vomit. He pounded his fist into the bed, clenching his teeth together to stifle a scream. Rising from his bed, he grabbed all the forms, the pictures and stormed out to the living room.

His father was sitting in his recliner, staring at the ceiling, a water glass half filled with scotch in his right hand.

Before Jacob could say anything, his father looked up at him. His eyes were rimmed in red, his nose running. He'd been crying too.

"You found it, didn't you?"

"If you mean these, yes," Jacob screamed, throwing the papers at his father.

"What does it mean? Tell me. Tell me everything," he demanded

"Sit down son," said Herbert.

Jacob recoiled upon hearing Herbert refer to him as "son."

"I'm not your son and I'd rather stand," he replied.

"Suit yourself," said Herbert, a slight slur to his speech. He drank the entire contents of the glass in one gulp.

"Are you going to tell me what they mean?" Jacob asked again, his voice rising.

"Some things are better left alone. You don't want to know these things," Herbert said, nodding towards the papers.

"No! No!" screamed Jacob. "I want to know the truth. Who are my parents? Who is this girl?," he said, waving the photo in Herbert's face. Herbert moved his face away as if he were smelling a piece of rotting meat.

"What do these papers mean? Damn you, tell me the truth. I've got to know," screamed Jacob, his voice becoming hoarse from yelling.

Herbert sat and stared at him for a moment. Then he took a deep breath and said, "Okay, but you aren't going to like it. Now, sit down."

Grudgingly, Jacob sat down on the sofa and waited.

"That girl in the picture was Lori Edgar. She was about thirteen. You can probably see from one of them that she was pregnant. That was about twenty years ago. Charles Edgar my brother was Lori Edgar's was his step daughter.

"Anyway she came here stayed about seven months or so, had the baby, and left. End of story." Here Herbert stopped, hoping he'd satisfied Jacob's curiosity. He hadn't.

"That's not all of it. What about the papers? Who was the father?" Jacob demanded.

"We don't know who the father was. They told us it was some boy in her class. It doesn't matter. She couldn't raise no baby. She was only a kid herself. Before she had the kid she signed papers giving it up. It was supposed to go to a family that belonged to our church. After she had the baby, she left, went back up north. Went on with her life."

Again Herbert stopped, waiting to see if he'd said enough.

"Where did the baby end up?" asked Jacob, almost afraid to ask, fearing what Herbert was about to say.

When he saw Jacob wasn't satisfied with only part of the story, he decided to let him have the whole thing.

"I told you, a church family adopted him."

"God damn! Stop the bull shit! I asked you to tell me the truth. Now tell me," screamed Jacob, rising slightly off the sofa face red, veins bulging on the side of his neck, fists clenched.

"The truth. You want the truth? Okay, here it is."

Taking a deep breath he began.

"Your mother couldn't have kids. All the years we were married, she never got pregnant. It was eating her up inside. All her lady friends at church were having kids, all except her.

111

She'd pray every night, get down on her knees and pray for a child of her own. When my brother sent his kid down here to have her baby, Edith thought her prayers had been answered. We arranged to take guardianship of the baby after it was born. Eventually, we adopted it."

"It was me, wasn't it? I was that baby, right?" said Jacob, tears welling up in his eyes and running down his cheeks.

"Yes. We raised you as if you were our own. We cared for you. Loved you. Your mother never wanted to see you hurt, we never meant to hurt you."

Herbert rose from his chair and went out into the kitchen. Jacob could hear the refrigerator door being opened and ice cubes dropping into a glass. A moment later Herbert returned with a full glass of scotch. He settled into his recliner, hoping his story telling was over.

"So you lied to me. All these years have been a lie. You're not my father. She wasn't my mother," said Jacob.

"She loved you more than any real mother ever could," said Herbert, now raising his voice. "Don't you know that? Didn't we give you everything we could?"

"Everything but the truth," Jacob shot back.

"Thank God your mother didn't live to see this day. It would have broken her heart," he muttered to himself. He looked at Jacob, hoping he could understand. But Jacob wasn't finished. He was only getting started.

"What about these?" asked Jacob, his voice still raised.

"What's that?" asked Herbert.

"It's a copy of a newspaper from New York. There's a story in there about a murder. There's a picture. The woman looks like Lori, only older with long, blonde hair. It says she was involved in the murder of her lover. A murder! That she had some guys torture him and then shoot him to death. It says she escaped, but was captured in Florida. Is she the same woman who stayed with us? Was she Lori Siegel?"

Herbert was through lying. Without raising his head, he said, "Yes."

Jacob rose from his seat. He stood over Herbert. He was sweating profusely and it mixed with his tears, mucous running from his nostrils.

"And this, this Lori Siegel, the Lori who stayed with us, she's the girl in those pictures, Lori Edgar. The girl who was pregnant! Isn't she?" he asked, spittle flying from his mouth as he spoke. He was obviously fighting to maintain control, but slowly losing the battle.

"Lori Edgar, Lori Siegel, she was my mother, wasn't she?" he screamed so loud it startled Herbert. Startled him so much he began to fear Jacob would attack him.

"Yes," Herbert shouted back, staring Jacob straight in the eyes.

"Oh my God. It's all been a lie. My whole life has been a lie. The people I thought were my parents aren't. They lied to me. This woman who gave birth to me, just left me behind. She never wanted me, never asked about me, never said anything when she was down here. She just left me and never cared what happened to me. She knew who I was and she . . . and we . . ." he stammered. But Jacob caught himself.

"She what?" asked Herbert.

113

"Nothing! Never mind. It's none of your business. I don't owe you anything. My real mother abandoned me. My real mother was a whore, a murderer. I'm a bastard. My real father was God knows who!?"

"And I had sex with my own mother," Jacob thought with horror, his stomach churning inside of him.

"I can't believe you. I can't believe anything you, or that woman who pretended to be my mother ever said," Jacob yelled before turning and running out the door. He ran across the driveway, jumped in the car, and roared off, the wheels spinning in the loose dirt and stone.

In the living room, Herbert sat with his head bowed, his face in his hands, sobbing. "It's all gone. I've lost everything now."

Jacob rode around for a while before ending up on a seldom used back road. He pulled over to the side of the road, got out of the car, and leaned against the fender. He began to cry uncontrollably. He thought of events in his life, happy times that were now corrupted by these new revelations. He remembered his mother encouraging him to visit Pastor Ruben's. How the "good pastor" tried to sodomize him, how he had killed him by pushing him down the stairs. Then his thoughts shifted to Lori.

He saw her blonde hair, her smile, the sound of her voice, the curve of her body. "How could she have abandoned me? Worse, how could she have sex with her own son?" Jacob felt dirty, disgusted with himself.

In his anguish, his thoughts shifted to the readings in the Bible. He remembered the Bible story of Adam and Eve. How Eve tempted Adam and as a result they were cast out of Paradise. Eve was the cause of man's suffering. A woman was the cause for his suffering, his shame, his anger.

These thoughts swirled like a tornado in his mind. He felt dizzy, nauseous. Suddenly, feeling of hatred welled up from inside him. He began to gag and then retch. He clung to the side of the car and vomited until only bile came up. Finally, the spasms passed and he was able to stand erect. He took a deep breath. He imagined he'd spewed up the evil from deep within him. He wiped his mouth on his sleeve.

Jacob stood there for several minutes, staring off into space. He kept clenching and unclenching his fists. He remembered that when Pastor Ruben had fallen down the stairs he'd felt glad it had happened. Jacob knew the pastor was an evil man who committed evil deeds. He knew that God wanted the evil person to be punished. He, Jacob had been the hand of God. Jacob knew that a woman, a mother who had abandoned her son committed an unspeakably evil act. Surely, God would want someone punished for such a deed.

A plan began to form in his mind. He would see that no one would escape punishment for these deeds.

Jacob returned to his house. He found his father where he'd left him, only now he was asleep in his recliner, snoring loudly, unconscious from too much scotch. Jacob went into the hall closet and, took out an old leather suitcase. He went into his bedroom and threw some clothes into the bag.

He grabbed his bank book from the top dresser drawer.

He was about to leave when he spotted the hunting knife Herbert had given him for his fifteenth birthday, nestled snugly in its leather sheath. Without a further thought, he grabbed it and shoved it into his back pocket.

On the way out, he stopped and picked up the papers and pictures he'd found in the old shoe box. He put them back inside the large manila envelope and shoved it inside a side pocket in his bag. In the kitchen he found a pencil and pad. He quickly scrawled a message to his father, or rather the man who had pretended to be his father all these years. When he was finished, he carried the pad out to the living room. Looking down at his "father" he placed the note on his lap. Then he picked up the suitcase, grabbed the car keys, and headed out the door. The screen door slammed shut, but Herbert never heard it.

Hours later, when Herbert woke up, it was already dark. He fumbled for the lamp switch on the table next to his recliner. When the light came on its brightness caused him to raise his hand to his eyes. As he did, he felt something slide off his lap. He looked down to see a pad on the floor at his feet. There was something written on it. He looked around and found his reading glasses. He picked up the pad and read the note.

"Dear Dad," it started, but the word "Dad" was crossed out so it read instead, "Dear Herbert,"

"I can't live here anymore. My life has been one big lie and this place will always remind me of that. I've taken the car and am leaving. I won't be coming back. I have to find out who I really am. I have to find my real mother, my real father. I have to make things right. Don't try to find me, you won't. Good bye, Jacob."

Herbert read the note twice more. When he'd read it the third time, he flung the pad across the room.

He rose from his chairs, legs shaking under him.

With arms raised over his head he screamed, "Damn you, son. Damn you to hell! See Edith, I told you we shouldn't take in someone else's kid. They are nothing but trouble. Now see what you've done?"

Tears started to run from his eyes again as he dropped to his knees and pounded the floor with his fists. Then clasping his hands to his chest he cried out, "Edith forgive me. God forgive me. Oh Jacob, Jacob, Jacob, what are you going to do?"

Chapter 9
(The present)

It was a monumental feat for Max to get out of bed this morning. He felt like he'd just fallen asleep when the alarm clock went off. The radio was tuned between stations and all he heard was ear-piercing static. He peeked at the clock with one eye. It read 11 A.M. With a groan, he threw his white, stubby legs over the side of the bed and sat up. After steadying himself, he pushed himself up and onto his feet. Scratching his head, then his crotch, he shuffled off to the bathroom.

Max didn't bother showering, only splashing some cold water on his face. After toweling off, he put on the same clothes he'd worn the day before. He walked down the narrow hallway towards the kitchen. There, he poured himself a mug of cold, stale coffee that he'd brewed the day before. He "nuked it" in his microwave and added some milk, happy to see it didn't curdle once it hit the coffee. Max grabbed his jacket, felt his keys in the pocket, and with mug in hand headed out the door.

The rain from the night before had stopped, but the air had turned cold. Winter wouldn't be far off. He drove the winding roads until he reached the highway. The Bronx River Parkway was nearly empty and he made good time. Exiting at Pelham Parkway, he headed towards the Long Island Sound and City Island. Just before the Island exit, he turned left, and drove through an industrial area until he came to the end of the road.

Here Max entered the parking lot in front of "Giggi's" Topless Bar." The lot was gravel with a minefield of water-filled potholes. Skillfully maneuvering through the mine field, he parked his Caddy alongside the bar.

Max grabbed his coffee mug and after much effort got his bulk out of the car. Weighing nearly three hundred pounds and standing only five feet ten, he'd had the unlikely nickname, "Tiny."

Max had struggled with his weight since high school. He'd tried "fad" diets, but never stuck with them. After each painful diet he would regain all the weight he'd lost, plus a few more pounds. At forty-two years of age, he'd almost given up. But then he'd think of Jennifer, the night-time waitress.

Jen was always kind to him, always ready with a smile and big hello. He knew her situation, being a single mother and all, but he could still dream. In those dreams he saw himself six feet tall and weighing no more than two hundred pounds.

He was ten years younger and walking down the aisle with his bride on his arm, Jennifer Sands Peterson. But like most of his dreams, this would never be. He knew he'd have to be content to just admire her from afar. However, the mere thought of knowing he'd see her later made coming to work almost bearable. With visions of Jennifer fresh in his mind, Max waddled towards the front of the bar.

As he was about to unlock the front door, he noticed a car parked on the far side of the lot. It looked like Jennifer's car.

"I wonder what she's doing here. Maybe she had car trouble last night. But if she had, she'd have come back in for help," he thought. Putting the set of keys back in his jacket pocket, he followed a zigzag path, towards the car, trying to avoid the potholes. As he got closer, he could see a figure inside the car, slumped over the wheel. He picked up his pace after realizing who was in the car.

"What happened?" he wondered as he approached the side door. Max took hold of the handle and pulled the door open. Max wrapped on the driver's side window, bending lower to look inside.

"Hey, Jen, what the hell are you doing . . . ?"

Max never finished the sentence. He could see something was wrong, very wrong, with Jen. Her head rested on the steering wheel, face turned slightly towards the left, her eyes open, but unblinking. He hesitantly reached in and touched her shoulder, hoping against hope she was okay. But before he could shake her, something on her lap caught his attention.

"Aaaahh!" was the sound he made, as he stumbled backwards. He stepped into a pothole, fell backwards, and landed hard on his ample butt, in the middle of a large puddle.

"Oh no! Oh no!" he gasped.

He suddenly grabbed his mouth, rolled over onto his side, and proceeded to vomit. The bile burnt his throat and came out his nose as well. Spitting into a puddle, Max tried to get the vile taste out of his mouth. He took one big, meaty hand and wiped his mouth.

Oblivious to his soggy pants and cold air, Max just sat and stared into the car. After a moment, he snapped out of it, regained his senses, and with much effort got back up onto his feet. Against his better judgment, he looked back inside the car.

"Maybe I didn't see what I thought I saw," he said to himself.

But at second glance his suspicions were confirmed. His stomach started to cramp again and he felt more bile rising in his throat. He turned and retreated back across the parking lot, his head bowed. He tugged at his soggy pants, which were plastered to his behind. Once he reached the front door, he struggled to get the key into the lock, his hands trembling. Finally, he managed to insert the key, unlock the door and enter the bar. He didn't bother putting on any of the lights. Instead, he walked over to and around the bar. Once there, he reached under the bar top and removed a worn telephone from underneath. Placing it on the counter and lifting the receiver to his, he punched in the numbers "9"-"1-" "1."

He heard the phone ring twice before it was answered.

A woman's voice said, "9-1-1. How may I help you?"

She sounded calm and in control, something that Max wasn't.

When he tried to speak nothing came out of his mouth.

"Hello," said the woman again.

Finally, after a deep breath Max said, "I need help! Someone's been murdered."

"A murder you said? May I have your name and location please?" asked the woman. Her voice revealing a hint of anxiety.

For a moment Max couldn't remember his name. All he could think of was the image of Jennifer in her car.

Shaking his head he stated, "My name is Maxwell Peterson. I'm the manager at "Giggi's Bar" out on Mosey Road. That's in Pelham Park. There's a woman in the parking lot. She's dead."

"One moment please. Don't hang up."

A pause followed. The longest pause in Max's life.

"Okay, Mr. Peterson, a police car is being dispatched to your location. Did you touch anything?" she asked.

"No. Wait a minute. Yeah, I think I touched the door handle, but that's all," said Max.

"Okay. Don't touch anything and keep everyone else who's there away from the scene."

"There's no one here, just me and Jennifer." He suddenly realized Jen wasn't with him any more. Max began to cry. He tried to keep the woman on the other end of the line from hearing him, but it was too late.

"Calm down now, Mr. Peterson. The police will be there soon. Just try to relax. Now, I want you to stay on the phone until the police arrive. Do you understand?"

"Yes, stay on the line," said Max as if in a trance. He kept the receiver next to his ear, but the 911 operator wasn't talking to him. He could hear her muffled conversation. She was talking to someone else. He heard her giving his name and address to some one and then a series of numbers that he didn't understand. While he waited, Max took a bottle of scotch down from the shelf behind the bar and poured some into a glass. He didn't bother to add any ice or water. He took a long drink. The scotch burned his throat, which had already been irritated when he threw up. He ignored the discomfort and drank some more. Then he refilled the glass and waited for the police to arrive.

It seemed like an eternity to Max before he heard a car pull up on the gravel outside the bar, when in fact it had only been a few minutes.

"They're here. The police are here," he said into the phone.

"Okay, Mr. Peterson. Put one of the officers on the line when they come in," she asked.

Max waited, leaning against the bar. He felt more comfortable there, safer. It was familiar territory for him. He prayed they wouldn't make him go back out to Jen's car again. He didn't think he could bear to look at Jen again. He was also afraid he'd throw up again.

The front door opened and two NYPD uniformed officers walked in. They looked young, like kids to Max. One was a black woman, the other a dark-skinned, Latino-looking man. The woman cop led the way over to the bar.

"You Max Peterson?" she asked.

Max nodded his head yes.

"Is 911 still on the phone?" she asked.

Max didn't reply, but handed her the phone. She spoke briefly to the operator, then hung up.

"You reported a murder?" she asked, looking around the bar.

"Yeah," Max managed to say.

"Where is the body?" asked the other cop.

"She's outside in the VW. across the parking lot," said Max, pointing towards the front door.

"We're going to take a look and be right back. You stay here. We'll want to talk to you," the female ordered and the two left through the front door.

Officers Janice Samson and Hector Soto walked across the gravel towards the VW.

As they approached, Janice asked her partner, "You ever cover a homicide before?"

"Nope," was his one word reply.

"Me neither," she said.

Taking a deep breath, Hector said, "Okay. Let's do this by the book."

Officer Samson arrived at the side of the car a step before Soto. She stepped around the driver's side door, which Max had left open after his grizzly find. She stepped around the door and looked inside. She immediately turned and grabbed her mouth. It took all her will power to keep from throwing up.

"What?" asked Hector, moving around her to see. Officer Samson just pointed towards the car.

"Oh, Jesus," he said, staring at the body. "Her guts are hanging out."

"We better call this in right away," said Officer Samson, after regaining her composure.

"Why don't you stay here. I'll go back to the car and make the call," she suggested. Without waiting for a reply, she headed off across the parking lot.

Officer Soto continued to look in the car. He saw an umbrella on the floor behind the front seat and a woman's pocket book on the passenger's seat.

"It doesn't look like a robbery," he thought. He looked at the woman's face. She was young and pretty.

There didn't appear to be any marks on her face. Her forehead rested against the top of the steering wheel. Soto noticed a small tear drop that apparently had run from her left eye, down her cheek, and stopped near the corner of her mouth. Her arms hung at her sides, hands open, relaxed. He glanced down at the ground. He could see what appeared to be diluted blood mixed with the muddy water collecting in a few of the potholes. He made sure he didn't step in it.

Backing away, he moved around to the other side of the car to have a look. It appeared clean. The passenger side door was closed and locked, judging from the position of the release button visible through the window. He decided to wait for the detectives to arrive before going any closer.

Officer Soto had told his partner that this was his first homicide, but it wasn't his first dead body. As a youth growing up in the Bronx, he'd seen his share of gang members and crake dealers killed. He'd once seen the results of a woman raped and thrown from the roof of the tenement building he lived in. It was all part of growing up in that part of the Bronx. Hector Soto had been one of the fortunate ones. He came from a good family. His parents were hard-working people. His father worked as a custodian in the local high school. The work was steady, the pay good. There was a pension, and they had health insurance coverage. The Soto children never knew what it was like to have to go without food, proper clothing, or health care.

Hector's mother worked in a dental office in the neighborhood. Her boss was considerate and allowed her time off to care for a sick child when necessary. In return, Mrs. Soto was a steady and loyal worker, frequently arriving early to open the office or working past her normal quitting time when needed. Hector was the middle of five children, the only boy with four sisters. It was like having three mothers the way his older sisters looked after him. He graduated high school at the age of seventeen and attended John Jay College, where he took courses in criminal justice.

When he reached the minimum age, he took the entrance exam for the NYPD. Hector earned his spot on merit in spite of the fact the police department was going out of its way to hire minorities. Hector Soto was a good cop and had the capability and qualities to get ahead in the department.

His partner, Officer Janice Samson, was five years older than he. However, she had the same length of time on the force. Janice had been raised by her mother. Her parents had divorced when she was a baby. Her father remained involved in her life. He provided support and visited on a regular basis. Janice couldn't understand why they divorced. Neither remarried and they seemed to get along well when together. She figured that though they were friends, they just couldn't live together. Janice had two older brothers, both police officers, like their father. Her mother wasn't happy to see her boys follow in their father's foot steps. She'd hoped they'd go on to college. But Mrs. Samson was proud when her daughter had been accepted to Fordham University in the Bronx. Janice had taken liberal arts and graduated with a degree in elementary education. Janice would be a teacher.

She applied through the city's Board of Education and was hired almost immediately. Janice was placed in a Bronx Elementary School near where she lived. For the first two years, she found teaching rewarding, but felt unappreciated due to the low pay. The salaries for city teachers was the lowest in the metropolitan area. Many teaches found it necessary to take on second jobs to make ends meet. Janice decided with her education she should be able to survive on one income and began losing interest in her job. It was time for a career changes. After speaking to her brothers, she decided to apply to the police academy.

After a year-long wait, she was hired. It was while a rookie at the Academy that she met Hector Soto. They hit it off immediately. When they were assigned to the same precinct house, they hoped to be teamed up.

However, as rookies, they were given more experienced officers to sort of "break them in." Two years later, they were placed in the same squad car. Janice and Hector worked well together. Some of the other officers teased them that they might as well be married. Janice and Hector would just laugh. They enjoyed each other's company and were on the same wave length as far as police work went, but there were no sparks between them. Both freely admitted it was better that way.

Janice took several deep breaths as she walked across the parking lot. When she returned to the squad car, she called headquarters. She told the supervisor what they had. He directed them to secure the area and wait for the homicide detectives to arrive. She went inside the bar to check on the man who'd reported the murder. Max was now seated at one of the small tables near a window overlooking the parking lot.

"You okay?," she asked.

"Yeah, thanks," said Max.

"The homicide detectives are coming down and will probably want to talk to you. You better go easy on the booze or you're not going to be any good to anyone," she offered.

"You're right. I'll put on some coffee. If you or your partner want any it should be ready in about ten minutes," said Max.

"Thanks. Maybe we'll take you up on the offer. I gotta go see how my partner is," said Officer Samson and walked outside to her car. She drove the car to the other side of the lot and stopped short of the area around the victim's car.

Rolling down the window, she yelled, "Hector, come on. Might as well wait in here until the detectives arrive." Officer Soto joined her inside the squad car. They sat next to each other in silence, staring at the VW.

Chapter 10

The "unmarked car" rounded a corner and screeched to an abrupt stop.

"Where the hell are we?" asked Detective Nancy Mooney.

"How the hell should I know?," answered her partner, Detective John Straub.

"I thought you said you knew the Bronx like the back of your hand," retorted Mooney.

"I do, just not this part," countered John Straub. Pushing the shift into reverse, John backed up hard until the rear wheels hit a curb. Then slamming it into drive, he spun the "unmarked" around facing the direction they'd just come from. Detective Mooney could see her partner's face turning red.

"Give me the cell phone," demanded John.

Mooney knew better than to ask why.

"Here," she said, thrusting it at him.

Because of "budgetary restraints" GPS positioning was not available to the cop on the street yet.

John took the phone and pushed one of the speed-dial numbers.

After a moment, John said, "Hi! Do me a favor and look something up on the map for me. It's Mosey Drive or Road in the Bronx."

Mooney couldn't tell who John was talking to, but she hoped he'd find out how to get to their next assignment.

"Yeah, that's it. Okay. Okay. Thanks, Ski," he said and broke the connection.

"He says it's just down the block in the industrial section."

"That was :Ski?" How's he doing?" asked Detective. Mooney.

"He's good. But he can't wait to get back full time."

Peter Zubriski, "Ski" to his friends, was just back from sick leave. Ski had been Detective. John Straub's partner up until about six months ago. During the arrest in a murder case, Zubriski suffered a shattered knee cap. It happened when the "perp" the police were trying to arrest fought back. The perp was skilled in karate. While trying to subdue the suspect, Ski took a side kick to his knee. His knee cap shattered like a dinner plate striking a stone floor. He dropped immediately to the floor in agony. The "perp" dropped on top of him and tried to take his gun from him. Through the pain Ski managed to hold onto his weapon and the perp until assistance arrived. They quickly subdued the suspect and called for an ambulance for their brother officer. In the hospital X-rays revealed the extent of his injury. One doctor in the "ER" suggested the knee cap or patella would have to be removed, leaving Ski a cripple. Through the fog of pain Ski demanded they do something to save his leg. Ski was taken immediately to the operating room where a team of skilled doctors were able to wire the knee cap back into place. After a few days in the hospital Ski was released to begin several long months of strenuous rehabilitation.

When he was finally cleared by the police department's doctor he was allowed to return to work. While he was eager to return to the streets his commanding officer placed him on restricted duty. Ski was "sentenced" to ride a desk for the next six months.

With his partner laid up, John Straub was teamed up with Detective Nancy Mooney. Straub resisted having her as a partner, but it had nothing to do with the fact that she was a woman. Straub knew Mooney from prior cases they'd worked on together. They were more than partners. They were lovers. They'd been living together almost a year. Being partners would surely put their relationship to the test.

Too much "togetherness" worried Straub.

John stepped on the gas, headed out onto Pelham Parkway, and turned south towards the Long Island Sound. After a few minutes, they saw a sign that read, "Mosey Industrial Park."

John turned the car right onto Mosey Ave. and headed down the block looking for an address. On either side there was nothing but warehouses, interspersed with abandoned buildings and lots, over grown with weeds.

At the very end of the block, they came to a chain-link fence surrounding a gravel parking lot. A large metal gate intended to prevent trespassers hung open, one hinge missing. At an opening in the fence was sign that read, "Giggi's."

John drove through the opening and into the parking lot. Across the graveled area stood a police cruiser. Its engine running. Next to it was a small car. A VW Beetle.

"I guess this is the place," said Detective Mooney, as John drove towards the squad car. Stopping their car near the VW, John put the car in park and shut off the engine.

"Let's go solve a crime," said John.

Sliding out from behind the wheel he put his left foot directly into a puddle. "Damn it," he said, looking down at the ground. "Son of a bitch." he added for emphasis.

"What's the matter?" asked Mooney.

"I just stepped into the mother of all potholes. My shoes are soaked."

Mooney stifled a laugh and declined to comment.

She almost said, "It wouldn't be a normal day if you didn't step into something," but kept it to herself.

"What?" demanded Straub. "What were you going to say?" he demanded.

"Nothing sweetheart."

"Don't call me sweetheart when we're on the job," he retorted.

She just grinned

They walked around the front of their car and were greeted by the two uniformed cops.

"Hi guys. I'm Detective Straub. This is my partner Detective Mooney," said Straub, introducing themselves.

"Officers Samson and Soto," said the female cop, nodding towards her partner.

"What have we got?" asked Straub as he shook hands with the two young cops.

"We've got a homicide, is what we got. She's in the car," said Officer Samson, heisting up her gun belt and trying to act like however a veteran cop was supposed to act.

"Has anyone touched anything?" asked Nancy.

"As far as we've been able to determine, no," responded Officer Soto, trying to include himself in the conversation.

Mooney walked towards the car and looked inside.

"Man. Somebody did a job on her. Who found her?" she asked.

"A guy named Maxwell Peterson. He's the manager of the topless joint over there. Said he came in around noon to open up and found her here," answered Soto.

"Anything else?" asked Straub. "Did he know her? See anyone around?"

"We didn't question him. We were told to protect the crime scene and that's what we did," offered Samson.

"Okay. Mooney, why don't you take one of these guys with you and see what you can learn from this Peterson character. I'll call in the M.E. and the lab people."

Mooney did as John requested.

"Samson is it? Why don't you come with me?" It was more of an order than a suggestion.

"Fine," said Samson.

She glanced at her partner as if to say, "Sorry. I get to play detective."

The two walked off towards the bar.

John moved around the car, keeping his distance, not touching anything. Soto followed right behind him, like a little puppy dog. Having the rookie looking over his shoulder made Straub uncomfortable.

"Tell me, Officer Soto, what do you make of this?"

The young officer looked at the detective in surprise. He hadn't thought he'd be asked anything other than was the scene secured. He decided, if he wanted his input, why not?.

"Well, the woman was killed with a knife. It had to be a long, sharp knife to cut through clothing and flesh like that. Plus, the guy was probably strong. He probably knew her."

"Why do you say that?" asked Detective. Straub.

"Well, as I see it, a knife is personal. Not like a gun. With a knife, you have to get up close to the person. Usually a stranger can't do that too easily. Get up close, I mean. This guy had a reason for killing her the way he did. Usually a '"knifer"' sticks once or twice, or slashes across the neck. This guy disemboweled her. That shows fore thought," said Soto.

"Very good, Soto. Where did you learn to think like that?" asked John.

"The streets," was Soto's replied.

"Yeah. I guess you'd get a good schooling about crime in the right neighborhood. Where are you from?"

"Right around here, the Bronx."

"You said it would be hard for a stranger to get this close. Why do you say that?" asked Straub.

"Her hands. They aren't cut. No defensive wounds. This guy got on her without any warning."

"Why do you keep saying 'guy' when you talk about the killer?" asked John.

"It's not a woman's style. A woman would go for the face first, disfigure the victim. Also, a woman wouldn't use a knife. A gun, maybe, but not a knife. It's too messy. And it took some strength to do this," Soto said, motioning towards the victim's abdomen. "You're good, kid," said John, causing the rookie's face to beam. "You see a lot," said Detective Straub with a smile. "You'd make a good detective."

Soto smiled with satisfaction.

John proceeded to walk around the car observing the distance from the bar and the puddles in the parking lot.

Thinking out loud, something he often did, Straub began to survey the crime scene.

"This happened sometime last night. The body is cold. No steam coming off the organs. The place is flooded. It was raining hard last night. My guess is the woman runs to the car. It's dark, the rain and wind is grabbing at the umbrella which she's holding in one hand while she tries to get the keys out of her pocketbook with the other. She probably didn't see anyone coming from behind.

"Look here," said Straub. "There's blood mixed with the water in the puddles. She was knifed outside the car, managed to get inside and then died. Probably from shock and loss of blood. Could have been the manager, a patron, a stranger. Figuring that part will take time."

John went back to their "unmarked car" and returned with a camera equipped with a flash. He proceeded to take pictures of the outside area around the car and several inside. He used the zoom lens and snapped a few shots of the passenger seat, where the victim's pocket book was sitting.

"Don't the guys from the lab take the pictures?" asked Soto.

"Oh, they will. I just like to take some of my own if I see something that strikes me. I'll ask the lab boys to take the same pictures, but this is in case I forget," said Straub. Noticing the look on the rookie's face, he said," "Don't look so surprised. We detectives aren't gods. We forget and make mistakes just like the rest of you mortals," he said with a smile.

John walked around to the other side of the car and tried the handle. It was locked.

"I'd love to get a look at her pocketbook," Straub said out loud.

"Here, use my night stick. If you're careful, you should be able to lift it out by the straps," offered Soto.

John took the stick and careful not to touch anything inside the car, reached across the body of the victim. He hooked one of the pocket book's straps with the night stick and lifted it over the woman and outside the car.

"Here, hold these for a second," requested Straub.

Once Soto took the stick and pocket book, John removed a pair of latex gloves from his pocket. He carefully lifted the strap off the night stick and opened the clasp to look inside. He could see a wallet sitting inside.

"It wasn't a robbery," he thought.

With the strap still looped over a gloved finger, he took a pen from his pocket and hooked the end of it through the folded wallet. He hung the pocket book back on the night stick and opened the wallet.

"Jennifer Sands," he read out loud. "At least we have a name and address."

He flipped open the sleeve of plastic inserts inside the wallet. They contained credit cards and a baby's picture. Then he spread the bill section open. In between the folds of the leather compartments he could see several bills, about sixty or seventy dollars in fives and tens, he guessed without removing them.

Next he took his pen and moved some of the items in the bottom of her pocket book around. Other than an assortment of lip sticks, compacts, a small comb and brush, and some tissues, there was nothing else Straub could see worth trying to look at in the parking lot. He returned the wallet to the pocket book and then, using the night stick, placed the pocket book back on the seat of the car. Then he put the camera back in his car.

Inside "Giggi's" Maxwell Peterson stood behind the bar where he felt most comfortable. Across the bar, Police Officer Samson stood next to Detective Mooney.

"I'll need your full name, address, and phone number," began Mooney. Max gave her the information. "Now, can you give me the victim's full name and address? Also, did she live with anyone, a husband, boyfriend, kids?"

Max gave the detective Jen's full name, address, and phone number.

"She lived alone as far as I know. She had a kid, but the welfare people took him away from her. She said they didn't think she could provide a healthy environment for the kid. Jen told me she thought it was the kid's father who put a call into the social workers just to bust her chops."

"Was Jen married?" asked Mooney.

"No. She said she'd lived with a guy for about a year. She got pregnant. She said that's when he took off. She said he wouldn't help her with the kid. Wouldn't pay any child support. She said she had him brought into court. They'd ordered him to pay, but he'd stop after a few months. Then she'd have to track him down and start all over again."

"Did she ever say whether this guy hurt her? Did he threaten her?" asked Mooney.

"She never said anything about it, but that don't mean it didn't happen," said Max.

"Any relatives around?" asked Mooney.

"I think her mother lives nearby. I may have her phone number in back. I'll check." Max walked into the back and returned with a tattered piece of paper.

"Yep, here it is," said Max, returning to his favorite spot. He handed the paper to Mooney, who put it into her pocket.

"Okay, so why don't you start with what happened this morning when you arrived at this place," said Mooney, looking around the place.

"Like I told the lady cop here, I drove into the lot around twelve. I saw Jen's car and went over to see what was going on. That's when I found . . ." Here Max stopped, swallowing several times to try to keep his stomach from revealing how strongly it had affected him.

"Okay. Try to relax. Take a deep breath," suggested Mooney.

"I'm all right. When I walked over to the car I found Jen inside. She was obviously dead," said Max, tears welling up in his eyes.

Mooney glanced at Officer Samson and shook her head.

"You really liked her, didn't you?" asked the officer.

"Yeah. I liked her. But I never told her. She'd never have anything to do with a guy like me," said Max.

"Is that why you killed her?" asked Mooney.

Max looked up with a start, eyes wide and glaring at the detective.

"I didn't kill her. I loved her," said Max, his face grimacing as he tried to control his emotions.

Mooney could see by his grief that he was sincere.

"Okay. Sorry, but I had to ask. Do you have any idea who would?" asked Mooney.

"No. Jen was liked by everyone. She didn't have a mean bone in her body."

"Do you know if anyone had a crush on her, besides yourself? Someone who she might have put off and might want to get even, hurt her?" Mooney continued.

"No. As far as I know she wasn't seeing anyone outside of work. At work she was all business with the customers. Oh, she flirted a little. You know, to try to increase her tips, but she never went too far. Not like some of the girls."

Max stopped, wondering if he'd said something that could come back to haunt him. The cops obviously knew what kind of a place he ran and what went on inside. Sometimes the girls did more than dance for the customers, but that was on their own time and off the premises. That was the rule. The last thing Max wanted was the place getting raided and closed down. He'd be out of work.

"Are you the owner of this place?," asked Mooney.

"No, I just manage it. Some guy with money to burn, owns it. He never comes around, just pays the bills and has his accountants keep track of the receipts. I guess it's just an investment with him."

"Do you have a name or address?" asked Nancy.

"Actually, no. If there are any problems I'm to call his lawyer or a management company for emergency repairs or maintenance," answered Max.

"Why did he put it back here? How does anyone find this place?" questioned Mooney.

"NIMBY," he said. The cops looked at each other.

"You know, no one wants a place like this in their neighborhood. The town council knows some people want places like this, but 'Not In My Back Yard,' NIMBY, you know?" Max didn't wait for a reply.

"So they let us open back here in the industrial districts. There aren't any private houses around. The businesses close down by six, so that leaves us here alone. Back here they figure where we can't corrupt the minds of their kids. That's a laugh. Their kids are seeing it on their own cable TV's, on videos, or doing it with the chick next door. As for how anyone finds us, that's easy. Word of mouth. People who want this kind of entertainment always know where to find it," added Max.

"Okay, let's get back to the lady outside. Tell me about last night," directed Mooney.

"It was slow. The weather kept the guys home. There were only a few customers left by eleven o'clock, so I decided to call it a night. We announced 'last call.' The dancers finished up their 'performances' and left. Jen and I were the last to leave.

"She left a little before me. When I closed down and went outside it was still raining pretty hard. The wind was blowing hard too. I just ran to my car and drove home. I never noticed Jen's car. I guess with all the rain, I just couldn't see anything."

"Did you notice anyone hanging around at closing. Maybe someone who was paying a little too much attention to the victim?" asked Mooney.

"No, I wish I did, but no. It was just the usual group of guys," concluded Max.

"How about names?" she asked.

"Just first names but my guess is that they aren't real. The guys that come in here don't want to be known. You know what I mean?

"What about the other girls? Did any of them ever say anything about being harassed or stalked by one of the patrons?"

"The girls are always having to deal with creeps who want to touch or 'get to know them.' You know. But the girls can handle them. I swear I can't think of any thing that might help you guys. I wish to God I could. I'd give anything to see you catch whoever did that," said Max.

Detective Mooney proceeded to look around the bar. She was searching for any signs of a struggle, blood, anything that might connect Max to the murder. There was nothing. Next, she went outside and looked through Max's car. It reeked of body odor and was cluttered with empty candy and potato chip bags, but there were no signs of blood. However the forensic people would probably take a closer look.

"It looks like this one's going to require some leg work," she thought and returned to the bar.

"Okay, Mr. Peterson," started Mooney, who then reached into her jacket pocket and removed one of her business cards and gave it to Max. "If you think of anything or hear anything, call me."

Detective Mooney and Officer Samson walked towards the door of the bar. "What is your opinion of the guy?" asked Mooney.

"I believe him. He looks like a big blob who never had a girl. He probably fantasizes a lot, but never gets any. She was probably nice to him, but that's all. I don't think he did it. He's too stupid to be such a good actor. Nope, I believe he's clean," she suggested.

"Me too. You have a good read on people. It'll come in handy in this job. Now, I'd like you to stay here and keep an eye on him. When the lab boys get here they'll want to swab his finger nails and stuff. I didn't notice any scratches or fight marks, but you never know. Anything that would put him close to the victim. Okay?" asked Mooney.

"Sure, Detective, glad to help," she said.

Mooney walked outside and headed over towards their car. She noticed the Police Crime Scene Lab Van had arrived and the boys in the white coats were going over the area and the car. Bright flashes from cameras illuminated the scene and the interior of the car. Parked next to the lab van and their "unmarked" was the ME's (medical examiner's) van.

They'd be removing the body once the detectives and lab boys were finished. Mooney approached her partner, who was standing next to Officer Soto and one of the guys from the lab. John noticed Mooney's approach and stopped his conversation.

"Get anything?" he asked.

"The usual. He discovered the body. Said she had an abusive boyfriend but says he doesn't know anything else. Oh, and she has a kid" she added.

"A kid?"

"Yeah, a boy but he's in foster care."

They compared notes and conferred with the crime scene technicians. A couple of hours later the "go ahead" for removal of the body was given. As the black M.E. van pulled out of the lot, Detectives Straub and Mooney were right behind. They headed back to their office to begin the task of assembling whatever information they had on the new case.

Chapter 11

Detectives Straub and Mooney walked into their office after spending most of the afternoon at the Bronx crime scene. John settled behind his desk, removing his wet shoes and soggy socks. Mooney pulled up a chair alongside Straub's desk and just stared at him.

"What?" asked John.

"I was just thinking about that woman. It's hard to believe how brutal one person can be towards another."

"I wish I could say you'll get used to it, but you don't. It's probably just as well. I think the bad guys will have won when this kind of stuff no longer bothers us," said John.

"So, partner, shall we get to work and try to solve this one?" asked Straub.

"Right. What do you want to do first?" asked Mooney.

"I'll run a check on Jennifer Sands. See what the system has on her," John said out loud.

"And what about me?" she asked.

"We won't get anything from the M.E.'s office for a day or two. Why don't you run a check on our manager,

Maxwell Peterson. See if you can track down the owner of the bar. Then go through the list of employees. See if any of them have a rap sheet."

"Gotcha," said Mooney and went off to her own desk and phone.

Straub got on the computer and ran a check through the system on the victim. He soon learned she'd never been arrested, not even a traffic ticket. But her name was in their data base. She was listed as a complainant in a domestic abuse case. She was also known to the Department of Social Services.

John placed a call to DSS. He was soon connected to Mary Clarke. She was a case worker at DSS and had helped him in the past. After exchanging pleasantries, John got to the point of his call. He told her about the new case he was working on. He gave her the victim's name and address and asked for anything they had on her. Mary said it would take a few minutes to gather the information. She promised to call him back as soon as possible.

Next, John returned to his computer and brought up the "domestic abuse" case in the police records. It revealed that Jennifer Sands was a complainant against one Bruce Krane. They were listed as "partners" and had lived together for a while at the same address she held at the time of her death. She'd called the police after being struck by her live-in boyfriend. The report said he'd been drinking and an argument over money had erupted. He'd struck her, giving her a black eye. She declined medical treatment and just wanted him out of the house. Following a "zero tolerance" departmental directive, the cops arrested Krane and charged him with assault. The case was later dropped when she refused to press charges. Bruce Krane moved out and that was the end of the report. It didn't give a current address for the ex-boyfriend.

John had just finished printing out a copy of the report when his phone rang. It was Mary Clarke from DSS. She said Ms. Sands' case involved child support. Jennifer had a son, Steven, who was three years old now. Bruce Krane was listed as the father. He never contested paternity, so he was ordered to pay child support. Jennifer was on welfare at the time. Therefore, any money he paid went to DSS to reimburse them for the support provided to Jennifer and her son.

Bruce wasn't very reliable. He was constantly in arrears. The only way the department got him to pay was to get a court order and "garnish" his salary. Unfortunately, Bruce rarely held a steady job. During one of the rare periods when he was working and paying support, he filed a complaint with DSS. He alleged that Jennifer Sands was a drug user, worked in a topless bar, and often brought her son with her to work.

The DSS investigation failed to find evidence that she was an addict. However, she did work in a topless bar and admitted on a couple of occasions to bringing her infant son to work with her. She claimed the woman who watched him was ill at those times. Because she couldn't find a baby sitter she was forced to bring her son to work with her. She insisted the infant stayed in the back of the bar, away from the customers. She claimed she could and would hear him and made sure he was fed and changed. She insisted he was never abused or abandoned in any way. She claimed Bruce was just trying to get back at her for making him pay support. The agency found enough cause to take the infant away from the mother and place him in a foster home. Jennifer was allowed to visit him and did so regularly.

Mary Clarke said the case was "inactive" and had no further information. The matter was referred to the "Foster Parent Placement Department," which monitored the child's welfare. She gave John the name and number of the supervisor of that section if he needed any further information. John thanked her for her help and promised to treat her to dinner in return. Mary just laughed when he made these promises. She'd known and helped Detective Straub over a two-year period. During that time, she'd never seen him in person. He was only a voice on the phone.

After hanging up the phone, John added what he'd learned to the growing file on Jennifer Sands.

While John pursued his own inquiries, Nancy was busy using her computer and telephone contacts, running down leads on others who might be connected to the Sands' murder. Using her computer, she checked the names of Maxwell Peterson and the other employees through the police arrest files. All, except one of the dancers came up clean.

The dancer, Jill Gomez, had an arrest five years ago for "loitering." "A nice word for prostitution," thought Nancy. When she went into the state's records, her suspicion was confirmed. Miss Gomez was arrested, held over night, and released the next day. She eventually plead guilty to a reduced charge and paid a fine.

Having hit a dead end, Nancy decided to give the M.E.'s office a call. As expected, they hadn't even gotten to open a file on the deceased yet. She was asked to call back tomorrow. Nancy swung around in her chair to see what John was up to.

John was sitting in his chair, leaning back so its two front legs were off the ground. He was staring at the ceiling.

"You ready to call it a day, old timer?" asked Nancy.

"Yeah, I guess so. What time is it?" he asked.

"Six thirty," she replied.

"Okay, then let's go."

They shut down their computers and headed out the door.

"What are you cooking for dinner tonight?" asked John.

"Excuse me?" returned Nancy. "Did I not get up the same time you did? Did I not work the same number of hours as you? Do you actually expect dinner? Wonder Woman I'm not," she said with a little bite in her voice.

"Wrong question," thought John.

Back pedaling, he corrected himself and asked, "I meant to ask what you wanted to do about dinner, as in which restaurant," added John, hoping this would get him off the hook. Nancy decided to give him a break.

"So why didn't you say that in the first place? I feel like lobster tails. Let's go down to one of those places in Sheepshead Bay for dinner," suggested Nancy.

"Ouch, lobster tails. That's going to set me back a pretty penny," thought John, but said instead, "Lobster, why not."

They found their car in the rear parking lot and headed across town, over the Brooklyn Bridge and onto the Brooklyn Queens Expressway, towards the Belt and Brooklyn. After about forty minutes of bumper to bumper traffic, they finally came to their exit and drove down to the water front. Once there, Nancy directed John to "Cirro's on the Water" and they parked in a nearby lot. As they walked to the front door, John wondered if there was a "Cirro's Not on the Water" some place.

Once inside, they were quickly seated and a waiter took their drink orders. Nancy had a glass of white wine, John a scotch on the rocks with a splash of water. The waiter gave them a few minutes to look over the menus. Nancy looked out the window at the ocean because she knew what she wanted, lobster.

Glancing at the menu John found the lobster tails. Forty dollars! Without fries!

"Forty bucks for lobster. Are they kidding?," he thought.

When the waiter returned John ordered the lobster for Nancy and swordfish for himself. Although the prices were a little steep for him on a cop's salary he decided to forget the cost and enjoy the company and view. He watched Nancy as she continued to gazed out the window. She still took his breath away. He liked it when she wore her hair down. The red tint gave it a fiery warmth. Her eyes glistened, and a slight smile played across her lips.

"God you're beautiful," he said softly.

Nancy turned from the window, reached across the table and took his hand in hers and said "You're beautiful too" and turned back to look at the ocean.

John blushed at the compliment. He still wasn't used to signs of affection. It had been a long time since his divorce and he had deliberately shied away from dating. "Once burned is enough," he'd often say when co-workers tried to "fix him up" with someone. But this was different. For the first time in his life, John was deeply in love.

He couldn't believe they'd been dating for almost a year now. Nancy had made the first move in their relationship. John had been divorce for almost two years when Nancy had approached him at a police watering hole one night after work. He'd resisted. He thought she was too forward and it was too soon after the break up with his wife. There was a rumor that she'd made her gold shield on her back. A rumor started probably out of jealousy. Many officers were still resistive to women on the force, so these kinds of lies were thrown about. The truth was she came from a police family. Nancy's dad was a retired New York City captain. But Nancy refused to accept any help. She had scored among the highest on all her police tests in the Academy,. She put in long hours accepted moves to often unpopular assignments just to get the experience under her belt. Despite stories to the contrary, she wasn't sleeping with any of the brass. Nancy earned her promotions and was proving to be a solid partner.

John's original partner, Pete Zubriski was on "sick leave" from a job-related injury. Although he didn't ask for Nancy to be assigned as his partner, it was turning out okay.

When they were teamed up together he feared too much time together would prove their undoing. So far that hadn't happened. Nancy managed to keep their work and off-duty relationship separate. At work, she willingly took John's "suggestions" in stride, admitting he had the experience. However, she wasn't afraid to add her two cents when she thought it appropriate.

"She's bright, good looking. What more could a guy want?" thought John.

Nancy was actually more than good looking. She was stunning. She was tall, almost five ten, with a sleek, athletic body, with a "great rake," as some of the other cops would say, but never in front of John. John hated that expression, thinking it vulgar and demeaning. She had wavy, reddish brown hair, which she wore long off duty. Her eyes were blue green and had a lot of life in them. She was quick and had a great sense of humor. She knew how to playfully push John's buttons without being mean. Nancy saw John's reflection in the glass and knew he was still looking at her. She turned towards him and smiled, showing perfect white teeth. John smiled back.

"What were you thinking?" asked John.

"Nothing, just admiring the view. What about you?" she asked in return.

"Me? I was admiring the view also," he said with a smile.

"Stop. Now you're making me blush," said Nancy, feigning embarrassment.

"I love you," said John impulsively.

"Of course you do," replied Nancy, teasing, but didn't respond to his acclamation of love.

"Well?" asked John slightly annoyed.

"Well what?" asked Nancy.

"Forget it," replied John, a tinge of anger in his voice.

Nancy laughed and reached across the table for his hand.

"You're so easy to tease," she said. "Are you so unsure of our relationship already?" she asked.

John hesitated for a moment before replying.

"As a matter of fact, yes. But I guess it is one sided," he added.

"John Michael Straub! How dare you?" said Nancy, feigning indignation. Still holding his hand she continued, "You are the most handsome, intelligent, kindest man I've ever known. Of course I love you," she said raising her voice. "Don't you go getting all insecure on me. After all it was your self-assuredness that drew me towards you in the first place," she added.

John smiled and squeezed her hand. "I guess I just like to hear you say it, that's all," he added. At that moment the waiter arrived with their dinners.

John and Nancy spent the next half hour eating, sharing their food with each other, and at times laughing for no apparent reasons. They looked cute together and more than one couple in the restaurant noticed them, envying their playful behavior. After dinner, they ordered decaf cappuccinos. John leaned back in his chair and sighed.

Nancy did likewise and as she moved her shoulders back let out a slight burp.

"Excuse me," she said putting her hand to her mouth.

"Nancy," said John. "How unlady like."

"Oh, don't be such a fuddy-duddy. I said excuse me. Besides, it's just natural," she said with a girlish grin on her face.

"Yeah, but if I did that you'd say it was rude."

"If you did that half the people in the place would have heard it."

"Do you want to take a walk along the water after we finish our coffee?" asked Nancy.

"Sure. It's a beautiful night," replied John.

They finished the last of their cappuccinos. John paid the bill with his American Express card, leaving a generous tip. On the way out, John grabbed a couple of free after-dinner mints from a bowl on the counter. He offered one to Nancy, but she declined. Instead, she looped her arm around John's back. They walked around the front of the restaurant towards the beach in the back. They'd no sooner gotten to the water's edge, then they noticed a group of people standing by the shore line a short distance down the beach.

"Hmm, I wonder what they're all looking at,?" said Nancy.

They turned and approached the group of about twenty people. There wasn't any moon that night and what light reached the water was cast by street lights more than thirty feet back from the water.

The ocean was black and the waves rolling up onto the beach cast a light spray. A small dog that appeared to be part beagle and probably belonged to one of the people in the crowd, was moving back and forth with each wave, barking at something in the water.

John and Nancy moved closer to the group.

John stood next to an elderly man. "What are they were looking at?" he asked.

"There's something in the water. Our dog, Toby, drew our attention to it," he said. Tilting his head towards an elderly woman standing next to him, he said, "The misses and I were walking him when he pulled away from us and ran down here. Some people were already here at the time," answered the man.

Without responding, John moved closer to the water. He tried to discern what it was that they were all looking at, but couldn't at first. Whatever it was, it rode the waves in and out without seeming to get any closer than five feet from the beach. Occasionally, what little street light reached this far, seemed to flash off something white, before the object rolled back towards the ocean. Finally, showing no fear, a young teen pulled his sneakers and socks off, rolled up his pants legs, and wadded out into the water.

As he got closer, he yelled back, "It looks like a pile of rags or something." Then without waiting for any comments, he reached out and grabbed hold of the material and pulled. It must have been heavy, because the young man had trouble moving it. Finally, he grabbed it with two hands, turned slightly, and began dragging the object through the shallow surf and up on the beach. As he maneuvered it onto the sand his back was towards it.

Suddenly, a young woman gave out a high pitched scream and turned away, hands covering her face.

"What is it?" asked the kid, turning to look at the object. He too gave out a yell, staggered backwards, falling onto the wet sand, then scrambled backwards, crab like, farther up the beach.

John moved around the people who stood staring. As he came closer, he recognized what the object was.

Turning to Nancy, he said, "Hon, go back to the car. Get the cell phone and call 911. It's a body."

Nancy didn't ask any questions. Instead, she headed up the beach towards their car.

Back on the beach, some people moved back several feet, while others pushed forward to get a better look.

"Stand back, please," said John as he reached in side his shirt and removed his detective's shield. He let it hang from a thin chain.

"I've summoned the police. I'd like you all to remain until they get here. They'll want to ask you some questions," said John to the crowd.

Upon hearing this, the youth who'd pulled the body from the water grabbed his sneakers and ran up the beach toward the road. He didn't bother to take his socks, or stop long enough to put on his sneakers.

"I guess he doesn't like cops," said a young man in the group.

John turned his attention back to the body. He didn't want to touch anything, but his police instincts got the better of him. He crouched down and tried to get a look at the person's face. A leather jacket was partially pulled off one arm and hung by its side, sand clinging to its surface. The body wore a pair of black cowboy boots and jeans. Some of its clothing, a sweater it appeared, had ridden up and was covering the face. However, with the clothes pulled up, the mid section of the body was exposed. John looked at the flesh and was immediately taken by the fact that there was a long, open gash up the abdomen. It seemed to begin well below the navel and continued up to the breast bone. He could see the lower part of a breast partially exposed. The victim was a woman and she wasn't wearing a bra. John stood up and glanced back up towards the road. He saw Nancy walking down the slopping sand, the cell phone in her hand.

"They're on their way," she said. "And guess what?" She didn't wait for John to reply. "They want us to stay and take the case. Looks like it's going to be a, not-so-lovely end, to an otherwise perfect night." John just shook his head in disgust. "It never ends," he said to no one in particular.

John and Nancy ended up spending the next four hours at the scene. They took down the names, addresses, and telephone numbers of the people who'd been at the crime scene. No one knew the name of the kid who pulled the body from the water.

Before leaving, they made sure the people from the M.E.'s office had their names, shield numbers, and phone numbers. They asked to be contacted once the M.E. was ready to go to work on the body.

By the time they got back to John's house, they were both too tired to think about anything but sleep.

"Boy you really know how to show a girl a good time," Nancy said sarcastically.

"Yeah. I guess any thought of sex is out of the question," John responded.

Nancy tilted her head to the side, fluttered her eyes, and smiled.

"Don't be so sure about that," she said with a devilish grin on her face.

Chapter 12

The next morning Detectives Straub and Mooney decided to visit the place where the murder victim, Jennifer Sands, had lived. John let Nancy drive for a change. Secretly, he wanted to be able to consult their map, so they didn't get lost again. They drove up the FDR Drive and, using the Willis Avenue Bridge, crossed the Harlem River and picked up the Major Deegan and onto Webster Ave. After a short distance on Webster they made a right onto Tremont and another right which put them on Third Avenue. A quick right off Third put them onto Hoffman, a right onto East 188 St. and a block down to Arthur Ave.

"Turn left."

They were now in the what was called the Fordham section of the Bronx.

John started scanning the buildings

"What are we looking for?" asked Nancy.

"Just drive," John said annoyed.

"Gotcha boss," replied Nancy knowing better than to argue with him when he was trying to read directions.

They'd almost reached East Fordham Road when John yelled "Stop!"

Nancy hit the brakes, stopping in the middle of the block. The guy in the car behind her blasted his horn and flipping her the finger as he drove past.

"Next time give a girl a little warning," she said, a touch of annoyance in her voice.

"Sorry. Go slow" John suggested in a softer tone.

Nancy drove slowly so John could check the numbers on the buildings.

"Here it is. Park the car," said John.

Nancy spotted a space and expertly pulled in. As they exited the "unmarked" car they both took deep breaths.

"Something smells good," said Nancy.

"That would be the Italian restaurants up ahead," said John, pointing to the other side of the block. There was a lot of activity for that hour of the morning, mostly people in their late teens and early twenties.

"A lot of young people in the area," commented Nancy.

"Most are students from Fordham University. It's just up the block. Some of the kids prefer living off campus. I guess it gives them a sense of independence," added John.

"Yeah, but in the Bronx?" replied Nancy.

"Believe it or not, this is a good area to live in. This is the "'Little Italy'" of the Bronx," said John. "See those old men sitting on chairs in front of that apartment?" he asked.

Nancy noticed two elderly men. They were dressed alike, each wearing white "T-" shirts and old dress pants, held up by suspenders. They leaned forward, elbows on their knees, talking, but looking up and down the street at the same time. In front of the next house were two women, also talking, their backs to baby carriages standing on the side walk.

"Those women could walk off and leave the baby carriage and no one would dare bother it. The two old men are the 'eyes' of the neighborhood. If they were to see anything that looked remotely like trouble, they'd give a signal. In less than ten seconds about a dozen men with baseball bats would be on the streets ready to take action. This neighborhood is pretty much policed by its own. The cops rarely have to respond to calls here. When they do, it's usually to mop up after the 'neighborhood' has taken care of matters."

"You weren't kidding when you referred to it as 'Little Italy.' We should come here for dinner some time," she suggested.

"See that place there?" said John, pointing across the street. That's 'Mamma's' and that one, 'Tony and Maria's.' They're both first class restaurants. You can't ask for better food or service. We'll come up sometime for dinner, I promise," he added, his mouth watering.

With that said, John motioned to the apartment building in front of them.

"This is the place," said John.

They walked up to the entrance and into a small foyer set between two doors. The interior door was locked. On the wall was a list of apartment numbers and names underneath.

"Here," pointed Nancy.

"3C, Sands," she read. Just out of curiosity, she pressed the button. Nothing. Then she pressed it again. Still nothing.

"Try that one," said John, pointing to the bottom button on the right.

Nancy pressed it and waited. She noticed the apartment number was listed as 1D and had the words "Super" under it. Nancy was about to press the button again when the inside door opened.

Standing in the doorway was a short, Latino-looking man. He wore a stained sweatshirt and dungarees, also stained.

"What do you want?" he asked, no hint of an accent. John showed the man his ID and introduced Nancy.

"My name's Sanchez. I'm the superintendent here. Come in, detectives." As Sanchez backed up, John and Nancy entered the hallway inside. John looked around. The place was spotless. It appeared to be freshly painted, the floors shined, as did the steps leading up to the second floor. He didn't see an elevator.

"You keep a nice building, Mr. Sanchez," said John. The super smiled and his chest seemed to puff out.

"That's my job," he said. "Now, what can I do for you?"

Now it was Nancy's turn to talk.

"Mr. Sanchez, we're here concerning one of your tenants, Jennifer Sands."

"Yes, Ms. Sands. She lives here, apartment 3D. She is a very nice lady. Has she done something?" asked the super.

"No," said Nancy. Seeing the puzzled look on his face, Nancy added, "I'm afraid Ms. Sands is dead."

"Oh no!," said Mr. Sanchez, moving his hand across his chest in the sign of the cross. The super appeared visibly shaken by the news. "She was such a nice lady. How could this happen?" he asked.

"That's what we're trying to find out," said John.

"Was it an auto accident?" asked Sanchez.

"No. We believe she was murdered," added John.

The super lowered his head and just shook it back and forth. Finally, he raised his head, his eyes moist.

"What can I do?" he asked.

"First, we'd like to see her apartment. Then, if you aren't busy, we'd like to ask you a few questions," said Nancy.

"Of course. Come with me. I'll get the keys. They're in my apartment."

He led them down the hall to the last door, 1D. He produced a key and opened the door. As he entered the apartment he yelled out, "Maria, we have company."

Mr. Sanchez's apartment showed as much, if not more care than they'd seen in the hallway. His place consisted of a TV/living room. A narrow hallway ran the length of the apartment. Off the hallway could be seen a kitchen with a round wooden table and four chairs. A baby's high chair stood in one corner. Farther down the hallway were the doors to what John assumed would be the bathroom and two bedrooms. The living room furniture was old, but appeared clean and well cared for. Mrs. Sanchez walked into the living room with an infant held on her right hip. She was Latino, like her husband, and smiled shyly as they were introduced. Also like her husband, she expressed shock and grief when told of the young woman's death.

John and Nancy asked the usual questions.

"What kind of a tenant was she? Did she cause any problems? Did she entertain much? Ever see anyone with her?" The usual.

Mr. and Mrs. Sanchez could offer nothing that helped to explain her sudden and tragic end. The super explained she'd been a tenant for less than two years. She was described as a pleasant young woman, who lived by herself. They didn't know what she did for a living other than it involved nights. She paid her rent on time and never caused any problems.

Next, Mr. Sanchez took them up to her apartment. John had been correct when he noticed the absence of an elevator.

The apartment complex was a three-story walk-up. Mr. Sanchez produced a key, unlocked the door, and stepped aside to let the detectives enter the apartment. He waited in the hall.

Nancy saw framed pictures throughout the apartment of a young boy, in various stages of development throughout the apartment. The front of the refrigerator held an assortment of snap shots of the boy, some by himself, some with his mother. The only thing missing were clothes and toys for a young boy. Jennifer's kitchen was similar to that of the Sanchez's except it had a more modern touch. Unlike the Sanchez's, this one had a microwave and a small color TV in the kitchen. It sat on one side of the kitchen table.

"Looks like that was her source of company," said Nancy, pointing towards the TV.

Other than a few dishes in the sink, the room and the rest of the apartment was neat and orderly. They moved down the hall to the rear of the apartment. Jennifer Sands' bedroom consisted of a single, twin-sized bed, a night table and lamp, a double dresser, mirror, and a small vanity positioned near a window to better catch the natural light. The bed was made and her clothes were arranged neatly in the dresser drawers or hung in the closet. Nancy rummaged through the drawers in the dresser. Nancy found nothing except a few more pictures of the boy she presumed was Jennifer's son.

John looked in the night table. There he found a small address and appointment book. He flipped through it. There were certain dates marked on the calendar. Jennifer had a doctor's appointment coming up in two weeks. It indicated "pap" test. John guessed it was her gynecologist. He hoped the doctor's name was listed among the addresses in the back of the book.

Further on there were a couple more items penciled in, "*Mom's Birthday,*" "*Visit Stevie at Gerard's,*" and "*Custody Hearing.*" John then flipped back to see what she'd marked down for the months before her murder. He found more of the same, mostly birthdays and anniversaries, a few doctor's appointments, and finally "*apply to Com. College.*" John decided to take the entire book with him back to the office.

While John was skimming through Jennifer's appointment book, Nancy was going through her closet. As she examined the collection of shirts, pants, jackets, and sweaters, the one thing that stood out was the fact that Jennifer didn't spend money on fancy clothes. She owned an assortment of outfits that allowed her to be presentable for most occasions. Judging from the labels, Jennifer shopped in discount stores and catalogues. Her shoes were sensible, but also, not expensive. She closed the closet door and turned her attention to the vanity.

Nancy sat down on a small wooden seat in front of the table. Bottles of make up and perfumes were scattered across the top of the vanity. She pulled open a small drawer and found a collection of "beauty implements."

Turning to John, Nancy said, "Nothing here. She certainly didn't spend money on herself. I wonder what she did with the money she made at the topless joint?"

Not getting a response from John, Nancy was about to get up when her knee caught on something under the vanity. Bending down and peering under, she saw an envelope taped beneath the table. She reached under, peeled the tape, and removed the envelope.

"Found something," she yelled.

As she held the envelope up towards the window she could see there was something inside. The envelope felt bulky. The flap wasn't sealed, so Nancy turned the envelope upside down and allowed the contents to slide out onto the top of the vanity. It was a bank book. Opening it, Nancy saw that Jennifer Sands had been making regular deposits to a savings account. While the amounts differed slightly, the deposits were consistent. After the last entry, which was on the past Friday, the book showed a total savings of $12,600.

"I found out what she did with her money," yelled Nancy.

"What are you yelling for? I'm right here," said John, suddenly popping up from the far side of the bed. "Nothing but dust bunnies under here."

"Dust bunnies? Did you say 'dust bunnies'?" she asked, teasing.

John ignored her.

"I found a bank book. She was saving her money. I wonder why.? It looks like she lived hand to mouth," added Nancy.

"I think she was saving it so she could get her kid back," said John. "The boy was placed with a family nearby by DSS. From her little date book, it appears she made a point to visit him regularly. The woman I'd spoken to at DSS said he'd been taken from her because of where she worked and the hours she kept. I guess she wanted to make a change with her life. Did you find anything else?"

"Nothing out of the ordinary, you?"

"Just the address and appointment book. I figure we can go through it back at headquarters," said John. "Come on. Let's go see if Mr. Sanchez has thought of anything."

John and Nancy walked through the apartment and found the super waiting in the hall.

"Did you think of anything while we were inside?" asked John.

"Only that she didn't deserve to die so young," said Mr. Sanchez.

"Mr. Sanchez, did Jennifer ever have a visitor, a guy named Bruce, Bruce Krane?" asked John.

"No, she never had anyone come over. But the name is familiar. Who is he" asked Mr. Sanchez.

"Bruce Krane, he was an old boyfriend. I think he was the father of her son," John replied.

"That's it. Yes, she mentioned him once. She'd come in and seemed very upset. She said she'd tried to get her son back, but the welfare people turned her down. She said it was all his fault. That he was trying to get even with her. But he was never here, as far as I know. If you want, I'll check with my wife on the way out," offered the super.

Once they were out of the apartment, Mr. Sanchez locked the door. He pulled on the door knob to make sure it was secure. They followed the super down the stairs to the first floor and headed to the Sanchez apartment. John and Nancy said they'd wait outside while he spoke to his wife. In a moment he returned, but admitted his wife had nothing new about Bruce Krane or Jennifer Sands. The detectives thanked him for his help and walked back to their cars. As they walked past the two old men who were still seated in the same spot, one of them looked up and waved.

"Wait a minute," said John to Nancy. He walked over to the two elderly men. After a moment, he returned to join Nancy as they headed to their car. "Have a good day, Detectives," said the man with a heavy Italian accent.

"Anything?" asked Nancy.

"Nah. They said they knew a young woman lived in the apartment house, but didn't know anything beyond that."

Nancy returned to the driver's seat and John rode "shotgun." As they were riding down the street, John's beeper went off. He pulled it off his belt and checked the number.

"It's the M.E.'s office," said John. He took the cell phone out of the glove compartment, dialed the Medical Examiner's number, and waited.

"Hi, Doc. It's John Straub. What have you got for me?. Okay, we'll be right there. In about half an hour," said John and broke the connection.

Nancy didn't ask any questions. She just headed back towards the city and the M E's office.

Chapter 13

In the Department of Social Services building caseworker, Mary Clarke leaned back and stretched her arms overhead. Glancing at her wrist watch she noted the time. It was almost three P.M.

"Two more hours and I'm out of here," she thought. She rubbed her eyes and returned to her computer.

As she aged, Mary Clarke found using the computer's monitor more and more difficult. It was time for a visit to the eye doctor. Mary had been going over her cases and compiling information for her monthly reports. She thought back to the "good old days" of case work. Back then she had youth, ambition, and a desire to help people. There were no more than fifty people assigned at any one time. She made home visits, got to know the people, their families. She helped them line up job interviews, gain admission to community colleges, and vocational schools. She saw to it that they got proper medical care. Back then she considered herself a "professional."

Now caseloads numbered in the hundreds, home visits were no longer permitted, and it was rare that she ever got to know the people's first names, let alone their family members or home lives. People became numbers.

"Move the numbers," was the catch phrase. Looking around the large open work area, portable partitions forming individual cubicles, she could see more than half were empty. They were empty not because the workers had left for the day. They were empty because half the workers had left, permanently. A hiring freeze had been in effect for the past three years. In order to ensure a modest raise for the current crop of workers, the unions had negotiated away a decent starting salary for any new hires. Recent college graduates entering the department today started at $18,000, with no vacation or sick time until their first anniversary. They had to pay part of their medical insurance premiums and contribute eight percent of their salaries toward their pensions. Then to top it all off, the earliest retirement date was pushed back from fifty-five to age sixty-five. It was no wonder there wasn't any new blood in the department. For the past few years she had been counting the days until her own fifty-fifth birthday. She was fortunate to be in a retirement tier that would allow her to retire at that age.

Mary sat before her computer, eyes following the information as it appeared across the screen. The little cursor moved just ahead of the letters that would form a series of names, addresses, and departmental codes. Codes would identify the type of case, the action taken, and the person assigned to the case. She decided to look into the case that Detective Straub had inquired about the day before. Mary found it a pleasant break from the tedium of her job and she felt she was doing something important.

Although they'd never met Detective Straub, she could tell from the sound of his voice and the way he spoke to her that he was a gentleman, a "dedicated professional." She liked to think of herself as professional as well. Unfortunately many of the younger workers just considered it a job.

Her fingers moved across the keyboard and within a few moments the case file she'd searched for appeared on her monitor. She read the information as she scrolled down.

SANDS, Jennifer (mother)   Krane, Bruce (father)
DOB 1/29/72   DOB unknown
ADDRESS: 1330 Arthur Avenue   ADDRESS: Unknown
Bronx, New York 10058
Tel: 212 555-2702
Child: Steven
DOB 9/9/96 (Currently in foster care)

The rest of the information on Ms. Sands would be found in the case folder. Mary called the records room and inquired as to the status of the case. She was advised that the folder was signed out to J. Edgar. Mary wasn't familiar with Mr. Edgar, so she went through her departmental telephone list. She decided to give him a call and see if he knew anything that might be helpful to the detective. When she dialed the number listed for the case worker, it was answered by his "voice mail." Mary chose not to leave a message, planning to try again later in the day.

In spite of her good intentions, Mary got involved in a new case she'd been assigned. She had received a frantic call from a young woman who'd applied for assistance. She was being evicted and needed help, as of "yesterday." In the rush to help the poor woman and move the papers along hoping to forestall the eviction, Mary forgot about the Sand's case. Before she realized it, five-thirty rolled around; quitting time. Mary shut down her computer, grabbed her purse, and headed for the subway and home.

Chapter 14

Nancy Mooney and John Straub had left the area called "Little Italy" in the Bronx and drove directly to the medical examiner's office. Parking in the rear, they entered through the loading platform. Once inside, the security guard entered their names and badge numbers into his log. He then directed them to the autopsy room, where the M.E. was waiting for them.

John had been here many times in the past. For Nancy this was her first since a "class trip" while in the Academy. Regardless of how many visits one made, though, the smell always caught you by surprise. It stuck in your throat. There was the over powering odor of formaldehyde, overlaid with the metallic smell associated with blood. And then there was the stench of death, of corruption and decomposition.

It is a sickeningly, sweet smell that made you gag. It is a smell unlike any other. Oh, you may think that the smell of food left too long in the refrigerator is bad, but can't compare. How about the smell from a skunk? Worse yet. Medical examiners live with it. To the M.E., this odor can be a clue, a source of information. It may help them judge the time of death, sometimes the cause. It could help solve the crime. Homicide detectives are familiar with the smell also. However unlike the M.E. they might be able to deal with the smell, but they never got use to it.

After donning paper coveralls, boots, and masks, the two detectives entered the autopsy room. The bright overhead lamps illuminated the room, the light reflected off stainless steel tables, instruments, and white tiled walls and floors. The tables had a raised border around them. Over each was suspended a hose with a shower head attached. These were where the autopsies were performed. Most of the dissection tables were occupied. Lab technicians, assistant medical examiners, and other homicide detectives hovered over the remains displayed on the tables. All but one of the workers remained intent on the work in front of them. It was Dr. Morrison, Chief Medical Examiner for New York City. Dr. Morrison was a tall, powerfully built black man, his hair cut short, and turning gray at the sides. Dr. Morrison had been lured from Washington D.C., where he'd been the assistant chief M.E. This was seen as a major coup for the mayor, while others viewed it as a smart political moves. But, unlike some of the city's former M.E.'s, Dr. Morrison maintained a low profile.

"Over here," he called out in a deep baritone voice. John and Nancy headed over to where he was working.

"Greetings, John. Welcome to my parlor. You're just in time. I was about to begin on the woman they brought in yesterday." said the doctor. "Jennifer Sands," he added after looking at a tag attached to the victim's toe.

"She's our case, Doc," replied John.

"And who is this lovely lady with you?" asked the M.E.

"This is my new partner, Nancy Mooney. She's replacing Ski while he's on the mend," said John.

The M.E. extended a gloved hand, which Nancy took in her equally gloved hand.

"I must admit, John, you are getting better looking partners. It's a pleasure, Detective Mooney," concluded the M.E.

"Got anything yet?" asked John.

"Well, we went through her clothing. Nothing unusual there. She was wearing some cheap jewelry. I was just beginning the autopsy when you came in, so you might as well hang around for a while. See what turns up," said Dr. Morrison as he reached up, adjusting the overhead light and clicking on a recording device attached to it.

He removed a plastic sheet that had been covering the woman's body. Dr. Morrison bent down to closely examine the hair, face, neck, and chest of the victim. Her skin had turned a glossy, bluish-gray color. Instead of a rosy glow, her cheeks were pale white, and there were dark circles under her eyes. Nancy unconsciously moved a step back, as the odor escaping the body cavity was overwhelming.

"The victim is a female, white, approximately twenty-six to thirty years of age, whose body appears well nourished and manifesting good muscle tone, indicative of one who exercised on a regular basis," said the M.E. into the concealed microphone. Bypassing the abdomen, he went down to her feet, examined the toes, the bottoms of the feet, and her legs.

"Lower extremities are absent of any abnormality."

He then grabbed hold of each ankle and moved them apart, exposing her genitalia.

John turned towards Nancy. Feeling his gaze on her she looked back. John had an odd look on his face. She wasn't sure if it was out of a sense of embarrassment for her, a woman, or to see if this was getting to her.

Without a word they both returned their attention to the table.

Bending low to the table and holding a magnifying glass to his eye he perused the area.

"No visible sign of sexual trauma," he said as he took an oversized "Q-tip" and swabbed the inside of her vagina. He placed the swab into a glass tube and secured it with a rubbed cap. He then wrote a case number, name, and date on a label attached to the side of the tube. Out of respect for the deceased he drew the sheet back over her lower torso. The M.E. then lifted each hand, turned it over, and examined the fingers.

"No sign of defensive wounds. There appears to be dried blood in the creases of the hands."

He took pieces of moistened gauze and rubbed some of the dried blood off the skin, placing the gauze pads into glass tubes. He then used a smaller sized Q-tip and a slender wooden instrument and scrapped under each fingernail. Each of these scrapings was placed in its own glass tube and labeled.

He then returned to the victims head. He carefully looked at her face, eyes, and nose, in her mouth and ears. Then he moved his gloved fingers through her hair and across her scalp. Using a large comb he ran it through her hair catching any particles into a small envelope. Next he examined her neck and chest area.

"No apparent signs of trauma to the head, neck, or chest areas."

Next, he gently rolled her over onto one side. He examined her back from the nape of her neck down to the backs of her thighs. Into the over head microphone, the M.E. stated.

"An entry wound, possibly caused by a knife in the lower right side of the back." Then, to the detectives, he said, "This was probably the initial strike." He turned her carefully and viewed the victim's front; his attention drawn to the victim's abdomen.

"Victim presents what appears to be a disembowelment." The M.E. took a small flash light, picking up the magnifying glass again he bent closer examining the gapping wound.

"How can he stand to be so close?" thought Nancy.

The M.E. carefully followed the edge of the incised flesh.

"No sign of tearing, incision smooth and complete to approximate depth of six inches."

John began jotting down notes as the M.E. spoke. Nancy glanced over John's shoulder to see what he'd written.

"Incision appears to have been caused by something very sharp, approximately six-inch-long, possibly hunting knife," was scrawled on John's pad.

The M.E. continued to follow the edge of the wound, at times having to lift part of the intestines, to get a better look. As he followed it he walked around the table to the side where the two detectives stood. They moved back a step to give him room.

"Ah, here is the point of entry, just above the pubic bone. There appears to be some tearing as if the weapon had a serrated edge on one side," said Dr. Morrison.

Without looking up, he said, "You might want to consider some kind of hunting knife, folding perhaps. The initial penetration is deeper than the rest of the incision. A one piece knife usually has a guard between the handle and blade. It is designed to keep the hand from sliding down the handle and being cut on the blade," added the M.E. "That kind of guard would cause bruising at the entry point. There is none here." He paused for a moment, reached up to adjust the overhead light and continued his examination.

"The person who did this was probably right handed. Maybe a hunter," he added.

"Why is that?" asked Nancy, then wondered if she should have said anything while he was dictating.

"Well, a right-handed person tends to make circles in a counter clockwise direction. Lefties go in the opposite direction. The wound, which began in the lower abdomen, moves to the right and then up and over the top. It hits the breast bone and goes back down to the pubic area. Therefore, probably right handed. Also this reminds me of how a hunter would gut a deer," concluded the M.E.

Nancy just nodded and smiled. She turned to John, "Write that down, probably a right handed hunter."

"Got it boss. Thanks," said John, then looked at the M.E. and winked.

"Now, it's time to get my hands dirty," said the M.E., which was strange considering he wore elbow-length rubber gloves.

Without another word, he reached under the organs that bulged from the gapping wound in the abdomen. He lifted and moved them to one side, letting them rest on the table. Leaning over, Nancy was afraid he'd fall into the cavity. The M.E. shown the light inside, probed the interior of the woman's torso, and then stood up. He stretched his back and groaned.

"I'll get the organs weighed. The fluid and tissue specimens will go to toxicology. I should get the test results by late tomorrow if you want to give me a call," offered the M.E.

"Thanks, Doc," said John, and he turned towards the door.

Nancy said goodbye to the M.E. and followed John out of the room. They changed out of their paper coveralls, throwing them into special waste containers with their booties and rubber gloves and masks. Once they stepped outside, Nancy took a deep breath of air.

"Boy, that'll clear your sinuses in a hurray," she said.

John just smiled. He admired her strength. Even though it was only her second time in the autopsy room, this had been a particularly messy one. She hadn't flinched once as far as he could tell.

"You hungry?" he asked.

"Give me a break. I may have held it together in there but a greasy spoon dinner is all I'd need right now to lose my cookies," she said, getting into the car.

Once seated and buckled in, she turned to John and asked, "What was with the wink?"

"What wink?" asked John in all seriousness.

"The wink you gave to the M.E. when I told you to write down that her murderer was probably right handed," said Nancy, a note of tension in her voice.

"Oh, that wink."

"Yes. That wink. I don't think you were flirting with the M.E. So what was the wink all about?"

"Nothing," answered John.

"Oh really? You couldn't have been indicating that my observation was foolish, amateurish, could you?"

"Where is this coming from?" asked John.

"I just want an answer to a simple question, that's all," she said.

"Well, I didn't mean anything by it. In fact, I was thinking how well you were handling the whole situation," replied John.

"Why? Because I'm a woman?" she asked.

"Oh for crying out loud, Nancy! No, because you're new at this and some veterans would get thrown by what we just saw. That's all."

With that he turned away from Nancy and looked out the window.

"Where to now?" asked Nancy, ice in her voice.

"The office," was all John could say.

They drove back to headquarters in complete silence.

The rest of the day was spent in silence. When six rolled around, John broke the ice by announcing it was time to head home. He hoped Nancy would have loosened up by then. She hadn't. Nancy made him stop at a Chinese take out place on the way home. They ate in front of the TV. For the remainder of the night the TV was on, but neither seemed to be watching what was on. When they went to bed, John gave Nancy a kiss on the cheek and rolled over onto his side.

After reading a few pages of a novel she'd picked up, Nancy finally shut off the light and went to sleep. John found it difficult falling off and spent a good half hour going over what had transpired during the entire day to see if he could figure out what went wrong. In time, he too fell asleep.

Chapter 15

The next morning John rose first and headed into the bathroom to shower. When he came out, the bed was empty and the covers straightened. While he got dressed, he heard Nancy call from the kitchen.

"Come on, handsome. Breakfast is ready."

"Now what?" he thought.

John walked into the kitchen, his head slightly pulled into his neck like a turtle's into its shell, not knowing what to expect. Nancy was standing with her back to him, busy at the stove. John helped himself to a cup of coffee and sat down at the table. The morning newspaper was sitting in front of his plate. He was about to open the paper and hide behind the pages when Nancy turned around. She walked over with a frying pan in her hand. John flinched. He was afraid she meant to hit him with it.

Instead, she held the pan under his face and asked, "Sunny or over easy?"

John looked at the two eggs frying in the pan. "Sunny is fine," he replied.

She tilted the pan and let the two fried eggs slide onto his plate. Then she put the pan back on the stove and went to the microwave. She hit one of the buttons and he could hear the fan blowing and see the light come on inside. After about ten seconds, Nancy removed a plate of bacon from it and placed it in front of John. Then she released the lever on the toaster and two halves of a toasted English muffin popped up.

"Butter or jelly?" she asked as she placed the hot muffins on his plate with the eggs.

"Butter is good," he said, still waiting for something to come flying at him.

Instead, Nancy brought the butter dish to the table, bent down, and kissed him on the forehead.

"I'm going to shower. Enjoy your breakfast," she said as she headed down the hall.

"Thanks," he said to an empty room. "What the hell?" he asked himself. He proceeded to eat his bacon and eggs.

John finished his breakfast, had a second cup of coffee, and then decided it was time to go have a talk with Nancy. As he walked into their bedroom, Nancy was just putting on a pair of black slacks. She turned to him as he came into the room.

"How was breakfast?"

"Great. Thanks," was all he could think to say.

"I'll be ready in five," said Nancy and continued getting dressed.

John went back to the kitchen, picked up the newspaper, and walked into the small living room. He sat in his recliner and read the news of the day. True to her word, Nancy emerged within five minutes ready to head off to work. John jumped up, not expecting her to be ready this fast, and ran into the bathroom. He brushed his teeth, used the toilet, and slipped on a pair of loafers. In the bedroom, John grabbed his Glock off the closet shelf, slipped a magazine in it, and charged a round into the firing position. Once holstered, he threw on a jacket and headed out the door.

When he stepped outside, he found Nancy was already sitting behind the wheel of their "unmarked" in front of the house.

As she drove towards the Queens Borough Bridge, Nancy hummed along with a song playing on the radio. John decided to break the ice.

"You seem in a good mood today," he began.

"I am," was her response.

"Is there anything you want to talk about?" he asked.

"No," was her answer, "Why?"

"Oh, I just thought after yesterday . . . ."

"Oh that. I guess it was just PMS. Sorry," she said.

John thought her response was a little flippant, considering they hadn't spoken the entire night. But then he figured it was better to let it drop.

Nancy went on, "I guess it's been a while since you've been around a lady. You're not used to our little mood swings," she added.

"Little mood swings?," thought John.

John was about to say something when some "primal" instinct went off in his head. Instead, he thought, "I was afraid to close my eyes, thinking you were going to bump me off in my sleep. And you say it was just a little mood swing. Jesus Christ, I guess I have been out of the loop too long. I'd forgotten that women are different from men. Well, if it was over, it was over. I'll just have to be more observant next time." The only

182

trouble was John had no idea when next time would be. Then he glanced at Nancy and smiled. He felt a warm feeling rise up inside.

"It was worth it, dealing with mood swings," he thought to himself.

The drive to the office went smoothly with little traffic to contend with. When they walked into their office, they were pleasantly surprised by the sight of John's old partner, Peter "Ski" Zubriski. He was sitting at his old desk, the same desk Nancy had been using. She wondered where she'd do her work as she entered the office. Once he saw them, "Ski" got up slowly from his seat. John gave him a big hug and a pat on the back. Nancy came over and once the men untangled arms, she gave him a kiss on the cheek.

"Welcome back," said Nancy, standing awkwardly to the side.

"Oh, I'm not back, not yet," said Ski. I had to come in to fill out some papers and drop off my doctor's report at Personnel. I thought I'd surprise you guys. Here, Nancy, sit. This must be your's now," said Ski, hobbling back, limping on his right leg.

"No. Sit," she said. "It's your desk."

"Not for a while I'm afraid," said Ski. "The bureau's doctors say I can't come back until I'm a hundred percent. That won't be for about another four, maybe six, months the way this knee is coming along."

"Where are your crutches?" asked John.

"I use a cane now," replied Ski.

"Okay, then, where's your cane?" he asked.

"It's out in the car. I hate using it. It makes me feel like a cripple," commented Ski.

"But you are a cripple," said John, a big grin on his face.

"Really, guys, sit down. I'll just pull one of these over," said Ski as he grabbed a nearby straight back side chair. John and Nancy dropped into their chairs.

"So, tell me, what's new around here?" asked Ski.

"Same old, same old," replied John. "We're working on a couple of female homicides, the usual, a family dispute gone too far, a few gang hits, etc., etc. The usual," said John.

"Boy, I miss the good times," said Ski sarcastically.

"Oh, and the new commissioner has decided to make crime cost efficient. No longer do we have separate divisions like homicide, narcotics, robbery in each of the five boroughs. Now everything is 'centralized' as he likes to call it."

"You're kidding? I saw on the news how he was trying to cut costs, but to have all the departments working out of headquarters is nuts," said Ski.

"Tell me about it. It may cut down on duplication, especially of brass, but it also means we gotta cover the whole friggin' area with less personnel. Worse, we get assignments in all areas. Places we've never worked in before. We don't know the neighborhoods, the local foot patrolmen, or the street people. It's like working blind. Take, for example, the two latest homicides. One was committed in the Bronx, the other in Brooklyn. Go figure," said John with a shrug of his shoulders.

"That's nuts," said Ski.

"Well, you better plan on getting used to it, because that's the rules for now. Are you sure you're still in a hurry to get back?" asked John.

"Well, I can see your current partner has me beat in the good looks department. How are you guys making out working together and dating?" asked Ski. He almost said "and living together," but didn't because he thought that was none of his business.

"So far, so good," piped up Nancy. John just nodded in agreement, not wanting to mention their little tiff the day before.

"By the way, if you guys aren't busy Betty and I would like you to come out for dinner this weekend," said Ski.

"Gee, I don't know. We may have plans," John started to say when Nancy interrupted.

"You tell your wife we'd love to. When and what time?" she asked.

"Sunday. Dinner is usually around three, but I'll have Betty give you a call," replied Ski.

"No. Tell Betty I'll call her tonight. Is nine okay? Will she be finished putting the kids to sleep by then?" asked Nancy.

"Putting them to sleep? Are you kidding? They've grown since the last time you guys were over. What was that, almost five months ago? Those two put us to bed some nights," said Ski, referring to his twins, Peter Jr. and Stacy.

"So, we got a date? Good. Betty will be glad to hear it," said Ski. Rising slowly from the chair he added, "I'll let you guys get to work now. I have to stop at the 'physical terrorist' on the way home." Seeing the confusion on their faces he said, "Physical terrorist, that's what I call my physical therapist. They seemed to love to inflict pain, ergo the name, "physical terrorist."

John and Nancy smiled and proceeded to walk Ski down the hall to the elevator. After saying their goodbyes they returned to their office to get working on their cases.

John reached for the Sands' folder. Inside he found the victim's address book. As he flipped through it he jotted down the names of acquaintances. Then he turned to Nancy.

"While I run these names through our files why don't you go through her appointment book. See if anything unusual pops out," suggested John. He passed the small book to Nancy and got busy on his computer.

The first name he entered was her ex-boyfriend, Bruce Krane. In a matter of minutes he saw that Bruce had an arrest record going back almost ten years to when he was a teenager. He'd been arrested for possession of stolen property. There was no disposition.

John knew from experience that first-time offenders, under the age of nineteen, received special consideration. It was called "youthful offender" treatment. It meant that the person didn't have a record of a conviction following him around his entire life.

Next he noticed that Krane had been arrested about two years ago and charged with possession of a weapon. This time he was placed on probation. Picking up his phone, he dialed the records room at the NYC Probation Department.

He learned that Krane was currently under the supervision of a Probation Officer Moran. He took a chance on catching the PO in his office and dialed his extension.

After two rings, a female voice answered. John told her who he was and asked for P.O. Moran.

"I'm Moran," came the reply.

"Oh," said John, a little taken aback by the fact the guy had a female PO.

"I'm Detective Straub."

Straub explained to her his interest in one of her cases.

"Give me a minute to get his file. I have to run down to the record room. It may take a minute. Do you want to wait?" she asked.

"Sure. Go ahead, I'll hold on."

PO Moran pulled Bruce Krane's folder from the record room. When she returned, she apologized for keeping him waiting. Moran said she had about two hundred cases and some of them got lost in the shuffle, but not Krane's.

The probation officer told Straub that Krane was on probation for possession of a weapon, which John already knew. She told him that he'd been picked up by police in Brooklyn on a domestic complaint. It seemed he had a girlfriend he liked to get rough with. As John suspected, the name of the complainant was Jennifer Sands.

When the police picked him up on the complaint, they found an unlicenced thirty-eight caliber revolver on him. He was charged, pled guilty, served six months at Riker's Island, and was released under probation supervision.

"Has he given you any trouble? Any more complaints from the girlfriend." Straub didn't mention that the woman filing the complaint was lying on a steel table at the city morgue.

P.O. Moran told him that Krane was a smooth operator. He was good looking and tried to use his charm to get his way. He was cooperative.

"I told him he needed to work and just like that, he walks in one night and plops down a union membership book on my desk. He says he's working construction and is a shop foreman. Can you imagine, a guy in his mid-twenties getting a construction job and being made a union rep right out of the box?" asked Moran.

John made no effort to reply.

"Anyway, he'd been working at this construction site in the Bronx for about a year."

"What about now?" asked John.

"Well, that's a problem. He's missed his last three appointments. I've sent him letters and called the place work, where he lives, nothing. I really thought he was going to make it through without violating his probation. I'm still trying to track him down," said Moran.

"You got an address on him?" asked John.

"Sure. It's over in the Little Italy section of the Bronx," replied Moran.

John could hear her flipping through papers. When she came back on the line she had an address.

"Here it is, 188-10 Lorillard Place. It's off Fordham Road."

"I know the area," said John, having just been there with Nancy to interview the victim's apartment building superintendent.

"How about family, friends? Who does he hang out with?" asked John.

"He seems to be a loner. The only family is a mother at the same address," added Moran.

"Any arrests since he's been on probation?" asked John.

"No arrests yet. But I'm getting ready to issue a warrant for failing to report." "Thanks, Officer Moran. If you hear anything from him, give me a call,"

"Will do. Same goes with you if anything turns up. By the way, how long you been with NYPD?"

John thought this to be a strange question, but figured there was no harm in telling.

"Almost fifteen years. Why?"

"Oh, I was just wondering if you knew my father, Tom Moran. He was a sergeant with the auto squad back in the eighties," she said.

"No, I haven't come across him. Is he still on the force?" asked John.

"No. He retired about five or six years ago. But he's a 'Piper' she stated.

"A 'piper'?" asked John.

"Yeah. As you can probably tell from the last name, we're Irish. My Dad is a member of the NYPD Bagpipers Marching Band," she said with pride.

"I haven't heard of him, but I'm sure I've seen him march. I never miss a Patty's Day Parade," commented John.

"You Irish?" asked P.O. Moran.

"Half, on my mother's side. Her maiden name was McNenny. She was as Irish as 'Patty's pig,' as they say," replied Straub.

"I knew you couldn't be all bad," said Moran, the sound of good humor in her voice.

"Well, thanks again for your help."

"Glad to be of help," said the P.O. and hung up.

John sat back and looked at his notes.

"I guess it's time for another visit to the Bronx," said John to himself.

"You say something?" asked Nancy.

"I didn't think I said it out loud. Just that the victim's ex-boyfriend lived near her, has an arrest record, and hasn't been seen by his probation officer in a while. What about you?" he asked.

"I've been going through her appointment book. The only thing that keeps coming up is her kid and a foster family named Gerard. I get the feeling she was trying to get the kid back," said Nancy.

"That would jibe with her saving money and planning on going back to school, maybe changing jobs," added John.

"Maybe Maxwell Peterson didn't want her leaving. Maybe he tried to get her to stay on and when she didn't, he killed her in a rage," suggested Nancy.

"That's possible. He had the opportunity and possible motive. But my money is on this Bruce Krane. I think if we can track him down, have a heart to heart, we might just crake this case. I don't think it's all that complicated. Girl meets guy. Girl falls in love with guy. Girl gets pregnant by guy. Guy takes off, leaving her to care for the kid on her own. Girls gets order of support. Guy gets pissed. Guy kills girl. Case closed," said John with a smile.

"Oh, are they all that easy to solve?" asked Nancy.

"Some," said John.

"Okay, let's put your theory to the test. Let's go find Bruce Krane," said Nancy, rising from her chair.

"You got the address?"

"Yep. Back to the Bronx."

"Good. Maybe this time you can treat me to a good Italian dinner at one of those restaurants we saw the other day," said Nancy.

"Maybe," offered John. "Boy, it's expensive having you as a partner," he quipped. "At least Ski would split the tab with me."

"But did he scrub your back in the shower?" she teased. Then added, "Never mind. I don't want to know. Here, you drive for a change," she said, throwing the car keys over her shoulder to him as they headed out of the office.

Chapter 16

John drove and they arrived in the "Little Italy" section of the Bronx without delay. They located Lorillard Place near Arthur Avenue and Fordham Road. They lucked out grabbing a place to park about half a block from Krane's apartment house. They identified the name under one of the "door buzzers" pressed it and waited. Nothing! After hitting it a second time, this time holding the button for half a minute, an annoyed voice came over the intercom.

"Who is it?"

Nancy guessed by the sound of the voice that she was an older woman, perhaps Krane's mother.

"Police. We'd like to speak to Bruce Krane," said Nancy.

"He ain't here," said the voice.

"Are you his mother?" asked Nancy again.

"Yes,.." was her one word answer.

"May we speak to you, please?" Nancy asked.

Without getting a reply, they could heard the door's lock being electronically released. John pushed through before the door could re-lock itself. The two detectives entered the dimly lit apartment hallway. It was, cluttered with bikes and baby carriages. The walls and ceiling were in need of paint. The building lacked the care that the super, Mr. Sanchez, devoted to his building just a few blocks away.

Bruce Krane's mother lived on the ground floor, apartment 1 E. John found the door at the end of the hall and knocked. A moment later the door opened, but only partially, apparently secured by a security chain. A slightly blood shot eye peeked through the opening.

"You got badges?" asked a crusty old woman.

John held his shield up to the door. The woman nodded and closed the door. They heard chains rattling inside and then the door opened all the way. The woman motioned them inside, leading them down a dingy hall to a small kitchen. She wore what John referred to as the traditional outfit of the seniors in the Bronx, an old house dress and slippers.

"I was just going to have a cup of tea. Want to join me?" asked the old lady.

"No thank you," John started to reply before Nancy cut him off.

"That would be fine. We'd love to," she said, giving John a look.

John just shrugged. Mrs. Krane put out three mugs, none of which matched, and dropped tea bags into each. The tea pot was sitting on an old, battered stove, steam escaping from its spout. The "whistle" had long since rusted out. The woman poured boiling water into each mug and returned the pot to the stove.

"Milk or honey?" asked Mrs. Krane.

"Milk's fine," replied John.

"Me too," Nancy added. An opened quart of milk was taken from the equally old-looking refrigerator.

"Don't mind the fancy china," said the woman, sliding the steaming tea cups in front of them. Then she eased herself into a kitchen chair, making a moaning sound as the chair creaked from under her weight.

"It's good to get off these old feet,." she added with a smile.

John noticed she was missing a couple of teeth.

Nancy guessed the woman had had a hard life. Her hair was gray and in need of a cutting. The front was tinged in yellow. Mrs. Krane's actions soon explained why as she lit a cigarette, Marlboro. She dropped the match in a glass ash tray that sat on her side of the table. Mrs. Krane looked to be in her late seventies, slightly stooped with arthritis. She wore bifocal glasses with one a piece of adhesive tape wrapped around the bridge, apparently holding them together.

"Now what do you want with my Bruce?" asked Mrs. Krane.

John was struck by the fact that the woman didn't seem to find it unusual for police to be paying her a visit or asking about her son.

"We'd like to talk to him about his ex-girlfriend, Jennifer Sands," answered Nancy.

"She making complaints against him again?" asked the old woman, as she drew in a lungful of smoke from her cigarette.

"No. We'd just like to talk to him, that's all," said John.

"Well, like I already told you, he ain't here. In fact I haven't seen him in about two weeks," she added.

"Is that unusual for him, not to come home at night?" asked Nancy.

"Not really. He's a man now. Has his own life. I see him when he needs clean clothes. Things like that," she said.

"Do you know where we might be able to find him?" asked Nancy.

Mrs. Krane rubbed her chin with her crooked fingers while she pondered the question. John noticed she had a number of stray hairs on her chin that needed plucking. "You might find him over on Randall's Island. They're doing a job on some of the old buildings there. If he ain't there you might try the union hall on Westchester Avenue," offered Mrs. Krane.

"Does he have a current girl friend, someone he might be staying with?" asked Nancy.

"Well, he may be with a woman named Christy. I don't remember her last name though. She lives someplace in Brooklyn. I think it's near Coney Island," she replied.

"Do you have an address?" asked John.

"I don't, but Bruce may have it in his room someplace."

"Would you mind if we looked around his room?" asked Nancy.

"I guess not, as long as you don't take nothing." She slowly got up from her chair.

"It's this way," she said as she shuffled off down the hall.

The two detectives followed Mrs. Krane to the rear of the apartment where the bedrooms were located. The door to her son's room was partially closed door. She pushed it open and allowed them to go inside. She remained in the hall way with her arms folded across her chest.

Bruce Krane's bedroom looked like it hadn't been cleaned in months. Nancy could see what looked like a half inch layer of dust on every flat surface. Clothes were thrown haphazardly around the room, on the unmade bed, over door knobs, on the floor. John walked over to a battered wooden chest of drawers. Some of the drawers were half open and with clothes hanging out. On top of the dresser, John found a small notepad. Turning around and glancing over his shoulder towards Mrs. Krane, he lifted the notepad. The old woman just waved her hand and nodded. With her tacit consent John scanned through the pages. As he did a business card fell to the floor. Picking it up, John found P.O. Moran's name on it. On the back a date had been scrawled. The date was several weeks old.

"His P.O., Ms. Moran, has she ever been here?," asked John.

"Her? Yeah, maybe three or four times. Nice lady from what I remember," responded Mrs. Krane.

Continuing flipping the notepad John. He came to a section with several names, addresses and phone numbers.

One was Jennifer Sands' and included her work place and written next to her name were the words, "*child support*" and below that a number for Child Protective Services.

After rummaging further through the little notepad, John came across the name, Christy Martin and an address: 2300 Avenue Y, Sheepshead Bay. There was also a telephone number. He turned towards Mrs. Krane.

"That girl you said your son might be living with, Christy. Her last name wouldn't be Martin, by any chance?" asked John.

"Martin. Yeah, I think that's her," she replied.

He also came across an address for the local union hall where Bruce belonged.

"Mind if I take this pad with me?" asked John.

"Only if you got a warrant. It ain't mine to give," Mrs. Krane snapped back.

He copied the names and addresses he'd found to a small pad of his own. Satisfied he'd gotten as much information as he could from the pad he returned it to the top of the dresser where he'd found it.

While John was looking through the notebook, Nancy was sifting through various items on a night stand next to the bed. She found a "crake pipe" sitting out in the open. She picked it up, examined it, and sniffed the burnt cup at the end.

"I could take this as evidence. But I don't know if this search would hold up in court. The hell with it. We're after bigger game than this," she thought and replaced the pipe.

Finally, John turned to Nancy and nodded towards the door.

"Well, we've taken enough of your time Mrs. Krane. Thanks for your cooperation," he said and walked towards the front of the apartment.

"Thank you for the tea, Mrs. Krane," said Nancy politely.

"No problem. If you find that no-good son of mine, tell him it might be nice to give his poor old, gray-haired mother a call once in a while."

"Will do," said Nancy as they exited the apartment. Once outside, they headed down the street towards their car.

As they walked the half block, Nancy turned to John and said, "I'm hungry. How about that Italian restaurant you showed me the last time we were here?"

John thought for a moment, looked at his watch, and grunted, "Okay."

They drove the few blocks to Arthur Avenue and parked in front a small restaurant called "Ann and Toni's." They walked inside and were shown a seat by a friendly waiter. The interior reflected the uniform design of many Italian restaurants. There were pictures with scenes from Italy hung on the stucco walls, along with a few photos signed by famous celebrities who'd dined there. The smell of garlic permeated the air. It made their mouths water. It was too early for drinks and they were still on duty, so they ordered Cokes with lemon. While they waited for the sodas to arrive they looked at the menu. The waiter returned and placed the drinks on the table, while another waiter appeared with a basket of fresh baked bread and a small plate. The first waiter told them the specials of the day.

"We have a chicken dinner called Chicken Napoli. It consists of a thinly sliced breast of chicken, wrapped in prosciuto, mozzarella cheese, and sliced tomato. It is fried in virgin olive oil. There is also a poached salmon," offered the waiter.

Listening to him describe the two dishes made their mouths water. Disregarding the menu they decided to go with the Chicken Napoli, a house salad and penne pasta with butter.

After the waiter left, John reached for the bread and foil wrapped pats of butter. Taking a slice he offered the basket to Nancy. He was about to put butter on the bread but stopped when he saw Nancy pour a small amount of olive oil on the small plate, dipping the bread into it before tasting it. He decided to try it her way.

"If I continue to work with you, I'll gain twenty pounds," commented John.

"No problem. I know how you can work it off," said Nancy with a smile.

John felt her foot rubbing up against his leg.

"Down, girl. I'm on duty," replied John.

Changing the subject Nancy asked, "What do you think about Mrs. Krane

"She's an old woman who lives by herself, no family, and a no-good son. I felt sorry for her," was John's response.

Nancy smiled at this answer. She was glad to see her man had a soft side to him. John suggested they drive over to Randall's Island after lunch and see if Bruce was there. If that didn't pan out, they'd try the union hall. Then if it wasn't too late, they'd run down to Brooklyn and try to find Christy Martin.

The waiter brought their meals and the two proceeded to eat. Few words were spoken as they consumed the delicious meal that had been put before them. It was as if they hadn't been fed in weeks.

"I had thought I'd end up bringing half of my dinner home in a doggy bag, but," said Nancy with a shrug, looking at her empty plate. "I guess I was hungry."

"It's just as well. I doubt it would have stayed fresh in the car for a couple of hours," said John as he mopped up the remaining sauce from his plate with a piece of Italian bread.

The waiter returned and asked if they wanted dessert. The both agreed they'd eaten enough and asked for cappuccinos.

John said, "I was going to order Tartuffe, but I'm too full."

"What's 'Tartuffe'?" asked Nancy.

"I don't know if that's how you say it. It sounds something like that, but the waiter would know what it is. It's three balls of ice cream, vanilla, chocolate, and strawberry, lumped together around a cherry. Then it's covered with chocolate," said John.

"Sounds sinful," said Nancy.

Out of curiosity, John asked the waiter if they had that on the dessert menu. He told them they did. He said some places call it a Bocce Ball, because of the way it looks. He warned, however, that each restaurant might have a different name for it. Here a Bocce Ball is a dessert. In another it might be a very alcoholic drink that's sweet and tastes like chocolate. He suggested it was always better to describe what they wanted to a waiter.

John and Nancy sipped their cappuccinos and talked about everything except the case. While they were talking, a group of young coeds from the local college came in and sat at a nearby table. They were all talking at once, giggling, and full of life. Nancy looked at them and grew sad. John noticed the change in her face.

"What's the matter?" he asked.

"Oh, I was just looking at those girls, how happy they look. They've got their whole lives ahead of them.

I wonder if they'll be happy. It's sad to think one of them could end up like Sands. Life can be so cruel."

"Don't go getting melancholy on me, now. Better we get angry and go find who took that girl's' life and future away."

They got up and John paid the bill, leaving a generous tip. They walked back to their car and John let Nancy drive. He wanted to look through a map to see what was the best way to get to Randall's Island from here.

They ended up taking Fordham Road to Southern Boulevard, then headed south where they got on the Bruckner Expressway. Following the signs towards the Triborough Bridge, they eventually came to Randall's Island. Nancy picked up a side road that took them through a park. They drove over a deeply rutted road at the end of which was an old psychiatric center. The buildings appeared abandoned with some of the windows sporting gapping holes. Off to one side John spotted a construction shack. Nancy drove slowly trying to avoid the potholes. Arriving at the shack she shut the engine off. John led the way into the shack. Inside they found a few men sitting around an old wooden desk drinking coffee.

John and Nancy flashed their shields.

"Which one of you guys is the yard boss?" asked John.

The guy behind the desk raised his hand.

"Guilty," he said. "What can I do for you?"

"We're looking for a guy named Bruce Krane. We were told he worked here," said John.

"Krane? Not here. He's a union rep. Union reps don't get their hands dirty. You'd probably find him back at the Union Hall," offered the yard boss.

"And that would be where?" asked Nancy.

"Up on Westchester Avenue," he said.

Nancy turned to John, "We just passed there," she said.

"What's going on around here?" asked John, motioning to the building outside.

"We're renovating the old psych wards. Some are going to be converted to administrative offices, others will be hospital space. The mayor wants to open an AIDS center. It will be connected with University Hospital where they're doing research."

"What about the psychiatric patients?" asked Nancy.

"Patients, are you kidding? Where have you been for the past ten years, under a rock? The last governor ordered across the board budget cuts in the mental health field. Most of the hospitals were forced to discharge the nuts. You ever wonder where all the homeless people came from?" asked the boss.

Neither Nancy nor John had a response. They thanked him for his help and went back outside.

"Boy, can you believe this place? These were filled with mentally ill people at one time. Now they're all empty. I wonder what 'Administration' is going to be moved up here?" asked Nancy, not expecting an answer.

They got back in their car and after a number of wrong turns found Westchester Avenue. From there they followed the numbers until they came to the Union Hall. They had little luck in finding the missing

Bruce Krane there. The union secretary said he would normally stop in around the end of the week, but they hadn't seen him for a couple of weeks.

Once back in the car, Nancy turned to John, "So where is our boy? He seems to have dropped off the face of the earth."

"Maybe he has a reason to be missing. He probably knows we're looking for him. For all we know, he might be just down the end of this block. Maybe we'll have some luck after we talk to Christy Martin," said John.

Glancing at his watch, he said, "It's only four. We can be there in a half hour. Let's go," suggested John.

"Okay, lead the way," said Nancy as she drove off.

Using his dog-eared road map, he gave her the best route to get them over to Brooklyn. The used the Shore Parkway and made good time. Most of the traffic was going in the opposite direction. Nancy pulled off the parkway at Coney Island and headed towards Sheepshead Bay.

John realized they weren't far from the seafood restaurant where they'd had dinner just the other nigh.

Then he was reminded of the fact that that was the night the body of an unidentified girl floated up on the beach.

They worked their way over to Avenue Y and found the Martin woman's address. It was a semi-attached house in a mixed neighborhood. John lead the way up to the woman's front door, pushed the door bell, and knocked just to make sure anyone inside knew someone was there. The two detectives stood patiently on the front stoop waiting. Several minutes passed before the door to the neighbor's apartment opened. An elderly man was backing out of the house, pulling the door closed tight and locking it. As he turned to his right he jumped and put his hand to his chest, having been startled by the sight of the two people standing there.

"Oh, I'm sorry. We didn't mean to scare you," said Nancy sympathetically.

"That's all right, young lady. But at my age a start like that, even if it's caused by such a lovely looking woman as yourself could be fatal," said the man with a smile. He had a heavy European accent.

"I'm Detective Mooney. This is Detective Straub."

"Sol. Sol Abraham. So what brings New York's Finest to my neighborhood?"

"We are looking for the woman who lives in this apartment," said Nancy pointing towards number 2300. "Do you know the woman who lives here, Christy Martin?" asked Nancy.

"Christina, yes, of course. A lovely lady," said the man.

"Do you know if she's home?" asked John.

"Maybe. Did you knock?" he asked.

"Knocked and rang the bell," was John's reply.

"That never works. Here, let me," he said, moving past them and striking the door hard with his knuckles. "There. That's how you ring a door bell," said the man.

Nancy smiled. A moment passed and still no one answered.

"I guess she's not home. She's probably still at work," he offered.

"Do you know where she works?" asked John.

"She works for the city."

"Do you know which agency?" asked Nancy.

"It's something to do with the elderly," he replied.

"Does she live with anyone?" asked Nancy.

"She has a boyfriend who stays with her once in a while. But I haven't seen him lately. Christina's mother lives nearby. She has a son who stays with her mother most of the time," he added.

"Do you happen to know her mother's address?" asked Nancy.

"Mrs. Martinez? Let me think. Sure I know. She lives on Avenue T, between East 26th and 27th I think. I'm sorry, I don't know the number." he added as he glanced at an old pocket watch. "Oh, look at the time. I have to go. My wife is in the hospital and I'm late for visiting hours," he said.

"We're sorry to have kept you. Thank you, Mr. Abraham," said Nancy.

"My name is Abraham. Sol Abraham," he said.

"I hope your wife gets well soon," said Nancy.

"I'm afraid it's too late for that. She's in God's hands now," said Mr. Abraham. Then lowering his voice, he whispered the word "cancer." With that he walked down the steps, turned left and continued towards the corner and a bus stop.

"Poor guy. It must be tough at his age seeing his wife dying," said Nancy. John just shook his head.

"Come on, partner. We still have time to see if we can find her mother."

They soon located the street where Mrs. Martinez was said to live and began looking for a place to park. There were none.

"I'll sit in the car. There's a mailman. Maybe he knows where the Martinez woman lives," said Nancy.

John got out and walked over to the mailman. After speaking to him he turned and pointed down the block. He started walking in that direction and Nancy followed slowly in the car. He stopped in front of a string of attached brownstones.

"Park down there, I'll wait," he yelled.

Nancy looked up ahead and saw the area he was talking about. It was an abandoned gas station. The pumps had been removed and the office was boarded up. A few other cars sat on the property.

As she pulled off the street and onto the lot she noticed a sign.

"No parking. Violators will be towed at owner's expense." She got out, locked the car, and headed back to join John.

Once she reached her partner they walked up to a door and John knocked. It was answered by a short, elderly Hispanic woman. She had a small boy clinging to her left leg.

"Yes?" she asked.

John showed his badge and the woman allowed them to enter. They were lead into a small parlor at front of the building. There were a couple of wicker chairs with large, over stuffed cushions. The woman told them to sit. She remained standing. Nancy smiled and waved to the little boy, who cowered behind the woman.

"You are Mrs. Martinez, correct?" asked John.

"Yes. Why? What is wrong?" she asked hesitantly.

"Nothing to worry about as far as we can say. We are conducting an investigation. We were just at your daughter's place, but she wasn't home. Her neighbor gave us your address. Is she here?"

"No," was her reply.

"We were hoping you could help us contact your daughter. We'd like to ask her some questions," said John.

"I don't see my daughter much," she said.

"Is this your daughter's son?" asked Nancy.

"Yes. This is Julio. But my Christina doesn't have anything to do with him," she said, her face forming a frown.

"How is that?" asked John.

"It's not something I like to talk about. My daughter, Christina, denies she is Latino. She calls herself Christy Martin now and wears a blonde wig all the time. She likes to go out with some unpleasant men. She had a drug problem. When Julio was born the doctors found heroin in him. He was taken from his mother at the hospital. That was over two years ago. Fortunately, I am strong enough to care for him, so the welfare people let me raise him. My daughter is too busy to visit her own son. Now she says her boyfriend doesn't want her to have anything to do with him," she replied.

Nancy could see that this was very upsetting for the woman.

"What is the boyfriend's name?" asked Nancy.

"His name/ Bruce Krane," she said.

John and Nancy exchanged glances.

"Do you happen to know where she works?" asked John.

"Work? She doesn't work," said Mrs. Martinez.

"That's strange. Her neighbor said she worked for the city," offered Nancy.

"My daughter is on welfare," she replied.

"So you don't know where she might be? where we might find her?" asked Nancy.

"You might try her boyfriend's place. I think he lives in the Bronx," she suggested.

"Well, we'll look into it. If you hear from your daughter, please ask her to contact us, Mrs. Martinez," said Nancy, handing her one of their business cards. They rose from their chairs, thanked her for her time and headed out to the car.

Once in the car, John turned to Nancy. "This guy, Bruce gets around. I wonder if he's the father of little Julio?" he asked.

"We'll never know if we don't talk to Christy or better yet, Bruce himself," said Nancy.

John looked at his watch. Seeing the time he suggested they call it a day. While Nancy headed back to the parkway and then to John's place in Queens, John called the office. The section's secretary read him their messages and told him she'd sign them off.

"Nothing for us at the office that can't wait until tomorrow," said John.

Nancy had noticed that John had a ritual that he'd perform after returning home from work. Each day after work, he'd strip and take a long, hot shower. Nancy saw it as something symbolic. He seemed to be trying to wash the grit and grime of the streets and the things he'd seen that day from his body. He'd emerge from the shower refreshed and usually in a noticeably better mood.

Today was no different. Nancy was sprawled across their bed and could see him through the partially open bathroom door. She watched him towel himself off. As he moved the towel across his body she could see his muscles ripple. Although tall and slim, John was well muscled. He had a habit of doing his sit-ups and push-ups each and every morning. Until she'd moved in, he'd been in the habit of jogging two or three miles a day before work. Now he didn't seem to have the time for that.

He was developing a slight roll of fat around his midsection.

Nancy debated with herself as to whether she should tease him about the weight gain. But thought it was better left unsaid for now. She was sure he'd notice it himself and return to jogging.

John walked out of the bathroom and saw Nancy staring at him.

"Good or bad?" he asked.

"Good or bad, what?" she returned.

"Do you have good or bad thoughts?" he asked with a gleam in his eye.

Nancy let her eyes roam up and down his body.

"Turn around," she ordered.

John complied, somewhat self consciously since he was naked. When he'd completed the turn he looked at Nancy.

"Well?" he asked.

"I don't know. You're getting older, you know. I like my men young and virile," she said with a smile.

"You'd have a teenager, if you thought you'd get away with it," he teased.

"You dirty old man," she yelled and threw a pillow at him. "And I suppose you don't fantasize about a teen in plaid jumpers and white bobby sox?" she replied.

"Nope, not me. At my age I'd have a heart attack," said John as he went to his dresser to get a fresh pair of underwear.

"Listen, before you do, I'd like you to do something for me?" she asked.

"Oh, what's that?" he asked.

"Come here," she commanded. "And forget the underwear."

John complied. Walking to the edge of the bed, he stood before Nancy. Nancy got up on her knees and wrapped her arms around his waist. She kissed his flat stomach and ran her tongue around his navel. John just stood there, eyes closed.

"Now, pleasure me," she commanded.

"Pleasure you? Now who's sounding old? I've never heard that expression except in the old movies.".

"Do you know what it means?" she asked with a smile.

"Of course I know," he answered.

"Then do it, before I get violent," she said, slapping his bare bottom.

John knelt down on the bed and straddled her. He bent down and began kissing her eyes, neck, and nibbled at her ear lobe. He sensed Nancy give a slight shiver as he passed his tongue over her throat and down her neck. Reaching down, he opened her blouse, one button at a time. Then he lifted her slightly off the bed. Moving his hands under her blouse, he found the hook to her bra. In one move he released the clasp. No longer restrained by the bra, Nancy's breasts fell slightly, exposing two brown nipples. Cupping each breast in his hands, John kissed them. He moved his tongue in a circular fashion around them until they became hard and erect. He couldn't help but notice that this foreplay was having an effect on him as well. He looked down into Nancy's face. She looked up at him, as if seeing him for the first time. She didn't blink, but held his gaze in hers.

John then slid down the length of her body. He moved his tongue across her naked flesh, causing goose bumps to form on her delicate skin. He found the top of her slacks and slipping his fingers inside the elastic band, pulled them down over her hips. Her panties, caught in the same movement, followed the slacks. John swung his leg back over Nancy and continued to pull the pants down and off her completely.

He took a moment to admire her body. It was lithe and toned from her own regular exercise routine. He could still discern tan line from her bathing suit. Nancy's legs were slim and long. Where they met, a small triangle of reddish, brown hair concealed the center of John's interest. He settled down on his right side and proceeded to kiss her stomach, moving down slowly to the area he most coveted. She could feel his warm breath and hot, wet tongue as it brushed her flesh. She knew where he was going. Her body tensed for a moment then released, muscles relaxing. She knew what was to follow. Not being able to wait a moment longer, she parted her legs and invited John to "pleasure her."

Chapter 17

The following day, when John and Nancy arrived at work. A message waiting for them from the M.E. John called Dr. Morrison's extension and waited. After three rings the M.E. answered the phone.

"What, no secretary?" asked John.

"It was my phone ringing so I assumed it's for me. Besides, she's busy," replied the doc. "I have some information on the Sands woman. The toxicology reports came back clean. No drugs, alcohol, or poisons. There was no evidence of sexual assault. Her body was clean, nothing under her nails. I didn't find any foreign matter, hairs, skin that the perp may have left behind. The rain may have washed them away or the killer was wearing gloves but there were no particulates. As I initially surmised the cause of death was exsanguination. When the killer sliced through her abdomen he nicked her aorta. She bled out. How is the investigation coming along on your end?"

"We think her ex-boyfriend may have done it. He certainly had it in for her. We're trying to locate him now," said John. "Anything else?"

"I've completed the exam on the other woman, the one found in Sheepshead Bay. She had track marks on her left forearm. Toxicology should have more, but I'd say she was an addict.

I got a good set of prints off her. The fingerprint people have them now. We should get the results soon. My guess is she has a record. She'd been in the water only a short time. She was still alive when she went into the water. There was salt water in her lungs. Oh, and you may have a serial killer on your hands. Her wounds were similar to those on the Sands woman."

Hearing this made the hairs on the back of John's neck stand on end. A chilling thought went through his brain. "A serial killer. That means there may be more victims."

The M.E. continued, "Like the first victim she was cut from the pubic area up to the sternum. It was a very clean cut. Like the other woman, no evidence of sexual abuse. No fibers, foreign matter, skin tracings not belonging to the victim. My guess is she was dead maybe ten, twelve hours, at most. You got anything?"

"Nothing concrete. Maybe the prints will help ID her. Let me know if you come up with anything else. Thanks, Doc," "said John as he hung up the phone. Without saying a word he turned to leave their office.

"Where you off to?" asked Nancy.

"I'm going down to records to get the case number for the file on the woman pulled from the water the other night. The M.E. says she was killed by a knife, deep and long. He thinks she may have been an addict. Once we get the prints back we can check the files, see if she has a record.

No sooner had John left, when his phone began to ring. Nancy swung over on her wheeled desk chair and picked it up.

"Homicide, Detective Mooney," she said.

Nancy listened without commenting to the person on the other end of the phone. She wrote down some information on a yellow legal pad John had on his desk.

When John returned, he had a case folder with a number on it. He also had a stack of forms. These were the beginnings of the case on the woman found off Sheepshead Bay. Before he could begin filling out the forms Nancy walked over to his desk dropping the yellow pad on his desk.

"Better look at this before you enter 'Jane Doe' on any of the forms," warned Nancy.

John picked up the pad and read what had been written on it. At the top, in large letters, was scrawled, "*Christina Martinez.*"

"So, what's this?" asked John.

"That's our Jane Doe," said Nancy, stopping to let that sink in.

"Shit! I don't believe it. She's the one we were looking for in connection with the Sands murder. She's Bruce Krane's girlfriend. The M.E. said the wounds were similar," he said, rubbing his forehead with his right hand.

"Ex-girlfriend," corrected Nancy. "Two girlfriends. Two murders, both knifing victims, and Bruce Krane knew them both," summarized Nancy.

"This guy's on a one-man murder spree," said John.

"We gotta catch this sick bastard before he strikes again," said Nancy.

John looked at the ceiling for a moment and then turned back to Nancy.

"The Martinez woman said her daughter was on welfare. But her neighbor said she worked for welfare. I'm going to call my contact over there and see if she can find anything else we could use," said John as he picked up his telephone and dialed.

"Mary Clarke? This is Detective Straub. How are you doing today? Sorry to hear that. There's a bug going around our office also. Listen, if you get a chance, I need some information on a Christina Martin or Martinez. You may have a Sheepshead Bay address on her. She's part of a homicide case we're working on. Yeah, a victim, I'm afraid. No, we haven't solved the last one I called about. Believe it or not, unlike the T.V. shows it usually takes us a little more than an hour to solve a case. Thanks Ms. Clarke," said John, hanging up.

When Mary Clarke awoke that morning she found she had a scratchy throat, headache, and itchy eyes. All the makings for a cold. She hoped it wasn't the flu. By the time she'd gotten into work she was sniffling and sneezing. With each sneeze her eyes grew blurry. Her head pounded harder.

Mary Clarke tossed another tissue into her waste basket. She slowly rose from her desk and walked down the hall to the records room. She could have gotten the information over the phone, but she wanted to get away from her desk. She thought the walk might clear her head.

When she got to the records room she asked the clerk for the file on Martinez. She indicated a homicide cop had called on the case and she needed it as soon as possible. After a moment, she was told it was signed out to some one else. Mary didn't care who had it, just that they forwarded it to her when it came back. She retraced her steps back to her office and tried to resume her work.

"Aughh chooo!!" came a huge sneeze before she could grab a tissue to cover her face.

"I hate it when people come into work with a cold. They just end up going home early. But first they have to make sure everyone else gets it too," she thought. But then looking around at the empty cubicles, she smiled. "Who the hell is going to catch it from me in here?" She went back to the stack of cases on her desk.

"I'm returning this," the records room clerk heard a male voice say behind her.

"Okay. Leave on the pile. Which case is it?" asked the clerk.

"Martinez," he said.

"Put it in the wire basket. I have to send it down to a case worker," she said.

The man frowned. "Who wants it?" he asked.

"Mary Clarke. She was just here. Said it had something to do with a police inquiry."

"Don't worry. I'll take it down to her," said the man and left. He walked towards Mary Clarke's area. He located her cubicle and peeked over the partition. It was empty.

"She's gone for the day," said a woman a few desks away. "A cold. Need something?"

"It can wait," he said. The man walked back to the records room and dropped the folder in the wire basket on the front counter. "Another time, Mary Clarke," he thought.

On the way home, Mary Clarke kept thinking about the recent calls from her friend, Detective. Straub. Two women who had been involved with the welfare department were found dead.

"Why should I find that strange?" she thought. "These people often come from the worst neighborhoods and have complicated lives."

While Mary thought it a shame, she also wondered if there was any kind of a connection. She began to connect the dots and was beginning to grasp something about the two women when she was seized by a series of horrendous sneezes. The other passengers on the subway all gave her a look and attempted to move as far away as possible.

"What's the matter? You think I have the plague or something?" she said out loud.

She wasn't the type to speak up like that. "I guess it's the cold," she thought.

Distracted by the sneezing fit, Mary lost her train of thought. Her head continued to pound.

"Cold, headache. I've probably got a fever," she thought. "Why didn't I stay home this morning?" she said to herself as she rummaged through her pocketbook looking for a tissue.

Chapter 18

While John had been talking to Mary Clarke at DSS, Nancy was running Bruce Krane's name through the DMV (Department of Motor Vehicles.) She found that there was a warrant out for Bruce's arrest for failing to appear on a traffic ticket. His driving record was indicative of a person who didn't care about rules. He had tickets going back to before he even had a license to drive. Right now his driving privileges were suspended. His current car was a 1997 Cadillac, Deville.

"Now why would a guy living in the Bronx, or Brooklyn, for that matter, want a car, especially a big boat like that?" she wondered. The DMV listed his mother's address as Bruce's legal residence.

John finished with Mrs. Clarke and headed out of the office. When he returned, he had two cups of Starbuck's coffee with him. He placed one in front of Nancy and pulled his chair around his desk so he could be closer to Nancy. He waited while she finished printing out a DMV record off her computer.

"I spoke to the woman at DSS. She's going to see what they have on our latest victim. What about you?"

he asked, taking a sip of coffee. "Whew, that's hot," he said.

John carefully removed the plastic cover and, leaning dangerously far, placed the cup on his desk. When he turned back, he saw Nancy smiling at him.

"What's the snicker for?" he asked.

"No snicker. I was just waiting to see if you were going to fall over backwards trying to put your coffee over there. Why didn't you just put it on my desk?" she asked.

John just looked at her as if she'd asked him what the overall weight of the sun was.

"Forget it. After last night's treat, I shouldn't be so critical," she said with a smile.

"Treat? You mean pleasured, don't you?" he said with glee in his eye.

Nancy's face turned a light shade of red. Trying to change the subject, she said, "Bruce Krane has a lengthy DMV record. I got a make on the car he drives. Maybe we can circulate it among the squad cars in the areas, see if they spot him."

"Okay. In the mean time, we should take a ride up to the old Martinez woman's place. Some one has to break the news that her daughter is dead. I'm afraid that falls on us. I'll get records to send me over the positive ID from her finger prints."

John drove and within forty-five minutes they reached the neighborhood in Sheepshead Bay where the victim and her mother lived. When Mrs. Martinez saw the two detectives from Homicide at her door, a feeling of dread overcame her. Without being told, she knew they'd come to give her bad news. She invited them inside and this time they all went into the kitchen and sat at the small metal and Formica table.

Nancy looked the woman in the eye and said, "Mrs. Martinez. I'm afraid we have very bad news." Not wanting to prolong the woman's agony, she came out with it.

"A body was found near here the other night. We got a call from the medical examiner's office this morning. It's Christina, your daughter."

Mrs. Martinez knees buckled slightly. Reaching out to the wall she regained her balance, bowed her head and began to cry. Her tears fell on the table in front of her. She didn't wail or carry on as most mothers would upon learning their daughter had been killed. Instead, she sobbed softly. Nancy and John gave the woman a moment to absorb the information Nancy had just given the woman. Finally, Mrs. Martinez rose from her chair, walked to the kitchen sink and turned on the tap.

She stood staring at the flow of water. Then she removed a glass from an overhead shelf and filled it part way. Shutting the tap off, she slowly drank from the glass. Then she removed a tissue from a pocket, dabbed at her eyes, and blew her nose.

Turning to the two detectives, she said, "Please excuse me."

"That's all right, Mrs. Martinez. I can't begin to imagine the pain you must be feeling now," said Nancy.

"I was afraid this would happen someday. I used to dream I'd get awakened in the middle of the night. A policeman would stand in the door way and tell me my daughter was dead. Oh, she wasn't a bad girl. She never broke the law, not really. But she couldn't stay away from the drugs. That's why I have her son with me. At least I'll always have a part of her in him." With this she returned to the table and sat down.

"Mrs. Martinez, your daughter is dead, but not from drugs. At least not directly as far as we know right now. She was murdered," said John. He paused, expecting the woman to start crying again. She didn't.

"Do you know any one who might want to harm your daughter, Mrs. Martinez?" asked Nancy.

The woman sat for a minute, as if mentally running through a list of suspects in her mind. Finally, she looked up.

"No. But I didn't know some of the people she was hanging around with since she moved out over a year ago. Do you think it was over drugs that she was killed?" asked the old woman.

"Again, I'm sorry, but we just don't know. What about her boy friend, Bruce Krane? Do you think he could do something like this?" asked John.

"Maybe. Do you think he killed my baby?" she asked.

"We haven't found him to talk to him yet," said John.

Using the tissue to wipe her eyes, Mrs. Martinez continued.

"I really didn't know him that well. I think I met him once when my daughter stopped by to see Julio. He was with her. He didn't say much that I remember. He seemed uncomfortable being here. He definitely didn't want to have anything to do with Julio. When my daughter offered to let him hold him he refused. I remember, he said 'he couldn't stand babies, that they were 'nothing but trouble.' My poor little girl,

God knows she didn't deserve this." Mrs. Martinez paused as she dabbed at her eyes with the tissue. After a moment she went on.

"I remember she had a kitten. Use to leave it with me and Julio when she'd go off for a few days. She stopped leaving the kitten a few months ago. I don't know if it's still there. Maybe you could check on the cat. I have a key to her apartment. You can have it if you like. I don't need it anymore," she added. She retrieved the key from a hook on the back of a cabinet door and gave it to the detectives.

John and Nancy stayed with Mrs. Martinez for a little while longer. They explained to her that the body would have to be identified. Mrs. Martinez said she'd call her brother, Christina's uncle. He would help her with the funeral arrangements. John and Nancy extended their regrets again and left the woman alone to grieve.

They returned to Christy's place and found the key Mrs. Martinez had given them still worked. They unlocked the door and entered the apartment. It was a ground floor one-bedroom affair. It was furnished with what looked like second hand pieces. The only thing new was a twenty-five inch color TV sitting in the living room. John and Nancy went through the apartment. There was the usual assortment of clothing and miscellaneous items. But nothing that could explain why this girl had been murdered.

They found a note pad with names, addresses, and dates scribbled in it. After looking through it, Nancy looked up at John, who was busy looking through pieces of mail that had been left on a small table in the hallway near the door.

"According to this, the girl was working part time for welfare to pay back some of the assistance she received."

"Here's something from welfare," said John, slipping the letter out of the envelope.

"According to this, she's was asked to furnish information about her son's father. It lists Bruce Krane. I guess Julio is his kid. Welfare is picking up the tab to keep the child in care of the grandmother. They're trying to get him to pay child support. Seems Bruce is quite the swordsman. This is the second kid he's not supporting," said John.

"Maybe the mother was trying to get him to pay support," says Nancy.

"We've got to find this guy," said John. "Let's stop down at the local precinct. We can ask around and give them a make on Krane's car," he suggested. They left the mail, but took the dead woman's notebook.

Returning to their car, they drove to nearby Coney Island and the police precinct. After identifying themselves, they asked for the precinct commander.

"Down the hall, last door on the left," said the desk sergeant.

John and Nancy walked the short distance down the hall. An elderly secretary sat "guard" outside the commander's office.

"Detectives Mooney and Straub. We're here to see the commander," said John.

The woman picked up her phone, said a few words, then hung up.

"The 'boss' will see you. Through that door," she directed.

The 'boss' was a large, black man. He appeared to be about six and a half feet tall and weighed about two hundred and fifty pounds, maybe more. Nancy saw by the stripes on his sleeve that he had over twenty-five years on the force. From the sound of his voice and diction, she guessed he was well educated, not one of your typical "TV actor type cops" with all "dees" and "does" in his vocabulary.

"Definitely college; that would have made him a rarity back when he probably entered the police academy, unless he went to school nights after joining," Nancy thought.

The precinct commander was signing some papers on his desk when they walked in. John waited for the commander to look up, then introduced himself and Nancy. The boss stood up and reached across his desk. He offered his hand, which easily engulfed Nancy's.

"Commander M. L. Grady. The M. L. is for Martin Luther. My mother was Lutheran. We were raised Lutheran, not Baptist like most other black kids. The name is after the original, before Martin Luther King Jr. came along," he said with a smile. The commander invited them to take seats.

"What can I do for you detectives?" he asked.

Between them, John and Nancy gave him a rundown on the two murder cases they'd been working on. They told him about the connection with Bruce Krane and how he'd dropped off the face of the earth. Giving the commander the make on Krane's car, they asked for his help in locating their suspect in the double homicide.

"I'll be glad to pass this on to my men, excuse me, men and women. But I'm afraid you'll have to get in line concerning this Bruce Krane," said the commander.

"How's that?" asked John.

"The Feds are interested in your boy too," said the commander.

"The Feds?" asked Nancy, looking at John.

"Yeah, as in F.B.I. They were here a few days ago. Do you remember the controversy surrounding the last union hauler's elections? The one where the incumbent was supposed to have taken money under the table, 'kick backs' to see that work moved smoothly at construction sites.

Their president was supposed to have had a 'goon squad' that roughed up members of the opposition team. Bruce Krane was supposed to be one of the 'enforcers.'

"But that's only half of it. There's more they have to talk to this Krane about. There was the big heist at the air terminal a while back. A shipment of gems that came in from Antwerp. They were being held overnight at an armored car warehouse," said Grady. He shifted in his chair and continued.

"One night, the place was hit by about a dozen masked and heavily armed men. They killed one of the security guards before hauling away over two hundred million dollars worth of uncut diamonds. The Feds are trying to keep it quiet. They're afraid of what this could mean on the world market. I hear even the people at De Beers, the International Diamond Syndicate, are sending a group of their own 'investigators' to look into it. These investigators are all ex CIA, KGB, and Mossad agents; all trained to kill in a hundred different ways. Oh, and the guard who was killed, he was one of ours, NYPD. He'd retired about six months before. He had a wife and two girls, one in college. They must have known he was a cop and singled him out. Maybe he recognized someone or knew something. Word on the street is that an informant has given them Bruce Krane as one of the members of the gang that pulled the job," concluded the commander.

"Man. This guy, Krane is all over the place. Are you sure there isn't more than one of him?" asked Nancy sarcastically.

The commander brought two street cops in who covered the Sheepshead Bay area. They knew the "street people" and promised to shake a few trees and flip over some rocks to see what crawled out. They compared notes and gathered as much as they could from the officers. When they'd finished John and Nancy thanked them for their help and left the precinct house.

"Do me a favor, honey, you drive. I want to make a call," said John.

"Stop calling me 'honey' on the job. People may get the wrong idea. Unless you called your old partner, Ski, honey also," she teased.

Suddenly she grew very quiet and the smile faded from her face. John picked up on the mood change.

"Oh no, not the PMS monster again," he thought.

Throwing caution to the wind, he asked, "What's the matter, Nancy? What's on your mind?"

"Nothing," was her response, as she turned the key in the ignition.

"Come on. No secrets," he demanded.

"It has nothing to do with the case."

"Okay, what?"

"I was just thinking about your old partner, Ski. He'll be coming back soon."

"Now don't think about that now. He won't be cleared for full duty for several months. Besides we might not be teamed up again," he said.

"Why not? You guys were partners about ten years, right?"

"Ten years? Yeah, something like that."

John had had these thoughts also. He didn't know how he was going to respond when his commander asked him to choose between Nancy and Ski. They both had their pluses and minuses. But like most major decisions in his life he'd wait until the last minute to decide. In the meantime he tried not to think about it.

John put his hand on her shoulder, then ran the back of his hand against the side of her cheek.

"Come on, smile," he asked.

They were suddenly distracted by whistles and hoots from outside the car. Three uniformed cops had just walked out of the precinct and saw them in an intimate exchange. Knowing they were fellow cops, they teased them and rubbed two fingers together, saying "shame, shame" like school kids. John turned red.

"Get us out of here," he said. Nancy complied.

Once they got a few blocks, John asked, "You okay?"

"Sure. I guess I just want you all to myself. I hate the idea of sharing you with anyone."

"I'll tell you what. We have that date with Ski and his family for dinner on Sunday. When he's not looking, I'll break his kneecap again so we can stay together another six months. How's that?" he asked.

"If I didn't know you better, I think you'd do it," she replied.

"Oh, you always say the most romantic things to a girl."

Chapter 19

The weekend finally arrived. John and Nancy were getting ready for their dinner with the Zubriskis. As was usual, Nancy was ready ahead of John. She'd learned very early in their relationship that John was meticulous about his appearance. He weighed himself almost every day. If he saw the pounds adding up, he'd go on a high protein diet and increase his exercise routine. The slight "love handles" she'd noticed on him only a few days ago, seemed to be disappearing already. Without her having said anything, he had spotted the extra flesh and was taking steps to get rid of it.

Nancy realized the time was quickly approaching when she'd have to start watching what she ate and begin to exercise more seriously. Nancy had been lucky so far. She'd taken after her mother, Sharon, who was also tall and slim, like Nancy. But she had bright red hair, rather than auburn, like Nancy's. She used to wear it long. Nancy remembered seeing pictures of her mother when she was her age. They could have passed for sisters. But after Sharon reached her mid-forties she began to gain weight. Her metabolism must have changed, slowed down or something. Maybe it was menopause.

"If I take after my Mom, I'm going to have a weight problem in a few years," she thought.

To kill time, Nancy began flipping through the notebook they'd gotten from Christy Martinez's place. Suddenly she stopped and stared at an entry.

"Listen to this?" she said but got no response from John.

Hey, can you hear me in there?"

"What? Did you say something?" asked John as he shut off the hair dryer he'd been using.

"I asked if you could hear me?" she repeated.

"I can now," he said after shutting the blower off. "What?"

"I was looking through the Martinez woman's note book. It has a couple of entries in there about foster care. Something about appointments to see one of the case workers," she said.

"So? Her son was being raised by the mother. The old lady was smart enough to apply for welfare assistance for the child. We didn't ask her what she did for money, but her place didn't look like she had an income in the six figure range. I guess she felt she deserved the help. Besides, whoever the foster parents were, welfare would give them assistance to help with the expenses," answered John.

"I know that. But why would the mother of the child be seeing a foster care worker? They deal with the people raising the child, not the mother. CPS (Child Protective Services) might be concerned or Work Fare could have something to do with the mother if she's getting assistance, even the Support Division. But why Foster Care?" she asked.

"I don't know. But I could ask my friend at DSS to check it out if you're that interested," promised John.

"I am. And the other woman, Jennifer Sands, she had appointments with Foster Care penciled in on her appointment book," added Nancy.

"Okay, Monday, I promise. Now put that away and get ready," said John.

"Get ready. I've been ready for the past half hour. I'm just waiting for you. I swear you're like an old lady," she countered.

"Don't you want me to look nice when we go out?" asked John.

"Nice, yes, but you're giving yourself a complete make over."

John didn't respond. He continued moving at his own pace.

John finally completed his ritual and they headed off to meet their friends. The drive out to Long Island was uneventful. The Zubriskis lived just over the Queens-Nassau County border, so it didn't take long before they were knocking on the front door of their modest cape. Ski greeted them with bear hugs and kisses. Bear hugs for John. Kisses for Nancy. As soon as they were inside they were greeted by the twins.

"Hi, Uncle John, Nancy," they yelled in unison.

"I can't believe how they've grown. At this rate, they'll be married with their own kids in no time," said John.

From inside came Betty's familiar voice. "Hey, I'm in the kitchen. Come on in," yelled Ski's wife, Betty.

Once in the kitchen, more hugs and kisses were exchanged.

"Gee, it's good to see you guys," said Betty.

"What can I get you to drink?" asked Ski.

"I'll have beer," said John.

"I'll have what Betty's having," added Nancy.

Ski got a cold beer from the refrigerator and opened it. "Mug or in the bottle?" he asked.

"The bottle's fine for me," said John.

Ski grabbed a bottle of white wine off the kitchen counter, poured a glass, and handed it to Nancy.

"Let's go sit for a while. We're having barbecued steaks, salad, and baked potatoes. Easy dinner. So we'll have a chance to spend some time with you. Get caught up on all that's been happening. And by happening I mean between you two, not the job," said Betty.

"Great," said Nancy.

They all walked back into the living room and settled down on the sofa and easy chairs.

"Something is different," commented Nancy once she sat down.

"Yeah. What did you do, redecorate?" asked John.

"Well, to be honest, Betty redecorated. It started out a few weeks after I got home from the hospital. I made her drive me to the big home outlet out in Farmingdale. We picked out paper, paint, the whole nine yards. Once we started, I realized I wasn't in any shape to do it. That surgery on my leg and laying around for so long must have taken a lot out of me," said Ski.

"Don't let him kid you. He did more than the doctor would have liked. I made sure he was careful on the ladder," said Betty with a smile.

"Get out of here!" exclaimed Nancy.

"She's kidding, Nancy. She wouldn't let me near a ladder. But I was able to do some plastering and use the roller for the paint. It took a while, but we managed to get it done," added Ski.

"We even got the kids' rooms redone, finally. We'd moved them into their own rooms about a year ago. But, believe it our not, one still had the original color that had been there when we moved in over ten years ago," said Betty.

"I'd love to see it," said Nancy.

With that, Betty rose from her chair, as did Nancy.

"What about you, John?" asked Nancy, giving him a look.

"Oh, okay. I'm right behind you, hon," he said, winking at Ski.

Betty led them down the hall to the twins' rooms.

"Little Peter's" as Betty liked to call him rather than Junior, had his room painted in a pale blue with a wall paper boarder of nautical scenes running around the top. The hard wood floor was bare and appeared to have been redone. It had a deep, rich shine to it. Against the longer inside wall was a pine bunk bed set. The bed covers were a darker blue and followed the nautical theme. There was a chest of drawers stained to match the floor. The single closet stood partially open and a full length mirror was attached to its inside surface.

"This is lovely," commented Nancy. Betty beamed.

"It smells so clean," said John.

"As opposed to what?" asked Betty, teasing him.

"No. It's just very nice," he stammered. He looked at Nancy for help, but she offered him none.

Then Betty took them to Stacy's room. This had been the twins' original bedroom. Now it had been redecorated to reflect the feminine occupant. Like Peter Junior, or "Little Peter's," room the carpet had been removed and the floor stripped and re-stained. The woodwork around the windows, door frames and base board had also been stripped to match the floor. Nancy wondered to herself if the other room had all its wood stripped also. She didn't recall. The walls were painted in white, but with the faintest hint of pink. The bed was a hide-away type and the bedspread was a rose, which matched the curtains.

"This is perfect," said Nancy. She noticed that a small vanity had been set up near the single window in the room. There was also a dresser with a mirror over it.

"You did a very nice job with the rooms," commented John. He glanced at Nancy to see if he'd said the correct thing this time. He guessed he must have, because she smiled at him.

"Why the bare floors?" asked Nancy. "Aren't they cold on their feet?"

"Actually, no. The furnace is on this side in the basement. When it's running, it gives off enough heat to warm the basement ceiling and the floors above. We also found out they both have allergies. They'd been getting one head cold after another, especially during the winter months.

Our doctor made us take them to an allergist. She tested them and found they were allergic to dust, mold, animal dander, everything. She suggested if we were redoing their rooms anyway to take out the rugs. Apparently, rugs were a big source of their allergies. You know, since they moved into the new rooms they haven't had a cold. The weekly allergy shots may be helping too. Who knows? All I know is they're healthy and that's the main thing," concluded Betty.

"Where are the two elves now?" asked John.

"They're downstairs in the den. We decided to put their toys and a TV down there to get them out of their bedrooms. Especially when they have friends over. Otherwise they'd be laying all over their beds with their dirty shoes or sneakers on."

Betty led them back to the living room, where they found Ski with his eyes closed, snoring away.

"Oh, he must be exhausted," said Nancy. Ski's eyes popped open and he smiled broadly.

"You were gone so long I figured I'd take a nap. So what do you think?" he asked.

"I think you guys do nice work. Do you take on outside jobs?" she asked.

"Nope, just domestic," replied Ski.

"Oh, well, John,. I guess you'll have to do it all by yourself," said Nancy.

"Oh, oh. That sounds like the nesting instinct coming out. I'm in deep trouble now," he thought.

They sat down again in the living room, resumed their idle chit chat, and shared stories covering the last six months of their lives. Finally, Betty said to her husband, "You better start the grill or we'll never eat."

Ski got up and turned to John.

"Come on. We'll go through the kitchen and grab a couple of fresh brews to take outside."

John followed his old partner from the room.

Nancy followed Betty into the kitchen, where she began washing the lettuce for the salad.

"I put the potatoes in the oven when you guys got here. They should be finished by the time the steak comes off the grill. Do you think I have enough? I've got the steak, baked potatoes, salad, fresh-made bread. Am I missing anything?" asked Betty.

Nancy didn't respond.

After a moment, Betty turned to Nancy and said, "Earth to Nancy. Come in, Nancy."

"What?" asked Nancy, turning away from the window to see what Betty was asking.

"I was just asking if you thought I had enough here to eat. Where were you? Is everything okay between you and John?"

"Everything is fine," replied Nancy.

"But?" asked Betty. "It sounds like there should be a but after that answer," commented Betty.

"Oh, I was just looking at the boys out there. They seem like brothers. It's as if they've been partners all their lives," said Nancy.

"So what's the problem? Oh, I get it. Sorry, I'm a little slow some times. It must be from dealing with twins all day. Sometimes I feel like I'm brain dead. You're worried about what's going to happen to you when Peter goes back to work, right?" asked Betty with a smile.

"It's just that I like working with John. He's taught me a lot in the past few months," replied Nancy.

"But I know he'll want Ski, I mean Peter, as his partner again, when he returns," said Nancy.

"Look, Nancy, you know I like you." Then she corrected herself. "No, I love you like a sister. I'm glad you and John have found each other. I think you were both meant for each other. So don't take this the wrong way. Look at them out there," said Betty, pointing to the men in the back yard.

Nancy looked. The two men must have been saying something that struck them both as funny. They were laughing and John was patting Ski on the shoulder.

"Those two guys are like bread and butter when it comes to the job. They know each other better than they know either one of us. And that's as it should be. It's what's kept them alive all these years.

I'll be the first to admit I get jealous at times. Maybe it's because they get to spend so much time together. But do you know what? I wouldn't trade it for the world. Peter has his life out there and leaves it there. He sees and does things no wife should see or know about. Inside this house we have each other, and the kids. When the time comes, you'll know what's the right thing to do. You'll do what's best for everyone, including you. So don't worry about it. Give it up to God," concluded Betty.

Nancy heard what Betty said and she had to agree with her. She'd heard Betty say that before, "Give it up to God." She wished she had her faith. But after thinking about it, wasn't everything "up to God," in one way or another?. We really couldn't control everything about our futures. There was always something unexpected coming along to throw our planned routine out of whack.

Nancy turned to Betty and gave her a big hug. "Thanks, Betty. Thanks for being my friend. Now what can I do to help?" she asked.

"More wine would be a big help," said Betty, holding up her empty glass.

"I can do that," said Nancy, her mood noticeably better.

Outside, Ski had the coals bright red and could feel the heat from the grill as he stood next to John.

"Now all I have to do is wait for the signal from the boss, throw these babies on the barbeque and we'll be all set," said Ski.

"So how is the leg coming along?" asked John.

"It was coming along fine. Then the other day I fell over one of the kids' toys and wrenched it pretty bad. I was afraid I'd broken something again. The doc checked it out and said I'd just strained it a little. But it let me know I'm not ready for work, at least not on the streets yet," admitted Ski.

He could see the disappointment in his old partner's face.

"What's the matter? Don't tell me you miss me. For crying out loud, maybe the guys back at headquarters are right when they tease us and say we're like an old married couple," said Ski.

This made John smile.

"I miss you, partner. I'll have to be honest, it's not the same," said John.

"Don't let Nancy hear you saying that. She's liable to put a contract out on me," teased Ski. "Speaking of which, how are you guys doing?"

"Great," said John.

Ski could see he meant it.

"I think she is the girl I'd like to spend the rest of my days with," added John.

"And what about the nights? Are they good too?" said Ski, knowing how to embarrass his partner. Ski knew John was a bit of a prude when it came to talking about sex, especially when it concerned a woman he cared about. Ski liked that in him. Ski had found that too many cops liked to use their uniforms as bait. They knew some women were attracted to it and they took advantage of it. Then they'd brag about their conquests. Ski thought they were all bullshit.

Ski's favorite expression was, "Me thinks he doth complain too much." He meant that the more guys bragged, the less they probably got. Neither Ski, nor John ever took advantage of a woman or used their positions as cops to get women. So, Ski had to admit, he was just as much a prude as John.

"How is it working with Nancy?" asked Ski, getting to the meat of the matter.

"She's good. She's smart, has good instincts. I'd trust her to cover my back anytime," said John.

"And?" asked Ski.

John was quiet for a moment and Ski let him think before speaking.

"I don't think it's good, the both of us working together. You know what I mean. I know she'd take a bullet that was meant for me, just like I would for her. It's just that I worry everyday that it might happen. I don't think I could live with that."

Ski knew what he meant and thought better than to try to make light of the situation.

"Man, you've really got it bad for this woman," replied Ski. "But you're right. If it was my woman with me, I may hesitate, worried about her, and that could be fatal for both of us. Bottom line, partner, she's got to go. You've got to separate your professional life from your home life. And she should be separate from you. Don't get me wrong. I'm not saying it because I want to come back as your partner. I do. I think your relationship could suffer if you continue to work together. Haven't you seen it already?" asked Ski.

"Yeah. I guess. But how do I tell her?" asked John. "How do I tell the woman I love I don't want to have her as a partner because I love her too much?"

"That's exactly it, though. You can't work together, be together both home and at work without it wearing on you. My advice, let it run its course. Don't worry about it so much. It's out of your hands anyway. The top brass usually makes those decisions for us.

Enough already of this heavy shit. Let's see if it's time to cook these steaks. Go get a couple of fresh ones and ask Betty if I should start," ordered Ski.

John gave him a mock salute and went inside.

Nancy saw John turn and walk towards the sliding glass door. She went to the refrigerator, grabbed two cold beers, ready to re-supply the troops when he came in. As John closed the door behind him he saw Nancy holding two beers at arm's length over her head. He walked over and put his arms around her and kissed her softly on the lips.

"Hey, you two, knock it off in my kitchen or I'll turn the hose on you," said Betty smiling.

As Nancy gave John the beers he asked, "Should we put the steaks on?"

"Absolutely, we're ready in here," said Betty.

Once the steaks came off the grill they all gathered around the dinning room table. After everyone was seated and the food placed around the table, Betty and Ski reached out to either side to hold hands for grace. The twins had managed to seat themselves on either side of "Uncle John" and "Aunt Nancy."

They placed their small hands in those of the grown ups and bowed their heads. Nancy looked at John and motioned for him to lower his head. John complied with a smile. Ski gave a brief grace, thanking God for the food, family, and friends gathered around the table.

He specifically said, "And Lord, if you are of a mind to, please let these crazy love birds live happily ever after, amen."

The twins yelled out "amen" and teased John and Nancy, calling them "love birds."

All smiled at their enthusiasm. John looked at Nancy and smiled. Nancy looked into John's eyes and felt herself getting choked up. She was actually afraid she was going to cry. At that moment, she felt the happiest she'd felt in many years. And it was all because of John Michael Straub.

Dinner was delicious. Everyone complimented the "chef" for his wonderful job on the steaks. After dinner the twins ran off to watch some TV before bed time. The "grown ups" remained at the table having coffee and dessert.

The conversation was light and there were several humorous anecdotes shared, many, it seemed, at John's expense. Nancy had mentioned how John hadn't been looking where he was walking and had stepped into a puddle at the last crime scene. Ski added that it was a tradition with John to step into something at the beginning of every new case. Ski said he thought of it as good luck.

The girls cleared the table and Nancy joined the men in the living room while Betty got the twins ready for bed. When she returned the twins were close behind. They'd been bathed and had gotten into fresh pajamas.

Stacy and Peter Jr. scrambled on top of "Uncle John and Aunt Nancy" to give them big good night kisses. Nancy returned their kisses and gave them each a big hug.

John noticed her holding them each for an ever so brief moment in her arms. The first thought that came to mind was, "first she fixes up my place, which they say is 'nesting' and now she's savoring the embrace of children. I'm in big trouble. But good trouble."

Nancy caught his look and gave him a warm smile and a wink. Betty caught the silent exchange and nudged her husband. Naturally, being a man, Ski had no idea what he'd missed. As she was leaving the room to go to bed, Stacy turned to Nancy.

"Aunt Nancy, if you don't marry Uncle John, I will," she said, giggling as she ran down the hall. John's face turned bright red.

"Out of the mouths of babes," said Betty, patting Stacy on the bottom as she ushered her to their bedrooms.

Once the twins were tucked in, Betty rejoined them in the living room.

"I apologize for the twins," said Betty.

"Don't be silly," replied Nancy.

"I think they are adorable. I'd feel blessed to have just one like them. You and Peter have done a wonderful job raising them."

"Thank you, Nancy, we try," said Ski.

Their conversation resumed and after about another hour of chatting, John announced it was past his bed time. They all hugged, the ladies exchanging kisses, and Betty warned them about being strangers.

"I'll tell you what," said Nancy. "I'll have John call in a week or so. Maybe you could come over with the twins for dinner at our place."

Betty didn't miss the "our place" and thought, "She's ready for the next step."

"That would be great. But would you mind terribly if we left the twins at my mother's for the night?" asked Betty.

"But we'd love to have them," countered Nancy.

"Yes, but we'd like a break, if it's okay with you guys?" asked Ski.

"Fine, just the four of us. We'll do it in a couple of weeks, promise," said John.

John and Nancy left with Betty and Peter standing in the doorway waving.

"What do you think?" asked Betty of her husband.

"I think she's hooked him good. The poor guy. It won't be long now. Another fine bachelor bites the dust," said Ski.

"Keep it up, Peter, and I'll break your knee cap again," she warned. Ski hugged her as they closed the door and started putting the lights off in the living room.

Later that night in Queens, John sat up in bed reading a new book by Clive Cussler. Ski had introduced him to the author. John found his writings interesting and informative.

They all had a historical twist to them. He heard Nancy coming from the bathroom after "preparing herself for bed," as she referred to it. He lowered his head to look over his "reading glasses."

"What are they always preparing themselves for?" thought John. But, seeing Nancy made him thankful she 'prepared' herself for him. Nancy wore a white, silky, short nightgown. She called it a "teddy." She saw him staring and smiled.

"I guess you are interested," she said.

"More than interested," asserted John. Nancy walked over and stood beside the bed.

"Can we talk?" she asked.

"Uh oh," said John.

"No, nothing too heavy. I've been thinking about something lately and I think you have too. Seeing you with Ski today just brought it to the surface. When Ski is ready to return full time, I'm going to request a transfer," said Nancy.

"Why?" asked John.

"First of all, I don't think it is good for a couple to spend so much time together. I think we should keep our professional lives separate from our private ones. Another thing, I think you secretly want to be back with Ski and I don't blame you. I think you have developed a sense about each other and how the other works. That's important in our line of work. It helps solve cases, but more importantly, it could save your lives," concluded Nancy.

"I don't know what to say," said John.

"There's nothing you can say. I'm right and you know it. Case closed," said Nancy. With that she straddled John's body and sat on his legs. "Now what are you thinking?" she asked.

"When you started with 'Can we talk?' I was afraid it was going to be the 'Dear John' talk," said John.

"You're kidding, right?" asked Nancy.

"No," said John.

"How can you be such a macho guy outside and such a wimp inside? You're so insecure. I can see I have to change that," she said.

"Now, let me see, you want a 'Dear John'?' How about this?" asked Nancy. She rose up on her knees, still straddling John and mimed strumming a guitar. Then, mimicking the country singer guys thought she looked like, Shania Twain, she began to sing in a Western twang.

"Dear John, oh how I hate to write. Dear John, but I must let you know tonight. That my love for you has gone, like manure from the barn, and my heart is with another, Dear John." She raised her imaginary guitar over her head as if waiting for an audience to give a rousing ovation.

"Cute! Real cute," said John. He sat up, grabbed hold of her by the shoulders, and pulled her down on top of him. He took his hands and held her head inches from his face.

"How did you become so beautiful and smart?" he asked.

"It's a gift," she said, shaking her long mane of auburn red hair.

"I love you," said John.

"I love you too," she said giggling, expecting him to kiss her and let the love making begin. Instead, he continued to hold her face in his hands.

"What John? What's on your mind?" she asked, realizing he was getting serious and was trying to say something.

"Nancy, I really love you."

Now it was Nancy's turn. She took his face in her hands playfully.

"John, I know you love me. What's not to love?" she asked, kidding, trying to make light of what ever he was trying to say so it wouldn't be so hard.

"Do you love me?" asked John.

"Yes, John Michael, I love you," she said.

John became quiet again and Nancy began to fidget. Finally, he said what was on his mind.

"Nancy Mooney, will you marry me?"

Nancy shook her head and opened her eyes wide.

"Excuse me?" she asked.

"I said, will you marry me?"

Now it was Nancy's turn to freeze. After digesting what he'd said, she responded with the only answer she could think of at the time.

"Yes."

Chapter 20

Monday morning came too fast for John and Nancy. After John "popped" the question and Nancy said "yes," they'd made long, slow love. It was unlike many of their previous sessions, which tended toward the rough and wild side. This was sweeter, Nancy thought. It was like John was taking his time to be sure that this was the best and most memorable night she'd ever had. It was. The love making lasted over an hour and when they'd finished they were both fully satisfied, but exhausted.

After the alarm clock went off, they entertained the thought of calling in sick, but didn't. They thought about calling Betty and Ski, but didn't. Instead, they went to work. By ten in the morning, John and Nancy were in Brooklyn. They decided to speak to some of the neighbors of Christina Martinez hoping to get any information that might lead them to Bruce Krane.

The first person they spoke to was the elderly man who lived next door. He offered nothing more than he conveyed the first time they'd met. He looked at a "mug" shot of Bruce Krane that the detectives had gotten from records.

"Sure. I recognize that man. He used to come around here all the time. I think he was living with Miss Martinez for a while." The man, Mr. Sol Abraham, clearly didn't like or approve of the man living with the woman.

"She seemed like a friendly girl, but every once in a while she'd have people over that weren't very nice," he said. "These people weren't clean. They looked like they could use a bath, clean clothes. You know what I mean?" he asked.

John nodded his head.

"Did you happen to catch any of their names?" asked Nancy.

"No," said Mr. Abraham, rubbing his chin. "But maybe the girl two doors down might have. She used to visit with Christina a lot. Her name is Ivy Brown."

The detectives asked a few more questions, but could gather no further information from the old man.

Before leaving, Nancy asked, "How is you wife doing?" She remembered he was going to see her at the hospital.

"Oh, my poor wife. The doctors say it is just a matter of time. Tell me, is it a crime to pray for some one to die?" he asked, a tear welling up in his eye.

"Gee, Mr. Abraham, I'm sure it's not," said Nancy.

"I asked my rabbi the same question. He said only God could decide when someone should die. But I pray that He takes my beautiful Mildred soon. She has suffered so much over the last few months. I'll miss her, of course, but it's time for her suffering to end. She suffered enough as a little girl, you know. She was in a German concentration camps during the war. She saw her entire family taken away to the gas chambers. She was the only one to survive. She would have died too, if the Russians hadn't come and freed them when they did. Me, I was lucky. My parents fled Poland before the war began.

"No, I'll pray that God takes her. If that is wrong then you can come and lock me up," he said, holding his wrists out to the two detectives.

"Don't worry, Mr. Abraham. No one is going to want to lock you up or punish you. Not even God, I'm sure," said Nancy softly to the poor man.

John and Nancy walked down the block to the home of Ivy Brown. After a few knocks, the door was opened by a young, black woman.

Ivy Brown appeared to be in her late twenties. She wore sweats that had the letters "CCNY" across the front. They identified themselves as detectives and Ms. Brown invited them inside.

Yes, she knew Christy Martinez she told them. She said she sometimes used the name Martin when she danced. Ivy told them Christy was a topless dancer in some of the clubs in the area and out on Long Island. She didn't know Bruce Krane, but had seen him occasionally. She thought Christy had a biker guy who "handled" all her dancing gigs. She didn't know his name, but he was with the Hell's Angels.

"Great," thought John. "Someone else to consider." John knew that the gangs often controlled the dancers at the topless bars. It had been known in the past that girls sometimes tried to break off from their "man." When this happened, their "handlers" would beat them. It was a good lesson for any other girls who might be thinking of leaving. At times, the beatings went too far and their battered bodies would be found alongside a back road somewhere.

"Could this be one of those cases? Was it possible Krane was not the killer?" John wondered.

Having gotten little new information from Miss Brown, John gave her his card and they left. Once back in the car, John drove down to the water. He wanted to think and bounce some thoughts off his "partner." He drove to the docks in Sheepshead Bay and parked the car.

"Let's compare notes before we do anything else," said John. He turned sideways in the front seat so he could look at Nancy as they talked. As soon as he looked into her eyes, he forgot some ideas about the case that had been bouncing around in his head.

"Damn," he thought to himself. "This wouldn't happen if I was with Ski."

Nancy waited patiently for him to speak first.

"Let me say this out loud. Listen and tell me what you think, okay?" asked John.

"Okay by me," answered Nancy.

"Okay. We have two women, both killed by a knife wound to the abdomen. The fact they were killed that way means something. Most people using a knife would want to stab and get out. Strike for the heart. Slit the throat. Kill the victim. It's like this guy is trying to do more than kill these women. Next, both women were acquaintances of Bruce Krane. Bruce Krane may have fathered children with them. He has an arrest record, can be mean, and has disappeared since the murders. Does that about sum it up?" asked John.

"My turn?" asked Nancy with a smile.

"Be my guest," said John.

"Both women had children, but neither woman is raising the child. Krane is connected to them. Both women worked at topless bars. We know one victim was killed outside a "Giggi's" where she worked. Her friend told us she'd worked as a dancer. And speaking of which, we don't know exactly where she was killed, only where her body was found. Did the other victim, Martinez, work at a place near where she was killed? That could be important," concluded Nancy.

"Good. Good points," said John, nodding his head. Without saying a word, John started the engine and swung back out onto the main road.

"Where are we going?" asked Nancy.

"Back to where the Martinez woman was found. The beach," said John.

They arrived at the water front and parked near the restaurant where they'd had dinner the night the victim was discovered. John got out of the car, as did Nancy, and they looked around. John started walking towards the restaurant's entrance.

"They won't be open yet," said Nancy.

"Maybe some of the help is in already." John went up to the front door and tried it. It was locked. He pressed his head against the glass and shielded the sunlight with his hand to see inside. In the back, he could see two men working. He tapped on the glass, but neither man looked up.

Nancy followed the outside deck around to the side. She found a side door standing open. She took her ID out of her pocket book and stepped inside. She immediately saw why neither man heard John's feeble tapping on the glass. They both wore ear phones over their heads. From several feet away, she could still hear a cacophony of sounds coming from the tiny ear pieces. They were attached to Walkman-type tape players. One was apparently listening to Latin music, the other to what sounded like a rap beat.

"Excuse me! Excuse me!" she yelled.

Neither turned. Finally, she walked up behind the black man and touched his shoulder. He nearly jumped out of his skin. He actually rose two feet in the air, turned partially towards her, and slipped on the wet wooden floor he'd been mopping.

"Sorry," said Nancy, holding her hands, palms up at her side.

The other worker must have seen her seconds coming because he wasn't frightened. Instead, he laughed hysterically at his co worker on the floor.

"Man, you must have crapped in your pants," he said as he removed his earphones and laughed heartily.

The other worker sat on the damp floor, a mean scowl on his face.

"What the hell you doing, coming in here when my back's turned? You could have given me a heart attack. Can't you see the place is closed?" he asked, getting up off the floor.

By his movements, Nancy could see nothing more than his ego had been hurt.

While this was going on, John had found his way around the side of the place and entered through the opened door. He reached inside his shirt and removed his gold badge to show them he was a cop also.

"Everyone okay in here?" he asked. The one listening to the rap music had removed his head set and was brushing his pants off.

"We're detectives with the NYPD. We're here investigating a murder that may have occurred here the other night. Either of you guys working when that woman was pulled from the ocean?," asked Nancy.

At first both workers looked at each other, having nothing to say. Then the "rapper" admitted he was. He told them he'd worked bussing tables that day and was helping out in the kitchen when the police started to arrive. Nancy produced a picture of the Martinez woman and asked him to look at it.

"Ever see her before?" asked John. The "rapper" shook his head no. The other worker reached over and took the picture. He looked at it a moment and handed it back to John.

"Well?" asked John.

"Yeah, I seen her," admitted the Latino music man.

"In here?" asked John.

"Not in here. Down the street," he said.

"Where down the street?" asked John, a frustrated look across his face.

They seemed to be incapable of expressing a complete thought. They would never elaborated. It was like pulling teeth to get information out of them.

"The bar down the street."

"What's the name of the bar?"

"It's called Bare Fortune."

"You mean bear as in B-E-A-R?"

"No. I mean bare as in N-A-K-E-D," replied the Latino.

"A smart ass," thought John. "Now don't get pissed at him and cause him to clam up," he warned himself.

"This is a topless bar, right?" he asked.

"Very good, man. Yeah, a topless bar," replied the Latino sarcastically.

Nancy could see John was losing his cool and decided to step in.

"Did she work there? Was she a waitress, a dancer?" asked Nancy.

Distracting the Latino and breaking the growing tension, Nancy saw that he seemed to relax.

"Yeah, she danced there once or twice a week. She was good," he said, his eyes rising to the ceiling.

Nancy could almost see him remembering the girl dancing on the stage.

"What's your name?" she asked.

"Miguel," he said.

"Well, Miguel, were you a regular there?" asked Nancy.

"No, not a regular. I'd only go about three or four times a week," he answered.

"I wonder what he'd consider a regular? Probably someone who slept there," she thought. Nancy turned to John.

"You got the guy's picture handy?" asked Nancy.

John removed the picture of Bruce Krane from inside his jacket.

"Does he look familiar, to either of you?" she asked, passing it first to Miguel, then to the "rapper."

"No, I never seen him before," said Miguel quickly, but then he took another look at the picture.

"Wait a minute. Yeah, I seen him there once or twice. He always sat at the bar. Never sat at a table up near where the dancers worked," replied Miguel.

"Did you ever see him with the woman?" asked Nancy.

"Naw, he'd stay at the bar. I ain't never seen them together though," he answered.

"Do you remember the last time you saw either of them there?" continued Nancy.

"About a week ago," he said.

"Do you think it was the night her body was found?" asked Nancy.

"When was that?" asked Miguel. She told him the date.

"No, I was off that night. My kid sister was having a baby at the hospital."

"Which one?" asked John.

"Which sister? Oh, you mean hospital, right? Coney Island Hospital. It's just down the block. The whole family was there except for the father," added Miguel.

"Who is the father?" asked John.

"Ricky, he's in jail. But he'll be getting out soon. He's going to marry my sister when he gets out. Do the right thing, or else," concluded Miguel, punching his right fist into his open left palm.

The two detectives asked a few more questions but got nothing of interest. Nancy apologized to the "rapper" for scaring him.

"I wasn't scared, lady. You just surprised me, that's all," he said defensively. They gave both workers business cards and asked them to call them if they remembered or heard anything new.

As they were leaving, Miguel yelled after them, "Hey, is there a reward?"

"The only reward is knowing you've been a good citizen," said John.

"Shit," said Miguel and spit on the floor.

"Hey, I just cleaned there," warned the "rapper."

Once in the car, John said to Nancy, "You feel like topless for lunch?"

"What the hell. If that's what it takes to get you in the mood, I'm game," she said with a smirk.

They drove about two and a half blocks before coming to the "Bare Fortune" topless bar. As they were getting out of their car, two men in business suits were strode purposefully towards the bar's entrance. They appeared to be headed for a "liquid" lunch and some ogling. Taking one look at Nancy and John getting out of their "unmarked" car, they instantly recognized they were cops. The "suits" simultaneously turned around and headed back towards their car. They got back into their car and drove off.

"Was it something I said?" asked Nancy.

"Come on," said John with a grin.

They walked into the dimly lit building and headed towards the bar. John walked up to the bartender and "flashed" his badge. Without a word, John produced a picture of Ms. Martinez and slid it across the surface of the bar.

"You know her?" asked John.

"No," replied the bartender without even looking at it. John reached across the top of the bar, grabbed a hold of the man's shirt, and pulled him half way across the bar top.

"Do I have to close the place and take you down to the precinct, or are you going to look at the picture?" asked John.

He held the man in his grip for a moment before releasing his hold. This time the bartender studied the picture more carefully.

"Yeah, I know her. It's Christy Martin. She used to dance here," he said, smoothing the front of his shirt and tucking the ends into his pants.

"Used to?" asked John.

"Used to, as in past. She was killed last week," he said.

"How do you know she was killed?" asked John.

"Everyone knows what happened. Hell, they pulled her from the ocean down in front of that seafood restaurant. I heard she'd been slit up the middle," was his response.

"What's your name?" asked Nancy.

"Jimmy. Jimmy Brady," he said.

"Okay, Jimmy. What can you tell us about Ms. Martinez?" she asked.

"Christy was one of our dancers. She worked the circuit. You know, floated from one place to another, here, out on the Island. She was a good dancer. She must have taken dancing lessons at one time because she knew how to move her body. Not like some of the other stiffs we get in here. She'd worked the night she was killed. Left around mid night, I guess," added Jimmy.

"Did she leave with anyone that night?" asked John.

"Yeah, I think a couple of the other girls may have left about that time too. I'm not sure," added Jimmy.

"Did you notice if any of the customers were, maybe overly interested in Ms. Martinez?" Nancy queried.

"No. Wait. Yeah. There was this one guy. Been here a few times; sat right over there," pointing to a side table. "The table by the fire exit. He acted like it was his private table. We almost had a fight one night when he ordered some guys to give up the table. I offered the guys a free drink and they moved without a hassle. The guy used to watch Christy. When she was finished he'd leave. Never bothered with the other girls, just Christy," said the bar tender.

"Did he leave with her?" asked Nancy as she showed him a picture.

"That the guy" asked John. The bar tender looked at the picture of Bruce Krane.

"Nope," he said. John looked at Nancy.

"Are you sure? Take another look," ordered John.

"I said no. This guy," the bartender said, poking his finger at the picture of Krane, "he was a friend of hers. But he always sat at the bar, never up close. He was quiet, never any trouble, ya know? But he looked like you didn't want any trouble from him either. Know what I mean? A tough guy," added Jimmy.

"Did Miss Martinez act like she was afraid of this guy?" referring to Bruce Krane asked Nancy.

"I said they were friends. She'd sit with him between sets. Some nights they'd leave together."

"Was he here the night she was killed?" asked Nancy.

"Nope. I think they must have split up. He stopped coming around about a week before she was murdered. I asked Christy what happened but she just shook her head," Jimmy answered.

"Do you mind if we talk to the girls?" asked John.

"Help yourself. Most of them are in the back. Come on, I'll show you the way," offered Jimmy.

Even though it wasn't even lunch time yet, about half the tables were occupied in the bar. Most were men in suits, nursing their drinks, staring at the dancers.

As Jimmy walked towards the other end of the bar, he called to one of the two waitresses working the room.

"Gail, cover the bar for a minute. I've got to go in the back," said the bar tender.

"Okay, Jimmy," replied the waitress.

John and Nancy followed Jimmy down a narrow hallway to the rear of the building. He opened a door without knocking, entered, and then held it wide for the two detectives to join him. John allowed Nancy to go first. Once inside they found a crowded changing room where the girls adjusted their make up and put on their costumes. John's mouth almost fell open.

There were about six or seven women, attractive, but in a hard-looking way, gathered in the small dressing room. They were all in various stages of dress. Or rather, undress. Some were trying to catch the best light from four light bulbs set on the side of a smoky mirror. None of the girls bothered to look up when the bartender walked into the room. John saw that the girls seemed to range in age from the early twenties to mid forties. The youngest seemed to be the least modest and most brazen. She was totally naked and sat on a wooden chair. She had her legs crossed and was applying polish to her toe nails. She made no attempt to conceal her body.

John caught or sensed Nancy's glare on the back of his neck. He looked away, not knowing where to place his eyes without getting into trouble with his partner.

"Ski would never make me feel like this," he thought.

"Ladies, these here are two detectives. They're looking into Christy's murder last week," said Jimmy.

"Fuck you," said one of the older women. Jimmy's face turned red.

"They're all yours. I'll be out front," said the bartender as he left.

"We'll try not to take up too much of your time, ladies," said Nancy trying to get their attention.

"Like he said, we're here concerning the murder of Christina Martinez, or Christy Martin, as some of you may have known her. We know she danced here. What we need is any information you may have concerning men who she may have hung around, shown an interest in her. My partner has a picture he'd like you to look at. If he looks familiar, we'd like to know," said Nancy in her most professional manner. All the naked flesh was beginning to bother Nancy as well.

John passed the picture to the first woman and smiled. She smiled back. She was a tall, dark skinned Latino woman. Nancy immediately noticed that she'd probably had implants. She also noticed that John was noticing too.

"You are so dead," she thought to herself.

As John passed the picture from one to the other, each tried, in their own way, to get a "rise" out of John. However, two of the women seemed to be more interested in Nancy.

One, a petite redhead, came over to her and said, "Hi! My name's Peaches. What's your's?" as she stroked her fingers across Nancy's arm.

Nancy felt a slight shiver run up her spine. Her eye lids fluttered involuntarily. Peaches smiled and moved closer, pressing her bare breast against Nancy's side. Nancy was so flustered she didn't know what to say. Then she heard John say,

"Well, thank you, ladies. You have my card. If you think of anything, please call," he said.

"And you know where to find us," said one of the dancers. As they were about to leave one of the ladies called out to them.

"Wait a minute. I remember that night. Christy had danced that night. She was good. She knew how to move. The guys loved her. I guess with that blonde wig she wore, they thought of her as the girl next door. You know, the "all-American" type, all sweetness and goodness. I thought she was sexier with her own long, dark hair, but then, to each his own," she commented.

"What about that night? See anyone leave with her?" asked Nancy.

"Not exactly. She had done her sets. One guy gave her a fifty," she said.

"How do you know?" asked John.

"In between dances we usually cruise the room. You know, get guys to buy us a drink. Nothing wrong with that, is there?' she asked, suddenly wondering if she'd done something illegal.

"Skip it. Now what about that night?" demanded John.

"Okay, okay. Well, I walked past this table where this guy was sitting by himself. He handed me a fifty and asked me to put it into her G-string. I told him he could do it himself, but he said he was too shy."

"And?" asked John impatiently.

"I did it," she replied.

"What did Christy do?" asked Nancy.

"Nothing. She waved and nodded to him, that's all," she added.

"What about after work, anything?" asked Nancy.

"We left together, no men if you're wondering," she said.

"I remember we walked outside. But I take the subway so I left Christy. She use to walk home by herself. She doesn't live that far from here."

"And you didn't see anyone walk out when you left?" asked John.

"I told you, no," she said, raising her voice. Her eyes began to get glassy and a tear slipped down her cheek.

"God, if only we'd stayed together that night, maybe she'd still be alive," she said, dabbing her eye with a tissue. Then she looked up, eyes wide.

"Wait a minute. I remember now. I was walking in the other direction, away from Christy, when I heard her say something. I thought she was calling to me. I remember turning and I saw her talking to someone down the block. It was dark but it was a man. I think he was wearing a raincoat, but I'm not sure. He was too far for me to see his face, but he was taller than Christy, maybe five ten, six feet, I'd guess. She was talking as if she knew him. I figured it was her boy friend hitting her up for money. I thought nothing of it.

"But then the other day we were talking about her murder. I mentioned the guy under the street light and how it might have been her old boy friend, Bruce. But one of the girls remembered Christy saying she wasn't supporting him anymore because he was out of town or something. I wish I'd gotten a look at that guy. Do you think he could have been the killer?" she asked.

"It may have been," said Nancy. She reached into her pocketbook and withdrew a picture of Bruce Krane. "Are you sure this wasn't the guy?"

The dancer looked at it and shook her head.

"No, that's her old boyfriend. I don't think it was him."

"How can you be sure?" asked John.

"The way Christy acted was like the way she acted when she's trying to sell drinks or get a guy to buy a lap dance, ya know?" she asked.

"No. I don't know," said John, somewhat indignantly.

Nancy smiled at his reaction.

After getting the names and addresses of all the girls in the room, they prepared to leave.

"Thanks for the information. It may help. If you hear anything else that you think might be helpful, call me," said John.

"Can I call you even if I don't have anything else?" flirted one of the girls.

John smiled and turned to open the door to leave the dressing room. He called back to Nancy.

"You coming?"

"Well, are you coming, Sweetie?" asked Peaches, still standing very close to Nancy. Peaches was crowding her space and it was making Nancy uncomfortable. Yet she was drawn to this woman.

"Oh, yeah," said Nancy.

They stepped out into the hall and before the door closed heard the women laughing and making "off-color" comments about both of them.

"A lot of hormones rushing around in there," said John.

John took Nancy's elbow and led her to the door.

He waved to the bartender on the way out and walked towards the car.

When they got to their car John noticed that Nancy hadn't said anything, so he turned to look at her. Her cheeks were red.

"You okay?" he asked.

"Yeah," she said, somewhat in a daze. Nancy continued to walk, but took several deep breaths as she did.

"John, I've got to ask you a serious question. Do you think I could be a lesbian?"

"What? Where is that coming from? You are definitely one-hundred-percent heterosexual."

"It's just that I felt . . . I don't know . . . kind of excited by that one, Peaches."

"She exudes a lot of heat. She was just messing with you. That's what they do. They can go either way I guess. But not you," he added emphatically.

On the return trip back to the squad room neither said a word. Both were lost in their own thoughts.

Chapter 21

Detective Straub was busy on the telephone talking to the "Feds" concerning Bruce Krane. Nancy Mooney sat at her desk looking through Christina Martinez's notebook for the tenth time.

"Is there something in here that I should be seeing?" she asked herself.

She went to the beginning of the small book and began turning the pages, one at a time.

"Pick up things at the cleaners. Sanitary pads, lipstick. Call Mom about Julio, see if she has a few bucks for the weekend. Dance at The Living room. Call Bruce. Call Foster Care," were some of the entries.

"Not much here," she thought.

She kept turning pages until she came to the day before Christina's body was found. "Dance at Bare Fortune."

"What happened that day, Christina?" she wondered.

For Christina Martinez's the last day in her short life had started out bad and gone down hill from there. She'd been required to go into the city to be interviewed by a Foster Care worker concerning her son. This was the first time "Foster Care" had requested an interview.

All her previous contacts concerning her son had been through her welfare case worker. Any papers she had to sign were done through her. She was concerned that they were going to cut the money off for Foster Care.

Christina knew her mother wouldn't keep her son if the money stopped. Christina loved her son, Julio, but she wasn't ready to change her lifestyle to take care of him.

Christina got dressed and took the subway, changing trains when necessary, and arriving five minutes early for her appointment. The worker had her wait over half an hour. It turned out all they wanted was for her to fill out some federal forms. She didn't know why they couldn't mail them to her, but she kept her feelings to herself. The last thing she wanted to do was to get this woman "pissed off" at her. She knew the worker had the power.

Once the papers had been signed, she rushed out of the building and down the block to the stairs leading down to the subway. She rode the old, crowded trains back to Brooklyn and walked the few blocks to her apartment. When Christina got home, she was in a bad mood. Besides having wasted half the day running into the city, now she had a splitting headache. She knew what the problem was, she needed some "crack." Unfortunately, there was none in the apartment and she was short on cash. She already owed money to her dealer, so she couldn't call him. She'd just have to "tough it out" until after work. She'd have the money then.

She took two aspirins and laid down on her bed. In two hours she had to be at the Bare Fortune. She was scheduled to dance from four until twelve. She set the alarm for three and closed her eyes.

Christina Martinez, or Christy Martin, as she was known around the topless bar circuit, believed she had only one resource worth anything, her body. She tried to take care of herself, watched her weight, exercised on a fairly regular basis. She'd taken dance classes as a teen and had developed new moves that drove the customers wild. They'd rewarded her with five and ten dollar bills which they stuck down her G-string. She rarely got singles like most of the other girls. When not dancing, she'd cruise the patrons trying to pick up a few "lap" dances. They were usually good for an extra fifty, maybe a hundred bucks.

While Christina readied herself for work, a man sat in a large car outside her apartment. He was slumped down in the driver's seat; parked only a short distance from her front door. When he first glanced at his watch, it was a little before two. He knew from observing her that she'd be leaving by three to go to one of the topless bars where she worked. Not knowing which one she was scheduled for tonight, he was forced to sit and wait. The day had turned cold and the windows were fogging up from his breath. He cracked the side window and wiped the inside of the front windshield with the palm of his hand. He didn't mind waiting. It was all part of the hunt, being patient. He'd studied her carefully. He, knew all about her. This one would give him great satisfaction.

"I am a rock. I am an island," he softly sang to himself. The words of the old Simon and Garfunkel song seemed to fit him to a "T." He rarely thought of his past, growing up in a family that had been a sham.

But from time to time his mind would drift to the events that brought him to this spot on this street. He allowed his memory to play out like a movie reel.

The day he'd left home, he had no idea where or what he was going to do with his life. The long drive from Florida to New York had given him time to think. He wondered if his real mother was actually dead or was it a lie also. He was going to find his mother, living or dead, get some answers, and some how make her pay for what she'd done to him. He replayed events from his past over and over in his mind.

He concluded his "real" mother had "abandoned" him; that the people he thought were his parents had deceived him. The pastor of his church, a man of God, had molested him. He recalled the relief he'd felt when he'd pushed his pastor down the basement stairs to his death. He felt it was justified, that he had it coming to him. It was as if God had guided him, given him the strength to do what needed to be done. And finally, his mother had returned to seduce him. He remembered how she looked. The light blonde hair and that body. His emotions swung from lust to loathing and it served only to enrage him all the more.

The first hundred miles of his journey was a blur. He'd been crying off so hard sometimes that he wondered how he managed to keep the car under control. Eventually the tears stopped and his sorrow was replaced with hatred. The anger rose in him like molten lava from a volcano. At one point his fury was so strong that he pulled over to the side of the interstate, gotten out of the car, his entire body trembling, overcome with rage. So strong was his anger that it squeezed his stomach like a vise, causing him to throw up on the side of the road. The very act of regurgitating seemed to rid him of some of the pain and helped clear his mind.

It was like he'd rid his body of a poison that had been eating away at him. Unfortunately, the poison had already done its harm. It had affected his outlook on life and attitude towards people, women in particular. The tiny seed of a plan formed in his mind as he got back into his car, a relatively new Caddy Deville and continued north.

He resumed driving until fatigue overcame him. Ahead he saw the neon "Vacancy" sign flashing at a motel on the interstate. Exiting the parkway, he drove up to the motel office, registered, and went to his room. He shed his clothes and lay naked upon the battered bed. In time he drifted off to sleep. However, his sleep was marred by nightmares. Flashes of past events passed through his mind.

The next morning he awoke shortly before sunrise. Took a shower and changed into fresh clothes. He walked over to the motel office, paid his bill in cash, and picked up the complimentary cup of steaming coffee and soft roll. As he walked through the parking lot towards his car, he took a deep breath of the cool morning air. A smile formed on his face. It felt good to be out on his own.

He had just closed the driver's side door when he saw a figure leaving the room two doors down from his. The person moved furtively, glancing from side to side, hunched over, carrying something in his arms.

He watched as the man moved towards a row of Dumpsters standing at the side of the motel. By his movements, he guessed he was young, a teenager maybe. He seemed frightened, nervous. He kept looking over his shoulder. He approached one of the large, steel bins. Again, looking quickly from side to side and satisfied he was not being observed, he quickly tossed the bundle he'd been carrying into the open container.

He started to leave, then turned and looked inside. He stood on his tip toes, peering inside the garbage bin. Finally, he turned and walked back to his room.

His curiosity piqued, the traveler continued to watch and wait. After a few minutes, the same young man came out of the room and got into a car. As he drove off, the motel room door opened and a girl stood in the doorway. She was crying and yelling something, but the man didn't appear to hear her. He'd already reached the entrance ramp of the interstate. The girl stomped back inside the motel room and slammed the door behind her.

Inquisitive, the traveler shut off the car and walked over to the garbage container where the man had placed the bundle. Stretching up on his toes, he looked inside. At first all he saw were green garbage bags. Then he spotted the towel. It was a large motel bath towel. It appeared stained with something. He grabbed a corner of the towel and lifted it. As he did he could feel something heavy inside. As he continued to lift the end of the towel an object, wrapped inside, rolled out into the garbage. It was a newborn baby.

Its skin was wet and seemed to be partially covered in some kind of waxy or cream substance. It had dark hair that was plastered down against its small skull. The umbilical cord hung, twisted around one leg. He nudged the infant with his finger. It didn't move. He looked closer at the newborn's face. It was bluish in color and something appeared to be stuffed in its mouth. It was a big, wad of toilet paper. The infant was dead.

He was moved by compassion for this little soul. Reaching under it, he grabbed the motel towel that still covered part of the body. Carefully, delicately, he lifted the lifeless body out of the filth. As he cradled it in his arms he saw it was a boy. Tears welled up in his eyes and he began to cry.

He carried the bundle back to his car, placed it on the passenger's seat, and closed the door. He stood there in the chill air, steam coming from his mouth. He walked around to the other side of the car and got in. He sat there, wondering what to do next.

"This was awful," he thought. "Why would they do it?"

He had to find out. He pushed open his door and started to slide out, but something caught on the edge of his seat. It was the handle of his hunting knife, the blade tucked down into its leather holder. The gift from his "supposed" father was always on his belt. He shifted to one side and moved the handle, freeing him from the material.

He nervously walked towards the motel door, not knowing what he was going to do, not knowing what to expect. Tapping tentatively at first, he got no response. Then he pounded his fist on the wooden door. After a moment, the door swung open.

"Oh Lyle, you came back," she started to say, but stopped upon seeing a stranger there. She wore a ski coat, opened in the front, that revealed a nightgown underneath. She was barefoot.

"Who are you?" she asked, her lips trembling.

He didn't respond to her question. He stood, staring at her. His eyes bore into her eyes.

Standing before him, was a young girl, "maybe fourteen," he guessed. She was pretty, had blonde hair, loosely tied back in a pony tail. Her eyes were red and swollen, with dark circles beneath. She reminded him of someone from his past. Suddenly, his mind was filled with a flurry of visions from his past. He felt rage rise up within him, an fury that was all consuming.

"Why? Why did you do it to me?" he screamed.

She looked at him, not comprehending what he was talking about.

"How could you?" he yelled.

The girl stood staring, as if in a daze.

"How could you? Your own son? How could you abandon me like that?"

Fear and confusion gripped her. She saw the fire in the stranger's eyes, his nostrils flared, spittle fly from his mouth. She moved slowly back into the room. He followed.

"Who is he? Where did he come from? Was he going to tell the police, my parents?" she thought.

As she began to comprehend the danger, he moved closer to her. She retreated until the back of her legs hit the bed. She teetered backwards, but managed to stop herself from falling. Finally, regaining her wits, she was about to tell him to get out, to scream for help. But before she could open her mouth he slapped her across the face. Her cheek stung. Tears welled up in her eyes. She brought her hands up to protect herself, when she saw light flash off something in his hand.

Before she could respond, the stranger thrust something into the pit of her stomach. The pain was extreme, her stomach still sore from child birth. Then she felt a piercing, burning sensation move up her stomach. Just as suddenly, the man moved back away from her. She looked down at the object in his hand.

It was a knife. A large, sharp hunting knife. The pain in her stomach grew worse. It brought back the memory of the labor pains she'd endured just a few hours earlier. She groaned and clutched her stomach, sliding down onto the floor next to the bed. She felt warm, sticky fluid on her open hands and saw it was her blood. She looked up at the man, bewilderment on her face.

"Who are you? Why are you doing this to me?" she tried to speak, but couldn't.

She looked into the man's face. He was nice looking, not much older than herself. He was even smiling at her. But his eyes, his eyes were cold as he stepped back away from her. She felt her head spinning. She couldn't focus on what was happening. The room seemed to be getting darker. The pain was still there, but not as severe. She felt cold and began to shiver in spite of the fact she wore her winter coat. As she sat on the worn, motel carpet, her head tilted to the right, she felt herself sliding over onto her side. She could tell the man was saying something, but wasn't sure what it was. For some strange reason she felt these words were important, might explain what had just happened. But the room began to spin before her eyes, sounds grew dim, and flashes of bright light appeared before her eyes. Gradually, the light grew steady. The light seemed to hold the promise of warmth and protection.

She continued to stare at the light, all else unseen by her eyes despite their open gaze.

He watched her gasping for breath, pink, foaming bubbles forming on her lips. Blood sprayed from her mid-section covering the front of his shirt.

"There, you bitch. That's for what you did. You didn't think you'd get away with it, did you?" he asked.

Afterwards he took his time, washing his hands and knife in the bathroom sink. Noticing his shirt was splattered with blood, he removed it, rolled it into a ball and carried it out to the car. He threw his wadded up shirt, the towel and the knife onto the floor in the back of his car. He drove out of the motel parking lot, got onto the interstate, and headed north. After a few hours, he exited the parkway, drove a few miles until he came upon a dirt road. Bouncing over ruts and occasionally scraping the bottom of the car on rocks he eventually came to a secluded area. Before exiting the car he grabbed his knife off the car floor and the bundle from the trunk, carrying it to the edge of the field. Using his hunting knife and his hands, he dug a shallow grave and gently placed the baby's body in the bottom. He looked down at the small, innocent figure beneath him. A tear formed in his eye and dropped onto the infants face. After carefully covering its face with part of the towel he slowly pushed the loose soil back over the bundle and patted it down. He knelt beside the grave and said a silent prayer for the soul of the infant. Tears ran from his eyes and down his cheeks. After a few moments he rose from the spot and walked back towards his car. Using the back of his hands he wiped tears from his faces. Walking back to the car he opened the trunk and removed an old rag. He wiped the tears and mud from his face and hands. Then he removed the mud from the blade and closed the knife. He returned the knife to a leather sheath and placed it back inside his knapsack.

He never returned to that spot, but every now and then, like now, the memory of that morning returned to him.

Several weeks later, while sitting in his New York apartment, he'd seen an article in the *Daily News*. It spoke of the murder of a girl by her boyfriend, Lyle Delaney. He was eighteen. She was sixteen. The police said she'd recently given birth to a child, but no infant was ever found. Naturally, the boy proclaimed his innocence.

"Innocent!" he'd thought. "How could he think of himself as innocent after killing his own son?" Despite checking the papers from time to time, there was never any more information about the case. That was almost two years ago.

A lot had happened since then. He had found an apartment, gotten a job, and continued to search for answers to why his mother abandoned him. The hatred was always there, just under the surface and he was resolved to see she was punished. His job gave him access to all sorts of information. He was able to verify that his mother was, in fact, dead. While unable to exact revenge on her for what she'd done, he set his mission in life to locating others who committed the same, selfish act. On them he rendered judgment and sentence. He found one "sinner," a woman who'd "abandoned" her son, working in a bar in the Bronx. He'd seen to it that she paid for "deserting" her son.

Like the act at the motel, the feeling of satisfaction overwhelmed him afterwards, but this soon passed. His actions brought only temporary respite before the rage returned.

Then he'd encountered Christy Martinez. She'd appeared one day in the building where he worked. She was slim and, blonde, like he remembered his mother.

He overheard the caseworker talking to her. He discovered that she had a son, a son in foster care. The rest of the hunt was easy. As if acting on instinct, he sought out her case record and studied her file. Sure enough, like his mother, the girl in the motel and the one in the parking lot in the Bronx, she too had abandoned her son. Now she was living a sinful life, carousing with men, using drugs, ignoring her duties as a mother. That would all end. He decide that she would pay for it.

Chapter 22

The alarm next to Christina's bed startled her out of a sound sleep.

"Oh, I'd love to stay in bed all day and sleep right through until tomorrow," she thought as she stretched her arms over her head. But sleeping didn't pay the rent. She reluctantly got out of bed and went into the shower. After toweling herself off, she felt a little more alert and prepared for the night ahead.

She sat at her vanity and carefully applied her makeup. She made a point of applying some to her legs and arms, trying to conceal her "track" marks. Some of the other dancers had tracks, but resorted to tattoos to conceal them. Oddly, Christina hated the thought of getting a tattoo. She didn't like the idea of permanently marking up her body. Track marks didn't count. After applying the body make up she turned to her face. She'd noticed it seemed to be taking longer to get the desired results these days.

"Either you're slowing down or your getting old," she said to herself in the mirror. She finished "putting her face on," then brushed her hair and, with a few well-placed pins, secured it up in the back.

Next she took the long, blonde wig off its Styrofoam head and slipped it on. Shaking her head from side to side, she allowed it to fall into place. With her dark complexion and the wig she thought she looked like one of the babes on "*Baywatch*," a popular TV show. She knew the look drove the guys wild. She could almost read their minds as they watched her dance. They pictured her as the teenager in high school they admired from afar so many years ago.

Going into her closet, she pulled out two long black dresses, each with a slit that ran up the side to her hip. She placed a long plastic bag over them and laid them on her bed. Next, she grabbed the jumper she wore during one of her routines. With the blonde wig pulled into a pony tail, she looked like the "all-American" girl. She placed it with the dresses. Finally, she threw a couple of clean G-strings and some costume jewelry into a small tote bag, along with a pair of spiked high heels. After putting on a pair of dungarees, a red, loose-fitting sweater, and black cowboy boots, she was ready to head off to work. As she opened the door leading to the street, she felt the chilly air. Going back inside, she grabbed a leather coat and put it on. Now she was ready.

Down the block the man still sat, watching. He saw her leave the house and start walking down the street. He waited for her to get about two blocks away before starting up the car. As he pulled away from the curb he saw her dart across the street to the other side. He checked his mirror to make sure there wasn't anyone behind him, especially cops, and drove slowly down the block. As he grew closer he watched her enter a local bar, "the Bare Fortune."

"So that's where you'll be tonight, flaunting yourself," he said to himself. He continued down the block and turned left at the next main intersection. He had time to grab a bite to eat before taking care of business.

At first the night dragged for Christina. There weren't many customers and the tips were poor. Finally, around six the crowd began to pick up. There were the usual assortment of blue collar workers and suits in the room. She noticed one or two women sitting at tables by themselves. Christina knew they were either lesbians or prostitutes looking to pick up a horny customer. The girls didn't like the competition, but the management didn't care as long as they bought drinks, didn't cause any trouble, and took their business outside. Every so often one of the prostitutes would get caught performing tricks of the trade in the men's room with a customer. This was definitely considered a taboo. All they needed was for an undercover cop to catch this going on and they'd close the place down.

There was the usual complement of six dancers tonight. They'd go on stage for ten minutes and then be off for fifty. What they did during that fifty was their own business.

In the rear of the bar was an area where private "lap dances" were held. The girls would cruise the bar in between dancing. The trick was to get a guy to agree to come into the back where for fifty bucks they get a glass of watered down Champagne and a dance. The guy or "John" as the girls called them were made to sit while a girl danced and slid her body up and down his. The guys were forbidden to touch the girls themselves. Sometimes the girls let the "John" kiss them in various places, but that was all. A bouncer stood in the archway between the main room and back cubicles to see that things didn't get out of hand. The fifty was split between the house and the girls.

Anything the girls coaxed out of the customer while doing the lap dance was their's to keep. On a good night, a girl could pick up an extra seven, eight hundred dollars doing this. That was in addition to tips they got while dancing.

There was no salary paid to the girls by the house. The girls were strictly "outside" contractors, self employed. There was no record kept and everything was cash. The IRS never got its cut.

So, if these girls could make such good money, why were they still doing it at forty years of age? Why were they living in small run down apartments? Why did they do it four, five times a week?

Simple. Expensive life style. Most of the girls either had drug habits or a man who drained them of most of their earnings. In Christina's case, she had both. She liked her crake cocaine, and occasionally heroin. She also had a boy friend, Bruce Krane, who managed to squeeze money out of her. But for now he was out of the picture. He'd left on a "business trip," according to one of his buddies. They said they didn't expect him back for a while so that meant a few extra bucks for her.

By eleven o'clock, Christina had gotten a few customers to "spring" for a private dance. She figured she'd picked up about three hundred dollars so far. One more score and she'd consider it a good night. When Christina was on the platform "dancing," she usually spaced out on the music, barely noticing the customers.

But tonight she needed money and made a point of making eye contact with the few men in the bar. She caught their gaze and read their desire. Swaying to the music, she undulated her body, revealing parts and movements some men only saw in their dreams.

So, when she'd finish her number, she'd stroll the room soliciting "watered-down" drinks and lap dances from the panting "jerks," as she called them. Tonight, while dancing she noticed a guy sitting at a table off to one side. He was watching her very closely. She made a point of covering that side of the stage as much as possible. "This could be sucker number four and the end," she thought. Unfortunately, she was prophetically correct.

Christina finished her routine. She picked up the bills that had been thrown on the dance floor or stuck inside her G-string by customers sitting ring side. She left the stage and went behind the bar, where she kept her pocketbook. She shoved the bills inside and closed the clasp. After she returned it to the shelf under the bar, she looked over to the table where the guy had been sitting. He was gone.

"Shit," she thought. Having lost what she thought was her next customer, she strolled up and down the bar flirting with customers. All she wore was the G-string and a smile. She'd deliberately rub her breasts against the guy's arm or back, until she got his attention.

If she couldn't get them to join her for a lap dance, she'd try to get them to buy her a drink. The girls always ordered "the best Champagne" at ten dollars a glass. The bar tender gave them ginger ale and they split the price of the drink.

If anyone criticized her life she'd say, "Hey, a girl's got to make a living," and give them a cold look that would force them to back off.

By midnight, the number of dancers outweighed the number of customers, so some of the girls decided to call it a night. Christina was one of them. The management didn't mind if they left early, as long as a few dancers remained to entertain the stragglers. These dancers were usually the older women. They had to wait until the younger, better looking girls left and the guys were drunk. Then it was the "seniors" turn to try to get a lap dance out of them.

"Survival of the fittest," was the motto and it was true.

Christina gathered up her things and grabbed her bag from under the bar. She threw two twenties at the bartender and headed out the door. The smart girls knew to take care of the bartenders because they could keep an eye out for them. They'd steer customers their way or warn them when there were any Vice cops in the place. As she stepped outside she pulled the collar up around her ears. One of the other girls joined her on the way out. They talked about heading off to a diner for some food but it was too cold and Christy was beat. Christina waved good night and started walking down the dark street towards her place. As she approached a street light, a man called to her from the shadows. At first he startled her, then she recognized him from the bar. He was the one at the table off to the side.

"Screw you. No freebies," she thought to herself and continued walking.

"Wait, please," he said, as he quickened his pace to catch up to her.

"What do you want?" she asked.

"I'm sorry, I didn't mean to startle you," he said.

"Hmm, he has a pleasant smile. Young but cute," she thought as she stopped.

"I saw you dance inside. You may have noticed me, I was sitting at the table on the left. You are very good. I wanted to invite you over for a drink when you finished, but my beeper went off and I had to make a call. When I came back you'd finished already. I was just going to my car when I heard your voice calling to your friends. I don't mean to be forward, but could I still buy you a drink?" he asked with a shy smile on his face.

"He's cute," thought Christina.

"Sure," she said, thinking she might still make a few more bucks.

She started to turn back towards the Bare Fortune, but he took her arm.

"Not back there. That's where you work. Let's go some place else," he suggested.

"I think there is a nice place along the board walk," he added.

Figuring she was safe in her own neighborhood, in a public bar, she thought, "Why not?"

With him leading the way, they walked two blocks to the dock area and proceeded down towards the boardwalk.

As they walked, he engaged her in idle conversation. He could see she was becoming relaxed, trusting. That was good.

"Do you mind if we stay outside for a few minutes? I want to have a smoke. You're not too cold, are you?" he asked.

"No, the air is good. I've been in that bar all night and could use the fresh air," she said.

He maneuvered her farther down the board walk towards the far end saying they could watch the water while he smoked. There were no buildings. No one taking a casual walk. It was dimly lit and deserted. Perfect for what he had planned. They reached the end and stopped. The only sound was from the waves breaking on the rocks below. He leaned against the rail, his elbows resting on the top rail, looking out at the dark expanse of the ocean beyond.

"It's peaceful out there, isn't it?" he asked gesturing towards the water. Not waiting for her to reply, he continued.

"It's kind of like the universe. It seems to just go on and on. It doesn't seem to have an end. Not like life. Imagine being in a boat out there, all alone. No one to help you. Care for you," he said.

She listened to his words and began to get a strange feeling. She began to sense that something, a sixth sense, you might say, was trying to alert her. He had positioned himself so that she was at the end against the corner rail. The last light pole on the pier was about fifty feet away. They were practically in total darkness.

"Do you know about being alone? Do you know about being abandoned?" he asked raising his voice.

Her fear began to grow.

"I'm feeling a little chilly," she said. "Let's go have that drink?" she suggested.

She wanting to get to the street, the restaurants, somewhere there were people. Without waiting for a reply she started to move past him, when he suddenly grabbed her arm. He pulled her back into the shadows and pushed her up against the railing.

"Did you think you'd get away with it? Did you think you could just walk away and leave him like that? Alone. No mother to care for him. No mother to love him. Did you think there wouldn't come a day when you had to make amends, had to pay for your sins?" he asked in a deep, threatening voice, his face inches away from hers.

"Who are you? What do you want?" she asked, her voice trembling with fear. She tried to push him away, but he was much bigger than she was, much stronger. He held her, pinned against the rail, the hard board digging into her back.

"Who am I?" he asked. "I am the right hand of the Lord. I am the avenging angel," he said, his mouth now close to her ear. "And now it's time to pay for abandoning your son."

She felt him move back from her, experiencing a moment of relief. It was too dark to see him move his hand into the pocket of his raincoat. She didn't see him take out the folded knife, or flip it opened. She didn't see his left hand come up, grabbing her jaw, covering her mouth. He pushed his body full up against hers, bending her body backwards over the rail, pushing her head back until it would go no farther.

She was afraid she was going to fall backwards into the ocean. She grabbed the top edge, felt the wood and splinters stabbing her palms. Christy tried to break loose, but he held her in place. She tried to scream, but his hand muffled the sound. Then she felt a blow to her stomach. Her first thought was that he'd punched her, but then she felt a searing, burning pain. She felt the knife enter her flesh, its sharp edge being drawn upwards.

She knew she'd been stabbed. As a teen she'd been stabbed while fighting with a street gang. But that had been a slashing cut across her arm. This time it was different. It wasn't like the slash from the box cutter the girls used in that fight. Instinctively, she knew this was worse. This was meant to kill. Christina heard herself scream.

After he stuck the knife deep into her flesh and ripped her open, he grabbed the waist band of her pants and lifted her up and over the wooden rail. With a final shove he sent her falling into the ocean below.

She felt herself tumbling backwards, turning up side down, then plunging into the frigid water of the Atlantic Ocean. She opened her mouth wide to take in air, but instead felt a stabbing pain in her lungs as salt water rushed in. She struggled, kicked, trying to reach the surface, trying to breathe. But as she thrashed the pain in her stomach grew worse. She opened her mouth to scream for help, but no sound came. Instead more salt water rushed up her nose, down her throat, into her stomach, her lungs. Now the pain in her abdomen was joined by a burning spasm in her chest. Her lungs felt on fire. Christina continued to kick, but more slowly, weaker. She saw the faint glow from a street light above growing dimmer. She felt herself descending into the depths of the ocean. Something brushed against her flailing hands. It was her blonde wig, floating away with the current. A few more involuntary jerks of her arms and legs, then all motion ceased, her heart stopped, and Christina drifted lifeless with the tide.

He glanced around furtively to see if anyone had observed him. There was no one to be seen. He was alone. He took a deep breath and slowly exhaled, a feeling of relief settled over him. He stood there in the gloom for several minutes, looking down into the murky water below, watching to see if she rose to the surface.

He slowly, casually, walked back to the street. He was confident now that his mother's image, the memory of what she'd done to him, would no longer haunt him.

Chapter 23

John hung up the phone and banged his fist on his desk. Nancy, who had been going through Christina Martinez's notebook, was startled enough that he made her jump.

"What's the matter?" she asked.

"Those idiots. Don't they realize that we're on the same side?" he asked, not expecting an answer.

"Who were you talking to, John?" she asked.

"The Feds, of course. I thought it would be good for inter departmental morale to share information. But not those guys. They act like we're one of the bad guys. All they want is information we've collected without giving any of theirs," he said, his face still red from temper.

She let John calm down before going on.

"Did they tell you anything?" she asked.

"Only that Bruce Krane is under investigation by Federal authorities. He's believed to be involved in an international theft of gems from the airport. They wouldn't tell me if they had any leads as to where he might be hiding out. They wouldn't give me the names of any of the others believed to have been involved. Nothing," he concluded.

"All right. Maybe that's all they've got," she replied.

"Bull shit! They're holding back information that could help solve a double homicide," said John, as he rose from his chair.

He stomped around the room for a couple of minutes muttering to himself. Out of the corner of one eye he caught Nancy looking at him. She was trying to cover a smile with her hand.

"What's so funny?" he demanded.

"You. You look like a mad man the way you're carrying on. Sit down and let's talk this through. Maybe there's something we missed," she suggested.

Finally, John took her advice and sat down in a chair next to her desk. He ran his fingers through his hair. Nancy started to laugh out loud this time.

"Now what?" he demanded.

"Look at your hair," she said. She handed him a small compact. He opened it and looked at himself in the small mirror. His hair was standing straight up in the air. Apparently his palms were sweaty from his ranting and raving. When he ran his fingers through his hair it lifted the hair so it stood on end.

"You look like that guy, the fight promoter. What's his name? Don King," she said, still laughing.

John ran his tongue over his palm and tried to flatten down his hair. He couldn't help himself and began to smile.

"Maybe it's a good look for me. What do you think?" he asked.

"This?" he asked, pointing to his hair flat.

"Or this?" as he ran his fingers through his hair, again causing it to stand up.

"I think you need a hair cut," she teased, glad to see him smile.

"Now, please, go to the men's room and do something with it. When you return we have work to do," she said and sent him on his way with a slap on his butt.

"Sexual harassment. That's sexual harassment," he said as he left.

"You wish," said Nancy as she turned back to the papers on her desk.

A few minutes later John returned, his hair neatly combed back into place. Upon seeing him return, Nancy turned.

"I think we may have gotten a break," she said.

"Really? What did you find?" he asked.

"Me? Nothing. But I just got a call from the precinct down in Coney Island. They'd received a call from JFK Airport. It seems they found Bruce Krane's car. It's in the long-term parking lot near the TWA terminal," she said.

"Any sign of Krane?" he asked.

"Not yet. But the Port Authority Police said they'd wait for us to get there before they do anything," she added.

"Great. Let's get going," he said, excitement in his voice.

Nancy grabbed her jacket and put it on as she chased after John down the hall and out to their car. In no time they were driving cross town to the tunnel, Queens, and the airport beyond. Nancy drove the "unmarked" past the various terminals, following the signs to the "long-term parking" lot. She pulled up to the booth, prepared to show her ID. However, when she looked inside, it was empty.

"Push the button," said John.

Nancy looked around and saw a large red knob. She pushed it and a ticket popped out of a slot. Nancy removed it and stuck it under the sun visor.

"Now where?" she asked.

John pointed off to the right where he could barely see the flashing red lights from the top of a Port Authority truck. Nancy worked her way through the aisles until she pulled up behind a police car, its lights flashing.

They exited the car and headed towards a group of men and women. Some were in uniform, some "plainclothes."

"Great, the Feds are here," he said, nodding towards a small group of men in suits standing off to one side. John and Nancy hung their ID around their necks and approached a woman in uniform. Her rank was captain. John extended his right hand and introduced himself and Nancy.

The woman was Captain Isabel Banderos, Port Authority Police. Since the vehicle was on airport property, she was in charge of the scene.

"Glad you could make it. We were just about to open it up," she said, motioning towards the Cadillac, which was surrounded by yellow crime scene tape.

"You got a warrant?" asked Nancy.

"Nope," answered the captain.

"What's your probable cause?" asked John.

He knew that although the vehicle plates and the "VIN" number checked out to Bruce Krane, so far he hadn't been charged with anything.

Captain. Banderos took his arm and led him closer to the car. He was immediately overcome by a putrid odor coming from the vehicle.

"That's as good a probable cause as any," he said, putting his hand over his nose and mouth. He walked back to where Nancy was talking to some "suits," as he called FBI agents.

"What did she say?" asked Nancy.

"Something's rotten in Denmark," he said, staring at the Feds. "It smells like there might be a body inside," he added.

He continued to glower at the two men standing next to Nancy. Nancy saw his look and stepped between them.

"These are Special Agents Brian Michaels and Todd Rawley," said Nancy.

John found it hard concealing his dislike for these men and their agency. It was a common animosity and like the legendary "Hatfield and McCoy "feud, no one really knew what started it. It may have had something to do with the fact that in the old days the FBI only hired lawyers and accountants, college boys, as the cops on the street called them. Police thought you learned about crime out on the streets, not sitting in some classroom. Plus, the Feds were usually better paid, than the average cop on the street. Whatever the reason, the dislike was there for all to see.

Nancy decided to try to defuse the situation.

"Why don't we go see what the car reveals?," she said, taking John by the arm and leading him away.

Although walking alongside Nancy, John continued to glance over his shoulder in the direction of the two

291

agents. As they got near the car, Nancy could smell the odor.

Three men in full bio-hazardous outfits and face masks worked on the driver's side door. Using the highest technology available, a "Slim Jim," they managed to pop the door lock. They opened the door and then hit the release for the other doors. With the car opened fully, the odor became more intense. But looking inside, they couldn't find the source of the smell. Leaning forward, one of the spacesuit boys hit the trunk release on the door. The trunk rose part way and stopped. Walking around to the rear of the car, the same man opened the lid to its full position. The group of onlookers moved closer and peered inside.

"It looks like we got a homicide," said one of the FBI suits.

"Oh dear lord, where do they get their insight from?" asked John in a whisper. "Any idiot could see the guy didn't crawl inside the trunk and die of natural causes. Half his face was blown away," thought John.

The body was folded in half and wedged inside the trunk between the spare tire and a small suit case.

"Better get the Crime Scene Van and lab boys down here ASAP," said John.

"Not so fast," said the FBI agent.

"This is a federal case. It's on federal property. I think we have jurisdiction here," he said with a sarcastic tone.

Before John could explode, Nancy stepped in.

"Excuse me. Since I don't think the deceased climbed into the trunk by accident, this is an apparent murder scene. I don't see any evidence of federal law being violated her unless overtime parking is a federal offense now. Therefore, I do believe this is our crime scene."

Captain Banderos stood back, watching the exchange. Finally, she decided to step in and calm the waters.

"Ladies, gentleman, may I remind you this is airport property. As such it falls under the jurisdiction of the Port Authority Police. Now, I'm sure if we can all play nice while we work together to get to the bottom of this." She paused to look each in the eye.

"Great! Now we're going to let 'toll collectors' work the crime scene," said one of the FBI agents.

Captain Banderos gave him a look that could have cut through a diamond.

"I'll make believe I didn't hear that for the sake of good inter-office cooperation."

In time, everyone's ego seemed to have been soothed and the "pecking order" established. It was suggested that the city M.E.'s office handle the autopsy, lab work, and hold the body. The Feds would work the crime scene with their lab boys. Then everyone would meet at Port Authority Headquarters in the airport to share information. They all reluctantly agreed and stepped back to let the scientists take over.

With nothing to do, but wait, John and Nancy returned to their office. Once there, they sat at their desks, the files on Martinez and Sands opened in front of them.

"It was too easy," said John.

"What was too easy?" asked Nancy.

"This whole thing. All the evidence pointed directly towards Bruce Krane. Now we find him dead. Case closed."

"Assuming the guy in the trunk is him," she reminded him. "And even if it turns out to be Krane, what's wrong?"

"It's too pat. There aren't any loose ends. There are always loose ends. The ends shouldn't fit yet. There's a piece missing. Something's not right. We're missing something and it's going to come up and bite us in the ass," he predicted, walking around to his desk.

"Will you please lighten up? You're handed a gift. Why do you have to look for the worm in the apple? Let's get the paperwork in order. Once the M.E. does the autopsy and we get the prints back proving it's Krane, we can close this one. There are plenty more cases in our drawers that need work. Plus, somebody's going to have to figure out who killed Krane and why. It might fall in our laps. Holy crap if you weren't such a good lay, pardon my French, I'd kick your sorry ass out into the cold," she added.

"Just one moment please," said John, holding up his hand like a traffic cop.

"Yes?" asked Nancy.

"If I recall correctly, you live in my house. If anyone's ass is going to be kicked out into the cold it won't be mine," said John.

Nancy walked around her desk and hovered over John. She looked down at him with her most menacing look.

"Be afraid, John Michael Straub. Be very afraid," said Nancy, trying to imitate a deep, scary voice.

They spent the rest of the day pushing papers and filling out mileage and overtime forms.

"Don't forget the receipt from the airport parking lot," she reminded him.

"I can't believe that idiot made us pay and for a full day's parking. Didn't he realize we were there on a murder case?" asked John.

"He was only doing his job. Now fill out the form, attach the receipt, and send in the claim. Please stop your griping. You sound like an old man," she pleaded.

John got up and walked over to where she was sitting. Seeing him coming, Nancy asked,

"What are you going to do?"

Without saying a word, he took his arm and swept it across her desk, sending all the papers onto the floor.

"John, what's gotten into you?" she asked, pulling back from him.

"Old Man! I'll show you old, right here, now, on the desk. Let's go," he said, breathing heavily, eyes glaring in mock aggression.

"John, stop it," she squealed as John pushed her back against her desk.

Without knocking a uniformed police woman stuck her head in the door.

"Excuse me, boys and girls. If you can't control yourselves, I'm going to have to use the fire hose on you."

John backed off and Nancy started straightening up her blouse.

"We were just . . . ." John started to say, but stopped.

Ignoring his attempted explanation the officer said, "I have a call from the M.E.'s office that came in at the front desk. I'll transfer it over to you," she said and left.

John walked back to his desk and waited for the phone to ring. But it was Nancy's phone that rang.

295

She picked it up and listened. John sat, impatiently drumming his fingers on the desk. He watched and listened to Nancy's side of the conversation, trying to figure out what the M.E. could have found already that he had to call. Finally, Nancy finished the call and, hung up.

"So, what did they say?" asked John.

"That was one of the assistants. She said Dr. Morrison finished his autopsy on trunk body. The toxicology reports won't be back for a day or two, but the cause of death is probably a single gun shot wound to the head."

"Sounds like a mob hit. What else did she say?" asked John.

"Well, the fingerprints, dental records, and ID on the body confirms it was Bruce Krane. He was probably dead about three, maybe four days. They're going to send a written report over when the lab results are finished. Port Authority has notified the victim's mother.

"Well, I guess that takes care of that," said John, a hint of sarcasm in his voice.

"You don't sound satisfied," said Nancy.

"Well, since this guy went out with little suffering, compared to the two women, I'd say he got off easy."

"And?" asked Nancy. She was beginning to understand John and knew he said more without words sometimes.

"Like I said before, it's just too easy," he said.

"Oh, come on, John. Take it as a gift. Not all of them have to be hard. All the evidence points to Bruce Krane. He killed Jennifer Sands and Christina Martinez."

With that John's phone rang. He took the call while Nancy returned to her desk to "close" out the Sands and Martinez folders. When he finished, he turned to Nancy and informed her that they were just given the Krane case.

"So, aren't you happy? Maybe you'll be able to close up some loose ends," said Nancy. John had a scowl on his face. "John, you got that look now. What are you thinking?"

"Just that we'll have to work with the Feds, that's all. I just love working with those 'college boys.' It's always a learning experience," he said sarcastically. Nancy just shook her head.

"Look, why don't you call up Krane's mother? Find out if she's been informed. If not we can run up there for a follow up. There might be something. I'll notify the M.E. that it's our case and to send everything over ASAP," concluded John.

John called the M.E. while Nancy dialed the number she had for Krane's mother. After three rings Mrs. Krane answered.

"Hello, Mrs. Krane. This is Detective Mooney. My partner and I were there last week. Do you remember? That's right. It was about Jennifer Sands. Before I go on, I'd like to express my our deepest sympathy to you. We just heard about your son's death. It must be very difficult for you. We'd like to come over. We have a few more questions. You might be able to tell us something that will help us find your son's killer. That would be fine. We'll see you then," said Nancy and hung up. She swiveled around and was about to tell John what Mrs. Krane said, but he raised his hand to wait. John listened and nodded as he wrote down whatever it was the M.E.'s office was telling him. When he hung up, he turned to Nancy and said, "You first."

"Mrs. Krane said she could see us in an hour. She sounded pretty upset. Said the Feds had been there all morning 'harassing her.' Those are her words, not mine. They said they wanted to search her son's room. She refused because they didn't have a warrant. She's a tough old lady. I asked her what they did and she said, 'They left.'

"She said, 'I know my rights from watching that lady judge on TV.' They will be back with the warrant soon enough. I think we better get there before the Feds return. I think the woman will talk to us. But, if the Feds get her riled up, no telling what she'll do. Did you get anything from the M.E.?" she asked.

"Just that the paperwork will be sent to us when it's available. So I guess we go see Mrs. Krane," suggested John.

They drove out to the Bronx and found Mrs. Krane waiting for them. She was eager to talk to them before the FBI returned.

"First, Mrs. Krane, let me say how truly sorry we are for your loss," said Nancy.

Mrs. Krane just nodded. "I know you two from the last time. You didn't say so, but I knew you thought my son killed the Sands and Martinez women. Now, I know you'll just say I'm his mother, but I know my son. He is far from perfect, but he didn't kill those women.

"Bruce got messed up with the wrong crowd ever since his father died. It's hard raising a son without a man around. I tried my best, but . . . ." Here she began to cry softly. Nancy tried to console her as best she could.

"I'll be okay. But he was always a little wild. You know, the usual. He started cutting school. Then he was caught stealing from the candy store. He spent time in Juvenile Hall. Later, they got him with a garage filled with stolen hair dryers.

"But lately he was doing better. He'd gotten a job and was working with the union. Now this," said Mrs. Krane, and she started to cry again.

"Someone killed my boy. Who'd want to kill my boy?" she asked, as she walked to a small table in the corner of the living room. She picked up a picture.

It was a photo of a boy, maybe sixteen years old. He had blonde hair and bright blue eyes. His smile filled his face and you could see a twinkle in his eye. Here was the picture of a boy with the world before him. John remembered the face on the body in the trunk of the car found at the airport. He recalled that face, half obliterated. It looked nothing like the picture Mrs. Krane held.

Now, the boy in that picture was dead. Brutally murdered for being with the wrong people for the wrong reason. Mrs. Krane hugged the picture to her breast.

Nancy waited for the woman to have her moment of grief. Then she put her hand gently on her shoulder.

"Mrs. Krane, with your help, we will find the people who killed your son," she said. She watched as the woman wiped tears from her face.

Mrs. Krane was thinking about her son, but also about what Nancy had said. She took a deep breath and tried to compose herself. She gently returned the picture of her son to its place on the table and turned to Nancy.

"I'll help. Come with me," she said and lead them into her son's bedroom.

"My son kept his personal things in a metal box in his closet."

She reached inside the small closet, moved aside a loose panel in the wall, and lifted out a metal box. It was about twelve inches long, six wide, and about four deep. There was a lock, preventing it from being easily opened by snoopy people.

"Bruce had this hiding place since he was a kid. He didn't think anyone knew, but a mother knows. I found this key in his dresser. I think it fits the lock," said Mrs. Krane, handing both the box and key to Nancy.

"May I?" asked Nancy, motioning with the key towards the lock.

"Yes," said the woman.

Nancy placed the box on top of the dresser and inserted the key into the lock. Turning it to the right, she released the clasp and the lid popped open. Inside were various envelopes, letters, cash, and a knife. Nancy motioned for John to come join her. He looked inside and saw the knife. He took out a pair of surgical gloves and after putting them on lifted the knife from the box.

As he held the knife up to the light, Mrs. Krane said, "That was Bruce's hunting knife. His Daddy gave it to him when he was ten. They never got to go hunting. My husband died a short time later."

"How did your husband die, Mrs. Krane?" asked John.

"He was hit by a bus crossing the street," said Mrs. Krane. "A lawyer we knew tried to sue the bus company, but the case was thrown out. They said my husband was drunk. That it was his own fault." Now, turning towards Nancy, she said, "Detective Mooney, my husband didn't drink. He was raised a Jehovah's Witness. He never drank alcohol," said Mrs. Krane bitterly.

John placed the knife on the top of the dresser and went through the other items. The envelopes contained copies of paternity papers from the court, his union card, and some cash. John counted out the bills. It came to roughly five thousand dollars. "Not much for a life," thought John. Then he found a sealed envelope. On the cover were hand written the words, "*In the event of my death, open.*"

He gave it to Nancy, who asked if they could open it. Mrs. Krane nodded her consent.

Nancy began to read out loud.

"To whom it may concern," read the opening line. It had been hand written, the penmanship reflecting printing rather than script.

"He wanted to be sure people could read his writing," thought Nancy.

She read on.

"My name is Bruce Krane. I am writing this so you will know what happened if I am found dead. I was part of the diamond heist at the armored car company at JFK. I was with Tony Guzzo, Pete Rodriguez, Jeff Troutman, and Sal Naplolio. It was Sal who killed the guard. He shot him with his 9 mm. He didn't have to, but when he found a cop's ID on the guy he killed him just for the hell of it. We got about a million in uncut diamonds. Tony and Jeff were supposed to fence the gems. We were supposed to each get a ten percent cut. The other fifty percent was to go to the Carlotti Family.

"Pete wanted his money up front and started bitching. They wacked him. He was dumped in the swamps along the Jersey Turnpike. Tony and Sal said the Family was afraid someone was going to break. We told them not to worry. We were all okay with it. The other night I spoke to Sal. He said the Family wanted to see me. He said they wanted to know why the cops were coming around to my Mom's house and Christy's, where I slept sometimes. I don't know what the cops want with me, but I'm afraid I'm in trouble with the Family. I hope I'll be able to straighten it out. If I don't, I want whoever is reading this, to take it to the cops." The name *Bruce Krane* was scrawled at the bottom.

"Mrs. Krane, does this look like your son's signature?" asked Nancy.

Mrs. Krane just glanced at it, nodding as she started to sob again.

"They killed my boy. Do whatever you have to, but get them," she said, a mixture of anger and sorrow in her voice.

"We'll do our best. We're going to have to take this stuff in as evidence. It may help us get the people who killed Bruce," said John.

She nodded her consent and John placed the letter inside a zip lock bag. He got a paper bag from the kitchen and placed the knife and box inside with the rest of its contents.

John and Nancy talked to Mrs. Krane for a while longer, before thanking her for her help, and leaving. As they walked out of the building, a black sedan pulled to the curb half way down the street. John bowed his head, took Nancy's arm, and turned her in the opposite direction. They walked slowly down the block until John saw three men, Feds, enter the building they'd just left.

"Come on," said John, turning around and heading back to their car. They got in and Nancy drove back towards the city. John started laughing.

"What's so funny?" asked Nancy.

"I love to screw the Feds. They just came back with the warrant to search the place. Too bad we beat them to it," he said, patting the bag with the metal box inside that sat on his lap.

Chapter 24

John and Nancy were reviewing the information on the two women's cases when John received a call from their supervisor's office.

"Why not? We got nothing better to do," he said and slammed the phone back down into its cradle. Nancy jumped.

"You've got to stop doing that. Every time you do you scare the hell out of me. Keep it up and you'll give me grey hair. What's got you all riled up this time?" she asked.

"I hope you don't have anything special planned for tomorrow," said John.

Nancy starred at him with a quizzical look on her face.

"You got a Glock, right?" he asked, referring to the gun she carried.

"Sure. You know I do. So do you, why?" she asked.

"Well, it seems we aren't supposed to be carrying it," he answered.

"What are you talking about?"

"That call was to inform us, you and me, the two of us, can't carry it until we go through 'transitional training,' according to the commissioner's office."

"What are we supposed to carry in the mean time?" she asked.

"I guess we carry our 'wheel guns.' The old Chiefs," he replied.

A "wheel gun" was what they called revolvers because the cylinders turned like a wheel. When the "bad guys" started using Uzis that held twenty or more bullets, the department ordered and distributed semi-automatics to their officers.

The manufacturer they used was Glock, an Austrian gun maker. The barrel and some of the parts were metal. The rest was made with composites making them lighter. The magazine carried fifteen shots which put the "good guys" on an almost equal footing with the "bad guys." All was well until the first shoot out. Bullets were flying all over the place. There was a public outcry saying it was like the wild west. Law suits followed and with that new training programs were put into effect. That's what caught up to Detectives Straub and Mooney. They had to report to the police pistol range the next day for certification. No excuses!

The next morning the small alarm clock announced to John and Nancy that it was time to get up. Looking at the digital read out, John had his doubts. It read 6:00 A.M. He reached across Nancy, who had pulled the pillow over her head, and knocked the clock onto the floor.

"What idiot decided that firearms training had to start before the sun came up?" he asked, not expecting an answer. He rolled over and pulled the covers up to his chin. Five minutes later the alarm went off again. This time the clock lay on the floor under the bed, well out of John's reach. He tried to muffle the sound with his pillow. Finally, he felt the covers shifting and Nancy rolling over towards her side. Instead of shutting off the alarm and going back to sleep, she picked the clock up, silenced it, and padded over to the bathroom. A few minutes later John heard the water in the shower running.

He'd just started to drift off when he felt his covers being ripped from his body. Nancy stood over him, wearing only a bra and panties. Seeing her began to arouse him, but it had nothing to do with the pistol range.

"Oh, come on. Let's call in sick and play house," he pleaded.

"No way, lazy bones. Get into the shower. I'll put the coffee on. What do you want for breakfast, Corn Flakes or Corn Flakes?" she asked.

"Why don't we stop at one of the fast food places and grab something on the way? I need something more substantial than Corn Flakes," he whined.

Nancy towered over him, until he finally got up and walked into the bathroom to shower.

With their coffee mugs in hand, John and Nancy headed to the police firing range for "transition" training. They stopped at a local McDonald's, each ordered Egg McMuffins, and munched as they drove.

They found the parking area outside the range and walked down a slopping gravel driveway towards the building that housed the classrooms. Before they'd gotten more than ten feet down the drive, they were greeted by a large sign.

In big red lettering it announced, "***All officers carrying weapons must draw and unload them. No weapons or live ammunition is permitted in the classroom.***"

It directed them to leave the bullets in empty Styrofoam cups on a shelf by the classroom door and to put their initials on the cups.

Nancy and John complied, removing the magazines from each Glock and cleared the round in the chamber. They placed the first magazine, a spare magazine that they always carried, and the loose bullets into the cups. When they entered the room, they were met by one of the range instructors. He stood no more than five feet eight, was thin and wiry, with a close cropped crew cut.

He looked like he'd just been discharged from the Marines. In fact, he'd been in the Corps for ten years prior to joining the police department.

His name was Sergeant. Bickel, which rhymes with "pickle," he said when he introduced himself. He told them to leave their weapons on a table where several other Glocks rested, having been deposited earlier by other students. They were all given a "firearms" card to fill out and leave under their weapons. In a far corner of the classroom was the ubiquitous coffee maker. Several officers were availing themselves of its dark, muddy fluid. John and Nancy decided to take a pass.

Not recognizing anyone else in the room, they took seats near the back of the room and prepared to be bored for the next eight hours. Sergeant Bickel called everyone to order and directed the stragglers to find seats. He passed out forms and asked each to fill out the information requested. Afterwards, the forms were collected and the class began.

Sergeant Bickel had a habit of pacing back and forth in front of the class with his hands clasped behind his back. As he spoke, John was reminded of a boxing referee, Miles Lane, who was also a district attorney and later a judge. Not so much in his mannerisms, but more in his voice. Sergeant Bickel definitely wasn't from Brooklyn, John decided.

The sergeant began his lecture by reminding the assembled officers of safety regulations at the range. He also shared stories about mishaps with the newly issued semi automatics. He told them about officers cleaning their "supposedly empty "weapon, only to have it discharge.

The bullet sometimes caused serious injuries and in one instance, death. He reminded them that they needed to change their mind set concerning the new weapon. It was totally different from their old revolvers.

This part of the lecture lasted almost an hour. John had to admit, it was not only interesting, but an eye opener. He found himself sitting more upright and noticed the other officers had also shifted from their usual "police slouch" positions. He had to admit, "this guy knew what he was talking about."

They took a coffee break, during which time he became acquainted with some of the other officers in the room. When it was time to resume, they were presented with a new instructor.

Her name was Sergeant Maureen Henry. She stood no more than five feet five and had a small, but athletic-looking body. She showed a brief film that reviewed the parts of the semi automatic. When the video tape ended, she read the names of some of those in the room off a piece of paper. John's name was among them. She asked them to see her after her lecture. Sergeant Henry proceeded to explain to them the training course and firing requirements. She reminded them that they would be scored at the end of the day. Anyone not passing would be required to surrender their weapons and be placed on desk duty until they are qualified.

"No pressure," thought John.

When she concluded her presentation and sent the officers on their meal break, she reminded those named earlier to see her before leaving.

John got up from his chair, a sheepish expression on his face.

"What did you do that you have to go down to the principal's office?" Nancy teased.

"How the hell should I know?" he said, annoyed, and walked over towards where Sergeant Henry standing.

Although there were four women in the class, including Nancy, none were in the group.

The sergeant looked up from her list and asked, "And you are?"

"John Straub," he answered.

"Well, John Straub, it seems you and these other officers need a lesson in the proper care and maintenance of your weapons," she said.

A few men made snide comments with a sexual overtone about "maintaining their weapon." Sergeant Henry just gave them a stare that quickly put them in their place.

"Seriously, gentlemen. The semi-automatic is an excellent weapon. However, unlike the revolver you're used to, it is very unforgiving when not properly maintained."

She picked up one of the weapons that had been gleaned from those of the other officers and displayed it to the officers.

"Safe," she announced, showing them the empty grip where the magazine had been removed, then flipping it sideways so they could see the slide had been pulled back. They could see there were no bullets chambered as well as through the top of the weapon and down the grip. Sergeant Henry then released the slide, closed the weapon, and proceeded to dismantle the gun.

She moved swiftly and skillfully, placing the parts on a piece of terry cloth that had been spread upon a table. The first thing she did was pick up the barrel. Holding it at arm's length, she allowed the men to look down its interior.

"You'll notice dust inside the barrel. There is also gunpowder and grime stuck to the sides."

Then she picked up the main gun frame, which was made of mostly composite type plastic with metal slides running the length on top. It was on these slides that the moving parts road.

She took a finger and wiped it along the length of the slides. Extending her hand palm out all could see the finger was covered in oil.

"This is unacceptable, gentlemen. When it comes to lubricating a semi-automatic less is better," and proceeded to wipe the oil on a cloth.

Too much oil will cause lint and dirt to collect on the weapon. This could in turn prevent the slide from functioning. Or it could get on the firing cap of the bullet. In either case the weapon malfunctions. Now, in the event of an attack on your person, all you have is a heavy metal object to throw at your assailant.

Sergeant Henry methodically went down the line of weapons on the table, inspecting each one quickly and methodically. After identifying the owner she pointed out the problems she had found and showed the owner how to correct them while offering suggestions on how to properly care for their weapon in the future. By the time she'd finished, each of the semi-automatics was in top notch working order and each officer knew how to correctly maintain his weapon.

"Please pick up your weapon before leaving the building and remember to reload at the designated area. You are now dismissed for lunch." she said with a smile on her face.

After picking up his Glock and reloading John met Nancy waiting for him outside. As they were walking up to their car, she asked what had happened.

"She's good," he admitted, referring to Sergeant Henry. "She gave us a crash course in how to maintain the piece. She really knows what she's talking about," he added.

"And you find that unusual because she's a woman?" asked Nancy.

"No," replied John, being smart enough not to pursue this line of conversation.

"What do you want to do about lunch?" he asked, changing the subject.

"How about the diner down the road? I don't want anything too heavy or it will make me drowsy. I'm sure I can get a salad there," she suggested. John agreed and they headed off to lunch.

When they returned to the firing range they took their seats in the classroom. This time the instructor was an older officer, a lieutenant, who outlined the training for the afternoon and explained the qualification course. Afterwards they were sent to retrieve their weapons.

They were given safety equipment, "eyes and ears," as they called them, consisting of headsets for their ears and safety glasses. They then headed down to the firing line.

For the next four hours all they did was fire their weapons. The officers lined up across the open field. In front of them was a sand berm, approximately fifty feet high.

Below this were the targets, all controlled by a range officer. He was located in a tower approximately twenty feet high directly behind the firing line. Standing directly behind the "shooters" were three range safety officers. It was their job to keep the line "safe" and correct any obvious problems, and problems there were. Many of the "shooters" hadn't been to a firing range in several years. Their last training involved the use of the revolvers. It was soon apparent to John and most of the others that they had some "learning to do."

Right off the bat, one officer had a problem. He'd held the grip in his right hand. Where he made his mistake was to wrap his left hand around the back of the right hand for support. This would not have presented a problem with a "wheel" gun. However when he fired first round, the slide flew back from the explosion and recoil as the gun fired. The slide had sliced two deep, parallel lines across the top of his left hand, between the index finger and thumb. The webbing between them was bleeding profusely. One down, nineteen to go.

The next mishap occurred when one of the "shooters" failed to push the magazine all the way into the handle. Upon drawing the gun, the magazine fell to the ground and he was left with an empty weapon. He was pulled from the line, made to empty the magazine, clean it thoroughly, making sure all the grit and sand was removed, and then reload before returning to the line.

But the most common and serious problem for the "shooters" was accuracy. It became apparent that some of the men were, "limp wristing" when they fired.

The safety officer explained that this occurred when the person failed to hold the weapon securely. Upon firing the weapon, their hand moved up and usually to one side, absorbing some of the recoil. By doing this, it took away some of the force from the slide mechanism. This momentum was needed so the slide would move completely to the rear. If this failed, and the slide road back part way, the "spent" cartridge might not be ejected or the next round might not move into position properly to be fired. In any event, the weapon jammed.

While the instructors attempted to correct these problems, they were also trying to break bad habits and cultivate good ones. At first, John thought this was an impossible task. However, after firing hundreds of rounds and clearing weapons that did jam, he became more confident in the weapon. He began to understand its little quirks and appreciate its capabilities. All in all, the Glock was a very effective weapon. He grudgingly had to admit that he was glad he'd taken the training course. By the end of the day and after the qualification round was run, three officers were sent packing without their firearms certification cards. They'd be riding a desk until the next available opening. To John's surprise, not only did all the women, including Nancy, pass the course, but they were among the top scorers. Nancy out-shot John by ten points. He dreaded the trip home and the rest of the day. He knew she'd have fun at his expense.

They spent the last hour breaking down and cleaning their weapons. John and Nancy thanked the instructors for their help and headed home. It took two blocks before Nancy started busting his chops.

"I'm the king! I'm the best! I beat you!" she went on teasing. Using her index finger and thumb to mimic a gun, she feigned shooting out small objects from great distances.

"Pow! Pow!" she said, making the sound of her "imaginary" gun firing. Each time she did, she'd sing,

"And another one bites the dust."

John couldn't help but smile at her teasing. He'd been put down a peg and reluctantly admitted that she was a better shot this time.

By the time they got home, John was well chastised and Nancy was glowing in the light of victory. For John, there did prove to be an "up side" to Nancy's crowing. She was in an extremely good mood, felt sorry for John, and made a point of consoling him in the best way she could. She treated him to dinner. And to show he could be gracious in defeat, he allowed her the top position during their love making that night.

All in all, it was a good day for John and Nancy. Good days would prove to be few and far between for the two detectives in the weeks and months to come.

Chapter 25

Mary Clarke sat in her darkened apartment, too weak to get up to turn on a light. She was in the third day of a battle with the flu. "I'm sick and tired of being sick and tired," she thought. With a mighty effort she managed to get up, shuffle out to her small kitchen and turn the stove on under a tea kettle. "A cup of hot tea and a piece of toast might help settle my stomach," she said to herself.

While recuperating, she'd been thinking about Detective Straub's call concerning both the Sands and Martinez women. She'd learned both had small children, sons, who were in foster care. Both folders had been signed out of the records room. She wanted to check and see who had pulled the folders and for what purpose. She didn't know why, but it was something that bothered her.

Mary had recovered enough by Monday to return to work. She arrived early, as was her habit. She used the time before the phones started ringing to get caught up on paper work. At nine, she pushed away from her desk and headed to the records room. The woman in charge of the records was seated at her desk as Mary entered the room.

"Hi Lois! Have the folders I requested come back yet?" she asked.

"Which one's were they?" asked the clerk.

"Sands and Martinez," said Mary.

"Yeah, the person who had them said he was going to bring them to your desk last Friday. Didn't you get them?" she asked.

"No. I've been out for a few days with the flu. I came in early and there weren't any folders on my desk. Who had them?" asked Mary.

"Just a minute. I'll check." The clerk turned to her PC and scrolled through the case names on the screen. "Here they are. J. Edgar, Foster Care. I think he's in the Investigations section," added the clerk.

"Edgar. I'll see if he's in yet. Thanks," said Mary and headed off to find J. Edgar.

She walked across the building to the Foster Care section. Once there, the unit secretary directed her to where J. Edgar sat. Mary found his cubicle, but it was empty. Sitting there on top of his desk were the folders she'd been looking for. Mary picked them up and began looking through the one marked "Sands." Not seeing anything out of the ordinary, she turned to the Martinez folder. She'd just opened the other one when she heard foot steps approaching. As she looked up, she saw a tall, young man standing over her.

"What are you looking for?" he asked.

"Oh! Are you Mr. Edgar?" she asked.

"Yes. Now why are you going through my cases?" he asked.

NO DEED UNPUNISHED

"I was looking for two cases," she answered, waving the two in her hand.

"The Sands and Martinez kids. I have them here. Are you finished with them?" asked Mary.

"Why are you interested in these?" asked Edgar, not answering her question.

Mary hesitated at first but decided to tell the truth.

"I received a call from a detective. They were both murdered."

"Really? Murdered, you say. That's terrible. Maybe I could be of some help. Why don't you give me this detective's telephone number and I'll call him myself?" said Edgar, grabbing the folders from Mary's hand. His gruffness startled her.

"I don't have his number with me. I'll have to call you when I get back to my desk," said Mary, suddenly eager to get away from the man.

"Yes, why don't you do that Ms . . . . ?" here a paused.

"Clarke. Mary Clarke," she said. "I'll call you later."

"Ms. Clarke," he said, stepping back, allowing her to leave.

"Mary Clarke. Now where do I know that name from?" wondered Edgar. He prided himself on having a good memory. Dropping the files on his desk and sat down.

"Mary Clarke? Oh, yeah. That's it," he thought to himself. Edgar recalled reading a book about "Jack the Ripper," the mass murderer who roamed around London, England, in the late 1880's. According to the story, when he approached his victims, he would ask, "Are you Mary Clarke?" Apparently, he was searching for a woman who he felt had wronged him in some

317

way. In a sick, perverse way Edgar identified with the killer. Mary Clarke was a prostitute as were other victims. While there really was a "Jack The Ripper" no one knows who he was or what he said to his victims before killing them. That was all fiction. In fact the first known victim's name was Mary Ann Nicholls who was killed in a section of London known as "Clarke Yard."

"The author took some liberties when telling his version of the story," thought Edgar.

"But how ironic," thought Edgar. Jack the Ripper slashed his victims with a knife. Now he wondered if this "present day" Mary Clarke presented a danger to him and might meet the same fate as the fictional Mary Clarke.

"No way is some frumpy old lady going to stop me from doing what has to be done," he thought.

After her encounter with Edgar, Mary headed back to her cubicle. She sat down and decided to call Detective Straub. She didn't have anything new, just a "feeling" about Edgar that bothered her. She wanted to explain it to him and see if he would want to talk to Edgar himself. After placing the call, a woman answered the phone. She identified herself as Detective Mooney. She said she was Straub's partner and as such was familiar with the case she was calling about. She knew Ms. Clarke's name from talking to John. Assuming the case had already been solved Nancy decided there was no harm in telling Ms. Clarke what they knew. She told them that they'd found a body believed to be Krane's and since he was the prime suspect, the case would probably be closed. Nancy thanked Ms. Clarke for her help and promised to tell her partner that she'd called.

For the remainder of the day, Mary Clarke played catch-up with her work. Her meeting with Mr. Edgar was forgotten. At the end of her work day she headed out of the building and home to her little apartment in Queens. Preoccupied with making a mental list of grocery items she needed for the week, Mary didn't notice the man following her. Mary took the subway to the Jamaica Avenue stop and walked up the steep hill towards Utopia Parkway, past St. John's University.

The neighborhood consisted of a mix of private homes and apartments. It was near the subway, which made travel easy. But most of all it was near the college. Mary managed to enroll in a variety of courses at St. John's. She followed their basketball team and attended many of their home games when they were held in their gym, Alumni Hall. She liked the way the students treated her, "with respect." Some she'd gotten to know over the years and they called her, "Mom." It was a convenient, quiet, and safe neighborhood. Or so she thought.

She had never married and lived alone. On the way she stopped at a small grocery store. so she only needed a few things. and picked up a frozen dinner, some milk, eggs, fruit and whole wheat bread. She went home, put the groceries away and threw the dinner in the microwave. Then she headed into the bedroom to get out of her work clothes. She slipped into a flannel nightgown and slippers, returning to the kitchen just as the timer on the microwave oven went off. She removed the dinner and stripped off the plastic cover. She didn't bother to transfer the contents onto a new plate. Instead, she carried the molded plastic tray into the living room and set it down on a TV tray. Falling wearily into her easy chair and using the remote turned on the TV. The channel was already set for the local news. She turned the volume up on the TV and prepared to eat her dinner. However, before she could put the first forkful into her mouth she thought she heard a knock at her door. She lowered the volume and listened. A moment later there was another knock. "Now who could that be?" she asked herself. She moved the tray back while rising slowly from her chair. She wondered who could be calling on her at that hour.

"Not someone from the building. They all knew when dinner time was," she thought. "Must be one of the neighbors since visitors needed to be 'buzzed in' to gain entry to the building." Mary looked through the peep hole in the door, but didn't see any one there. Out of curiosity, she unlocked the door and opened it.

As she was about to stick her head into the hallway, a hand grabbed her face and shoved her back into her apartment. She was pushed with such force that she fell over backwards. From her position on the floor she was too shocked to realize who the intruder was. She looked up, a puzzled look on her face.

The intruder kicked the door closed with his foot and quickly knelt down beside her, his face only inches from hers. Now she recognized who it was. It was that Edgar guy.

"What are you doing here?" she asked, her voice trembling.

"You're asking too many questions, Mary Clarke. I'm afraid you may have placed me in great danger. You need to be stopped before it is too late," he said.

"Danger? Late? What are you talking about? Get off of me! What do you want?"

"Why, isn't it obvious, Ms. Clarke? I'm here to kill you!"

But before she could respond, his right hand came out from behind his back. She caught a glimpse of a knife just before plunged it into her abdomen. Mary felt the searing pain as the knife slid through her flesh. She felt herself lifted slightly as the blade was drawn upward through her stomach. The cold steel sliced through organs and muscle; severing the aorta and nicking her heart, causing it to go into spasms.

Once he sliced her, Edgar moved to the side, thus avoiding the gush of blood from the open wound. He watched the color drain from Mary's face. Her breathing became labored. She shuddered once or twice, and then she ceased to move. He watched her for another minute before he was satisfied that she would no longer cause him any concern.

Ignoring the gore all around him, he reached down and sampled a piece of meat from her TV dinner. He took one bite and then spit it out onto the floor.

"Disgusting," he said.

He wiped his knife on the fabric of her nightgown. then he went into the bathroom and examined himself in a full-length mirror on the back of the door.

"It wouldn't do for me to walk outside covered in blood," he said out loud. Satisfied with his appearance, he walked back through the apartment and left by the front entrance.

"Piece of cake," he said as he stepped out onto the street and headed home.

Mary Clarke wasn't a woman who had abandoned her son. She wasn't someone who needed to be punished. She had simply gotten in the way and Jacob Edgar felt nothing afterwards. With her death he had crossed a line. No longer could he be seen as an avenging angel. Now he was simply a cold blooded killer who needed to be stopped.

Chapter 26

They'd lucked out with the weather at the range. It had been a "picture perfect" day. But the next morning came with a leaden grey sky. Dark clouds moved over the city and rain drops began to fall as John and Nancy pulled into the police parking lot. They had just made it inside the building when the skies opened up. By mutual consent, they decided it would be an "office" day. They had plenty of paperwork to catch up on. Although Nancy thought the Sands and Martinez cases were closed, she knew John had bad vibes about them. But contrary to his "gut feeling," as far as they could tell, Bruce Krane had killed both women. End of story.

John sat at his desk, the ever-present cup of coffee sitting within easy reach. He was reviewing the notes on the Martinez and Sands cases. As he flipped through pages, he came across Mary Clarke's name. He realized he hadn't spoken to her in a while.

"I should give her a call. See if she found out anything on the victims," he thought to himself. He picked up his phone and dialed Ms. Clarke's number at DSS. In the chaos of the past few days, Nancy had forgotten to mention that Ms. Clarke had called him.

The phone at DSS rang several times before a woman's voice came on the line.

"Mary Clarke?" he asked.

"No, this is Mrs. Winski," she replied.

"May I ask who is calling?"

"This is John Straub. I'm a detective with the city. May I speak to Mary Clarke?" he asked.

"I'm afraid that's not possible," she responded.

"Oh. Then I'd like to leave a message," said John.

"I'm afraid you don't understand. Ms. Clarke is dead," responded the woman.

John was speechless for a moment.

"I'm sorry. I didn't know she was sick," he said.

"She wasn't. Mary was murdered," said the woman, emotion in her voice.

"Murdered?" repeated John.

"Yes. She was killed in her home. The police believe it was, what did they call it? A 'push in,' I think it was," said the woman.

"Oh my God. That's terrible," he said sincerely. "I'm sorry to hear that. When did this happen?" asked John.

"It was only a few days ago. We haven't fully gotten over the shock yet," she added.

"I guess not," said John.

"Was there something you needed from Ms. Clarke?" asked the woman.

"No. I guess not," he said, then asked, "By the way where did she live?"

"In Queens, near St. John's University," answered the woman.

Again, expressing his sympathy, John hung up the phone.

Stunned, John sat for a moment, thinking about the nice lady who had been so helpful to him over the years. He regretted never having met her personally. Knowing that she lived near St. John's, he called the local precinct. After identifying himself, he was transferred to the Detective's Division.

The phone was answered by a Detective Lynn Morgan. John explained his interest to the detective.

Detective Morgan explained that the desk sergeant had gotten a call from a woman who worked with the deceased. She said she was concerned when Ms. Clarke hadn't reported for work that morning. Further, the caller said Ms. Clarke didn't call in, which wasn't like her. They tried to reach her at home, but got no answer. The co-worker had the name of one of victim's neighbors and called her. The neighbor went to Ms. Clarke's apartment, knocked on the door several times, but no one answered. She said she hear a TV or radio playing inside.

Thinking she might be hurt and in need of help, the neighbor called the police. When the officers arrived they found the door to the apartment wasn't locked. When they entered they found her body on the living room floor. They think she'd been dead a day or two. It appeared to be a 'push in', added Detective Morgan.

"Either that, or she knew the person who killed her. There was no sign of forced entry. The killer used a knife," added the detective.

"A knife and you think it was a robbery gone bad?" asked John.

"Could be. Nothing appeared to have been taken. So, either the killer wasn't there to rob her, or he got scared off before he could take anything. The neighbors were interviewed, but couldn't give us much. We got a video tape from a surveillance camera mounted over the front entrance to the building. The homicide detectives took it to their lab to see if it could be enhanced," added the detective.

She gave John the names of the homicide detectives assigned to the case. He thanked the detective for her help and left his name and number in case anything new came up.

John slowly lowered the phone to its cradle and sat at his desk, staring off into space. He felt saddened by the news of the woman's death. Even though they'd never met, he'd grown to like Ms. Clarke. He thought of calling DSS back to see if they had any information about funeral plans so he could pay his respects. However, before he could make the call, Nancy interrupted him.

"What's up, John?" she asked, seeing his look.

"Do you remember the woman at DSS I would call from time to time for information?"

"Sure, Mary Clarke. I spoke to her the other day. Why?" asked Nancy.

"She's dead," said John simply.

"Oh, that's terrible. How did it happen? Was she ill?," asked Nancy.

"No. I asked the same thing when I heard. She wasn't sick. She was murdered. It happened a few days ago," said John.

"I wonder if it was the same day I'd spoken to her?" said Nancy.

"What? She called?" asked John.

"She called about the Martinez and Sands cases. I told her we'd identified the killer. I forgot to tell you. I'm sorry. Think she had information?" Nancy added.

"We'll never know," he said. "I called the Queens precinct where she lived. They gave me some information. I'm going to check in records to see who got the case."

But instead of getting up he continued to sit. Something was on his mind.

"What are you thinking about?" she asked.

"I was just wondering if Clarke's murder had anything to do with the Sands and Martinez cases," said John.

"I doubt it. How could it? Besides, Bruce Krane was their killer. He died before Mary Clarke was killed," she added.

"I'm still not sure about that."

Nancy chose to ignore him and went back to the files on her desk.

John picked up his phone and called the Police Records Department. After speaking to one of the clerks he had the name of the detectives working the Clarke murder. Hanging up the phone, he turned to Nancy.

"I'm going down the hall. Newel and Falcone got the case. I'll be back in a few minutes," he said as he walked out of their office.

John kept thinking about Mary Clarke.

"God, I hope I didn't have anything to do with that poor woman's death," he thought as he walked down the hall. He found the two detectives in their office.

Detective Dani Newel was a twelve year veteran who'd come over from Vice. She'd been one of the best undercover cops with Vice. She'd often be called on to act as a prostitute. Standing just over five feet, she'd wear spiked heels or boots to make herself look taller. Her straight red hair and fair skin turned heads. She was a woman who could easily pass for a teenager. She'd used this to her advantage on many assignments. Her arrest record for drugs and prostitution was impressive.

In time, it was decided that she'd become too well-known on the street to continue undercover. She was transferred to Homicide, where she was teamed up with Jim Falcone.

Jim Falcone was born and bred in Brooklyn. He was a tall, slim, Italian with short black hair. To hear him talk, one would never guess that he held a B.A. from John Jay College in psychology and was working on a masters. Some said he deliberately exaggerated any Brooklyn accent he might have to catch people off guard. The biggest mistake one could make with Jim was underestimating him.

Jim had been a good foot cop assigned to the Coney Island section of Brooklyn. Being a good "beat cop," he knew his territory. Through contacts, he'd helped the detectives make busts for drugs, larcenies, and gang assaults. In time, he earned his gold shield and worked his way over to Homicide. About a year ago, he was teamed up with Newel. They made an odd couple because he was over a foot taller than she. To some it looked like he was bringing his kid sister to work with him.

They worked well together. Despite being petite, Newel could handle guys twice her size. She was described as "scrappy." To John, that meant that she was a dirty fighter. But that was okay by him as long as he wasn't the one up against her.

As John entered their office, Dani looked up from her desk.

"Well, look what the cat dragged in. How are you doing, stranger?" she asked, a big smile on her face.

"Yo, John," said Jim in his best "Rocky Balboa" accent.

"Hi, guys. You got a minute?"

Without waiting for a reply, he continued, "Listen, I hear you just got a case, Mary Clarke."

"Yep. Just got it yesterday," said Dani. "You got something on it for us?"

"I don't know. I've been working on a couple of homicides. Two women, both knifed. I thought I'd found a link between them through DSS. My contact was Mary Clarke. She was running down some leads for me. My partner, Nancy Mooney, got a call from her the afternoon she was killed. Clarke didn't say what she wanted, but I was wondering if she may have been on to something," said John.

"Do you think she was killed by someone connected to your cases?" asked Jim.

"I don't know. Our prime suspect was found dead in the trunk of his car. It looks like a 'mob hit' but it was done before she died. I thought our cases were closed, but now this," John replied.

"You think there's someone else?" asked Dani.

"I got a strange feeling on this one. The evidence all pointed to our perp, but now I have my doubts. The

Clarke woman was murder with a knife just like our victims," added John.

"I see what you mean. What do you want from us?" asked Jim.

"Could you keep me in the loop on this one? I feel I owe it to her. I'd hate to think I'd put her in danger because of my questions," said John.

"Sure. No problem," said Dani.

"If we find anything we'll let you know," promised Jim.

"Thanks, guys. I appreciate it," said John and returned to his office.

When he walked into his office, he found Nancy sitting at her desk with the chair turned towards the doorway.

"Well, I hope you're happy," said Nancy.

"What?" asked John.

"Do you remember the knife we found at Bruce Krane's?" she asked.

"Sure. The hunting knife. It was probably the one used in the murders, right?" asked John.

"Wrong," said Nancy. "I got a call from the lab. There was some trace of blood, but it turned out to be fish blood, not human.

"Then I called the coroner's office. After I described the knife to the doc, he said it was unlikely it was used to kill our women. He said the blade was too long and the one used on the victims was shorter and probably folded."

"So, he had more than one knife," said John.

"Maybe, but it turns out Krane was left handed. Our two 'vics' were killed by someone who was right handed. He said it had something to do with the angle of penetration and cutting. Whatever. The bottom line is Bruce Krane didn't kill them. So I guess you were right after all," added Nancy.

John walked over to his desk and sat down heavily into his chair. He ran his fingers through his long brown hair.

"Aren't you happy?" she asked.

"Being right and being happy are two different things. I'd just about convinced myself we had our killer and our case was closed. I was also hoping ours had nothing to do with the murder of Mary Clarke. But now I'm not so sure," replied John.

"So where do you want to start first, Krane or the women?" asked Nancy.

"Krane was a mob hit. My guess is more bodies will turn up over the next day or so. He was involved in something big. He was in over his head and got rubbed out to keep his mouth shut. These things eventually fall apart. There are plenty of agencies working that case. We can put Krane on the back burner for now. It's the women's murderer we concentrate on. I have a feeling this is deeper than we originally thought. I hate to use the term, but we may have a serial killer on our hands," added John glumly. "There's a connection here. But what?" he added.

"Well, let's start with what we know. They both had kids; kids who were taken away from them. They were both stabbed to death," said Nancy.

"Yeah. But the way they were stabbed. The killer didn't just stick the knife in their chests or slit their throats. He disemboweled them," said John.

Nancy sat quietly, mulling things over in her head. Then she bolted up right and grabbed her phone.

"Who are you calling?" asked John.

"One of my professors over at John Jay. He taught a course in forensic psychology. If I can catch him, I'll run this past him. He may be able to give us some insight as to who or what we're looking for," answered Nancy.

"I need some coffee. You want one?" asked John.

Nancy nodded and mouthed the words, "My usual."

"Hello, Professor Mangini? Nancy Mooney here. How have you been?"

When John returned, he placed the cup of coffee on Nancy's desk sat at his own desk and sipped his coffee.

"Did you get your professor?" he inquired.

"Yes. It was good talking to him. He still remembered me from his class," she said with a smile.

"Do I detect a teacher's crush?," teased John.

"God, no. He's married with three kids. A nice guy though. Insisted I call him Gary instead of Professor Mangini."

"Oh, it's Gary now," quipped John.

"Stop your teasing and listen to this," admonished Nancy.

John went around to his chair and sat down.

"Okay, I'm all ears."

"Gary," Nancy caught herself and smiled. She continued.

"Professor Mangini said from the way I described the murders the sounded like the guy was 'ritual' killer. He said the method of disemboweling someone shows rage, a possible hatred of women, but control.

"He said that you could kill someone quickly with a knife simply by slitting the throat from behind or plunging it into the heart. But to deliberately disembowel someone takes skill, strength, and time. This guy wasn't in a rush and he wanted the victims to know they were dying and why. He probably gets off by watching the life slowly drain out of them."

"But the real kicker is that it may be an attempt on his part to stop the reproduction process," she said, pausing to drink some coffee.

"I'd say," said John. "Dead people can't reproduce."

"Yes, but it's more than that. He said some primitive cultures removed the hearts of their enemies after battle and ate them in a ritual feast. By doing this they absorbed the spirit and bravery of their victims.

"Professor Mangini said that our killer is trying to undo something that was done to him. Or prevent it from happening again. Now he admitted he was going out on a limb here, but he said the killer probably is searching for his birth mother or sees her in these women. He probably stalks them first, knows all about their lives. He might know the children were in foster care which to him would be the same as being abandoned by their mother. He may identify with the children. He may have been abandoned also," concluded Nancy.

John mulled this over in his head for a moment, then grabbed his phone and punched in a series of numbers.

"Jim, it's John Straub. How was the Clarke woman killed? Yeah, I know she was stabbed, but how? Right. I may want to go along with you," said John and hung up.

"That was Jim Falcone. He and Dani Newel are working the Mary Clarke murder. He said she was sliced up the middle, just like our two victims. They are going over to DSS to talk to some of her co-workers. I'm going with them."

"That could be the connection, both women's kids were in foster care," said Nancy

"Listen, would you stay here and work the Krane case while I run over there with them? See if our F.B.I. friends have anything they want to share now? I'll be about an hour," he added.

"Sure. But call if you come up with anything," she said, making.

"Will do."

Chapter 27

The three detectives walked into the office of Mary Clarke's supervisor. Marge Rainey was a heavy set woman with too much make up and over-dyed black hair. She wore a large, almost tent-like dress with what appeared to be slippers on her feet. It appeared to be an effort getting up from her chair to greet them as they introduced themselves.

Jim Falcone explained the purpose of their visit. They wanted to look through Ms. Clarke's desk, maybe interview her co workers. Huffing and puffing, Ms. Rainey said she didn't know if that would be possible, because there was a question of confidentiality involved. She said she had to protect the privacy of her clients. At this, Dani rose to her full five feet and leaned over Ms. Rainey's desk.

"Listen. The privacy of Mary Clarke was violated the other night and her guts were left all over her apartment floor. Someone killed her and we think that it had something to do with her work. Now either you cooperate or we get a judge to open up all the files in this department for scrutiny. Now, do you think your section could withstand a full audit by the mayor's office?" asked Dani, a sinister smile on her face.

Ms. Rainey's face turned bright red and her breathing became labored. Finally, she was able to speak.

"Of course we'll cooperate. I just meant that we have to be careful who looks at our files. But I'm sure under these circumstances there shouldn't be a problem. As long as nothing leaves the office," she added.

"We may need to make copies of material," warned Jim.

"That shouldn't be a problem. Now where do you want to start?" she asked.

The three detectives followed Ms. Rainey as she walked down a narrow hall and into a large open space. The room had been partitioned off into cubicles. Most were empty. They were soon directed to the one assigned to the late Mary Clarke.

There was no way all three detectives and Ms. Rainey could fit into the cubicle at the same time. Taking her leave, Ms. Rainey offered to provide any assistance they might need and returned to her office.

John walked around to the far side of the desk and sat in the chair. He looked across the top of the desk. There was a computer monitor, keyboard, and telephone on one side. The other was empty except a calendar blotter. There were no pictures, no souvenirs, no plants one might expect to find on the desk. It seemed sad to John thinking all she had was her job.

"She must have been a lonely woman," thought John. He glanced at the blotter and a telephone number penciled in a week ago caught his eye. It was his office number. It had been underlined in red several times.

Aside from a few "doodles" and stray numbers, the rest of the calendar was empty.

While the other two detectives went through two small file cabinets, John rummaged through the desk. In the top center drawer he found an assortment of pens, pencils, paper clips, a postage stamp, and a yellow pad. The top page appeared blank. John removed it and placed it on top of the desk. He looked at it from different angles. Then, on a chance, he took a pencil out of the drawer and, using the side of the lead point, ran the pencil over the surface of the top page. He could barely make out what had been written on the previous page before it was removed.

He could make out two letters, "*J E*," followed by two more letters, "*FC*," but nothing else. "I wonder who or what this could be? JE and FC?" said John out loud.

"JE and FC? Is there a telephone list around anywhere?" asked Dani.

"Here's one," said Jim, picking up a list from on top of a file cabinet. He handed it to John.

John skimmed down the list of names. He came across several with the last name beginning with "C," but none with a first name starting with "F."

"No 'FC' here," said John.

"Maybe the 'F' is a nickname. We could ask Rainey. She might know," suggested Dani.

"What about 'JE'?" asked Jim.

"Just a minute. I'm getting to the 'E's' now," answered John as he glanced down the page.

There were several workers with last names starting with the letter "E," but only three with the first initial "J." One of those was a Janice Eigner, who worked in the Medicaid section. John doubted it could be a woman, but wrote the name on a piece of paper anyway. The next two were men. One was Jose Escobar, who also worked in Medicaid and the other, Jacob Edgar, assigned to "support collections."

"Whatever that was," thought John. Looking up from the list, he told Jim and Dani what he had found.

"I guess we check them out. See what they have to say," suggested Jim.

They returned to Ms. Rainey's office and got directions to Mr. Esobar's area. It turned out that he was an elderly man who looked to have suffered a stroke at one time. He had limited use of his right hand and the right side of his face sagged. It was difficult understanding him due to his heavy Spanish accent and the damage from the stroke. After several minutes of questioning, it was apparent he couldn't be involved in Ms. Clarke's death. Next was Jacob Edgar.

When they located Edgar's desk, it was empty. A supervisor informed them that he was "in the field" and wouldn't return until the next morning. The detectives learned that Edgar's job entailed his tracking down and getting fathers to pay their court-ordered child support. In most cases, any money received by DSS went towards reimbursing it for money it paid out in benefits for the man's child. Sometimes they were lucky and they could garnish his salary through a payroll deduction. But in most cases, even when the father was found, more than likely he, too, was on welfare.

So as not to have made it a waste of time, they asked to see Edgar's personnel folder. They were sent to the Human Resources office, where, after much coaxing and not a few threats, they were given his folder. The three detectives removed various pages from the folder and read over them carefully. They had the secretary make copies of some of the material as they went through it. After about an hour of passing the pages around so each could read them for themselves, they returned the folder to the clerk.

Stepping into the hallway, the three detectives found an empty room and huddled up.

"Well, it seems Jacob Edgar is a new comer to the Big Apple," said Jim, starting off the discussion.

"According to his file, he shows up here about a year ago, no work history, no references, and gets a job in civil service without taking a test," declared Jim.

From time to time various city agencies would hire people "provisionally" to fulfill some special need within the department. Later, if the position was made permanent, then the person would have to go through the civil service commission and file for the job. This usually included passing a written test. So far, Jacob Edgar hadn't been required to do that. The job he filled was a "seasonal" position, usually reserved for college students on summer break. But Edgar had finagled his way into remaining employed for over a year. His supervisor had registered no complaints against him, his attendance was good, and he seemed a model employee.

"He looks like 'Joe College,' not a killer," said Dani, as she examined his picture. "But then neither did Ted Bundy," she added.

"Let's head back to the office. It's time to run this guy through the wringer and see what we can squeeze out. Either later today or tomorrow, we pay him a visit," declared Jim.

Later that afternoon, John returned to his office and filled Nancy in on what they'd learned.

"Do you think this guy, Edgar, is our killer?" she asked.

"On the surface, no. There doesn't seem to be any motive. But we'll know more after Jim and Dani run a background check on him. Anything new on Krane?" he asked.

"Well, I spoke to the guys in Organized Crime. The word on the street is that Krane was involved in the diamond heist at the airport. Sources say it was done by a group from the "old" Carlino crime family. They operate out of New Jersey, shake downs, truck high jackings, stuff like that. Some of their top guys were convicted in that union pension scam a few years ago.

"Joey Carlino's son, Anthony runs the show now. Any way, after a few too many drinks at a local bar, Bruce was heard talking about a big score. That was the week before he disappeared. They think it got back to the 'family' and they were afraid he was going to spill the beans. So they had him whacked," concluded Nancy.

"So, we let the Feds and Organized Crime work the case. They have the money to pay off the snitch and then they'll get their killers. I want to concentrate on the women's murders right now. We may have a nut case on our hands, a serial killer," added John.

On the way home from work, that afternoon, Nancy had John swing past her co-op in Bayside. After dropping her off at the front door, John cruised the area looking for a place to park. Nancy went inside to check the mail box and see that everything was in order at her place. Aside from the usual assortment of flyers and magazines, the only letter of importance was from her parents in Florida. She went on up to her apartment and threw the mail on the kitchen table. Ten minutes later, John finally came in.

"I hate coming here," he complained. "There's never a place to park. When are you going to sell this place?" he asked. Not getting a reply, he looked at Nancy, who was sitting on the sofa, a letter opened on her lap. She was crying.

"Hey, what's the matter, hon?" asked John.

"Nothing," replied Nancy.

"Then why are you crying?"

"I don't know," she said.

"Is there anything wrong? Who's the letter from?" he asked.

"It's from my mom," she said through sobs.

"Is she okay? Is your dad all right?" he said, sitting alongside her on the coach. "Let me see," he said, taking the letter from her hand.

John read the letter and turned to Nancy with a puzzled look on his face. By this time Nancy had stopped crying. John put his arm around her shoulders and pulled her towards him. He held her close for several moments, then, tipping his head back, looked into her eyes.

"Well?"

"I miss them," she finally said.

"How long has it been since you visited them?" asked John.

"I went down last Christmas. No, wait, that was two Christmases ago," she added.

"It's no wonder you miss them. Why don't you take some time and fly down?. Visit for a while," suggested John.

"I can't. Not with this case hanging over us," she replied.

"There will always be cases to solve. You have the time. Go," he said.

"I don't want to go without you," she said.

John didn't answer at first. He knew this moment would come, eventually. He loved Nancy and planned on marrying her. But he didn't look forward to meeting her parents. John's relationship with his own parents had been cool. There was love, but little emotion, expressed in his home. On the other hand, he knew Nancy came from a close, "Irish" family. He'd met the brothers once or twice, but dreaded meeting her father.

Captain Benjamin Mooney was a legend in the police department. He'd been around in the "old days" and had been involved in the solving of several high profile cases. One case in particular was the "Garbrera hit" in Little Italy. It had been one of the last open gangland slayings in New York City. Carlo Garbrera was gunned down as he left Momma's Italian Restaurant. The *Daily News* had a "front page" picture of him lying on the side walk. He was bringing some leftovers home for his dog. He still had a "doggie bag" clutched in his hand.

For some reason, the mention of this fact under the picture made him sound like a sweetheart of a guy, in stead of the cold-blooded killer he really was. In any event, Ben Mooney had cracked the case and managed to get three of the top bosses put away for life.

After hearing the stories, seeing his picture hanging in headquarters, and the way Nancy admired him, Captain Ben Mooney seemed larger than life to John.

He was afraid he wouldn't measure up or meet Nancy's father's expectations of the type of person his little girl should marry.

From his silence, Nancy intuitively knew what John was thinking.

"It's Dad, isn't it?" she asked.

"No. Well, yeah. What if he doesn't like me?" stammered John.

It was unusual to see John so ill at ease about anything. Nancy thought it was cute. It gave John a sort of vulnerable quality.

"Don't be silly. He'll like you. Besides, I'm the one marrying you, not him," she replied.

John sat quiet for a moment.

"What else are you thinking?" she asked.

"What about us living together? That's sure to piss him off," said John.

"John, please. We're not a couple of teenagers. We're both adults. Actually, we are more than adults. Soon we'll be considered middle age," she said, punching him gently on the shoulder.

John absent mindedly rubbed his shoulder as if the punch hurt.

"Middle age. No way. Now a days that isn't until your fifties. People live longer now, so middle age comes later," he said.

"You are so vain. Are you really afraid of aging?" she asked.

John just smiled at her. "Maybe I'm afraid you'll get tired of being with an old fart like me," he said.

"Come here, you old fart. I'll show you how tired I am of you," she said and kissed him long and hard.

They held each other for a moment longer and then Nancy pulled away.

"We'll see. Maybe we'll get lucky with this case and get a break soon," she suggested. "In the meantime, I'll give them a call when we get back to your house," she added.

"Our house," John corrected her.

John and Nancy did a quick walk through the apartment, checking faucets, pipes, appliances, making sure everything was running properly. She double checked the answering machine to make sure her calls were "being bounced" over to the "voice mail" on her cell phone. With one look over her shoulder, Nancy locked the door and joined John at the elevator. Holding hands like teenagers, they rode down to the main floor and got off.

As they stepped into the lobby, a man carrying two grocery bags passed them and entered the elevator they'd just left. John got a quick look at him. As he turned to look closer, the door on the elevator closed.

"Who's that?" asked Nancy.

"I don't know. He just looked familiar, that's all. Probably someone I'd seen before when you still lived here," he said. "Oh well, let's head home."

Chapter 28

Jacob Edgar had spent the day running around Brooklyn and Queens doing his job of searching for men named in paternity suits. He'd been lucky. He'd tracked down five "dead beat dads," as he called them. Now he had an address on them and knew where they worked. He could get a court order to bring them back before a judge and they could be made to pay child support. Jacob loved the power this gave him. He even had a small silver badge that he liked to flash at people. Upon closer inspection the person would see that he was an investigator for the Department of Social Services, not a cop. But they rarely made the effort.

Stopping at a local Waldbaum's, he bought some food and household items he needed before heading home. Glancing at his gas gauge, he noticed he had just a quarter of a tank. He thought about filling up the car, then changed his mind.

"I'll take a run over the boarder to Nassau in the morning before I go into work," he thought. The gas was a few cents cheaper there and the Caddy he drove was a gas guzzler. Jacob swung the car off Northern

Boulevard and down the block to the apartment building where he lived.

When he'd arrived from Florida he'd been living in motels. Then, through a woman at work, he had learned of a fully furnished co-op that was for rent in Bayside. He liked the area. There was a spectacular view of the water from the small patio off the living room, and the price was right.

The place came with its own parking spot in a lot next door. That was a real luxury in New York. Jacob parked, popped the trunk release on the arm rest, retrieved his two bundles and headed to the entrance of his building. He checked his mail box, found it empty as usual, and walked across the lobby. Most days he took the stairs, climbing the five floors just for the exercise. But with the packages he decided to indulge himself and use the elevator.

As he was about to push the "up" button, the doors opened and a couple stepped off. He didn't recognize the man or woman. She was attractive. Jacob thought he knew all the women in the building, but not this one. He entered the elevator and faced front, pushing the button for the fifth floor. He made eye contact with the man who had just stepped out. He was about to verbally challenge the man for staring, but the doors closed before he could say anything. One thing Jacob learned after arriving in the city was never to show fear. If you looked scared, you were asking for trouble. Besides, he had joined a local gym and considered himself in excellent shape. He thought he could handle himself in most situations. So far, just a look had enabled him to avoid confrontations.

Jacob Edgar had kept to himself and avoided his neighbors, giving them no more than a nod of his head when he encountered them in the hallway. Tall, blonde, with rugged good looks for a young man, he would have no trouble finding girls to date. But he shied away from them, not wanting anyone to get too close to him.

He had promised himself on the long drive up from Florida almost two years ago, that he would never let anyone get too close. No one would hurt him again.

"If there was to be any hurting, he'd be the one to do it," he had vowed.

After putting his groceries away, he began thinking about his days as a kid growing up outside Tarpon Springs, Florida. Everything seemed so peaceful and predictable. But, then he'd had the encounter with his pastor. This had left a deep scare on his soul. However, it was nothing compared to what he'd learned about the couple he'd been led to believe were his parents. This, capped off with the encounter with his biological mother, had created a rift in Jacob's soul so deep that no man or woman could ever heal it. Never again would he let that happen.

Jacob had these "recollections" from time to time and each time he found his resentment and hatred stronger. He blamed everyone for his anguish, but especially his mother.

"How could she just abandon me? How could she never call or try to see me? And how could she thrust herself on me sexually, her own son?" He'd say these things out loud as he'd stormed through the empty rooms of his apartment. Sometimes he'd pick up an object and smash it against a wall. But usually he'd slowly calm down and think about ways to "get even."

He'd spent several months searching for his mother after arriving in New York. He started with her married name, as he knew it, "Siegel." He knew her husband had given them the car he now drove, so he knew he was an auto dealer. The Siegel Auto Dealership's logo stood out prominently on the license plate's frame. Jacob did find three Siegel showrooms on Long Island.

One Friday morning, he called in to work and said he was sick. He drove out to one of the showrooms and asked to see Murray Siegel. The woman at the dealership informed him that the founder, Murray Siegel, had passed away a few months earlier and that his son ran the business now. Acting shocked at the news, he inquired about Mr. Siegel's wife, Lori. He told her he wanted to pay his respects to the widow.

The woman's face suddenly changed. Her plastic smile disappeared and she seemed at a loss for words. Jacob reasoned there was probably a good reason for this, but doubted she'd reveal what that was to a perfect stranger. Jacob told her that he was a relative of the Siegels from Florida. He even showed her his car, which bore the Siegel logo. Although reluctant at first, she eventually told him where the family estate was located and how to get there. He thought about going out there, but decided it would serve no purpose unless it could help him find his mother.

Jacob drove around until he found a library near the Siegel estate. Searching through the library's computer, he found what he was looking for, copies of old newspapers. With a little help from the librarian, he found the issue of the paper he was seeking. It contained the story of Lori Edgar Siegel, wife of millionaire, Murray Siegel. It explained how she'd been suspected of being involved in the brutal murder of a man described as her "lover." It never said whether she was convicted of the crime, but it did say she'd died while being treated for a "mental" problem at a state psychiatric facility. Jacob stared at the picture of his biological mother's dead lover. He saw no resemblance between himself and that man. Murray Siegel wasn't his true father he reasoned since he was definitely too old when they'd been married.

So now he knew for sure that his mother was dead, but what about his father. "How can I solve that part of the puzzle?" he said out loud. A woman seated at the next computer monitor turned to "shush" him. Jacob just glared at her a moment, then rose from his seat and left the library.

Jacob felt satisfaction at having tracked her down, but cheated for now because he couldn't ask her the questions that gnawed at his mind. He couldn't confront her and make her pay for what she'd done. On the drive back to his apartment, Jacob wondered what the future held for him. He knew he wouldn't rest until he'd had some measure of revenge for what was done to him. "Maybe I can find my father and get some answers," he thought to himself. "She was only a kid herself when she'd gotten pregnant." He assumed it was a high school sweetheart. Unfortunately, as far as he could tell, everyone was dead. Even the man she'd been married to when she'd visited them in Florida. As it turned out Murray Siegel had died of a heart attack only months before Edgar came to New York. Jacob discovered he was a man of extreme wealth. His grown son's from a previous marriage inherited it all. He was a bastard child without any claim to the name or fortune.

This thought bothered him for he often wondered what his life might have been like if his mother had kept him.

Once he got back to his apartment he did something he'd vowed he'd never do. He called the only man he ever knew as his father, Herbert Edgar. The phone rang several times before a male voice answered. The speech was slow and slurred. His father had been drinking.

"Hi, it's Jacob," he said. There was a long pause.

"I said it's Jacob. Can you hear me?"

"I can hear you fine," said Herbert. "What do you want?" he asked belligerently.

"I just called to see how you were," he lied.

"It took you almost two years?" asked Herbert.

Jacob could sense a sadness in Herbert's voice through the booze.

"Well, I've been busy, but I'm calling now. So how have you been?" he asked.

"I've been better. What about yourself?" asked Herbert, finding it difficult to think of what to say to the only son he'd ever known.

"I'm good. I got a job up here in New York and have a nice place to live. I'm doing good," he added.

There was a long moment of silence before Herbert spoke.

"Are you coming home?"

Again, another long silence.

"No," said Jacob emphatically. "There's nothing down there for me." Jacob immediately regret having said that. He knew it probably hurt his father and the memory of his mother.

"If you say so," said Herbert, trying to sound indifferent.

Finally, Jacob decided to get to the reason for his call.

"Listen, Dad," said Jacob, the word "Dad" almost sticking in his throat.

"You remember when that Lori woman came to visit us?" knowing full well that Herbert remembered.

"Yeah. What about her?"

"Well, she is related on your side of the family, right?" asked Jacob.

"Yeah. She was my brother Charles's step daughter."

"Is he still alive?" asked Jacob.

"Nope. He died in a construction accident years ago. Why?"

Ignoring the question, Jacob pressed on.

"What about Charles's wife? What is her name? Is she still alive?"

"Her name's Judith. I think it was Moore before she married Charles. Lives in Sparta, New Jersey, last I heard. What are you getting at?" asked Herbert.

"Nothing. I'm just curious, that's all. Well, I've got to go now. It was good talking to you. Bye," he said and hung up.

"Okay, now I know my mother's step father's name, her mother's name, and where she lives. It's a beginning. But at least now I have a place to continue my search," thought Jacob. But search for what? What did he hope to find?

When Jacob landed the job as an investigator for the Department of Social Services, he felt everything had fallen into place. He found fathers and made them pay child support. Due to a personnel shortage in the department, he'd also been assigned to keeping track of the mothers who'd given up custody of their children, mothers who had "abandoned" them. He was to monitor their employment status. If they were working, they could be made to pay for some of the cost of raising their child. The city could order them to reimburse the DSS for some of the cost of foster care. Naturally, Jacob found himself identifying with the children.

He proved to be an eager and effective worker. He was responsible for bringing considerable money back to the department through his efforts.

However, what his supervisors didn't know was that Jacob was motivated beyond the "duty" of doing a day's work for a day's pay. Jacob was on a mission. To Jacob, he was searching out the "evil" ones, as he saw them, and seeing to it that their deeds didn't go unpunished.

On that long drive up from Florida, when he'd encountered the young girl in the motel, he'd justified her killing by saying he was doing God's will, even though at times he doubted the existence of God.

"How could there really be a God, considering what has already happened to me in my short life?"

Now when he took his knife to a woman it was for revenge, pure and simple. He couldn't get at his real mother. She was beyond his reach. If he couldn't stop the women from abandoning their sons like his did to him, at least he could see that they were punished for it.

That night Jacob barbequed a small steak on the gas grill he kept on his patio. As he stood over the sizzling piece of meat, a bottle of beer in his hand, he looked out on the Long Island Sound. It would be dark soon and the lights on the Throgs Neck Bridge would come on.

Some nights he'd sit outside and watch the cars as they drove along the nearby parkway. He could see young people walking, jogging, some just strolling hand in hand on the path along the water's edge.

A wave of sadness might come over him and he'd wonder why he didn't have some one to hold close. But Jacob knew this was an impossibility for him. He'd gone out on a few dates over the past year, but he'd discovered that the women he met were too demanding. They wanted a "commitment" before they even got to know each other. A commitment was something that frightened Jacob. It meant opening up to some one, being vulnerable, and he couldn't do that. So Jacob resigned himself to his life as it was.

He shut the gas burner off and brought the medium rare steak into the small kitchen. He'd prepared a tossed salad with fresh vegetables and a small baked potato for himself. He set a place on a small table in the living room and turned on the TV. The evening news was on. The second story was about the police discovering the body of a DSS worker named Mary Clarke. They showed a picture of the deceased, which looked like it had been taken many years ago.

"Probably got it from Human Resources at work," thought Jacob.

They also played a short piece of video tape. The reporter said they'd gotten it from a surveillance camera outside her building. It went by very fast and the person looked like a blur on the TV. He noticed that he'd kept his head down and they only got a picture of the top of his head. He doubted they could ever identify him from that tape. Just the same, Jacob decided he'd take a walk over to Clarke's old desk and look around once he got to work the next day. He wanted to make sure there wasn't anything there that might connect him to her.

He continued eating his dinner and flipped channels with his remote. He found a rerun of "*Friends*" and decided to watch it rather than the news.

"The news can be so depressing," he thought to himself.

Chapter 29

John and Nancy were busy reviewing information they had gotten at DSS on Mary Clarke and Jacob Edgar. There didn't seem to be a connection, other than they both worked in the same building. John decided to run a background check on Edgar. Right off the bat he discovered he was from out of state, Florida in fact.

Nancy went over some of the data they had gotten on Mary Clarke. She was particularly interested in determining what cases she had been working on or had pulled from the DSS records room. She had a hunch that the poor woman may have stumbled onto something related to the Sands and Martinez cases that ultimately caused her murder. While she called DSS Records, John got on the phone to Florida's state capital.

John contacted their Department of Motor Vehicles. He learned that Jacob Edgar had been licensed to drive in Florida at the age of sixteen. He lived in a town called Tarpon Springs. Next, he called the local sheriff's department in Tarpon Springs. He spoke to a captain by the name of Cocoran. It turned out that he was a retired NYPD cop who had relocated to Florida with his wife over ten years earlier.

Cocoran said the boredom of retirement was driving both him and his wife nuts, so he decided to go back to work. Because of his experience, he was hired as a captain right off the street. Cocoran was quick to point out that the title might be impressive, but the pay stunk. If it wasn't for his pension, he'd never be able to live on his salary. He admitted that this didn't sit well with some of the "native" cops, but tough. Being a fellow New Yorker, he promised his full cooperation.

John explained he was investigating a double, possibly a triple, homicide. The name Jacob Edgar had come up and he needed some information on his years in Florida. Captain Cocoran said he had do some checking and call him back.

Nancy was still on her phone talking to someone when John hung up his phone. He waited until she finished, then walked around to her desk.

"I'll show you mine, if you show me yours," said John with a grin on his face.

"That's definitely sexual harassment. I ought to bring you up on charges," she said without conviction.

"I meant I'd like to know if you learned anything we can use," said John as he sat on the edge of her desk.

"As a matter of fact, I did. It may not be anything, but it seems Mary Clarke had gone to the record room the day before she died looking for the files on Sands and Martinez."

"Yeah. That was probably after I'd spoken to her. Damn, I had a lousy feeling I may have had something to do with that poor woman getting herself killed," commented John, his head down.

"Stop beating yourself up. The best thing you can do for her now is catch her killer," said Nancy.

"You're right. What else did you get?"

"Seems the woman in records remembers the cases she wanted weren't there. They were signed out to Jacob Edgar. She may have told Edgar that Mary Clarke was looking for the files also. He said he would give them to her himself, but he never did.

It seems the next day Mary Clarke came to the records room looking for the files. Now, supposing she learns Edgar has them, goes down to get them, and runs into him. She doesn't know any better and tells him she's doing a favor for the police, that they are investigating two murders and want the files. If this guy Edgar is involved some how, he might have panicked and decided to keep her from going any further with it. What do you think?" asked Nancy with a satisfied smile on her face.

"Makes sense. But without some proof we've got crap," said John.

"What about you? Find anything?" asked Nancy.

"No. Edgar is from Florida originally. I have a guy checking on him but nothing so far," replied John.

"Then I suggest you get back to your own desk and get to work. Go on. Shoo! Shoo!" she said, waving her hands dismissively at him.

John smiled, got up from her desk, and started to walk back to his own desk. Then, as a second thought, he turned and kissed Nancy on the cheek.

"What was that for?" she asked.

"Nothing. I just wanted to, that's all," he said, blushing slightly.

Nancy smiled and passed the back of the fingers of her right hand over the spot on her cheek where he kissed her.

John busied himself filling out forms for the next hour. He was about to call Florida back when the phone rang. It was Captain Cocoran calling him back.

"That was fast," said John.

"Listen. I got a guy here, an old timer who's been on the force since before they had alligators here. He knows all about this, Edgar guy. You might want to talk to him. Here, let me put him on," said the captain.

"Hello, Detective Straub?" asked a voice with a southern twang.

"Call me John," said Straub.

"Mine's Bill. Bill Prescott. That's with two "t's," added Prescott.

"Hi, Bill. The captain said you might have some information on Jacob Edgar," said John.

"Yep, I know Jacob and his whole family. They lived just out of town. What's your interest?" asked Bill.

"His name came up in a case we're working on up here," replied John.

Being a good cop, Bill Prescott knew better than to ask any more questions.

He continued, "Jacob lived with Edith and Herbert Edgar. Edith Edgar died a few years back. The big "C" he said, referring to cancer.

John thought it strange how older folks never said the word "cancer." Usually they just referred to it by the letter C. When they did say the word, "cancer" it was always in a hushed voice. It was as if they feared the word alone could cause death.

"They were good, church-going folks. Oddly enough, Herb just died. His neighbor found him yesterday, dead in that old easy chair of his. He had a bad heart, but the booze didn't help none. Ever since poor Edith died he just kept to himself and drank. It was like he wanted to die just to be with her," he said.

Impatiently, John asked, "What about Jacob, their son?"

"I'm getting to him. That was a funny thing. Jacob wasn't their son, not really. You see, Edith was barren."

"She was what?" asked John.

"Barren. You know, she couldn't have kids."

"Oh. How is it you knew that?" asked John.

"It's a small town here. Everyone's related one way or another. And everyone knows everyone else's business, if you know what I mean," added Officer Prescott. "Any way, all those years without a kid, then when you'd think they were too old to raise a kid, they go and adopt one."

"Do you know anything about the adoption?"

"Is the Pope Catholic?" asked the officer.

Not waiting for John to reply, he went on.

"One day they get a visit from a relative from up north. A young girl in her early teens. Hear tell she was a relative on Herb's side of the family. Anyway, it turns out this kid is pregnant. She stays with them, has her baby, and then disappears. Guess she headed back north."

"What about the baby?" John asked.

"That's who Edith and Herb adopted. Ain't you following me, son?" asked Prescott.

"Yeah. The Edgars adopted her kid. And this kid turned out to be Jacob Edgar, right?"

"Now you're cooking. They raised him as their own."

"What can you tell me about the kid? What was he like growing up?" asked John.

"Nothing unusual. He was a normal kid, a little on the quiet side. Reason I know is one of my own kids was in the same grade as the Edgar kid. She said he was a little wimpy. Kept getting picked on by the other boys. They teased him. You know, called him a momma's boy. Stuff like that."

"Anything else? Was he ever in trouble?" pressed John.

"Well, there was that business with the pastor from their church," added Prescott.

"What kind of business," asked John impatiently. He felt like he was pulling teeth trying to get information out of this guy.

"One day, while Jacob was visiting him at his house, the pastor fell down his cellar stairs and broke his neck. He was dead by the time anyone got there. The kid was the only witness."

"Anything ever come of it?"

"Nope. Like I said, there were no witnesses except Jacob and he was just a kid. We figured it was just an accident. That was that."

"Anything else?" asked John, thinking he'd learned all he was going to from this "cracker."

"Nope. That's about it. It's just a shame, though."

"How so?" asked John.

"Well, poor old Herb dying by himself like that. Especially after all they'd done for that boy. If you ask me, for all their sacrifice Jacob didn't appreciate it," added Bill.

"Why's that?" asked John.

"Well, after Edith died, you'd a thought Jacob would stay and care for his father. But nope. Not him. He took that new Caddy they drove and headed north."

"A Caddy? Did the Edgar's have money?," asked John.

"Not really. Hard working folks, like most of us down here."

"Then where did they get the Caddy from?"

"Beats the hell out of me. Maybe it was a gift or something. Strange, if you ask me. Any way, that's about all I can tell you. I hope it helps," said Bill.

"I'm sure it will. Do you remember when he left Florida?" asked John.

"I ain't sure, but I guess it was around the time of Edith's death. Let me check on something," he said.

John heard the phone being dropped on a hard surface. After several minutes of waiting, John was about to hang up when Bill came back on.

"Here it is, July 19th. Almost two years ago."

"Well, thanks for your help, Bill," said John and hung up.

After hanging up the phone, John glanced over at Nancy. She was turned half way around in her chair looking at him.

"Anything?"

"That was some 'old timer' from Florida, name of Bill Prescott. He's a cop in the town where Edgar grew up. Knew the family. It seems Edgar was adopted. His mother was some teenager who came to stay with them when she was pregnant."

"Any trouble down there?" Nancy inquired.

"Not unless you think pushing some minister down a flight of stairs and breaking his neck is trouble," added John.

"What?" asked Nancy, eyes wide.

John told her the story about the pastor's death.

"Could have been an accident," commented Nancy.

"Yeah, and our victims could have died from self-inflicted wounds," said John sarcastically. He sat quiet for a minute, staring across the room, a vacant look on his face.

"Say, if someone were driving up from Florida, what parkways would they likely use?" he asked.

"I don't know. Why don't you call AAA and ask them?" she suggested.

"Good idea," he said.

John called Triple A and found out it was probably I-95. His next task was to trace the path Edgar took just in case there was something out there that might help. He went down the hall and returned with a beat-up road map of the east coast. Opening it on his desk, he stood over it.

"Got this from Pete next door. Said he used it on his last trip to Disney World with the family." There was a yellow highlighted line running from New York through New Jersey and all the way down the right side of the page. It ended abruptly at the bottom.

Anxiously, John turned the map over. It was upside down. He spun it around and smoothed its wrinkled edges out so it sat flat. At the bottom, he found the end of the yellow high lighted line with a circle around the town of Orlando. Moving his right index figure along an east-west parkway, John found Tarpon Springs on the west coast of Florida.

"So this is where it all started," said John out loud.

Nancy had moved around to his side of the desk and pressed against his back, looking at the map. John got a whiff of her perfume. It was called "Chance." For a moment he lost track of what he was doing. Shaking his head to clear his thoughts, he turned around. He smiled at Nancy and, placing his hands gently on her shoulder, held her away from him.

"Please, you're distracting me."

Nancy smiled, happy she still had that effect on her man.

"What can I do?" she asked, a twinkle in her eye.

"Help me find our killer," he stammered.

"Yes, boss," she said, giving him a mock salute.

"Here, jot down the states along I-95. Call the county and state police, starting from the top. Ask them if they had any assaults or murders of females in the past two years. Mention you're interested in one's where a large knife may have been used. It's a long shot, but I have a feeling our boy Jacob left Florida in a hurry. He may have been running away from or trying to find something. The more I learn about him the more I think he has more to do with these deaths," concluded John.

Nancy jotted down the states and counties off the map starting with Jersey while John worked up from Florida.

John made more than twenty calls, working his way north from Florida, through Georgia, and the Carolinas, and Virginia. Using a large police directory, he called the police headquarters along the route. He explained who he was and what he was searching for. Homicides and assaults on women, preferably with a knife. He added the dates Edgar would most likely have passed through the particular state. Nothing.

So far Nancy hadn't found anything either. He was about ready to give up when he reached Maryland. He asked his litany of questions and sat waiting, the phone nestled in the crook of his neck. He could hear the familiar sound of the clerk's fingers clicking the computer keys over the long distance lines. Absent mindedly, he stretched his arms over his head. He waited to hear the usual reply, "Sorry."

"Got something," said the voice at the other end of the line.

"Talk to me, sweetheart," said John, suddenly sitting straight up in his chair, pen ready in his right hand to take notes.

"Well, we have the usual record of crimes along our stretch of the interstate. A lot of transients passing through, some transporting drugs. But this might be what you're looking for. A double homicide at a motel just off the parkway."

"Two women?" asked John.

"Not exactly. A woman, a teenager really, and a new born, a little boy. Oops, it is closed though. Seems they arrested the girl's boyfriend. He was convicted of second degree murder. He's doing time up state. Sorry," she added.

"That's okay. Does it say how they were killed?"

"No. I just have the particulars. I'd have to pull the file for more."

"Could you, please? It's probably a dead end, but I'd really appreciate it," pleaded John.

"I'll see what I can find and call you back. It might take a while. Those files are in storage."

"That's okay. Anything you can give me. Thanks."

John hung up, not knowing if he'd just wasted the last four hours or may have busted the case wide open.

"You got anything?" he asked Nancy, who had just hung up her own phone.

"Nada," she replied. "You?"

"Maybe. The woman I was talking to is checking something for me. She's going to call back."

John and Nancy decided to take a break and get some lunch. An hour later, when they returned to their desks, there was a message waiting for John. The woman from Maryland State Police had called back. John immediately punched in her number and waited. After two rings, her now-familiar voice answered the phone.

"I have the file in front of me," she began, ready to read the police notes.

"A teenage girl was found dead in a motel room. The autopsy showed she'd recently given birth to a baby. A little investigating revealed she'd been dating a local high school jock. He admitted they'd gone to the motel where she gave birth to a baby boy.

The kid insisted the baby wasn't breathing when it was delivered. They panicked, didn't know what to do. The baby was blue and he assumed it was dead. He wrapped the baby in a towel and tossed its lifeless body in a Dumpsters nearby. He said he and the girl had a fight. She was hysterical, crying, saying her life was ruined. He couldn't deal with her so he left. He insisted that when he left the girl was alive," concluded the clerk.

"How was she killed?" asked John.

"Let me see," she said. "Here it is. She was, oh, gross. It says she was 'disemboweled.' Can you believe it? How disgusting."

"Are you sure? Read the M.E.'s report," he pleaded.

Reluctantly, she complied. When she'd finished, John felt the hairs on the back of his neck standing on end.

"Can you send me a copy of the case?" he asked.

"Sure. I'll have my supervisor fax it to you. Anything else?" she asked.

"What about the baby?" he asked.

"Let's see. The guys on the scene checked the Dumpsters but it wasn't there."

"Had it been emptied already?" asked John.

"No. In fact, it says there was blood found on some newspapers inside. The blood was human and matched the girl's type. They assumed it was from the new born," added the clerk. Then she continued.

"Wait a minute. It says about a week after the girl was found, a farmer called. He said he was walking his land with his dog, looking for a stray calf when his dog took off. He found the dog under a tree. He was sniffing around and scratching at a dirt mound.

The dog must have smelled the scent of the baby or the blood and started digging. The next thing the farmer knew the dog was pulling at some kind of material. It was a towel. The farmer cleared more dirt away and found the body of a new born infant. He called the local sheriff, who notified the state police. It was the missing infant. The towel it was wrapped in had the name of the motel on it.

"The autopsy report showed the baby had never expanded its lungs after birth. It couldn't be determined if the baby would have survived or not if born in a hospital. In any event, the dead girl's boyfriend was charged with the girl's murder. He was sentenced to life and is serving time in the state pen," she concluded.

"Did the kid plead guilty?" asked John.

"No. He insisted the girl was alive when he left."

"Well, I don't want you to get the boy's hopes up, but you may need to reopen the case. Could you give me the name of the detective who covered the case?" he asked.

She did and then transferred his call directly to the detective's office. The detective's name was Evans. John explained what his interest was and what he believed. He promised to let the detective know if he got any more information that might play on his case in Maryland.

John hung up the phone, leaned back in his chair, and put his feet up on his desk.

"You look very pleased with yourself," said Nancy, seeing his smile and posture.

"I may have busted this wide open," he said.

"Do you want to share?" she asked.

"Don't say 'share.' It sounds like social worker jargon," he pleaded. "It's what they use in therapy. 'Let's share.' I hate that expression," he added.

Nancy knew better than to ask how he knew what went on in therapy sessions. She would learn later that John and his ex-wife had gone through marriage

367

counseling before their divorce. The counselor probably used the word during their sessions, so the term probably dragged up bad memories for him. She didn't comment.

"Okay, how's this? What do you have? Is that better?" she asked with a smile.

He saw her smile and lightened up. Bad memories weren't going to spoil his mood.

"I got a break after a call to a police squad in Maryland. It seems that a young girl was killed in a motel off the interstate. The same Interstate our boy, Edgar would have used to come north. The way she was killed is the same as that used on the Sands and Martinez women. They'd pinned it on some teenage lover, but I think it was our boy, Edgar. It's too much of a coincidence. Like the Mary Clarke case. She was knifed too. It seems our boy likes it up front and personal," he concluded.

"We still need some hard evidence to connect them all together," reminded Nancy.

"How is the investigation into the Clarke woman's death coming along?" asked Nancy.

"I don't know. I'll check with Dani," replied John.

"Oh, it's Dani now, is it?" she said with a grin.

"Come on. She's just a kid. Besides, I've got you," he added.

"You think?" she scolded.

"I think what?" asked John, playing dumb.

"You think you got me?" she teased.

"I'd like to think so," he said grinning. Nancy returned his smile.

John spoke to Detectives Newel and Falcone. He learned that the lab boys had found a half-chewed piece of meat on the floor in her living room. Since Clarke was such a meticulous person, they doubted she'd deliberately spit food on her own floor. They'd run a DNA test, but the saliva on the meat didn't match hers.

They wondered, "Could the killer have left it?"

John knew without a DNA sample from Edgar they still didn't have anything. He had a hunch they were headed in the right direction. In fact, he was sure of it. He stood up from his desk and said, "It's time we found Edgar and shook his cage."

Chapter 30

Jacob Edgar made a point of getting into work early. The building was practically deserted. He wanted to be able to look through Mary Clarke's desk undisturbed. He went straight to her desk and sat down. Rummaging through her desk drawers, he didn't find anything that caused him to be concerned. Then he picked up her small desk calendar. The page was still on the day she'd died. He flipped back several days and then slowly turned each page. He read her notes and reminders. Finally, his eyes came to rest on an entry written in red. "Detective Mooney 555-3954 Cases: Sands/Martinez closed? Call Straub next week."

"So, that's why she wanted to see those cases. Mooney and Straub. They must be the ones on the case. Still nothing connecting me to them," he thought to himself. He returned the calendar to the desk and turned the pages to her last date. Feeling contented, he got up from his desk and headed towards his office.

He was passing the "Administration" section when one of the secretaries passed him on the way to her desk. She was slipping off her jacket when she saw him. She immediately brightened up and gave him a big smile.

"Hi, Jay. How are you doing? You're in early?" she said flirtatiously.

"I got some paper work to knock off before I go out into the field," he said.

"By the way, did those detectives ever get a hold of you?" she asked.

Jacob felt the blood drain from his head. The room began to spin before he steadied himself against a doorjamb.

"What detectives?" he asked.

"I don't know. Something about poor Mary. They were interviewing everyone who worked with her," she answered.

"Why would they be interested in me? I don't work in her department," he asked.

"Beats me. All I know is they were looking for you. They even asked to see your personnel file. I guess they wanted your address or something," she added.

He excused himself and headed off to his cubicle. He sat behind his desk, his head pounding, sweat forming on his forehead.

"What did they want? What were they looking for?" he thought. He had no answer, but all he knew was he had to get out of there. He grabbed his jacket and walked out of the building.

He got into his car and, drove from the lot, before stopping for a red light.

"Slow down. Think," he said to himself.

But he couldn't think. He drove aimlessly for almost an hour before ending up at his apartment. He parked his car and headed into the building's lobby. Out of habit, he went to the mail boxes. As he opened his mail box, he happened to glance at the names of the other tenants. Suddenly, one stood out from the others.

"MOONEY, N."

"Jesus Christ. It can't be the same person," he thought as he locked the door on his mail box. "3C," he said to himself. "She lives in 3C."

Jacob entered his apartment and double locked his door. For the first time, he began to worry that he might get caught. In the past, he'd been so sure of his "righteousness" and later, his cleverness, that it never occurred to him that one day he might get caught. He wandered from room to room. He went out on his patio and looked at the water. Nothing helped. Finally, he went back inside and sat at his dinning room table. He reviewed the murders in his mind. Except for the fuzzy video tape, there was no evidence linking him to any of them. It never occurred to him that it would be the sixteen-year old down in Maryland who would prove his undoing.

"If I just keep my mouth shut, they can't prove anything," he thought to himself.

To get his mind off the police, he decided to go to work. He had some folders in his attaché case that he'd planned on pursuing that day. He left his apartment and pulled his car out of the parking lot. His first stop was a warehouse in Brooklyn. A guy worked there who was supposed to be paying child support. His plan was to confront him at work, threaten to speak to his boss, and, in that way, scare him into paying up. If that failed, he could always go through the courts and have the money deducted from his salary.

Forty-five minutes later he pulled up in front of a warehouse that advertised it wholesaled auto parts. He parked his Caddy and swaggered into the building. He entered through a small door cut into a double garage door and found himself standing in a large, dimly lit open area. Scattered around the place were different makes and models of autos in various stages of disassembly.

"A chop shop," he thought to himself.

Realizing he may have wandered into someplace he shouldn't be, he started to turn back the way he came in. But before he could reach the door, a large-framed man in greasy coveralls and a sweaty "T" shirt, came up to him.

"What do you want?" asked the man in a deep voice.

Jacob was not short, standing just over six feet himself. But this guy was a giant, towering head and shoulders over him. He didn't know what to say, so he said the first thing that came to mind.

"I'm looking for Raymond DePitri."

"What do you want with him?" asked the giant.

"It's personal," said Jacob, trying to sound confident.

"Okay. Come with me."

Feeling he didn't have a choice, he followed the guy through the warehouse and up a flight of steps to an office overlooking the work area below. From there he could see an assortment of expensive cars, BMW's, Jags, Mercedes, and a few Caddies. He began to think he'd seen too much and his fear was turned up a notch. He slowly slid his right hand into his pocket and curled his fingers around the knife he always carried.

The "office" was a cluttered mess. The furniture consisted of a beat-up desk, pushed into one corner, three chairs, their seat covers split, stuffing spilling out, and a battered drab olive file cabinet. Although there were chairs in the room, the two men in the office were standing.

One was short, bald, with a beer belly hanging over the tops of a battered leather belt. He wore dungarees and a sweatshirt. His clothing didn't appeared to have seen the inside of a washing machine in its life time. The other man was about Jacob's height, but heavier. He was dressed casually, but not for work on cars. He wore dress pants, a crew neck sweater that looked expensive, and lots of jewelry. A large cigar was clenched in his teeth on the left side of his mouth. Jacob knew he was definitely in over his head. All he wanted to do was get out of there.

"Who the hell is this?" asked the short one.

"He says he's looking for DePetri," said the giant he had met downstairs.

"I'm DePitri," said the well-dressed one. "Who are you?"

"My name is Jacob Edgar. I work for the Department of Social Services. There's a paternity suit on file with our agency that says you're the father of a child DSS is supporting," Jacob said, attempting to sound official.

"Who says I'm the father?" asked the man through clenched teeth.

"I really can't say. I'd need to review the case in my office. I may have the wrong guy. I'd have to check my files," stammered Jacob.

"Why don't you do that?" said DePetri.

"Yes. I'll do that. Then I'll call you and set up an appointment. I'll get back to you in a few days," said Jacob, backing up towards the door.

"You do that, sonny boy," said DePetri.

Jacob turned and bumped into the giant, who was hovering behind him.

"Let him go, Andre," said DePetri.

"Andre the Giant! That was the name of a wrestler a few years back. He was a giant too, over seven feet tall," thought Jacob.

Finally, to his relief, the giant stepped aside and opened the door.

Jacob proceeded down the stairs, across the garage floor, and out into the sunshine. He almost ran to his car, got in, started the engine, and roared out of there. Jacob's shirt was soaked with sweat. He decided he'd had enough trouble for one day.

He drove down to the Coney Island shore and parked outside a strip joint he frequented from time to time. He went inside and sat at a table in the corner. An aging waitress came to his table and he ordered a double scotch on the rocks. When the drink arrived, he took a long belt. The fiery liquid ran down his throat and into his empty stomach. He felt himself relax. He looked up at the stage. A dancer, long past her prime, moved mechanically around a brass pole. Jazz music blared from large speakers suspended from the ceiling. Jacob Edgar ended up spending the next six hours there. By the time he was ready to leave, it was dark and he had quite a buzz on.

Jacob had consumed more than his usual amount of alcohol. As he left the bar, he decided to take a chance and drive home. He figured there wouldn't be any cops on the road this time of night and doubted he'd get stopped. However, as he walked towards his Caddy, he happened to notice the outline of a car parked a short distance behind his. The windows were fogged up. At first he assumed it was two "lovers" in the car. Then, a passing vehicle's head lights illuminated the parked car. It was a police squad car.

"Son of a bitch," he thought to himself. "Just waiting for some poor bastard to come out of the bar so you can nail him. Well, you're not going to get me."

Jacob turned and went back into the bar. Once inside the door, he took out his cell phone and called for a cab. Ten minutes later, he was sitting comfortably in the back seat of a yellow cab headed home.

"I'll have to go back early tomorrow and get my car," he thought. The weather had turned nasty, with an easterly wind off the water and a steady drizzle was coming down. He figured on a night like this, no, self-respecting car thief would be out and about. He hoped his car would be safe.

Chapter 31

The same afternoon that Jacob Edgar was talking to the guys at the chop shop, Detectives Straub and Mooney were pouring over his personnel file from DSS.

"Oh shit!" said Nancy.

John looked up, amazed. Nancy wasn't one to use crude language, except when they were having sex.

"What?" he asked.

"This guy lives in my building," she said.

"Shit!" responded John.

"I already said that. Look at his picture. Does he look familiar to you?" she asked, passing a page with a passport-size picture attached to it.

"No," said John after looking at it.

"The guy we passed getting off the elevator the other day. It was him," said Nancy with conviction.

Without saying a word, John picked up his phone and made a call. After speaking to someone, he hung up.

"That was Edgar's supervisor at work. It seems he came in early and went out to the 'field' already. This guy is a slippery son of a bitch," said John.

"You know, I've been going over what we have on Edgar and I've been trying to figure him out. From what you learned from the people in Florida, he may see himself as having been abandoned by his mother.

He leaves Florida, heads north, passing through Maryland about the same time a young girl gets murdered after delivering and 'abandoning' a dead baby. A baby boy that was dumped in a garbage bin. He may have seen the teenage father dump its lifeless body in the Dumpsters. He finds the girl and kills her.

"He comes to New York where he gets a job tracking down wayward fathers. But in doing so he finds out that some of the mothers have given up their kids . . . their sons," she adds, correcting herself.

"The two women, Sands and Martinez, both had sons in foster care. From what the clerk in the DSS records room told us, Edgar had their folders just before they were killed. Then Ms. Clarke starts asking questions and she gets killed," said Nancy.

"And they were all killed by knife, same manner, in the belly," added John.

"It sounds like this guy is on a revenge kick. He's trying to get even for being abandoned by his own mother. He's trying to punish his mother," said Nancy.

"Wow, that's some theory we've got here. Too bad we don't have any evidence connecting him to the crimes," said John.

"Wait a minute. What about the motel where the girl was killed in Maryland? Do you think the cops have a list of who was staying there at the time?" she asked.

"I don't know. But I can sure find out," replied John, picking up his phone. Flipping through his notes, he found the number for the detective he'd spoken to in Maryland.

"Detective Evans? This is John Straub, NYPD. We spoke the other day about the motel murder a few years back. Did you get a list of the people who were registered at the motel at the time of the killing? Could you fax it to me? Great," said John.

He gave the detective the fax number and hung up.

"He's going to pull it and send it up. I'll go next door and get it when it comes off the fax machine," said John as he rose from his desk.

While John was down the hall, his phone rang. Nancy reached across and answered it.

A few moments later John returned, a big smile on his face.

"Bingo!" he said, waving the fax.

"Jacob Edgar, home address Tarpon Springs, Florida. He was checked in the night before the girl was killed. We got you, you bastard," said John with enthusiasm. He leaned back into his chair and was about to put his feet up on his desk when he noticed writing on the yellow legal size pad on his blotter. He dropped his feet to the floor and hunched over his desk.

A single word or name was printed on the paper, "Siegel."

"What's this?" he asked.

"Oh, while you were down the hall I took a call for you. That cop from Florida called back. He said after he hung up he was thinking about what you'd discussed. He said he remembered that the Edgar family was connected some how to a woman named Siegel. He said she was a fugitive who was busted at a Winne

Dixie down there." Nancy paused picking up a note pad from her desk. Scanning her notes she continued.

"Seems she'd been living with the Edgars. The cops were from New York who picked her up. They questioned the Edgars, but nothing ever came of it. He never did find out who she was or what they wanted with her. He just figured it might be helpful," concluded Nancy.

"Son of a bitch! Son of a bitch!" yelled John, bounding out of his chair. He stomped around the office, running his hand through his hair, looking up at the ceiling, and continuing to curse.

Nancy watched his ranting and figured he'd lost it and she'd have to call the "goon squad" in to pick him up.

"Mind telling me what's going on?" she asked finally.

John didn't answer her at first. He continued to walk around shaking his head. He was muttering something to himself about a "Breezy Point" case and a woman scorned. Finally, he seemed to calm down and returned to his desk.

"Sorry," he said.

"Okay, now take a deep breath, slowly, now exhale, and tell me what that was all about," she commanded as if talking to a small child.

John did as he was told. After taking several deep breaths, he looked at Nancy, a big smile on his face.

"You know that saying, 'The nut doesn't fall far from the tree'?" he asked.

"Sure. You're the poster boy, aren't you?"

"Very funny. But, seriously. Did you ever hear of a case "Ski" and I worked a few years back?

The case involved a woman married to a wealthy guy who happened to be the owner of a Caddy dealership on Long Island. I guess her husband wasn't keeping her satisfied because she gets herself a young stud. They had a falling out so she hired two guys to kill the boyfriend. He owned a motorcycle shop, remember?" asked John.

"Vaguely. It was around the time I got transferred over from Vice, right?"

"Right. Well, guess whose name just came up in connection with Jacob Edgar?" Without waiting for a reply, John went on.

"Lori Siegel, a.k.a. Lori Edgar," John said proudly.

"You think they're related?" asked Nancy wide eyed.

"What do you think? Lori Siegel was Lori Edgar before she married her wealthy husband. Now, according to my friend in Florida, a little over twenty years before the Edgars have a teenage relative staying with them who just happens to be pregnant. He checked the birth certificate and bingo it was Lori Edgar. She has a kid, a boy, and right after that leaves town. Later, the Edgars adopt the baby and name him Jacob. Then, twenty years pass and Lori Edgar, the teenager, is now Lori Siegel, the murder suspect. She runs away from a psych ward, ends up in Florida, living again with the Edgars. By this time Jacob is all grown up. He was there living with Lori Siegel. Who knows what happened between them or if he knew she was his real mother. Anyway, she's eventually tracked down, arrested and returned to New York. Only before she can go to trial she dies, cancer, I think. Short time after that the woman Jacob thinks is his mother, Edith

Edgar, also dies. Something happens and our boy Jacob suddenly leaves home in the family car. A Caddy they got as a gift but from guess who?"

"You think Lori Siegel's husband gave them the car as payback for hiding his wife," added Nancy.

"Correct. Now suppose Jacob finds his birth certificate, sees Lori Edgar is his real mother and then discovers fugitive Lori Siegel is the same person, his natural mother. He flips out."

"Yeah!" says Nancy. "His life is turned upside down. The people who raised him have lied to him. He goes looking for his real mother, only she's dead. Thus, one crazy guy on a rampage to right the injustices in his life," Nancy blurts out.

"How do we prove it?" asked John, somewhat deflated.

"By hard work and detectiving," says Nancy.

"Detectiving? That's not a word," said John, smiling.

"It is now. So let's find Jacob Edgar and put the screws to him."

"Now you're talking like an old-time cop. Let's go," ordered John.

"Okay. We've got to stop this crazy bastard before he kills again," said Nancy.

Nancy went on her computer and ran Edgar's name through the Department of Motor Vehicles. She found his record, which included a two year old Cadillac registered under his name. Further checking revealed he'd been ticketed for parking too close to a hydrant. The location was the block where the Martinez woman lived in Brooklyn. The date was a few days before the Martinez woman was killed.

"I got him in the area of one of the women a few days before her death," said Nancy. However, she couldn't find anything else to link him to the crimes.

"Why don't we take a ride to some of these bars? Let's check back with the guy who managed the place where Sands worked. Max something. Show him Edgar's picture. See if he recognizes him," suggested John.

"Fine by me. Anything to get out of the office," said Nancy.

John called the topless bar and confirmed that Max was working that afternoon.

John drove for a change, heading up to the Bronx and the scene of the first murder. After crawling through traffic for almost an hour, they reached their destination. The parking lot outside was half full. John parked the car and the two of them walked inside.

As soon as Nancy entered the place, all eyes turned in her direction. It was rare to see a woman coming into the place, except for the employees. Some of the patrons quickly averted their eyes, apparently embarrassed to be seen in a place like that. John spotted Max behind the bar and they headed over.

They didn't bother with idle chit chat. John just wanted an "ID" and Max wanted the cops out of there as soon as possible. It wasn't good for business. Already, two guys had gotten up from their tables and had slunk out through the front door. John passed Edgar's picture to Max. Max looked at it carefully. He said the guy was familiar, but he couldn't be sure. John asked if any of the girls working that night were there today. As it turned out, one was. Tina which was her stage name.

Max said she was back getting ready for her turn on stage.

John knocked hesitantly on the dressing room door. When they didn't get a response, Nancy turned the door knob and entered. There were two girls in the cramped dressing room. Except for "G" strings, they were both naked.

"Lucky you," said Nancy in a whisper over her shoulder to John. "Which one of you is Tina?" asked Nancy.

"That would be me," said the girl nearest them. Tina was Latino, small, and didn't look over sixteen. Nancy decided not to go there.

"I understand you were working the night the Sands woman was killed," said Nancy.

"What night was that?" asked the girl in a tough, Spanish accent.

Nancy told her the date and reminded her what day of the week it was.

"Yeah. I was working that night. Why?"

John leaned past Nancy and held out a picture of Edgar for her to look at.

"Ever see this guy before?"

"Him. I think he's been in here once or twice. I can't be sure if he was here the night Jen was murdered. That was a while ago," she added.

"How about you. Ever see him?" asked John, showing the other girl the picture.

"Nope," was her one-word reply.

Without another word, Nancy turned and pushed John ahead of her out the door.

"That was a waste of time," said John.

"Ya think?" asked Nancy. "I saw you eye balling the Spanish kid," she said with a frown.

John decided it was better not to reply. They waved to Max on the way out.

Max waved back and under his breath said, "Stay the hell away from here."

Once in the car, John said, "Now what?"

Nancy suggested they go to her co-op and see if they could catch Edgar at home. They left the Bronx, crossed over the Throgs Neck Bridge, and stopped in front of her Bayside apartment.

A call to her superintendent at the building earlier had confirmed Edgar's address and they learned he had an assigned parking space. They checked for his car, but the Caddy wasn't there.

"Let's go bang on his door anyway," suggested Nancy.

They found Edgar's fifth floor apartment, but despite repeated banging on the door, got not response.

"Where the hell is this guy?" asked John. "He's like a ghost."

They called it a day and headed back to John's house on the other side of Queens. Tomorrow was another day. Meanwhile, back at the Bayside co-op, Jacob Edgar awakened from a drunken sleep with a pounding in his head. He got up, went to the bathroom, and downed two aspirins. After which he crawled back into bed. What Edgar didn't realize was that the pounding wasn't in his head. It had been on his front door.

Chapter 32

Rap music suddenly filled the bedroom. Jacob's eyes opened as wide as saucers. He clumsily reached for the "snooze" button on top of the clock radio, but only succeeded in pushing it onto the floor. The jolt must have caused the tuner to move because now instead of so called music, only static blared from the tiny speakers. It started his head pounding all over again. Reluctantly, he threw the covers off and sat up, his feet dangling over the side of the bed. He reached down and grabbed the radio. After hitting several buttons and switches, he managed to shut the thing off. Scratching himself, he staggered into the bathroom, took two more aspirin, then climbed into the shower. As he prepared for work, he began thinking about the cases on his desk. There was one in particular that had his attention.

The name on the folder was Wallace. Like all his assignments, it was a paternity case where the father wasn't paying child support. But what caught his attention was the fact the mother, single and on welfare herself, had given her son up for adoption. The record showed the baby was born "crack" addicted.

In these types of cases, the mother usually lost custody until she could show she was fit to care for the infant. The baby was almost a year old and it didn't look like the mother had any intention of cleaning up her act. As he thought about it, he felt his anger rising.

It was always the same. These cases started him thinking about his own mother and situation. Then the bile would come up from deep inside of him. It would fester until he found himself obsessed with it. He wouldn't be able to think of anything else. Then he'd move to the next step.

She didn't deserve to have a child. She shouldn't be allowed to do this again. She had to be punished for her actions.

"I think I'll pay Miss Wallace a visit today," he thought.

Edgar downed a cup of coffee and was about to leave when he remembered he didn't have a car. Cursing to himself, he called a cab company and arranged to be driven to Coney Island, where he'd left his car the night before. He knew he'd be late, so he called his supervisor. He got her voice mail and left a message. He said he had a "client" to see before coming to work and would be in by 10 A.M.

Forty-five minutes later the cab dropped him off outside the topless bar where he'd spent the previous day. He was grateful to find his car still there and in one piece. The only cloud was there was a parking ticket stuck under his windshield wiper. He grabbed the ticket and threw it into his glove compartment. He headed for the Belt Parkway and the bridges to the city for work.

Nancy called Edgar's supervisor when they got to their desks that morning. She was told he'd be coming in at ten o'clock, but should definitely be there. Today was a scheduled office day for him. John and Nancy reviewed the areas they wanted to question him about. They had to be careful not to over step his "rights." They weren't planning on "Mirandizing" him, not unless he admitted something they could use against him.

At nine thirty they headed over to the DSS building. Once there, they met Edgar's supervisor in her office. They arranged to use a small conference room for the interview. They were only there a few minutes when the supervisor spotted Edgar signing in. She called him into her office and introduced him to the two detectives. She then escorted them down the hall to the room for their questioning.

Nancy noticed that Edgar didn't even blink when he was introduced to them. Aside from looking tired, his eyes bloodshot, he seemed alert and pleasant.

"Cool customer," she thought.

Once in the room, Nancy and John sat at a conference table with chairs arranged around it. Instead of both sitting across from him, John sat across, while Nancy took a chair a few seats away and on Edgar's left. This way the two detectives could make eye contact with each other and still talk to their suspect. Further, it would keep Edgar turning from one to the other during the interview. They knew that this simple action could unnerve a guilty suspect. But before they could begin, Edgar paused at the seat they'd directed him towards.

"Listen. I just got in and could use a cup of coffee. There's a pot down the hall. Can I get you guys any?" he asked as if inviting them for tea.

"As a matter of fact, yes," said Nancy.

"Me too," said John.

"Here, I'll come with you to give you a hand," added John.

The last thing John wanted was Edgar bolting on them now. He wanted to keep him in his sights. They walked down the hall, found the coffee machine, and soon returned with a cup for each.

After settling into their chairs, John began.

"Mr. Edgar, as you may know, we are investigating the murders of women, one of whom worked in this building. You may have known her, Mary Clarke," said John.

"Yes. I knew Ms. Clarke, not well though. It was awful what happened to her," he added.

"Yes, it was. Do you have any idea who might have wanted her dead?" asked Nancy.

"I'd assumed she was killed by a robber," answered Edgar.

"Why do you say that?" asked John.

"Well, I heard that she was killed in her place, so I figured someone had broken in and she caught them there," he replied.

"Have you ever been to Ms. Clarke's apartment?" asked John.

"No," was Jacob's quick response. "They're fishing," he thought to himself. "Just stay calm. They ain't got nothing on me."

Changing directions, Nancy asked, "Where are you from, Mr. Edgar?"

"I was born in Florida. I moved here a short time ago," he said.

"And your parents, they're still alive?" asked John.

"No. They're dead," was his response.

"I'm sorry to hear that. Are you married?" asked Nancy.

"No."

"Are you dating anyone?" asked Nancy.

"No."

"Do you frequent topless bars," asked Nancy.

Edgar blushed, but said nothing.

"Ever been to a topless place in Coney Island?" pressed John.

"I may have," was Edgar's curt reply.

"How do you spend your time?" asked John.

"I stay by myself. Why do you ask?" said Edgar.

"No particular reason."

Then, John slid two photos across the table.

"Have you ever seen either of these women before?" asked John, showing him the autopsy pictures of Sands and Martinez.

Jacob stared at the pictures, a slight smirk on his mouth.

"No," he said with confidence.

"No? Didn't you investigate their cases as they related to child support? Didn't you have their folders recently?" pressed John.

"I may have. But I don't remember them looking like that."

"I guess you wouldn't. They would have been alive when you saw them, right?" asked Nancy.

"I have so many cases, they become a blur after a while."

"What about this one? Ever see her before?" asked John, sliding a picture of the teenage girl killed in the Maryland motel.

Nancy noticed Edgar's eyes open wide and sweat begin to form on his brow and upper lip.

"No. I never saw her before," said Edgar.

The detectives could see he'd recognized the girl and knew they'd touched on a nerve.

"Ever been in Maryland,?" Mr. Edgar?".

"I may have," he answered.

"Ever stay in the Maryland Motor Lodge off I-95?" asked John.

"I don't remember," stammered Edgar.

"What kind of a car do you drive?," asked Nancy.

"A four year old Caddy Deville," he said.

"That's an expensive car for someone just starting out at work," said John.

"I got it from my parents. It was their car."

Nancy and John could see that he was rattled, but they still didn't have anything concrete on him. They didn't want to over step his rights and blow the case on a technicality, so they decided to back off.

"Well, I'd like to thank you for your time, Mr. Edgar," said John, rising from his chair. He extended his right hand and Edgar took it in his. John noticed Edgar's palms were damp. As they shook hands, Nancy reached across the table and grabbed the coffee cups.

"I'll throw these in the garbage on the way out." She made a point of picking up the lids and placing one on Edgar's cup. They then walked down the hall and out of the building. On the way, Nancy dropped two coffee cups in a receptacle. When they got into their car, John turned to Nancy.

"Whatchu got?"

"Edgar's coffee cup. Might as well run a DNA on him. You never know," she added. They drove away from the DSS building and back towards police headquarters.

Following the interview Jacob Edgar returned to his office cubicle. The underarms of his shirt were soaked with perspiration. He thought he'd done well, until they showed him the picture of that kid from Maryland.

"How did they find out about her? And how could they connect her to him?"

He had a million questions, but no answers. He thought he'd been so very careful, so smart. He still thought he was in the clear. But just in case, he decided to stop at the bank and withdraw his savings.

"Might as well be ready to move," he thought.

In another part of New York City was a young girl by the name of Patty Wallace, age nineteen. She lay on her bed, head fuzzy from smoking pot. She knew she had to get up and hit the streets soon. She had to turn a "few tricks" or else her man would give her a beating. What Patty Wallace didn't know was that a visit to the DSS by two detectives had changed the course of events planned for that day. They'd distracted one Jacob Edgar and in so doing had prevented him from following through with his own plans for Miss Wallace. She was able to live one more day, if you could call her life living.

Chapter 33

John and Nancy sat in their "unmarked" outside the DSS building's parking lot. They didn't have to wait long before they saw Jacob's distinctive Caddy pull out of the lot. John turned the key and the engine started. He waited for a car to pass before pulling away from the curb. He kept at least one car between them and their prey. After several turns, the Caddy parked in front of a Chase Bank. They watched as, Jacob exited the car. He didn't bother to check the time on the parking meter and walked swiftly into the bank.

"What do you think? Is he getting ready to run?" asked Nancy.

"Could be. I guess we can follow him for a while and see," replied John.

Jacob soon came out and drove on down the block. John followed, but not too closely. They continued to follow, with him eventually leading them to his and Nancy's apartment complex in Queens.

"Now what?" said John.

"I guess we could make a social call. After all, we are neighbors," said Nancy.

"Okay. At least he'll know we are on to him. He may get spooked and do something stupid," commented John.

John parked down the block and they walked to the front of the building and entered it. They boarded the elevator and headed up to Edgar's apartment on the fifth floor.

Watching from behind the exit door to the left of the lobby was Jacob Edgar. He'd spotted the cops tailing him and saw them walk into the elevator of his building. While he knew the woman lived in his building, he thought it too much of a coincidence for them to just happen to end up there.

Not knowing what to do next, he snuck out the side of the building, got back in his car, and started to drive. Cruising along the Cross Island Parkway, he reviewed his actions over the past few years. He tried to imagine what he could have left behind that would have tied him to any of the murders. He couldn't think of anything.

"They probably asked the same questions of everyone else at work," he thought. "But not the Maryland thing," he remembered. But then they knew he'd come up from Florida. Maybe they were checking for unsolved crimes along the interstate and just lucked out. But the papers said they had a killer, the girl's boyfriend.

Riding without a destination in mind, he eventually found himself back in the Coney Island section of Brooklyn. He exited the parkway and drove to the same topless bar he'd been at the night before.

"Might as well kill some time and think what to do next," he thought to himself as he entered the dimly lit bar.

Back in Queens, John and Nancy's repeated knocking failed to elicit a response at Edgar's apartment door.

"Come on. Either he's in there and not answering or he gave us the slip," said John.

As they walked out the front of the building, John noticed that the spot where Edgar had parked his car was empty.

"Damn sneaky bastard. He's gone," said John disgustedly.

"Well, there's nothing more we can do here. Let's head back to the office and drop the coffee cup off at the lab. Maybe they can connect him to one of the crime scenes through DNA."

Two weeks would pass before the two detectives got a break in their murder investigations. In the mean time, they learned that Edgar had not skipped town, but was nonchalantly carrying on with his life as if he didn't have a care in the world. His apparent smugness galled the detectives.

They had completely forgotten about the Bruce Krane case until a call from the FBI revealed another "punk" linked to the big heist at the airport showed up. This time the body was found in the marshes outside Newark airport in New Jersey. "Something about airports appeals to this gang," commented John when he heard. The FBI agent seemed confident that it was just a matter of time before someone connected to the crime decided it was safer and healthier to deal with the Feds than to keep his mouth shut.

John and Nancy continued to investigate a shopping list of murders on their desk, but always returned to the Sands and Martinez cases before long. They continued to interview Edgar's co-workers, bartenders, dancers, and bouncers at local topless bars, and even made several long distance calls to police from Florida north along the interstate he'd used. But nothing new materialized.

Then, out of the blue, Nancy got a call from Detective Dani Newel.

"You remember that Mary Clarke case John was interested in?" she asked.

"Sure," replied Nancy.

"Well, we just got a report from the lab in California that does our DNA testing. Apparently, you guys had sent a sample to them for testing. The report was just faxed to us because the case listed next to the specimen was Clarke. Did you guys send something for evaluation?" asked Newel.

"Yeah. Didn't John tell you?" Nancy said.

"No. You wouldn't be doubling up on our case, would you?" asked Dani accusingly.

"No. The day we turned in the sample had been a bummer for us and I guess he just forgot. Sorry if we stepped on anyone's toes," apologized Nancy.

"That's okay. Who is this guy Jacob Edgar?" asked Newel.

"Edgar is a guy who works with, or I should say, worked with Mary Clarke. We think he killed her because of something she found that may have linked him to multiple murders we're investigating. We'd interviewed him at work in connection with our cases and lifted a coffee cup he'd used while we were there.

We'd hoped the DNA might connect him to one of our cases, but so far we got zip," responded Nancy.

"Well, I don't know about yours, but we got him in Mary Clarke's apartment," said Dani excitedly.

"Get out of here," replied Nancy.

"No. Get this. We picked up a chewed piece of meat off the floor at Clarke's apartment. We doubted it was thrown there by the victim. She seemed to keep a neat place and it seemed out of character for her to spit a piece of food on her own carpet."

"Unless she had it in her mouth when she was being killed," interjected Nancy.

"That could have been, but DNA from the saliva on the meat didn't match the victim's. Then we get the test report back on that coffee cup. The DNA matches the saliva on the meat. Whoever chewed on that piece of meat and spit it out is the same person who drank from that coffee cup," concluded Dani.

"And that would be our guy, Jacob Edgar," said Nancy, equally excited.

"So I guess we're on the same trail after all," remarked Dani.

"Wait until I tell John. He's going to flip," said Nancy.

"How close are you to this Edgar guy anyway?" asked Detective. Newel.

"Hmm, that's a good question. We have an idea we're dealing with a psycho here. The latest theory is he's trying to kill his mother," responded Nancy.

"Stop. What did his mother do to him?" asked Newel.

"It's not what she did, but rather, didn't do. She seems to have 'abandoned' him. At least that's the way we see it. We haven't run it past any of our forensic people, but it seems this guy's mother had him when she was just a kid herself. She left him in the hospital and he was raised by her relatives. They apparently adopted him, but failed to tell him the truth. Somehow he found out and flipped out," said Nancy.

"Okay. So let's get our 'lesser' halves in on this and make our move. When do you expect John back?" asked Newel.

"He went across the street for coffee. He should be back any minute."

"Went out for coffee. What's the matter with the company pot?" asked Newel.

"If you have to ask, you're not a real coffee drinker. He insists on running over to Starbucks or Dunkin' Donuts for our coffee. Who am I to object as long as he's doing the running?" said Nancy.

"Right. I drink tea, so I can't comment on our in-house coffee. Suppose you call me when he comes back. I'll get Falcone and meet you in your office. We can compare notes," added Newel.

"Sounds good to me. Later," said Nancy and hung up her phone.

When John returned from his "coffee" run, Nancy told him what she'd learned from Dani Newel.

"See if you can get them down here," said John enthusiastically.

In ten minutes the four detectives were huddled around John's desk.

"I'll show you mine, if you show me yours," said Jim Falcone, holding the Mary Clarke folder out in front of him.

They swapped files and began reviewing each others' notes.

"Wow! This guy hates women," said Jim.

"Not just women. Women who he thinks deserted their sons. My guess is Mary Clarke was too close to linking him to the Sands and Martinez murders and got herself killed for it," said John, trailing off at the end and lowering his gaze to the desk.

"Stop beating up on yourself," said Nancy, placing an arm around his shoulder.

Jim and Dani exchanged questioning glances.

Nancy caught the look and replied.

"Ms. Clarke had helped John gather information in the past and he'd asked for her help on these," she said, nodding towards the two case folders the others were reviewing. "John thinks it was because of him that she got killed."

"Man, that's a rough call," said Jim.

"But maybe her help will stop him from killing again," added Detective Newel. "You just can't figure life out sometimes."

John raised his head. All could see that his eyes were glazed over, as if he were fighting back tears.

"Now, let's get this bastard. That's the least we can do for these women."

Chapter 34

Two weeks passed and Jacob Edgar began to believe he'd gotten away with murder. Because the detectives hadn't returned to question him, or lock him up, he figured they had been on a fishing expedition. He submerged himself in his work and put them out of his mind. Then one day, while sitting on his small outside patio admiring the bridge and water beyond, he thought of Nancy Mooney.

"I wonder if she still lives in the building?" he thought to himself.

This was still on his mind when he was walking down the hall to the trash chute. Walking in the opposite direction was the building's superintendent, Mr. Higgins.

"Hi, Mr. H," said Edgar, a big smile on his face.

Mr. Higgins nodded back.

"Say, I got somebody's mail in my box by mistake," said Edgar. "A Nancy Mooney. Does she live in the building?"

"Sure, on the third floor," replied Higgins.

"That's what I thought. But I went down and knocked on her door several times, no answer. Finally, I just slipped the stuff under her door," he lied.

"Ms. Mooney spends most of her time with her fiancée, Detective Straub. He lives in another part of Queens somewhere," responded Higgins.

"Oh, she's dating a cop?" asked Edgar.

"She's a cop, herself," returned Higgins.

"No kidding. That must be cozy," said Edgar.

Mr. Higgins frowned and continued on his way down the hall.

"So Detective Mooney, you spend most of your time at your boyfriend's. Maybe I can just take a peek around your place and see what I can learn about you. I wonder how you'd like to be investigated for a change," he wondered.

Later that night, when most of the other residents were asleep, Jacob paid a visit to the Mooney apartment. Knowing the apartment number from the mail box in the lobby, he went down the two flights of stairs to her floor. Once outside, he knocked several times to make sure no one was home. Satisfied, he removed his hunting knife from its ever-present leather sheath on his belt. He slide the long, thin blade between the door and the jamb until he came to the door's bolt. Carefully sliding and wiggling the blade, he managed to work the metal bar out of its seat and popped the door open.

Jacob quickly slipped inside Nancy's apartment and closed the door. He leaned against the hall door, waiting in the dark. Gradually, his breathing eased and he was satisfied there was no one home. He reached along the wall, found the light switch, and pushed it up. The living room area was suddenly bathed in light. He blinked, his eyes momentarily blinded from the light. After a moment, his eyes to the brightness and he began to move through the apartment.

First, he checked the bedroom, just to be sure. It was empty, the bed neatly made, and the room in perfect order. Moving back down the hallway he checked the bath room and kitchen, all empty, as was the living room. Realizing he was alone, Jacob began a methodical search of Detective Mooney's apartment.

He rummaged through kitchen drawers, but didn't find what he wanted. However, the bedroom held the treasure he sought. In a night table drawer was an address book. He sat on her bed and flipped through the various pages.

"She has a neat, printed-type penmanship," thought Jacob. It was easy to read, not like his "chicken scratch," as his teachers used to call it.

There was the usual assortment of names, family, friends, co-workers. But the name he was most interested in appeared under "S." There at the top of the page was the name, "Straub, John," followed by an address and telephone number. There were several casual "doodles" on either side of the name. Some consisted of little hearts with arrows running through them.

"How precious," said Jacob sarcastically to himself. "I wonder how he'd like it if my knife were thrust through his heart instead of one of Cupid's arrows," he thought, a smirk on his face. Jacob found a small pad and pen in the drawer and copied the information he needed. He then returned the book to the drawer and closed it. As he stood up from the bed he took a moment to smooth out the spread and with his handkerchief wiped off the surface and handle of the table. On his way out, he did the same to any surfaces he thought he might have touched.

After returning to his own apartment, Jacob was too excited to sleep. Instead, he got in his car and went for a drive.

It was almost three in the morning at Detective Straub's house. John and Nancy lay wrapped in each other's arms, fast asleep. They didn't hear the sound of a dog barking in the neighbor's yard. They didn't notice the headlights of a car, slowly cruising past their home. John and Nancy slept peacefully, unaware that a killer was stalking them.

Chapter 35

It was the beginning of a new week for Detectives Straub and Mooney. They had spent the weekend cleaning the house and attending a dinner party at John's old partner, Pete Zubriski's house. "Ski" was excited about returning to work. His leg was finally healed and he was cleared to return to active duty. It wasn't discussed, but "Ski" hoped he would be reassigned as John's partner. He knew this was selfish on his part, but he felt it wasn't safe teaming up a man and woman who were involved with each other. He thought this was true in most lines of work. Emotions, both good and bad, might get in the way of how they handled themselves. In their line of work, any hesitation on a partner's part could be fatal. Ski didn't know that Nancy agreed with him and was prepared to request an assignment change once Ski returned to work.

John and Nancy's conference with Detectives Newel and Falcone the week before had resulted in their obtaining a search warrant for Jacob Edgar's apartment in Queens. They planned on executing it that night. That way, they hoped to catch Edgar home and, if the search proved fruitful, make an arrest as well. They believed they had enough on him to at least charge him with the murder of Mary Clarke. With any luck, they might be able to link him to the other killings as well.

In the mean time, Jacob Edgar was keeping himself busy at work. He'd used his contacts at the New York Department of Motor Vehicles to track down more "dead beat" dads.

He filed the necessary paperwork and would haul their "sorry asses" before a Family Court Judge. Then, maybe they'd start paying support again for the kids they'd produced.

Jacob sat idly scanning through a DMV list on his computer when he had a thought. For the longest time, he felt he had exhausted all the leads and found everything he needed to know about his "real" mother. But, working on the numerous paternity" cases had sparked an idea. "Who is or was my father?"

He sat staring off into space for several moments before snapping out of it. For some reason, this information had never been that important to him. He'd been so fixated on the issues surrounding his mother that the other half of the equation rarely came up. Even when it did, Jacob tended to blame his mother for all his troubles. "Probably all my Bible reading, the story of Eve tempting Adam and all," he reasoned. But now he wanted to know. Jacob tried to remember what his father had told him about his real mother. He'd told Jacob that his mother Lori was from Sussex, New Jersey. After a struggle with his memory, he recalled that her mother's name was Ann Marie. He thought her maiden name was Moore but couldn't be sure. She'd been married to his Herbert's brother, Charles Edgar.

Edgar picked up his phone and on a chance dialed the New Jersey DMV. He identified himself as an investigator from New York's DSS. He was searching for an Ann Marie or Charles Edgar, last address, someplace in Sussex. The man at the DMV informed him that the only Charles Edgar he had was deceased and no Ann Marie Edgar.

Then, Jacob asked him to check under the last name Moore. Moments later, the clerk told him there were three Ann Marie Moores in the state, but only one living in Sussex. The date of birth made her old enough to have had a daughter about Lori Edgar's age. No if only she was still alive. Jacob copied down the address and thanked the clerk for his help. Not having any specific plans for the rest of the day, Jacob decided to take a drive to Sussex, New Jersey.

It took about two hours for Edgar to get out of the city and to the northern part of New Jersey, where the small town of Sussex was located. It was in the western portion of the state, not far from the Pennsylvania border. There was a mixture of farms and small communities. Since Interstate 80 had been completed, this part of the state was within commuting distance to New York City, all be it, an hour and a half trip on a good day.

He pulled into the little Village of Sussex and found a diner where he hoped to get a bite to eat and gather some information. Sliding into a booth, he ordered a "BLT" and coffee from the waitress. He used his smile and charm to engage the woman in idle conversation when she returned with his order.

It was mid-afternoon and business was slow. In no time, he learned her name was Joan Kelly. She was married in her mid-thirties, and had no children. Her husband was a supervisor with the local highway construction crew. As it turned out, the waitress knew Ann Marie Moore. It seems Moore had worked at that very diner as a waitress when Joan, the current waitress, was growing up. She told him that Moore was a widow, lived alone, even gave her directions to her house. Leaving a generous tip, Jacob headed out the door and off to meet his "grandmother."

It was now late afternoon and Jacob drove slowly through the back streets of the sleepy town. He followed the directions the waitress had given him and soon stopped in front of a small bungalow-style home. It was small but appeared well cared for. The outside was freshly painted and the lawn mowed, the shrubs trimmed. Jacob reached over the back of his seat into the rear of the car. He grabbed a black loose leaf binder that held notes from a prior investigations. He knew that when people saw him with the binder, they relaxed, thinking he wasn't a cop and they weren't in any kind of trouble. Putting on his best social worker's face, he headed up the walk to the home of Ann Marie Moore Edgar.

Inside, Judith was watching the early edition of the evening news when the front door bell rang. Glancing at the small clock on the mantle, she frowned. "Who could be coming by at this hour?" she wondered out loud. She approached the door and peeked through the small glass opening. Outside, she saw a nice looking young man, glancing off down the block. The first thought that came to Judith was "Jehovah's Witness." She was about to ignore him when the young man turned and caught her face in the window. He smiled.

"Something familiar about that face," crossed Judith's mind as she opened the door.

"Yes? Can I help you?" she asked.

"Good afternoon, madam. My name is Jacob, Jacob Waters," he lied. "I'm with the Department of Social Services. Is your name Ann Marie Moore?" he inquired.

"Yes, it is. Why?" she asked.

"Well, we are doing a background check on one of your neighbors. They are in the process of adopting a child and gave your name as a reference," said Jacob.

"Really. Who is that?" she asked surprised.

"Let me see, I have the name here some place," he said as he fumbled with the loose leaf book stalling for time

"Would you mind if I came in? It would be easier and more private. You understand," he said, trailing off.

Taken in by his pleasant looks, gentle manner, and the gnawing sense that she recognized him from somewhere, she agreed. Judith opened the door and allowed the stranger to enter her home.

Chapter 36

The four detectives pulled up in front of the building where both Nancy Mooney and Jacob Edgar lived. A patrol car with two uniformed cops accompanied them for support. Because this was a murder investigation, the assistant D.A. had managed to get a "no knock" search warrant from a local judge for the detectives. "No knocks" were rare. Usually they were only granted when there were drugs involved and there was a concern the suspects would, if given enough time, dispose of the drugs. However, in this case, the detectives furnished enough credible evidence to convince the judge this suspect was a threat to others and himself.

The four detectives, Straub, Mooney, Falcone, and Newel, entered the elevator. The uniformed cops remained outside, guarding the entrance and exits. As the detectives stepped off the elevator, they moved cautiously down the hall to Edgar's apartment. They had a heavy lead-filled pipe with handles on either side. They would use it as a battering ram to take the metal door down.

Once in position, Jim Falcone moved in front of the door. Being the biggest of the group, the heavy work of knocking in the door fell to him. Checking to see that the other detectives had their shields out and guns drawn, he swung the heavy pipe. In one smooth but shuddering blow, the door swung open. Falcone stepped aside and the other detectives quickly entered. Crouching, guns extended in front of them, they moved quickly through the rooms of the apartment. Once they'd searched the rooms, closets, bathroom, and balconies, they returned their weapons to their holsters.

"Empty!" exclaimed Straub, disappointed.

"Well, we're here. Let's search the place and see what we find," said Nancy.

The next three hours was spent going through every drawer, closet, and cubby hole they could find in Jacob Edgar's apartment. John and Jim weren't even trying to be neat. They deliberately pulled each drawer out and turned it upside down, spilling its contents on the nearest flat surface. They then scattered the items around looking for anything incriminating.

"Nothing!" John would exclaim after each area was thrashed.

The ladies were a little neater and more organized. They removed the clothing from the closets and went through the pockets, carefully patting each item for hidden folds. Next they went through the shelves. But like their male counter parts, they too found nothing.

"Nobody's that good," said Falcone. "They always keep some kind of souvenir, something," he exclaimed.

"What are you doing?" asked John when Nancy began going over a room he'd already been through.

"Just double checking," she said.

"I've already been through there," he said angrily.

Nancy chose to ignore him and began going over some of the closets and drawers he had already been through. She was about to admit defeat when she happened to turn a drawer upside down. There, taped to the bottom, was a large manila envelope.

"What have we here?" she said as she peeled the tape away and raised the envelope in the air. The other detectives quickly gathered around her.

"Clear a spot for me," said Nancy, referring to the kitchen table, which was littered with knives, spoons, and pieces of paper. John took his arm and brushed everything onto the floor.

"There, cleared," he said.

"Nice," said Nancy sarcastically. She couldn't understand why some cops had to trash a place when they searched it. It was like they were venting their frustrations on the suspect's possessions. They didn't seem to realize that neat meant careful.

Nancy pulled up a chair and sat at the table. She removed a pair of surgical gloves from her pocket, put them on and proceeded to open the envelope. She carefully spilled the contents across the empty table. Various sections of what appeared to be newspaper clippings and legal documents lay before them. Nancy pushed them apart with a gloved finger.

"Some of these are old. Look how yellow the pages are. I bet they're twenty years or more," said Detective Newel.

Each of the other detectives had pulled up chairs, donned gloves, and were opening the folded sheets of newspaper.

"Here's an article about that girl who was killed in the Maryland motel," exclaimed John.

411

"And here's one about the Sands murder," said Nancy.

"Martinez and Clarke," added Jim Falcone.

"Here's something from a Florida paper. It's several years old. It's an obituary. Looks like the guy's mother, Edith Edgar," commented Dani Newel.

In the mean time, John was busy opening legal size envelopes. "These look like birth certificates and adoption papers." John paused, examining the faded type of one of the papers. "Jacob Edgar was the son of Lori Edgar. She's that same bitch only her last name was Siegel involved in the contract killing a few years back. Just like I thought."

"From what I'm getting here is that this guy is the son of Lori Siegel. He was adopted by the Edgars, also family," interjected Nancy. "After his supposed mother dies, he finds out he's adopted, and takes off. He's enraged and on the way decides to kill the girl in Maryland. Then he lands in the Big Apple and gets a job pursuing wayward parents. He sees these women as doing the same thing to their sons as was done to him. So he decides to play God," said Nancy, stopping only when she ran out of breath.

"Then Mary Clarke starts snooping around and he kills her too," adds Dani Newel.

"So, we have motive, opportunity, DNA evidence, and now all we have to do is get our suspect and getting a confession out of him," said John, through clenched teeth.

The detectives took all the papers, returning them to the original manila envelope. On the way out, they closed the door and placed yellow "police" tape across the entrance. Once downstairs, they ordered the uniformed cops to "sit" on the place in case Edgar showed up. They warned them not to do anything, just call for them and back up if they spotted him.

The four detectives returned to their own cars and headed back to their offices. The next step was to get an arrest warrant for Jacob Edgar.

At the same time his apartment was being ransacked by four of New York's detectives, Jacob Edgar sat at a kitchen table across from the woman he suspected to be his grandmother.

Chapter 37

Ann Marie Moore had invited Jacob Edgar into her home. She lead him into the kitchen and, at her invitation, took a seat beside a small metal table. She offered him tea, which he accepted. A red and white checkerboard table cloth covered the surface. There was a plastic vase with artificial flowers placed in the middle of the table. The room was neat, though showing its age, like the woman placing a steeping cup of tea in front of him.

The woman took a seat opposite him, clasped her hands together on the table and looked at Jacob. She couldn't shake the feeling that they'd met before. He looked so familiar.

"Are you from around here, Mr. Waters?" she asked.

"No. I'm from Newark. But working for the state, I travel a lot."

"Now, you said you are investigating the adoption of a baby," she said.

"Well, it's a two year old, actually. A little boy abandoned by his mother. She was a drug addict and couldn't care for him. He's been in a foster home since he was a few weeks old."

"How tragic, And who are the people you are investigating?"

"I guess the word "investigating' is a little harsh. I'm actually just doing a back ground check on the family that has applied for adoption."

"And you say I know them?" she asked, a puzzled look on her face. She couldn't imagine anyone she knew who might be adopting a baby. Most of her friends were her age, or older.

"The couple are the Kellys. Joan Kelly works at the diner in town."

"Oh, Joan. I didn't know she and Bert were looking to adopt," she said.

"Well, I guess they were keeping it quiet in case it fell through. You know, they wouldn't want people maybe . . . , what? Pitying them."

"Oh for goodness sakes. That's wonderful. They have been married over ten years. Joan confided to me once that she'd given up having a child of her own. I just assumed they were resigned to being without. Imagine that. The Kellys with a baby," she said gleefully.

Jacob watched her face change. The expression, her smile. He tried to imagine her as a young woman. He could see his own mother's features in her face. At least what he recalled appearing in a wrinkled, old black and white photo of a teenage girl.

Jacob continued to ask her questions about the Kelly family, taking notes, and nodding or smiling at her various comments. When he felt he'd had the elderly woman totally at ease he began to move the conversation around to what he was really interested in. His mother. His father.

"You've been very helpful, Mrs. Moore. I think with what you've told me and what others have said, the Kellys shouldn't have any trouble with the adoption."

"You must get great satisfaction out of your job, Mr. Waters."

"Please, call me Jacob, Mrs. Moore," he offered.

"Thank you, Jacob. But it's Miss Moore," she corrected.

"Oh, I apologize. I just thought you were married. Maybe it was something Joan Kelly had said."

"I was married, once," she said, looking off into another part of the house.

Jacob could see she was recalling her past event or time, something unpleasant.

"Divorced?" he asked.

"Widowed," she replied.

"I'm sorry. I didn't mean to bring up anything unpleasant," he said.

"That's all right. It was a long time ago." She paused, as if trying to make a decision about something. Then she went on, "Besides, he was no good. I know one shouldn't say anything bad about the dead, but God forgive me, that man was evil."

Jacob was shocked by her openness. He decided to press the issue.

"That's okay. Your feelings can't hurt him. They can only hurt you."

She looked at him a moment. "That's very mature, wise even. You know, I've never spoken to anyone about my late husband. But for some reason I feel comfortable talking to you," she said.

"Funny. My late mother used to say I had a way with people. She said if I'd been raised Catholic I'd

416

have made a good priest. People can't seem to help sharing their thoughts and concerns with me. I guess that's why I came to be in this line of work."

"Well, you're very good at what you do. You have a very calming way about you."

"Thank you, Mrs . . . . I mean, Miss Moore," he said, lowering his head, feigning embarrassment.

Ms. Moore found this very disarming.

"Do you have time, Mr. Waters?" she asked.

"As much as you like. I'm single and don't have anyone to rush home to. Not yet anyway."

"Are you seeing someone special?"

"No. Why, do you have a daughter for me?" Jacob saw the hurt expression flash across her face. He knew he'd hit a nerve.

"No," she answered after a moment's hesitation. Then, as if to clarify her answer, said, "She passed away."

"I'm so sorry. I seem to be dredging up a lot of bad memories for you."

"That's okay. I haven't talked about it in a long time. Maybe I should. You know, get it out. But I don't want to burden you."

"No burden. Really. Do you want to talk about it?" he asked hopefully.

She sat for what seemed to Jacob like an eternity. Then she told him about her daughter.

"Her name was Lori, Lori Edgar."

Upon hearing this, even though he expected it, Jacob felt his stomach flip.

"That was my late husband's name. Edgar, Charles Edgar. He was a construction worker in town. I was young and did waitressing at a local bar." Here she

417

stopped, apparently searching for the right way to tell him her story.

"How can I say this without sounding like a tramp? Well, I guess I was, back then anyway."

Jacob was about to say something, but she raised her hand and stopped him.

"No, that's the truth. In my youth I drank too much, an occupational hazard I guess. I made the mistake of sleeping with one of the local patrons. He was already married, but I didn't care. He was good looking, older, and I found it all very exciting. Anyway, I got pregnant. They didn't allow abortions back then, so I staid home and had the baby. I gave birth to a beautiful seven pound little girl. God forgive me, but if I knew then, what I know now, I would have found a doctor and had it done.

"My parents died around that time, a car accident. Anyway, there I was, single, an out of work waitress, no means of support. I'm alone and along comes Charles Edgar. Not a bad looking guy. Anyway we got married and he agreed to raise Lori as his own.

"Charles' work wasn't steady and we needed a roof over our heads so I went back to being a waitress. I'd work nights, while he had his days free to look for jobs. My biggest mistake," she said, head bowed.

"Why is that?" asked Jacob.

"Well, Charles was a drinker. You never knew how he was going to be from one day, no from one moment to the next. He could be fun, care free, a real charmer. But then he'd turn ugly, like that horror guy. What's his name?"

"You mean a Jeckle and Hyde," offered Jacob.

"Yeah. That's it. A real Jeckle and Hyde. Well, I didn't know this, but he'd drink while he was home with little Lori. I'd be at work and he'd be home doing things to her," she said hesitantly.

"Like what?" asked Jacob.

"How can I say this? He would give her a bath at night before putting her to bed. He used to do things to her when she was in the tub."

"You mean he was abusing her?" asked Jacob.

"Abusing her. Yes, that's the word. He abused her. I didn't know about it. Not in the beginning. Lori never said anything to me. If she had, I'd have thrown his ass out in the street," she said, raising her voice.

Jacob could see tears welling up in her eyes. "Can I get you a glass of water?" he asked.

"No, I'm all right. As I was about to say, I didn't know he was doing these things. Then one night I came home and found him in bed with her. He tried to tell me he was just comforting her. That she'd had a nightmare. But I knew differently. I threatened to report him to the authorities. He promised nothing happened and nothing would. But as it turned out, I was too late. Lori had already had her period and she became pregnant."

"By her own father?" asked Jacob, amazed.

"He wasn't her real father. He was her step father, but still, it was a sick thing to do. She was only a baby. We decided to send her down to live with a relative of Charles, his brother and wife. They lived in Florida.

Lori eventually had a baby and that was that. She put it up for adoption. Like I said, she was only a kid herself. She came home and acted like nothing had happened. That was about the time my husband was killed in a construction accident."

"What about the baby? Do you know what happened to it? Was it a boy or girl?" asked Jacob.

"We heard it was a boy. Lori signed some papers. They said a family Charles' brother knew from their church adopted him. They said they were good people and would take good care of him. A few years later, I got a Christmas card and a note in it. Charles' brother's wife said the family that adopted him had moved away. I have no idea what happened to him after that," concluded Judith.

"And what about your daughter? Did she ever ask about him, the baby, I mean?," asked Jacob, fearing the answer.

"Lori never mentioned the baby or talked about her time in Florida. But some nights I'd hear her crying in her room. She'd have nightmares and she'd call out, 'My baby. Give me back my baby boy.' In time, I guess she locked her pain away in some dark part of her mind."

"When did she die? What did she die from?" asked Jacob eagerly.

Ms. Moore wondered why he was so interested in her daughter. However she felt a great weight rising from her as she related the story.

After a moment she continued.

"Lori graduated from high school. We got some money from a court settlement after my husband was killed at that construction site. I gave her some of it. After that she took off for New York to make a life for herself. I'd get a call from her every once in a while, but she never came back. I guess considering her background, it's no wonder she ended up the way she did," added Judith.

"How is that?" asked Jacob.

"Well, Lori came back from Florida, after having her baby, a changed person. She seemed angry, wild, ya know? I don't know other than what I read in the papers and what a lawyer told me, but she got involved with a wild group. She married an older man, but continued to run around." Here she paused. Jacob wondered if he'd heard all he was going to but then she continued.

"I can't believe I'm saying all this to a perfect stranger."

"You can stop if you want," offered Jacob, but afraid she would.

"No, I've gone this far. I might as well finish the story. As I was saying, even though she was married Lori found a lover. But the guy turned out to be only interested in her money. My understanding of it is the guy was into drugs. He did something that got some drug dealers mad at him and they killed him. They tried to implicate Lori, but she was never convicted of any thing. She died a young woman from cancer. Her husband didn't have the decency to give her a Christian burial. He had her cremated. I have no idea what he did with the ashes. I don't even have a grave to visit, a place to put some flowers, nothing."

"Did you ever hear from your late husband's family again?"

"I got a few cards at the holidays, but we lost touch after my husband was killed. I did hear my daughter visited them before she died, but I'm not sure why. It was something a lawyer said to me after she died."

"Why were you contacted by a lawyer after her death?" asked Jacob.

"You're going to think this weird, but Lori had a life insurance policy. It was worth $100,000. She designated the beneficiary, as 'my son,' no name, just 'my son.' I guess if I could ever locate him, I'd have to give it to him. It's sitting in a trust account now. I get a monthly interest check but can't touch the principle. If he doesn't come forward and I die, the money is supposed to go to a cancer research organization, ovarian cancer I think."

The woman sat back and sighed. She looked across at the young man from DSS. She could swear she saw a tear running down his cheek.

"I didn't mean to upset you. I'm sorry," she said, placing her hand on his arm. He slowly withdrew it from her touch.

"You've been very kind to sit through my story, Mr. Waters. It's late. Would you like to stay for dinner? I have more than enough.?" she asked, almost pleading.

Jacob could see she was a lonely woman, but didn't want to stay. He had a lot of thoughts racing through his head. He needed to think. Ann Marie Moore Edgar's story had unnerved him.

"No, that's very nice of you, but I feel I've taken up too much of your time already."

"Are you sure?" she asked.

Jacob nodded "yes," so she dropped it.

He rose slowly from the table. He thanked her for her time and the cup of tea. When he reached the door, she reached out to stop him.

"Would you mind if I did something and you could just chalk it up to a senile old lady?"

"Sure. What?" he asked, facing her in the doorway.

"May I kiss you on the cheek?" she asked.

Jacob didn't reply, but his expression indicated it would be all right. The poor woman reached up on her toes and kissed him gently on the left cheek. Jacob instinctively embraced her and returned her kiss. Tears began to stream down his face. He turned suddenly and headed down the walk towards his car.

"It was nice meeting you, Jacob," said Ms. Moore to his retreating back. Jacob waved a hand over his head without turning around. She thought she heard him say something but couldn't be sure. It sounded like he said, "Goodbye, Grandma." but that didn't make any sense.

She watched him get into his car and pull away from the curb. She felt a sudden chill run down her spine. The kind of chill people say happens when someone walks on your grave. She had trouble sleeping that night, often waking up with a start.

"Bad dream," she thought. She could remember remnants of the dream. It had to do with her daughter, Lori, her late husband, and a baby, but that was all she could recall. "Weird" she thought as she turned over onto her other side and tried to get back to sleep.

Jacob drove back to New York as if in a fog. He kept replaying what she had told him. Tears had welled up in his eyes and ran down his cheeks as he drove. He kept wiping them with his sleeve. But soon the tears stopped and his normal state of mind returned. One of anger towards the world and women for what they'd done to him. He realized that he'd gone there with the intention of killing her. Punishing her for her role in his life. In the end he decided to spare her. After all she was his last real kin and then there was that life insurance money waiting for him. He might need good old "Granny" to get at it some day.

He had no idea how he'd found his way out of Sussex, gotten onto Interstate 80, or back to his old neighborhood. However once he crossed the George Washington Bridge and entered New York his senses were heightened. It was like when he'd go hunting for deer down south. But this time he wasn't sure if he was the hunter or the hunted.

Chapter 38

It was after nine o'clock by the time Jacob entered the block where he lived. He slowed as he approached the building, pulling to the curb a block away. He wondered if the police were watching for him again. He got out of the car and walked the last block. From a corner across the street, Jacob saw the police patrol car. There were two cops in the front seat drinking what he guessed was coffee.

"Shit," Jacob said to himself. Not knowing where else to go, he circled the block and entered his building from the far side. He found a rear exit slightly ajar and entered the building. Avoiding the lobby he climbed the five flights to his floor. Cautiously, he opened the door and peeked down the hall. He immediately spotted a piece of yellow tape dangling from across his doorway. Not seeing anyone around, he moved quietly down the hall to his apartment. As he'd guessed, the tape was from the police department. It crisscrossed the entrance from one side of the door frame to the other. The door was pulled closed, but he could see a large dent in the door, the paint scratched and chipped as if it had been struck with a heavy object. He pushed against the door and it moved slightly open.

"Jesus, they must have been here," he thought. From working with the courts, Jacob knew the police routine for searching a person's place. Smash in the door and search the premises. If they didn't find anything, some believed they came equipped with evidence that would always result in an arrest. It really galled him to think there were crooked cops working in New York.

He ducked under the yellow tape and entered his apartment. Running his hand down the wall he found the light switch. When he turned it on the room was illuminated by a lamp lying on its side next to an end table. The place was a mess. Chairs were over turned, cushions from the sofa on the floor, items from shelves scattered about, some broken.

"Son of a bitch," he cursed out loud. He hurriedly ran through the rooms and was greeted by the same evidence of mayhem. In the kitchen, even the refrigerator had been moved away from the wall. There was breakfast cereal poured on the counter and floor. All the cabinet doors stood open and the drawers had been pulled out. Looking around the room, he suddenly froze. There on the small kitchen table was the drawer. It was emptied of its contents and lying upside down on the table, a lone piece of adhesive tape dangled from its underside.

"Oh my God. They found it." Jacob knew immediately what they'd found. All the newspaper clippings, the birth certificate, even the adoption papers he'd found in his late mother's closet. They were in a large manila envelope he'd hidden under that drawer.

He also had articles about the three women he'd killed hidden there.

"Jesus, why did I save those things?" he asked himself.

Jacob now knew why the police car was stationed outside the building. They were waiting for him. He ran to the window and peered down at the street in front of his apartment. The car was there but one of the cops stood outside. He was looking up at the side of the building. Jacob ducked back from the window.

"Too late," he knew. "They must have seen the lights in his apartment." As if to verify this thought two more police cars pulled up outside. He saw several uniformed cops get out and run toward the building. They had their guns drawn.

In a panic, Jacob ran into his bedroom. He gathered clothes, most of which had been removed from his closet and were scattered about the room. He pulled a small overnight bag out of the closet and shoved the clothes inside. Spinning around several times, he looked for something worth taking. Instinctively, he patted his side. The hunting knife was where it should be, in its leather case, strapped to his side. He had money in his wallet.

"Thank God I took the cash out this morning," he thought.

Knowing he didn't have any more time, he ran towards the door. As he brushed past the yellow police tape, he heard the bell of the elevator ring. Wheeling in the other direction, he made a dash for the stairs. He no sooner entered the stairwell then he heard feet pounding up from below.

"Damn. Now what?" he asked. Instinctively, he headed up the stairs, towards the roof.

"Maybe I can get across to the next building or go down the fire escape," he thought. Pushing open the steel door, he emerged onto the flat graveled roof of the apartment complex. Jacob ran to the edge and looked out at the Throgs Neck Bridge and the Long Island Sound beyond. The bridge was outlined in its evening glitter of lights. A soft, cool breeze came off the water and gave Jacob a chill. His face and neck were soaked in sweat.

He frantically looked around the roof for an avenue of escape. Immediately, he realized the nearest building was too far for him to reach if he jumped. He ran to the opposite side to where the fire escape was located. Down below he saw the lights from a police car that had pulled into the parking lot. Two officers stood with flash lights aimed up the side of the building.

Jacob ran back to the door that opened onto the roof. The same door he'd just emerged from. He expected the police to burst through the door at any moment. Lying on the ground, he found a metal rake, like one used in the garden. It had tar and pebbles stuck to its metal teeth. He guessed roofers had left it behind the last time they'd done repair work up there. He grabbed the rake and jammed the handle under the door handle. It acted as a wedge and would stop or at least slow down anyone trying to get onto the roof. Off in the distance, Jacob heard the sound of police sirens. The flashing red lights on Northern Boulevard were all headed his way. The police had reinforcements coming.

Chapter 39

John Straub, Nancy Mooney, Jim Falcone, and Dani Newel were sitting around Straub's desk when the call came in. The squad car on duty at Jacob Edgar's place had spotted the lights going on inside the apartment. They believed they saw someone looking down at them from the living room window. Assuming it was the suspect, they called for assistance and notified the detectives that their quarry was back in the nest.

John went to a small closet behind his desk and removed two bullet proof vests. He tossed one to Nancy and threw the other over his shoulder.

"We got ours in our car," volunteered Dani.

"Okay, let's go. I don't want to lose him this time," said John, heading out the door.

When the two unmarked cars arrived at Edgar's place, several police cars and emergency vehicles were parked in front. The block was cordoned off by more yellow tape.

Lifting the tape over his head, John said to Nancy, "I wish I had the concession on this stuff. The way the police use it I'd be able to retire to Florida and live in the lap of luxury."

The four detectives approached the sergeant on the scene.

"He inside?" asked John.

The sergeant knew the homicide cops by name, having worked scenes before with them.

"He's on the roof," replied the sergeant. "We got the place surrounded. The stairs are covered, the fire escape, and the occupants have all been evacuated. Most of them are over there," he said, pointing over his shoulder towards the other side of Northern Boulevard. "EMS is here too, just in case."

"Has any one spoken to him?" asked John.

"Nope. Figured we'd let you guys do that."

Turning to Nancy, John asked, "Feel like taking a ride to the top?"

"With you? Anytime," she replied.

John and Nancy donned their vests, placed their badges outside them so the other cops would see they were the "good guys," and headed into the building.

The elevator, so familiar to Nancy, having lived there for many years, now took on a menacing feeling. The door stood open and a uniformed cop waited, ready to send them on their way.

John and Nancy boarded the elevator and rode the ten floors in silence. As they exited the car, one of the cops in the hall turned towards them, his gun pointed in their direction.

"Easy, kid. We're the good guys," said Nancy, holding her hands up in front of her, shield in hand. The cop lowered his gun.

"Have you tried the door?" asked John.

"I could open it a little. But he's got something wedged behind it. I'm waiting for 'Tactical' to get here with something to bust it down," said the young cop, breathlessly.

"Good. Now why don't you holster that weapon and let us take it from here," said John, trying to calm the rookie down. The cop did as he was told and moved away from the door, relieved to be free of the responsibility.

John and Nancy moved to either side of the exit door, their own guns drawn and pointed at the ceiling. Nancy pushed at the door and it moved open a fraction. John knelt down and peeked through the small opening. Across the roof, John could make out the dark outline of a man.

"Edgar! Jacob Edgar! This is Detective Straub. I have Detective Mooney with me. Remember us? We spoke to you at work," said John, trying to put him at ease.

At first, Jacob didn't respond. Then he shouted over his shoulder towards the door.

"Don't come here! Don't come near me!" he shouted.

"Don't worry. We don't want to hurt you. And we don't want you to hurt anyone including yourself," said Nancy.

Hearing Nancy's voice, Jacob turned and looked towards the door.

John saw this and said to Nancy. "He seems to respond to your voice. You talk to him."

"What should I say?" she asked.

"Just talk to him. Try to calm him down. The longer he talks, the less chance this thing is going to turn ugly," added John.

"Okay," said Nancy and moved closer to the door. Putting her weight against it, the opening widened just a bit more.

"Stop!" yelled Jacob.

"Don't worry, Jacob. I just want to be able to see you, that's all. I'm not going to do anything unless you say it's okay. Talk to me, Jacob," she asked softly.

"What's to talk about?" he asked.

Nancy could sense a quivering in his voice, like he was fighting to maintain control of his emotions. Like he was ready to cry or something.

"Why don't we talk about why you're here? Why we're here?" she added.

Nancy continued to push against the door as she spoke. The rake handle kept sliding on the gravel, allowing the door to open more. Finally, it was wide enough that Nancy thought she could slip through.

"Jacob, do you mind if I come out there with you? I'm alone. I'll stay here by the door. Come on, what do you say?" she asked as she worked her head and shoulders through the narrow opening.

Seeing that she was almost through the door already, Jacob agreed.

"Okay. But stay by the door. Don't try to come near me," he said and waved his hunting knife in her direction.

"Don't try anything stupid," warned John from behind her. "Stay by the door. At the first sign of trouble, I'm coming through shooting," he added.

Nancy wiggled the rest of the way through the narrow opening. "I'll sit here, okay?" asked Nancy.

Jacob nodded "yes."

As she slid down into a squatting position she pushed the handle of the rake away from the door knob, freeing it so John could get through quickly, if needed.

"So Jacob, I guess we're neighbors," Nancy began. "How long have you lived in the building?"

Distracted by the conversation and her soothing voice, Jacob replied, "About two years."

"Two years and we never met before," said Nancy, trying to sound calm.

"I'd seen you before. You were with that other guy, the one you were with when you talked to me at work."

"That would be my partner, Detective Straub," she said.

Jacob remained quiet, looking off towards the bridge and water beyond.

"It's a beautiful sight, isn't it?" asked Nancy.

Again, he didn't reply.

From behind the door, John whispered, "Keep talking. You're getting to him."

Nancy took a deep breath and let half out before going on.

"You like work, John?"

"It's okay."

"You must get some satisfaction out of helping kids, mothers, stuff like that," she added.

"The kids, yeah. But the mothers are mostly whores," he said, anger in his voice.

"Is that why you kill them, Jacob?" she pressed.

"They deserve to die. They're no good. They abandoned their kids. They gotta be punished," he replied.

433

"You are right, Jacob. Some of them are no good. But shouldn't that be up to the courts. To God? The punishment part, I mean."

"The courts don't do nothing. I was doing it because God wanted me to. I was getting even," he said, his voice once again quivering.

"Getting even for what?"

"I thought I was getting even, that's all."

"Do you mean you were trying to get even? Was something bad done to you?" she pressed.

"Yeah. I thought my whole life has been a lie. I was abandoned. I was hurt. Like those kids were hurt by their mothers," he said with more force in his voice.

"Who hurt you, your mother, Jacob? Is that it?" she asked.

"That's what I thought."

"And now, what do you think?"

"Now, I don't know. I found someone. I spoke to her. Now I think I was wrong. It was all a mistake," he said. Now he was sobbing.

Sensing a shift in mood, Nancy rose to her feet. Jacob ignored her movements and continued gazing off into space.

"Tell me about it, Jacob. What went wrong?" she asked.

"My mother didn't abandon me. She was just a kid. She'd been raped by her own step father. What could she do?" he asked, continuing to sob.

"You're right, Jacob. A child can't be responsible for the acts of a wicked grown up. It wasn't her fault he forced himself on her. It must have been terrible for her. She must have been frightened, confused," said Nancy wondering what changed his mind.

"I found my grandmother she told me the truth. They sent my mother away, to live with strangers, to go through that alone. Then they made her give up her baby. She didn't want to, but they made her. She didn't know she had a son. She never forgot him. She thought of me often," said Jacob. His voice began to sound more like a child's than a grown man's.

Nancy picked up on the fact he had switched from the third to the first person. This was about him. He was agonizing over what he'd done, what he was about to do

"You made a mistake. You didn't know. How could you know?" she asked.

"But I thought I was doing the right thing. I even thought I was doing God's will. That girl in the motel. The one in the parking lot, the dancer. I thought they were all evil, mean for deserting their sons. I didn't realize they had no choice. Sometimes we have no choice. Sometimes we have to do things that hurt. Things that hurt you, that hurt others. How could I have been so sure I knew what they thought? How could I have imagined what they were going through? They didn't deserve to die," he said, now turning towards Nancy. She could see his face was wet from tears. His nose was running and saliva was dripping from the corner of his mouth.

While Jacob was telling Nancy how he'd misinterpreted life, she had moved slowly towards him. Behind her John had emerged through the door and stood, his gun raised in Jacob's direction.

Suddenly, Jacob seemed to snap out of his reverie.

435

"Get back, I'm warning you," he shouted, arm extended in front. The hunting knife reflected light from a nearby street light. Nancy moved closer.

"Stop," shouted Jacob.

"Nancy! No, don't do it," warned John.

But it was too late. Nancy had moved within reach of Jacob. She approached him, her right hand extended in front of her.

"It's okay, Jacob. Give me the knife," she pleaded.

In one swift motion, Jacob grabbed Nancy's hand and spun her around so she was shielding him from John and the gun. He brought the knife up to her throat, the sharp blade pressed into the flesh. With one motion, he could slit her throat from ear to ear.

"Don't move, John," said Nancy. "Lower your gun."

John did as she asked, but stood ready. He prayed he didn't have to shoot. He remembered how poorly he'd done at the police pistol range with the new semi automatic. He doubted he'd be able to hit Edgar without possibly hitting Nancy as well.

"It's your move, Edgar. What will it be?" asked John.

Edgar squeezed harder, pressing Nancy closer to him. He could smell her perfume. It smelled clean and fresh, pure. Not like him. He felt dirty, corrupt, evil. He felt Nancy's chest expand and contract with each breath. It was regular and rhythmic. Not like his, short and gasping.

"Jacob, you don't want to do this," she said, struggling to turn towards him.

"Hold still. I'll kill you. I swear!" he screamed into her ear.

Nancy squeezed her eyes tight and willed herself to remain calm.

"Put the knife down, Jacob. We, I can get you help."

"I don't need your help! I'm not crazy," he yelled, fighting to catch his breath.

Nancy knew he was scared and confused. She also knew that any sudden move would set him off.

"Okay, Jacob. I won't do anything." Nancy deliberately willed her body to relax and she leaned against him, fighting back her own urge to pull away and scream.

Responding to her, Jacob also relaxed his hold on her. He allowed the knife to move slightly away from her throat.

Less than ten feet away, John stood, gun in hand, but pointed down towards the roof.

"Let her go, Edgar," he pleaded. "There's no way off this roof. The place is surrounded. Let's end this now."

Jacob Edgar looked up towards the sky, eyes were blurred by his tears.

Sensing that he was distracted Nancy let her head drop forward towards her chest.

Thinking she was crying, Jacob lessened his grip ever so slightly, lowering the knife away from her flesh as her head moved forward and down.

"This is it," thought Nancy. Then, with all her might, she thrust her head back, smashing the back of her skull into Edgar's face. She could hear the crack of bone, as she broke his nose.

Jacob instinctively released his grip and threw his hands up to his face. It was wet with blood. He blinked his eyes several times, but could only see flashes of light like tiny flash bulbs going off before him.

Nancy threw herself forward and to the right. John immediately raised his gun to eye level and put the end of the barrel square in the middle of Edgar's head.

"Drop the knife!" John yelled. "Drop it, now!"

Edgar slowly removed his hands from his face. They were covered in his blood and tears. Ignoring the orders from the detective, Edgar turned around and moved towards the edge of the roof. Off in the distance, he saw the lights of the bridge. The smell of salt in the air came off the Sound.

"Judgment is mine, sayeth the Lord," Jacob screamed and stepped out into the darkness of the night.

The two detectives ran to the edge and looked down. They heard a sickening thud but in the darkness couldn't see the asphalt ten stories below.

"Jesus Christ," said John.

Nancy turned towards him and buried her head in his chest. She began to cry uncontrollably.

"It's okay. Let it out. Let go of it," he whispered into her ear, holding her tight, shielding her from the night and the darkness beyond.

Several dozen people walked over to the spot where Edgar had landed. Police, emergency personnel, people from the nearby fire department that had responded. Like flies, the media arrived on the scene with their cameras, reporters surged forward bright lights flashing. Everyone wanted a peek at the killer.

Jacob Edgar had fallen ten stories, over one hundred feet. The initial impact of the fall had been taken by his legs. The force from landing feet first drove the femurs up into his midsection. His head, which would normally have struck first and exploded like a watermelon, escaped the full impact from the fall. However, it was apparent to the bystanders that from the twisted posture of his back and neck, he was surely dead. It would be learned later that nearly every bone and organ in his body had suffered massive injury. Emergency services went through the motions of transporting the body to the nearest emergency room.

Once in the ER, the young doctors did their best to stabilize him, but he arrested at least twice before he was taken him into surgery. They were amazed that he was still alive.

As the gurney was wheeled onto the elevator, one intern was heard saying, "Waste of time. This guy is mush."

Chapter 40

John and Nancy stood in the back of Patty's Tavern, where they'd had their first meal together. That seemed like years ago.

But tonight was a special night also. Tonight they'd be the brunt of non-stop kidding by their fellow officers and friends.

Terry, the owner, had gladly turned the place over to them and their friends when he heard they were engaged. He organized a first class party for them and closed the place for the night so they'd have it all to themselves. They drank too much beer, ate too much corned beef and cabbage, and. sang so many songs that their throats were hoarse. At times tears ran down their cheeks from laughing so hard.

Their fellow officer shared stories about either John's or Nancy's past escapades, both on and off the force. All was said in jest. Inevitably the conversation would turn to their work in stopping the string of killings by Jacob Edgar.

The wives had taken their turns admiring the engagement ring on Nancy's hand. John had spared no expense and was proud of the ring. It had almost cleaned out his secret "mad money" account, but he knew she was worth it.

Nancy announced that they planned a wedding the following year, probably in October. "I guess it won't be a shotgun wedding then," shouted Ski.

"Amazing! The Polski can count," John yelled back.

To her joy, Nancy asked Betty to be her matron of honor. It was a "given" that John would have his old partner, Ski as his best man.

Towards the end of the evening, during one of the last rounds of toasts, John turned to Jim Falcone and Dani Newel. Raising his glass, he said, "What about you guys? Do you want to jump in? The water's fine," John said, referring to his engagement.

Dani, being a natural red head, couldn't help turning several shades of red with embarrassment.

Jim just smiled and waved. "All in due time, my friend. All in due time."

It was after midnight. The guests began to say their good nights and work their way towards the door when Terry, the bar owner, called for their attention.

"Just a minute. Not so fast, you guys," he yelled over the noise. He moved out from behind the bar and approached the group of well wishers.

"Everyone step back and give me some room," he directed. Then he took a chair and stood it in the middle of the clearing.

"Nancy, Ski, if you'd be good enough," he said and motioned for them to come towards him. He took each by the hand and positioned them on either side of the chair.

The guests all looked at each other, a puzzled look on their faces.

"Now, we all know that a detective can have only one partner. John, you have two, Nancy and Ski," said Terry as he moved back behind the bar. Reaching underneath and throwing a switch, he suddenly flooded the tavern with the sounds of an Irish jig.

"Now, Nancy and Ski, march around that chair there until the music stops. When it does, whoever gets the seat is John's partner. Now march," ordered Terry.

Everyone began clapping and tapping their feet in time with the music. Nancy and Ski looked at each other and smiled. Keeping their eyes set on each other and leaning over the chair, they began to move sideways around the chair in time with the music. Terry kept them going for over a minute; their pace quickened with the beat of the music and the stomping of feet.

Suddenly, the music stopped.

Nancy and Ski both dove for the chair.

As they did, Terry hit another switch and doused the lights.

On the street one could hear laughter and cheers from the group inside the now darkened pub.

Chapter 41

Belleview Hospital in New York City has a long and historic past. It's name is often associated with the mentally ill. However, it also possessed a renowned emergency care unit as well as areas of other medical specialties. Tucked away on the top floor is a floor devoted totally to coma patients. There the patients, no more than living shells of humanity, are cared for by a dwindling staff of dedicated nurses. On rare occasions a doctor, usually a neurologist, will enter to check the status of one of these "unfortunates."

A skeleton staff of nurses rarely touched the patients. Their job was to monitor the electrical screens that recorded the patients' vital signs.

One bed nearest the far wall held what was left of a young man who had suffered serious trauma. Virtually every bone in his body had been broken. Major organs had been seriously injured. Through the skilled hands of many surgeons this patient had survived his injuries.

His body was twisted and misshapen, both legs amputated at the hips. Electrodes were attached to discolored flesh. Tubes, inserted into every orifice, fed, flushed, and drained his body. His heart continued to pump slowly in his sunken chest. Wires attached to his head confirmed there was life, but what kind of life was open to debate. From all indications the body refused to respond to any form of stimuli.

They believed the patient had no sense of himself, where he was, no pain, no sensations, nothing. As far as the doctors and nurses were concerned, he was already dead, but his brain just didn't know it yet.

Medical staff and residents-in-training would stick and prod this patient, searching for any response. There was none. They would discuss the case openly while examining him, certain he could no longer comprehend. But they were wrong.

This shell of a person had a name. His name was Jacob Edgar. Jacob knew he was in a hospital, but for several weeks had no recollection as to how he got there. He didn't remember the fall from the building. He didn't remember his name or his life prior to being in the hospital. His ability to communicate was gone. In spite of what the hospital people said, he did feel pain. He felt every pin stick. He felt the pain in his lower back from lying in the same spot for hours and days at a time. People worked on him as if he were an inanimate object. They never talked to him, only about him. No one seemed to care.

Then one day he overheard two nurses talking about a patient in their care. They said he was a serial killer, a monster who didn't deserve to live.

"He is the devil himself and deserves to suffer for what he did," whispered one woman, each word dripping venom.

Who were they talking about? In time, he learned who that person was. It was himself.

Jacob Edgar didn't die in the fall from the roof of the ten story building as he'd expected, as he intended. He was the one who decided life and death for those woman. He was going to decide how and when he would die, not some court. That's why he jumped. But by some miracle, or curse, he survived.

Now he was imprisoned in a body that could feel pain but refused to act according to his will. For the remaining seconds, minutes, hours, days, years, all he could do was feel the pain and stare at the ceiling. Oh yes, and he could think. He began to recall his life and what he had done to those women. He could also think about what was ahead for him and it frightened the hell out of him.

From time to time he would drift off to sleep. He longed for those times because he would be free of the pain. Sometimes he would dream. He would dream about a little boy sitting on the edge of a dock in Tarpon Springs, Florida watching the fishing boats return with their daily catch. He could smell the aroma of baked bread from the nearby Greek restaurant. The air was warm and caressing on his tanned skin. He would play with the new hunting knife his fathered had given him. He would long to return to those days, but his dream wouldn't last. A nurse or orderly would come along to administer some form of torture. Pain shooting through his body would rouse him from his dream. In time sleep would return. He would escape from his prison and the pain. In another dream he was a little boy sitting in a pew at church. Music was playing and a soft, warm breeze came through an open window and caressed his body.

Next to him sat a woman he knew as "mother." She would look down at him and smile. He would look up into her tired brown eyes and return the smile.

He was a good little boy, always attentive in church. He could hear the words from the pastor as he preached to his flock. The sermon, like most, was about sin and damnation. Funny that he should remember those particular words. The pastor would raise his voice and remind the parishioners:

"No good deed goes unrewarded; no evil deed unpunished."

THE END

About the Author

Richard Tegnander writes under the pen name "Richard Anders." Richard was born in Brooklyn and raised on Long Island, New York. After graduating college he worked briefly as a high school teacher before entering the field of law enforcement. He spent the next 35 years working in the criminal justice system. He investigated hundreds of crimes ranging from petty theft to murder. He witnessed first hand the highest good and lowest evil one person can do to another. Much of what you read in his stories is based on these cases.

After retiring and at the urging of his first wife, Carole he decided to pursue full-time writing. His first work, a murder mystery entitled SCORNED was published in 2004 under the pen name Richard Anders. "NO DEED UNPUNISHED" a sequel was begun shortly thereafter. In 2006 after a long illness Carole passed away. NO DEED UNPUNISHED was forgotten and went unfinished.

Then in 2009, as Richard would describe it, "lightening struck a second time." He met, fell in love and married his present wife, Cindi, a retired high school French teacher. Having read SCORNED and after reviewing the rough draft of NO DEED UNPUNISHED Cindi encouraged Richard to finish the work. With her assistance the sequel to SCORNED was finally completed. They are currently collaborating on a third novel, which continues to follow the exploits of NYC Homicide Detective John Straub. It's tentative title is "Oh Carol."

Richard and Cindi currently reside in Bethel, New York, an upstate New York community not far from the site where in the 1960s phenomenon known as Woodstock was held.